# The Mozart Forgeries

# The Mozart Forgeries

*Daniel N. Leeson*

iUniverse, Inc.

New York  Lincoln  Shanghai

# The Mozart Forgeries

iUniverse, Inc.

For information address:
iUniverse, Inc.
2021 Pine Lake Road, Suite 100
Lincoln, NE 68512
www.iuniverse.com

ISBN: 0-595-31676-X (pbk)
ISBN: 0-595-66366-4 (cloth)

Printed in the United States of America

This book is affectionately and respectfully dedicated to Eva Harriet Einstein, the only child of the late and distinguished Mozart scholar Alfred Einstein (1880–1952) and his wife, Hertha Heumann (1881–1967), both of whom lie buried in the Mountain View Cemetery, El Cerrito, California.

At the age of ninety-two, while a resident of a retirement home in Oakland, California, Ms. Einstein proofread the text of this novel on several occasions, finding and correcting many errors and making helpful and constructive suggestions about pacing, plot, narrative, and continuity.

Ms. Einstein is a music lover who insists that she knows little about Mozart. However, it would have been impossible to be her father's daughter, particularly during his preparation of the third edition of the Köchel catalog in the 1930s, and not be knowledgeable about a variety of details that enabled her to be much more than a proofreader when she examined the tangled threads of this entirely fictitious story.

A 1945 biography, *Mozart, His Character, His Work*, by Ms. Einstein's father, is dedicated "To My Three Ladies," presumed, by those familiar with Mozart's music, to be the three ladies who act as handmaidens to the Queen of the Night in his opera, *The Magic Flute*. In fact, Einstein was saluting his wife, Hertha; his sister, Bertha; and his daughter, Eva. She has been a good friend for more than twenty-five years and it is to the last of "The Three Ladies" that this book is gratefully dedicated.

# Contents

## BOOK 3: FROM THEORY TO PRACTICE

## BOOK 4: CREATING AND DISCOVERING THE MANUSCRIPTS

## BOOK 5: THE COVER STORY

## BOOK 6: AUTHENTICATION

## BOOK 7: TRIUMPH, TRAGEDY, AND RESURRECTION

### FINALE: DA CAPO SENZA REPLICHE

# OVERTURE: FROM THE NEW YORK *TIMES*

The early edition of the New York *Times* hit the street around 10 p.m., though there were no places in Paterson where Librarian could get a copy of it at that hour. It was at an all-night newsstand in nearby Ridgewood that he bought it around midnight.

There, just below the fold on the front page, was the photo of the first surface of the concerto's manuscript—the one he had made available to Sotheby's for publicity. The headline read:

## "TWO MOZART MANUSCRIPTS REDISCOVERED"

Below that were two subheads, followed by the story.

### "FOUND AFTER TWO CENTURIES"
### "HOLOGRAPHS ASTONISH MUSIC WORLD"

In a stunning noon announcement made today in the New York offices of Sotheby's, the complete manuscripts of two of Mozart's most mature compositions, the *Concerto* for Clarinet in A, K. 622, and the *Quintet* for Clarinet and String Quartet in A, K. 581, were put on public display for the first time since their recent rediscovery by an anonymous individual. Lost for more than two centuries, the works were found inside an old briefcase in a thrift shop in Scherwiller, France, an Alsatian village near the German border, and on the main north-south autoroute halfway between Strasbourg and Colmar.

Sotheby's reported that the briefcase was purchased for 3€, about

1

$3.88. The holographs have been given a presale auction estimate of $20,000,000.

The manuscripts were examined and authenticated by experts, one from the Salzburg *Mozarteum* and another from the Berlin *Staatsbibliothek*. Both authorities inspected the manuscripts in New York only one week ago.

Professor Alfred Elias of Princeton University, one of America's leading Mozart scholars, examined and authenticated both holographs prior to the involvement of the European experts. It was at his suggestion that the Austrian and German authorities were consulted for corroboration of his findings. When contacted by the *Times*, Elias said, "I am honored to have confirmed the authenticity of these remarkable documents."

Mozart wrote the clarinet concerto in 1791 and the clarinet quintet in 1789, both compositions having been composed for clarinetist Anton Stadler, who, it is assumed, took possession of the manuscripts sometime before Mozart's death in 1791. Based on a letter from Mozart's widow, Stadler is said to have pawned a briefcase containing both manuscripts *ca.* 1800, at which point the holographs disappeared for more than two centuries. It appears that the briefcase found in the Scherwiller thrift shop, also on display at Sotheby's, is the one that Stadler pawned, containing the original manuscripts.

An auction of both holographs will be held in Sotheby's London offices in two months. News of the event is already generating considerable excitement since there has never been a discovery of previously vanished complete music manuscripts of this importance and in such perfect condition.

Communication with some of America's leading musicians has brought expressions of both amazement and joy. In a telephone conversation, Stanley Drucker, principal clarinet with the New York Philharmonic, said, "It's terrific! I'd love to play the first public performance of the concerto based on the original manuscript." Larry Combs, principal clarinet of the Chicago Symphony, said, "I never thought that I would see this day. It's a magnificent thing that has happened." Frank Cohen, principal clarinet with the Cleveland Orchestra said, "I am overwhelmed by this news. It was with this concerto and quintet that I first became acquainted with Mozart's music. And I've never forgotten the happiness that both works have always given me, to say nothing of the pleasure that the rest of the world receives from these magnificent compositions almost on a daily basis." Richard Stolzman, one of the few clarinetists to devote full time to a solo career, said that he was speechless when he heard the news. "Clearly, I am going to have to have a basset clarinet made for me now," referring to the unique instrument for which Mozart composed the work.

In speaking of the concerto, Gerard Schwarz, conductor of the Seattle Symphony and former conductor of New York's Mostly Mozart Festival, and George Cleve, conductor of San Francisco's Midsummer Mozart Festival, expressed their happiness at the discovery and intend to conduct a new edition of the familiar concerto based entirely on the autograph whenever it is made available. Cleve stated his intentions to include the quintet in an edition based on the manuscript as part of his summer festival's chamber music series.

Reactions from European musicians have been equally favorable, with the English clarinetist, Tony Pay, saying, "These two works are the most important solo compositions ever written for the clarinet. All clarinet concerti are measured against Mozart's, with every other one suffering by comparison. The quintet is the most glorious piece of chamber music with clarinet ever conceived. It is an astonishing and remarkable discovery, without parallel in music history."

For further details of this unprecedented event and a photograph of the first page of the quintet manuscript, see page B1.

Librarian was rereading the material in his Paterson house at 1 a.m. when the phone rang. Answering it, he heard the Sotheby's representative begin to talk without identifying himself.

"It's a madhouse here! We've had calls from Vienna, London, Berlin, and Frankfurt. The manager of the Vienna Philharmonic offered us $100,000 for an exclusive photographic copy of the manuscript, along with the rights for both a first performance and the first recording of an edition made from it. They have an editor all ready to go. We received an e-mail from Professor Doctor von Waldersee in Salzburg—remember him?—who offered us $30,000,000 for the two autographs, plus payment of *both* your and my commissions. The funds are to be supplied to the Mozarteum by the Volkswagen Corporation. I think he wants to avoid the perils of an auction and is making a generous offer right out of the gate. It's your stuff. Do you want to sell it at that price?"

"Absolutely not," Librarian said. "Do you think that I am going to give up the pleasure of living through the chaos of the next eight weeks?"

"What about the Vienna Phil's offer?" Sotheby's man asked.

"Just tell them that the owner will consider it, but not now," he replied. "Say that we'll get back to them."

"Did you see the *Times* article?" Sotheby's asked.

"I've got it in front of me right now," Librarian answered. "I was rereading it for about the fifth time when you called, and I was amazed to see that the story appeared on the front page."

"Are you serious?" the Sotheby's rep asked in astonishment. "It's scheduled to be on the front pages of Vienna's *Die Presse*, *Der Standard*, and the *Wiener Zeitung*, the Berliner *Morgenpost*, and Frankfurt's *Neue Presse* and *Rundschau*. I suspect that it will be front-page news on every major German language newspaper. And in France, the entire first page of both the Strasbourg and Colmar editions of the *Dernières Nouvelles d'Alsace* will be devoted to the discovery, including interviews with Benjamin Hemmerdinger and his aunt Ella. There's even a battle going on between those two cities as to which one has the closer cultural and emotional affinity to Scherwiller. That's so very French!"

Librarian interrupted him to ask, "Did Sotheby's French representative speak to the Hemmerdingers as I requested, asking them not to divulge my name?"

"He did, indeed," answered Sotheby's, "and both of them, while astounded at the magnitude of your discovery, refused to give any information about you in their interviews."

"Was there any newspaper publicity in France outside of Alsace?" Librarian asked.

"Oh, yes," Sotheby's rep responded. "It's already on the front page of *Le Monde*, *Nice-Matin*, and every major newspaper in France. The London *Times* made a big splash of the fact that the sale will be in that city; the Art and Drama section of next Sunday's New York *Times* will have a special article by Anthony Tommasini on the Mozart manuscripts of the Pierpont Morgan Library, and the Washington *Post* is doing the same thing for the Library of Congress.

"I think your discovery has tapped an enormous well of interest in music manuscripts, as well as igniting the greatest curiosity about Mozart's music since *Amadeus*. Someone sent me a FAX asking for comments about a piece scheduled for tomorrow's Austin, Texas newspaper. The governor is pointing out that there are no Mozart manuscripts anywhere in the state and he is making a request for some patriotic Texan to buy both of yours and house them at the University of Texas in Austin. Only in Texas could something like that happen!"

"That kind of activity will be good for the auction," Librarian pointed out. "The price will skyrocket if the public's fascination remains at this kind of a fever pitch."

"You are quite correct," Sotheby's rep said, "and in light of all this hullaba-loo, do you want to drop by tomorrow and increase the insurance coverage?"

"I don't think that's necessary," Librarian said. "I'm not coming over to your office to sign new insurance documents every time the price goes up a few dollars. Besides, I don't think it's necessary. Did you ever lose a major sale item?"

"Never," he replied, "though I understand that another auction house—not in New York, but in Milan—misplaced a Rembrandt for two weeks. They finally found it on top of a refrigerator in the cafeteria with a bowl of basil leaves sitting on it, and no one ever figured out how that happened."

"I am going to try and get to bed," Librarian said, interrupting the chitchat, "but before I do, tell me how the press conference went."

"Well," Sotheby's rep said, "Rothstein, from the New York *Times*, stood in front of the two manuscripts for fifteen minutes and every time I went near him all I heard was, 'I don't believe it. I simply don't believe it.' We were asked over and over why the owner wishes to remain anonymous."

"How did you answer that question?" Librarian asked.

"Cleverly," Sotheby's rep answered. "After about the tenth inquiry on that subject, I said, 'As soon as she decides to become unanonymous, you can ask her that question,' at which point I was asked to confirm that the discoverer was a woman. I deliberately looked very embarrassed, saying that I was not at liberty to give that information, and figured that my 'accidental' gender error would throw them off the track. Some day, I am going to become an actor."

"And some day I'm going to get to sleep," Librarian said. "Let me contem-plate my recent sex-change operation, thanks to you."

"I'll keep you posted," the response came back, "but the fun is just begin-ning. Goodnight and sleep well."

Librarian went upstairs to his second-floor bedroom and, astonishingly, was asleep in fifteen minutes. He had a night of erotic dreams about his first wife, which was astounding, because she was a profoundly unerotic woman. His second wife, from whom he was also divorced, was far more responsive, so much so that she ran away with an ophthalmologist who had gotten tired of the practice of medicine following a serious malpractice suit. There must have been something very Freudian in that dream, but Librarian had no idea what it was.

Now that the story of the rediscovery of the manuscripts was out, the sale seemed likely to make him and his silent partner into rich men. They had both worked on the problem since his confederate had gotten out of prison, and they were the only people in the world who could appreciate the magnitude of what they had done.

The two of them had constructed a pair of completely fraudulent manuscripts, created an airtight cover story about their rediscovery, and had them authenticated by three unimpeachable, world-class authorities.

That called for pancakes in the morning.

# BOOK 1:
# PRELIMINARIES

# 1

# FAIRTON FEDERAL PRISON

At 9 a.m. on the bright fall morning that begins this story, the parking lot of southern New Jersey's Fairton Federal Prison was half full. Eight rows from the steps leading to the prison's administrative entrance, the density of parked cars was considerably reduced. Almost alone in that eighth row, sat the only vehicle that wasn't empty. In it, awaiting the release of a particular prisoner, was one of the two principle characters of this tale.

Because of the nature of the activities in which he had been involved in the past, and one in particular—the central event of this story—in which he intended to be involved in the not-too-distant future, he is not identified by name. Instead, his profession, Librarian, will be used to make reference to him. Despite the occupational title, his job had little to do with the traditional activities of a public library, and while there were other specialists who duplicated his highly-trained occupation, few exceeded him in ability.

Not knowing the time of day when inmates were released, Librarian had inquired on the matter by calling the prison's administrative offices a few days earlier. In speaking to a gruff voice at the other end of the line—one that conveyed the impression that its owner was trained not to communicate a great deal of technical information about the prison—Librarian said, "I'm driving to Fairton to pick up an inmate scheduled for release this Friday. Can you tell me what time that happens?"

On being told that the time of discharge for freed offenders was variable, but generally sometime between 9 a.m. and the middle of the afternoon, Librarian thanked the voice and hung up. A six-hour window of opportunity did not speak well for federal precision in maintaining on-time events.

9

In a crazy combination of fastidiousness on one hand, while planning for a criminal act on the other, Librarian made himself available for the pickup by taking a paid vacation day from work, rather than the unethical choice of a sick day. It was his nature to be scrupulous about behaving responsibly towards his employer. Besides, keeping his time card accurately filled out was a neurotic compulsion.

The trip from Librarian's home in the northern New Jersey city of Paterson to Fairton prison was almost three hours. This was due by and large to the density of the traffic on the Garden State Parkway at the journey's northern end and the reduced speeds of the state routes after exiting the New Jersey Turnpike at its southern end. So in order to be at the prison on time—whenever that time was—he left his house early and was on the Garden State Parkway at 6 a.m., switching to the New Jersey Turnpike where the two intersected in the center of the state, and arriving at the prison at 8:50 a.m., following a stop for breakfast near Trenton.

The other principal of this story, the prisoner whom Librarian intended to pick up, was a man who will be referred to as "Forger." Like "Librarian," his reference was also profession related, though in this case its owner took great care never to advertise his occupation. There were a considerable number of very qualified people, including some in the US Treasury Department, who believed that his skill at making copies of things was among the world's finest.

Forger was completing a four-year sentence without even so much as a reduction of one day in the imposed judgment. That was a government-influenced decision, made whenever confronted by someone with a technique as remarkable as his. In fact, they viewed their attitude as one of great governmental generosity. Had it not been for Forger's technical cooperation, his incarceration almost certainly would have been considerably longer.

So instead of Librarian being at work, managing the rare and occasionally priceless music manuscripts that were part of the Special Collections of the Music Division of the New York Public Library at Lincoln Center, he sat in his car on the blacktop in the parking lot of the prison, waiting for the officials in charge to release that day's quota of prisoners.

With nothing else to do while biding his time—he could never read while waiting for an event because he constantly interrupted himself to check his watch—Librarian mused on the details of an opportunity that he envisioned for himself and Forger. It was an undertaking that few people could have imagined, and only members of the specialized community who had his training and knowledge would have even fantasized it. In Librarian's professional opinion, the opportunity had a $20,000,000 potential, maybe more. That was a lot of money for a counterfeit, but what he had in mind was a forgery of a kind that had never before been attempted, much less achieved.

It was only the exceptional skill possessed by Forger, coupled with the remarkable technical expertise of Librarian, that gave his project a glimmer of hope.

# 2

# THE BONDING BEGINS

Librarian and Forger had known each other since their childhood. In fact, they worked their first paid job together at the remarkably young age of five, in the summer preceding their entry into kindergarten at PS 3 in Paterson, 136 miles north of the prison.

Their job, about ninety minutes of effort that was more fun than work, involved helping Librarian's grocer father, and it was in two stages. First, around 10 a.m., they were taken to the nearby jute mill, where the father went every workday to collect orders for luncheon sandwiches. The children's task was easy enough: go through the three floors of the mill, pick up the 300 empty Pepsi Cola bottles delivered on the previous work day, and turn them upside down.

Then they shook out the ugly-looking cockroaches that had crawled in overnight to sip the remaining sweetened liquid and stepped on them. By the next morning, the squashed cockroach corpses had been cannibalized by their living brethren, and not a trace of them remained. It was a self-regulating system in that on a daily basis the living ate the dead.

The two carried the unwashed empty bottles to a central location on that floor, put them in the wooden crates left in the mill on the previous workday, and went back for more cockroach stomping. Their work normally filled six cases and took forty-five minutes.

Librarian's father, having completed his recording of that day's sandwich orders, carried the heavy cases to the truck two at a time. Then they would return to the grocery store, where Librarian's mother and her cousin Florence had already begun making the 300 sandwiches after the individual details had been copied down by Librarian's father. About eighty percent of the sandwiches were made in advance of receiving the orders, but their estimate of the sandwich-type distribution was, based on previous experience, fairly accurate. Making a few extra here and there, they closed out the exact quantity of sandwiches needed, using that day's live order data.

The customers had a choice of four variations: ham, ham and cheese, cheese, or baloney, all on seeded Kaiser rolls with lots of Gulden's golden mustard. Just before noon, the truck was loaded with cold soda, twelve boxes of sandwiches—four boxes per floor with each holding one of the four available sandwich types—and a thirteenth box that held little cups filled with potato salad, throwaway forks, and napkins. Then the three returned to the jute mills.

Librarian's father carried the heavy stuff. Each of the three floors received four boxes, corresponding to the four sandwich types, two cases of soda, and about one-third of the napkins, forks, and cups of potato salad. Then the two children began scampering around, delivering orders to the first-floor workers who would tell them what kind of sandwiches they had ordered. Both Librarian and Forger had their first reading lessons by recognizing sandwich names written on the sides of the four cardboard boxes. Along with each sandwich came one twelve-ounce bottle of cold Pepsi Cola and, if ordered, the potato salad.

On delivery, each child collected forty cents—forty-five cents with potato salad—before proceeding to the next customer. No one took advantage of their youth with false coins or short change, though some paid entirely in pennies. A mill worker might try to scam an adult, but they were honest with children. Counting coins was how the children learned the number system before their first day of public school.

While Librarian and Forger worked the first floor, Librarian's father worked the third. The children, a great deal faster, were half way done with the second floor by the time the father finished his third floor customers. By 12:45 everything was delivered. The two children rarely made a mistake, never lost a cent, had a marvelous time, and were paid fifty cents each for their day of work. They left the jute mills with two empty soda bottle crates placed on each of the three floors, the father took out all the empty cardboard boxes, and the next day they did it all over again.

That is how far back the friendship of Librarian and Forger went.

# 3

# FORGER'S EARLY YEARS

Librarian looked at the prison entrance, hoping to see Forger come out at any moment, but apparently the officials were not yet ready to release him. That gave Librarian more time to woolgather. In the part of southern New Jersey where the prison was located, it was a great deal more pleasant, and certainly more rural than Paterson, which is where Librarian still lived and where both he and Forger had had their education from kindergarten all the way through high school. It would be in Paterson where the day's journey would end, though, if Librarian's planning schedule held, not until well after dark.

Forger's mother was a French Catholic, raised in Lyon. She met his father when he was in the army during the Second World War. They married in late 1945 and came to Paterson, where her husband had been raised, though he was orphaned following the death of his parents in a 1939 car accident. She never spoke to her husband about her experiences between 1939 and 1945, and he never inquired. That was good, because he would not have been pleased with the details of what she went through to survive in those years.

Forger, their only child, was five years old when his father died in a worker's accident, which left his wife and son almost indigent. His mother was a remarkably beautiful woman who was extremely fastidious about her appearance. After her husband's death, she wanted to go back to France with her son, but had no family there any longer, her parents having died after the war and her only sibling being a sister who lived in a home for the mentally impaired outside of Lyon. Besides, she could not have afforded the trip. The insurance company, examining the details of her husband's accident concluded after some money quietly changed hands, that management was not at fault, so she received nothing.

Thus she remained in Paterson, went to work at the jute mill in which her husband was killed, and appreciated that her son worked for Librarian's father during the summer. This was partly because she was grateful for the money that her son got, and partly because, as a thrifty Frenchwoman who had worked as a child herself in the 1920s, she realized the contribution that labor, even child labor, brought to the formation of character.

Forger's mother spoke only French to her son, though she spoke an excellent but accented English to Librarian when he visited. It was quite a rarity to have a French-speaking child in the neighborhood. Mostly what was heard was Italian, Gaelic, German, Polish, Turkish, Arabic, and, more rarely, Yiddish.

Within a short time after her husband's death, a number of men tried to interest Forger's mother in some sort of liaison, or even marriage, but she rebuffed them all. Except for Forger's father, her experience with men was entirely negative. She was devoted to raising her son, was a strict Catholic, and had a peculiar but highly personal set of middle-class moral standards, this contradicting the general belief that all single Frenchwomen were sexual athletes. Rumors abounded, fed by the distorted memories of men who still remembered their service in wartime France and who would often speak of their involvement in those terrible events.

America was still very Victorian, and a woman in that area of Paterson who ventured into any kind of non-marital sex would have been unmercifully ostracized. This was particularly true in a community with a large number of married Irish Catholic women for whom sex of any kind—even when imposed by their conjugal duties—was seen as an unpleasant burden thrust on them by God because of Eve's sin.

# 4

# LIBRARIAN'S CHILDHOOD

Whenever the authorities of Fairton Federal Prison decided to release Forger, it was Librarian's intention that the two would take a short trip to a place where the view was far superior, the surroundings idyllic, and the circumstances perfect for a serious, uninterrupted business discussion, the end result of which might be something like the aforementioned $20,000,000, split down the middle.

One could smell the waters of Delaware Bay from the parking lot in Fairton, it being just a few miles south as the crow flew. Those waters, which separate southern New Jersey from northern Delaware, were where Librarian intended that they would have a long and detailed conversation.

Even when he was a child, it was clear that Librarian was an extraordinarily structured creature. How he learned that the alphabet had an order to it was unclear, but he used this facility in order to completely redeploy the soup cans on the shelves of his father's grocery store. For example, despite the fact that "Tomato Soup" should have been at eye-level because it was the most popular of the Campbell inventory his father sold, Librarian had placed it on a lower shelf because alphabetization required it to be there.

It was even worse. He had originally put it after cans of "Ravioli" and "Sardines" because brand names interfered with the kind of structure into which he felt compelled to systematize things. That drove his parents crazy, because they needed the canned goods ordered by ease of availability on the shelves so as to minimize bending, not by the democratic process of alphabetic order.

When he began music lessons, it took him some time to realize that rearranging the notes of a melody so everything went up or down in chromatic order produced very uninteresting tunes, and there was nothing he could do to fix that problem. He tried, but gave up as hopelessly impossible, the idea of arranging the notes by rhythmic duration—long ones first, though he later tried short ones first. Even though he abandoned the effort, he perceived it as an idea consistent with order and structure.

Librarian's mother, who was an avid reader, took him to the public library when he was quite young and deposited him in the children's room to look at picture books while she went to the adult section to find something suiting her own preference. When she returned, he was sitting on the floor, surrounded by the books taken from a nearby shelf, trying to figure out the classification system implied by the numbers written in white ink on the spine of each book. A few years later, as part of an essay he wrote for a seventh grade English class, he submitted a well-argued contrast of the Dewey decimal system with that of the Library of Congress classification method, stating which of the two was superior for the purpose of categorizing, organizing, and locating library materials.

What interested him most was history, a strange choice for the youngster, particularly because almost all historical events were random. His parents thought the interest would fade with time. It never did, though his curiosity became more specialized as he discovered that history was not one broad subject but became subdivided by topic. He was astonished when he learned that there were histories of individual disciplines, most of which he was not ready to tackle, such as a history of mathematics, a history of science, a history of food, and even one of the language in which he thought.

It was in the history of music where he found his true place, and not a week went by when he didn't take another book about the life of a specific composer home for a thorough read. As he got older and the books more sophisticated, he discovered a phenomenon that amazed him—namely that the data presented was, in some very important details, different from author to author. These people actually disagreed with one another. How was it possible to advance knowledge if certain fundamental facts were not firmly fixed?

For example, he learned from one author that Mozart's death was as a result of kidney problems, while another suggested that he died of a concussion after falling from a horse. Later, he learned that there were more than 100 different proposals offered about the cause of the composer's death. Didn't they know? Couldn't they come to a single conclusion?

Librarian's parents were not quite sure how to raise him. They were flabbergasted by his intellectual pursuits. Both had come from poor families, and neither had much education. This was not because they didn't want it, but rather because when they were young they had to leave school at an early age, get a job, and help support a large family. Librarian's mother was one of eleven, and his father one of ten. Both were intelligent, but neither had much education.

Whatever their circumstances, they made certain that their child would not be required to leave school and go to work at a young age. Instead, they intended him to have a proper education, though they were not quite sure what such a thing entailed.

# 5

# EARLY SCHOOLING

When Librarian and Forger were in the second grade of PS 3, the teacher was named Miss Spetgang. Hers was the only classroom that had a piano and she played it, at least to the children's eyes and ears, miraculously. They learned songs which both sang together, not only in class, but also on the stoop of Librarian's house where they spent a lot of time studying the words of the songs. The one that gave them, simultaneously, the most pleasure and the greatest confusion was called "The Lost Cord," or so they thought it to be titled, because both perceived it as a story about a man who found and then lost some rope that had an unclear purpose related to his organ.

The problem derived from the fact that one of Paterson's most important industries—what there was left of it—was the making of twine, rope, jute, and cloth, a heritage of its days as a great silk-manufacturing city. So what they heard when Miss Spetgang spoke the song's title were the words "The Lost C-o-r-d," and not the actual title of "The Lost C-h-o-r-d."

The two discussed the song because they could not understand how the narrator was unable to find the lost item. Also, they were not exactly sure what an organ was, though Forger, being Catholic, knew that it was a musical instrument played at Sunday church. He just didn't know what it looked like or how one could lose his cord while seated at it. To the very structured Librarian, the organist's search technique was completely incomprehensible.

The song's text wasn't very explicit in its details and didn't describe how the beautiful cord had somehow become lost. The narrator searched for it unsuccessfully, and paradoxically suggested that he might find it after he died.

The two children went to St. Joseph's Cathedral, on the corner of Main and Grand Streets, to see an organ. They found and looked at it for a few minutes, but one of the priests thought them to be vandals and shooed them out. Now, having seen an organ, though only for a few minutes, the boys spent hours attempting to understand the cryptic meaning of the song's message, and as far as either of them could remember, the only positive thing to come out of their analyses was that Forger got interested in playing the piano and Miss Spetgang began to teach him, within the limitations of her available time. After school, Forger would stay to study with Miss Spetgang and Librarian was permitted to watch silently.

One of the teaching tools Miss Spetgang used with Forger turned out to be of enormous importance to the two of them a number of years later. She gave him a specialized music nib from a little box she kept in her closet of treasures. The nib had five points and was inserted into a straight pen so as to enable him to create music staffs on plain paper. He used it for the simple music-writing exercises she gave him and kept it for years. Only when the nib was accidentally bent and he was unable to fix it or find another to replace it did he stop the practice of writing out fragments of music. The gift didn't sound like much, but no one can predict what potential exists in small packages.

Following the end of the school year, both boys went on to the third grade and Forger lost his chance to practice on the piano, though he wanted very much to continue his study in some way. Even with the few lessons he took with Miss Spetgang, he could play simple tunes. But he was an undisciplined student, constantly altering themes, changing them as it suited him. He even tried to modify the underlying harmonies, though he was not successful in figuring out how to do that. He did manage to change the meter frequently, and in doing so he might make a waltz into a march, or vice-versa. And he went mad with excitement when he figured out how to add an extra beat in a melody, changing it from 4/4 to 5/4 time. It drove Miss Spetgang crazy.

At some point in his lessons, Forger was taught what a "chord" was, and Librarian, being in the room at the time, had the titular misunderstanding of their favorite song cleared up.

# 6

# A KID SHOWS HIS COUNTERFEITING MUSCLE

In the opinion of those whose views on this sort of thing mattered, Fairton Federal Prison was about to let a counterfeiting genius out of jail. He was such a brilliant forger that, to the absolute shock of the US Treasury Department, he had, within only three months of its initial appearance, successfully passed something close to 500 perfectly-counterfeited US $100 bills—the new ones with an oversized picture of Benjamin Franklin. Their creation was done with such consummate skill that it was almost impossible to detect that the bills were forgeries. Furthermore, because the counterfeits followed so closely on the government's release of the new note, the Treasury Department was completely unprepared for the assault. They thought they had a few worry-free years available to them.

The speed of Forger's attack, coupled with the quality of his product, presented the authorities with a technical accomplishment, the dimensions of which had been thought by them to be unattainable.

In order to appreciate how young Forger was when his remarkable skills began to display themselves, an incident about his brief involvement with a famous American sports hero is recalled.

When Forger and Librarian were of an age to appreciate baseball—both around nine—Librarian's father took the two of them to Ebbets Field to see the Brooklyn Dodgers play. The two young baseball freaks, delirious with anticipation of the actual event, went crazy when Jackie Robinson, in his penultimate season, hit a double, two singles, walked, stole two bases, and made a spectacular, diving catch. The man was an artist.

When the game was over, the children wanted to get some of the player's autographs and were taken where they might see the athletes as they left the stadium. There were lots of kids there, all with the same idea, and many of them had baseballs they hoped would be autographed by someone. *Anyone!*

When Robinson came through from the player's dressing room in a suit—strange that he looked so ordinary when out of his uniform—a pile of kids ran over and asked him to sign their baseballs. Robinson, using a special pen that he kept just for that purpose, signed a half-dozen, and then left with another three-dozen kids jumping up and down with their unsigned baseballs in their waving hands.

One boy of about seven, small for his age, sat down on the cement walkway and began to cry because Robinson had not signed his ball. On impulse, because he felt bad about it, Librarian went over to him and said, "Give me your ball, kid. I'll get it signed for you."

But before running after Robinson, Librarian got hold of a ball that Robinson had signed and showed it to Forger before giving it back to its owner. Forger, who had stared at Robinson's signature only for about ten seconds, took the unsigned ball from Librarian and the two of them ran after Robinson, who was almost at his car by that time. Forger flagged him down and said, "Hey, Jackie, can I borrow your pen for a second?"

More surprised than anything—no kid had ever asked to use his pen before—Robinson handed it to Forger, who wrote something on the sweet spot of the crying child's unsigned ball. Then he returned the pen to Robinson, thanked him, and the two headed back to where the kid was sitting on the concrete runway, still blubbering over his misfortune.

Robinson, a puzzled expression of his face, stopped them and said to Forger, "What did you write on that ball, son?"

Forger replied, "Your name, Jackie. The kid is crying. You should'a signed his ball. So I signed it with your name."

"Can I see that ball, please?" asked Robinson.

Forger handed it to the great second baseman, whose eyes suddenly widened in surprise. Then he said, "Well I'll be damned!" And turning to the player who was riding with him added, "Look what that kid did!"

The other player examined the ball and the two of them broke out laughing. Robinson gave the ball back to Forger and got in the car, smiling and shaking his head, and the two children returned the baseball to the crying boy.

When Forger handed him the prize, the boy read its words aloud: "Jackie Robinson, Brooklyn Dodgers." The name was an absolutely perfect copy of what Jackie had written on the other kid's baseball—the one Forger had examined for ten seconds to fix Robinson's signature in his head. The identification of the team—made difficult by the fact that Robinson's name did not use the letters "B," "l," "y," "D," "d," or "g" and which required some improvisation on Forger's part—was his idea.

Years later, long after Robinson's death, that ball went for a very high price at an auction because it was the only one having both Robinson's signature, and the team designation on it. However, no one alive besides Forger and Librarian knew that it was a counterfeit done by a nine-year old boy with ten seconds of preparation and some heavy-duty extemporization.

Today, just a few years after Forger's passing of the first of his counterfeit bills, the $100 note is being duplicated more frequently, though the authorities try to minimize the extent of the injury. Clumsy amateurs with laptops do much of the work. If anyone took a moment to examine the bills being passed, few would get by.

The portraits on these poor counterfeits are either unclear or unnaturally white. The feel of the paper is weak because the cotton/linen content is low. The artwork of intricate, crisscrossing lines along the border is smudged and broken. The watermark is the wrong size, badly placed, fuzzy, or all three. The tiny red and blue fibers supposed to be embedded in the paper are not present in most of the samples found. The security thread, which is polyester material, cannot be reproduced. It has to be woven into the paper and is absent in the bills being passed. And the microprinted "United States of America" which should appear in miniature letters around the border emerges as a solid black line in the forgeries.

The fact is that today, none of the laptop amateurs are quality counterfeiters, nor do they have Forger's eye, skill, and ingenuity. They also are light-years away from having his expertise in paper, watermarks, and ink. The fact that he was also an excellent jazz pianist—the peculiar details of which are to be related shortly—is a skill that turned out to be essential to Librarian's plan, too.

# 7

# THE SACRIFICE FOR
# A PIANO

Now in the fifth grade, Forger wanted to play the piano and Librarian, the cornet, because that was what his father played. In the case of Librarian, having an instrument was no problem, because he could use his father's. A neighbor, Professore Maestro Giuseppe Carrafiello, said that he would teach Librarian for one dollar a lesson.

Carrafiello had been a cornetist with the *Banda Sinfonica di Napoli*, but that was many years ago. Now, he too worked in the jute mills, played cornet on the weekends with an Italian band in Lodi, New Jersey, and annually made a rich, homemade, heady red wine from Zinfandel grapes that were imported from California. Of this lush wine, he permitted both Forger and Librarian to have one glass each year.

Forger's mother took the matter of getting a piano for her son directly to heart. Lacking funds, she intended to use skills honed in the unspoken-of days between 1939 and 1945, expertise that she had hoped there would never be a need to rekindle.

Visiting Paterson's local Campbell-Templett piano factory and standing outside, she examined the few salesmen through a large double plate-glass window, paying particular attention to their method of approach to customers and their hand and body gestures. Finally, her gaze narrowed as she focused on one hawk-faced man, bald and with a pencil-thin mustache, the rest having suddenly lost her interest.

Whatever her criteria of choices were, she went inside and marched directly to him, asking about a used piano. The least expensive upright model, with delivery, would cost almost $45, an amount that was totally out of reach, even with her normal French frugality.

She took the salesman by the arm to a corner of the store where their conversation could not be overheard and spoke to him very quietly and with great seriousness of purpose. He turned bright red in the face, but nodded his head in assent to whatever it was he was asked. She took a slip of paper, wrote something on it, gave it to the salesman, and left the store. Later, she asked Librarian's mother if her son might spend several hours with her family that evening because she had some important personal business. Librarian's mother agreed and the two boys whiled away the hours playing Monopoly.

The piano salesman came to Forger's house, spent several hours there, and left limping, bruised, with a bloody nose, several noticeable abrasions that turned black and blue, and long, straight marks on his backside made with a switch, all inflicted noiselessly because of a gag in his mouth.

That evening's events were duplicated twice more, the visits being far enough apart for the piano salesman's bruises to repair themselves. Following those three visits, a piano was delivered to Forger's house and the salesman appeared twice more. Following those five visits, which turned out to be the contracted number, he attempted to see her a sixth time. She then threw him down two flights of stairs, tied him to the bannister on the ground floor with his own belt, and called the police.

When they came, she accused him of attempting to foist unwanted advances on her and that was the last time anyone ever saw him in Paterson. The police returned to comfort Forger's mother, saying that the man was clearly insane. The stories he told of this beautiful, gentle, and modest widow's behavior were so disgusting and repulsive, particularly in light of her spotless reputation, that he was put on a westbound passenger train at Paterson's Erie Railroad station and told never to come back to the city again.

He disembarked in Cleveland and curiously died there a few years later when a piano that he had just sold, which was being hoisted up seven stories under his supervision, broke its ropes and fell on him. The newspapers commented on the irony of his being killed by his merchandise.

It was on that piano delivered to his home that Forger learned to be an extremely competent and imaginative jazz player. First, however, his mother had to arrange for proper piano lessons to put him on that path.

# 8

# MUSIC LESSONS

Having solved the problem of securing a piano, Forger's mother addressed the matter of piano lessons. This presented a more difficult challenge because her task required an interview, easily done in a public room with a number of salesmen available, but more difficult for a piano teacher working out of a private studio in his home.

It took her only one Sunday morning to solve the problem, and she did it in the most practical manner possible. Calling Paterson's Local 248 of the American Federation of Musicians earlier in the week, she asked the party on duty for the names of several reliable, male, middle-aged, single piano teachers who might help her son learn to play. Her pretense for insisting that they be single was that her son was very shy around women and would not learn well if one were present, or even nearby while getting lessons.

It was the third interview on Sunday morning that she found exactly what she was looking for in a certain Mr. Lammie, an immigrant Scot who taught piano either in his home or, at a higher fee, at the client's home. With this man, whom she recognized in some unknown way as a sexually starved person, a sample of the currency used for payment was presented, and it almost unhinged his mind. A bargain was struck, and Forger began his lessons at Mr. Lammie's home on the other side of Paterson, which he reached by bus after school on the following Monday.

Forger's mother made very competent and generously-received payments for her son's lessons every fourth Saturday afternoon, followed by a splendid dinner, cooked and served by Mr. Lammie, who had become absolutely besotted with her beauty, charming personality, and erotic skills. He offered to take her out to dinner on several occasions, but she rejected this with a variety of excuses. Her real motivation was, of course, not to be seen in public with him because it would have created gossip. This bizarre liaison continued until Forger stopped taking lessons at the age of seventeen, by which time he was making very good money as a jazz pianist.

Following the pianistic basics, Mr. Lammie tried hard to steer Forger into the classical realm by giving him the Beethoven and Mozart piano sonatas, later Mendelssohn, Chopin, Rachmaninoff, Elgar, Prokofiev, Bartok, and even Scriabin, as weekly studies, but those didn't work. In fact, no music that had fixed and unchangeable melodies worked. While Forger played them all well—and learned to be an excellent sight-reader because of this aspect of his piano education—he used the melodic content of those works as springboards for his improvisational fantasies. It drove Mr. Lammie to distraction when Forger used the fixed melodies of, for example, Beethoven's *Moonlight* Sonata as a vehicle for his imaginative extemporizations.

But the world of classical music was not what Forger's internal artistic motivation needed. He appeared to be genetically unable to play the same melody twice in the same way. Unlike forging, where one had to stay within strict bounds—for instance no goatee on Benjamin Franklin and no happy face below Lincoln's signature—he needed the freedom available to him through jazz improvisations, where nothing was the same the second time around. He was a jazz player, and that was that.

Except for one final meeting, Forger's mother never saw Mr. Lammie after her son stopped studying piano with him. That last visit took place when he came to her house and asked if she would marry him, but she refused on the grounds that he was not a Catholic. He agreed to convert to Catholicism, but then she rejected him on the grounds that he was not French. He reminded her that her dead husband was an American, which she countered by saying that her late beloved husband had shown mettle by serving in the army. Mr. Lammie retorted that he had been in his country's army before coming to America, but she rejected that argument by pointing out that England was not at war during the time of his service, thus discounting the heroism of his act. Then she added that he smelled bad and she really did not care for him.

Shortly after that he left Paterson, moved to Nevada, and worked as a night clerk in a motel in the isolated town of Ely, near the Utah border. There he spent his nights, reminiscing about Forger's mother and where, many years later, as we shall see, Forger saw and behaved kindly to him.

# 9

# SLOGGING THROUGH ADOLESCENCE

In high school, Forger learned to play the tenor sax so he and Librarian could be in the band together. Because the school supplied an instrument, Librarian switched from his father's cornet to trumpet, a fact that irritated his teacher, Professore Carafiello. He felt—and said so at every possible occasion—that the character of the trumpet was too shrill and unmusical. He would say, "Eh! You tink 'arry James 'ee play good. *Ma non*. He'sa got 'n ugly cruda soun'. An' he can no transposa trompetto in La. Joost a-play *Chiribiribin*, wid' *molto vibrato*. You tink he can play 'Torna a Sorrento' *con delicatezza* ona da *trompetto*, you *stupido*?"

Despite all this, Librarian turned out to be an excellent player, though performance of music did not interest him as much as music history, a fact that was of vital importance to our story and his plan.

Forger was not a good tenor player. For one thing, he always wanted to improvise, and that didn't work in Sousa marches any more than it worked in Chopin nocturnes. For another thing, he never practiced, mostly because he was more interested in the drilling needed to copy people's handwriting. He loved to write letters to potential girlfriends, sometimes considerably older ones, too, in the hand of the romantic poet, Lord Byron, saying, "This is the penmanship of one of the greatest of love poets. That should tell you how I feel about you!" The women would go all gooey, and the next thing they knew he had his hand up their skirts.

Librarian could never emulate Forger's skill with women. With him it was a case of a lot of groping in the dark and a few rare kissing games at parties. He even went to the main branch of Paterson's public library to research the formal rules for both Post Office and Spin-the-Bottle because he found the actual occasions too unstructured. For example, when someone got what was called "a special delivery letter," they simply disappeared into the closet for five minutes. There had to be a rule on that matter and he searched for it, unsuccessfully, for some time.

As he got older, there was some heavy necking, and a few occasions when he got his hand inside some girl's blouse. In fact, the first time Librarian went on a date—it was a double date with Forger, who was squiring a cheerleader from Pompton Lakes—he had his arm around the girl's shoulder and rubbed her bony elbow for twenty minutes, thinking it was her breast.

The best part of being in the band was that the two got to go to football games, and during that season, Forger plowed his way through the entire cheerleading squad, while simultaneously mastering the handwritings of both Abraham Lincoln and Thomas Jefferson. His ability to mimic the hand of another person was no longer a childish prank. It was an awesome talent, and his reputation in that arena was growing a lot faster—and being brought to the attention of a different class of observer—than his piano playing skills.

# 10

# ADVANCED PROFESSIONAL
# EDUCATION

After the two graduated from high school, Forger left Paterson for Europe to study the practice of making eighteenth-century style paper, because he realized that it was an essential skill for him to learn. His talent at copying things was so immense that he gravitated into forging documents as naturally as a bird sings. But he realized that he required special training in the making of eighteenth-century paper. Without it, what he intended to do would get him into trouble very quickly.

So in late June of the year of their high-school graduation, he went to France as a passenger on the Queen Elizabeth and fell in love with water travel. There, at his mother's request, he took a train to Lyon, visited the graves of his grandparents, and made an emotionally difficult visit to his aunt, still in a mental institution outside of Lyon. She had no idea who he was, was unable to speak coherently, and remembered nothing of Forger's mother—her sister.

Then Forger took a train to Arnhem in the Netherlands, where he began his apprenticeship at a working eighteenth-century paper mill. It was almost six years before he and Librarian were reunited.

Librarian was accepted into Columbia College on a full scholarship, getting a major in European history with a minor in music in three years. After graduating *summa cum laude*, he went to graduate school at Columbia University School of Library Service for a Masters Degree, intending to specialize in the care and preservation of rare manuscripts following a doctorate in the history of music. He received that in two years and then got his first job with the Rare Manuscripts Division of the New York Public Library, located on Forty-second Street in Manhattan.

Forger completed his apprenticeship in The Netherlands the same year that Librarian entered graduate school. However, he chose to go on for another three years of work in a different eighteenth-century paper mill—this one located in Germany—because it specialized in techniques of making eighteenth-century watermarks. He deliberately chose it because of its prominent affiliation with the International Association of Paper Historians.

Forger came back to America around the time that Librarian began work at the New York Public Library. Getting his telephone number from Librarian's mother, who still lived on Grand Street in Paterson, he was told that her husband, Librarian's father and Forger's first employer, had passed away.

In a call to Librarian, Forger indicated that he needed help with something and wanted to talk with Librarian about a possible long-term business arrangement.

# 11

# A JOINT BUSINESS
# VENTURE BEGINS

By the time the two men were in their mid-twenties, Forger had created and sold his first important counterfeit to a New York dealer. It was an entirely invented letter of Abraham Lincoln that spoke about the evils of slavery. The dealer, a well-known Lincoln specialist, too, was convinced that the letter was genuine. To have bypassed successfully the watchdogs represented by that particular expert was an eye-opening demonstration of Forger's talents.

However, it was the accidental but remarkably comfortable symbiosis between Librarian's job on one hand and Forger's skills on the other that made the partnership between them a natural. It was this very issue that Forger had cryptically alluded to as "a long-term business opportunity" when he contacted Librarian following Forger's return from Germany.

Because the Rare Books and Manuscripts Division of the New York Public Library had authentic originals from almost every period of American and World history, when Forger wanted to create a document with someone's signature, Librarian would research an item in the holdings of the NYPL that enormously minimized the risks and substantially increased the chances of technical and financial success.

For example, once Librarian xerographically reproduced for Forger both sides of a genuine discharge certificate from the American Revolutionary Army, signed by George Washington. That item was part of the NYPL's fabulous collection of rare manuscripts. Forger made a perfect counterfeit of it, with a few changes to make that particular discharge unique.

The document wasn't a one-of-a-kind, because Washington signed many such discharges—most of which no longer existed—but it was quite valuable, despite the fact that it was not unique. In reality, most of the text was a standard handwritten discharge form with a lot of boilerplate. The date and name were filled in at the time of discharge and then signed. Generally, the only thing on the page in Washington's handwriting was his signature, but if a clerk had failed to enter data prior to Washington's signing, he might also write the missing information such as the dischargee's name or the date of the soldier's separation from the army.

The name of the person being discharged was important, but not critical, because record keeping in the Revolutionary Army was not the highest priority. Though registers did exist for many of the men in the Continental Army at the time of the American Revolution, presenting a document allegedly from that period and which made reference to a person whose name did not appear in the official records was not a showstopper.

On the other hand, one could not make up just any name arbitrarily, so visits to cemeteries dating from after the American Revolution was a part of the research effort, and any name possibility required further investigation at state registry offices and birth/death archives. For example, it did their efforts no good to produce a discharge certificate for a man who at the time of his alleged release from the military was documented somewhere else as being an amputee of some years standing and who never served in the military.

Almost any handwriting would do for the boilerplate, provided the style of the period and the penmanship were maintained. Forger did his professional job on those things, and also the forging of Washington's signature. Then he sold the discharge certificate—after he folded and ironed the paper many times to get the creases right—to a dealer who had a client with a very big itch for exactly such an item.

Librarian acted for Forger in the sale and got him almost $30,000 for his efforts—though the dealer originally offered only $5,000—at which point Librarian's manuscript expertise took over, allowing him to earn his commission. The dealer sold it for $80,000, so everyone was happy, including the buyer who would some day sell it for twice that price. It's out there, somewhere, appreciating like a good blue chip, and will never be discovered for the fake it is. That's the quality of counterfeits Forger is capable of making.

# 12

# TECHNICAL
# CONSIDERATIONS

Forger stated that the essential elements of any good counterfeit were handwriting and formatting, and if those were good enough, you were seventy-five percent home. However, he recognized that paper, ink, and pens were essential for the final twenty-five percent of the journey.

In effect, no matter how good the handwriting was, if one forged Washington's signature on a piece of contemporary Hammermill Bond, eighty percent rag-content paper—or even real but bleached-out eighteenth-century paper with an anomalous watermark—using a steel nibbed pen with modern ink, you'd soon be standing in the middle of Main Street without your pants on, surrounded by a lot of policemen and some very angry manuscript dealers. But it was in solving exactly those additional problems at which Forger's specialized skills were at their apex.

It was for the purpose of becoming a master at these, and a thousand other technical details, that he spent six years at two paper mills in Europe, honing his skills on almost every aspect of the production of documents with a perfect eighteenth-century patina. So when he finished a forgery, the paper was spot-on to the era with which it needed to be identified. With his perfect handwriting, as well as his scrupulous attention to the many things that are not handwriting but relate to the formatting and placement of text on the page, the fact that he had perfect paper with the correct watermarks of that era, written with a handmade replica of an eighteenth-century goose quill and using specially crafted inks, gave him breathing room.

The handwriting of his forgeries was so spot-on accurate, with such authentic-looking paper and period inks, that his copies were accepted almost without question. Never once was he asked to submit his documents to the kinds of scientific tests that might have shown that the paper on which the text was written was more contemporary than it was supposed to be.

With respect to watermarks, Forger was especially skilled. He knew everything about creating and properly placing watermarks in paper, including the fact that watermarks of handmade paper came in twin mirror-imaged pairs. In effect, he was capable of managing the multiple pieces of the watermark technology jigsaw puzzle that needed to be in place when an expert examined the document. When those specialists found each piece of that puzzle interconnecting perfectly with every other piece, it stopped being a contest.

Mind you, he did not know which watermarks were needed for which paper, but if you told him that you required a watermark of the Mannequin Pis or the Statue of Liberty of a certain size, standing in the middle of Times Square and placed at a specific location on the page, you'd get a work of art embedded into the very fibers of the paper and viewable on a watermark lightbox display or a Beta-radiograph of the page.

When Forger decided to counterfeit a Lincoln, Washington, or Adams letter, he made authentic-style paper that perfectly matched those of the period and with the very watermarks that were used in real Lincoln, Washington, and Adams documents. It was the need for these things that was probably the most significant contribution that Librarian made to their partnership.

If, for example, Forger intended to create a Franklin Roosevelt letter—which was unusual, because forging documents of the earlier Presidents brought far more money—he needed to know about the kinds of paper, including watermarks, that Roosevelt used during the era of the document that he intended to create. Then Librarian would examine the Roosevelt manuscripts held by the New York Public Library, of which there were eight letters in the collection. Using a light box, Librarian did a tracing of the watermarks of all eight—actually only five were needed, because one of the watermarks was identical in three of the letters and another in two—and Forger took his pick from the one written nearest the date of the document he was creating.

On the other hand, if the NYPL did not have a manuscript for the person or period needed, Librarian's job, coupled with his authentic identification documents, gained him entry into the rare manuscript division of any library in the world. He'd call the Roosevelt archives in Hyde Park, NY, identify himself, and state that he was making a watermark catalog of the NYPL's Roosevelt letters and needed to contrast them with those in the Hyde Park collection.

When he got to that facility, he would show them his ID, which was absolutely genuine, and instantly get permission to examine their collection at whatever level of detail he required. A call to the NYPL would always confirm that he was who he said he was, and that meant that Hyde Park could be comfortable in his knowledge of how to handle old manuscripts. He was, after all, an expert on the subject. It worked every time.

It may have sounded hypocritical for a man who had a responsibility to protect and preserve rare documents to use his skill and position to help create forgeries, yet he saw it differently. Librarian would never have stolen a document, even if he had the opportunity to do so, because he had no personal need for possession of such things. Besides, that was only a shortcut to public and professional disgrace. A few now-jailed scholars tried to create their own private library of valuable manuscripts, but all were eventually caught.

Librarian had good reason to think of his work as research, rather than a criminal enterprise. He perceived it as a simple examination of historic documents so as to obtain certain technical details about which his business partner needed to know. In that way, Librarian always felt that he was not at all involved in counterfeiting, just scholarly research that enabled another party to do more perfect work. It is quite safe to say that without Librarian's assistance, Forger's efforts in this arena would never have passed the technical inspections to which his documents were subjected.

Later, when the counterfeit document went up for sale, the things most thoroughly examined by experts were the handwriting, author-typical formatting, paper, ink, and watermarks. Forger's manuscripts always came through without difficulties, and the two of them made a handsome profit for some time.

Only the necessity to keep volume low prevented them from becoming really rich. After all, how many times can one discover an unknown and valuable manuscript without arousing suspicion? That meant that they worked manuscript dealers in Boston, Philadelphia, and as far west as Los Angeles.

On several occasions, Forger's manuscripts were even sold in Europe, with an especially high price paid at Sotheby's in London for a letter about plans for an enormous soirée at Versailles. It was advertised as a rare example of a letter written by France's Louis XVI—whose total indifference to the horrendous costs of the event was seen as further historic evidence of his disinterest in the desperate state of French citizenry.

The forgery, dated some years before the revolution robbed both him and his wife of their heads, was made especially difficult by the need for the vocabulary and style of eighteenth-century court French. The fact that Forger was fluent in French because of his mother allowed him to plow through a great deal of literature from that era to capture the style and grammar of the epoch, particularly when written by the royal hand, itself a rare event. That document was sold to the *Bibliothèque Nationale* in Paris for almost $250,000.

Librarian and Forger used a network of reliable agents—which reduced their income but was necessary for continued success—because they could not afford to become known, or even noticed. For example, if it became public knowledge that the same person who sold a Poe letter in New York also sold an Adams letter in Los Angeles, they would have been exposed quickly.

It was a few years before Forger's detour into the world of the new $100 bill dried up their revenue stream and injured their collaborative efforts to the tune of four years' worth of income, but until that happened, they had a very successful business going. Librarian bought the Paterson home with his share of the proceeds, and Forger rented a number of safe deposit boxes—none closer than fifty miles from Paterson—in which he stored a great deal of cash. He also had some real estate interests, but preferred liquidity above all other money management techniques, and he never used credit cards.

Occasionally, one of their agents would advise them of a manuscript dealer looking for a special item because of a specific customer's request. Those always paid the best. As it turned out, Forger's hiatus in prison was a sort of small blessing, though at the time they didn't feel that way about it. Since they hadn't produced anything for four years, the manuscript dealers were as ripe as summer plums for the kind of things they did.

However, for the idea that Librarian now had in mind—one radically different from anything they had ever done before—Forger would have to be kept out of sight for some time, and the fact that they knew each other needed to be guarded information. For one thing, there were some men who had a business proposition with Forger in mind—a variation of the very scheme that had gotten him his four-year vacation. For another, it would do Librarian's plans no good were any of the auction houses with which he did business to know that he had a friend who was a convicted felon and counterfeiter. This was information that Forger's would-be colleagues would gladly have advertised on his backside in 200 point Gothic type, given the opportunity.

# 13

# WHAT ABOUT RADIOACTIVE DECAY?

Following Forger's return from Germany and his reestablishing contact with Librarian for the purpose of discussing "a long-term business opportunity," they thrashed out plans for the making and selling of forged, historically important manuscripts. Depending on the contents of these documents—over which they had complete control and much of which would be entirely invented—their expectations were for some very high-priced sales. But the central problem, one that in Librarian's opinion was not unimportant but came up far more frequently than it deserved, had to do with a specific fear that Forger displayed and about which it was clear that he had some concerns.

It was based on his misperception of a technical issue, and before they could really begin, Librarian had to put it in proper perspective so as to ease Forger's mind on the subject. Despite Forger's training, talent, and absolute mastery of every significant element of the art of creating handwritten documents, each with a patina from a specific era, he had one overriding fear. Librarian's most significant contribution to the beginning of their work was the way he eliminated that fear.

What had crept into Forger's mind was that no matter what skills he brought to the counterfeiting art, his forgeries ran the risk of discovery through recourse to what he called "the scientific dating tests."

"I hear that science has ways," he mused, "to recognize forgeries in a minute. They use a giant gizmo or something. You put a piece of paper in it and dial a date on its knobs. Then it clicks and flashes until a computer-generated voice says, 'Fake! Fake! Fake!' Now, how am I ever going to get around that?"

Like most people with little serious scientific expertise, Forger had dozens of preconceptions about how technical things were accomplished. Knowing little, he believed in simple solutions to complicated problems. When it came to the science of dating paper documents, he held an exaggerated belief that a simple technique would nullify his years of specialized training.

"Didn't you discuss this problem with your teachers in Europe?" Librarian finally asked, exasperated with the frequency of Forger's pursuit of the subject.

"We sort of alluded to the matter," Forger answered, "but the schools I went to were not forgery academies licensed by the state. They were simply places where everything about the art of papermaking was studied and practiced. While techniques of document reproduction were also studied, of course, scientific methods of determining forgeries were not part of the curriculum. I suspect that if I ever really told anyone what was on my mind, they would have refused to train me.

"Whenever I brought up the subject of dating tests," he continued, "the response was invariably, 'That's something you don't have to worry about.' I'd ask why and be told that the answer was technical. It never satisfied me."

So, in a discussion no more detailed than it had to be, Librarian—who was an absolute wizard on the subject of paper dating because it was essential to his business—told Forger what the technique was really all about. It was, so to speak, getting over this hump that made their partnership a functioning enterprise.

Librarian began by saying that Forger's information was partly correct, but very misleading. Then he complimented him on the few things he had learned. Next, he agreed with Forger that there was a testing process that, if implemented, would present hard evidence that a paper document was not from an advertised era. Finally, he stated that the accuracy of the science, having nothing to do with opinion, was almost beyond question.

Now, having laid out all of the presumed truths of paper age testing, Librarian set about to crush every one of the arguments with the practical facts of the matter. The greatest impediments to the invoking of the tests were the consequences of using it. When asked for an explanation of that cryptic statement, Librarian said, "What I mean to say is that age tests reduce the value and worth of the document being tested." Then he explained the details.

"The first mistaken idea about the test," he continued, "is that it is performed even when other means exist to examine legitimacy. Mostly, the tests are employed when the calligraphy of the party who wrote the text is not known and no handwriting samples of that person exist for comparison. For example, were a document presented that purported to be theologically important—such as an assertion of personal involvement with a miraculous event—such tests would be used because they are the only way to approach the issue of authenticity. But that is not always necessary—or even desirable—for a document whose genuineness can be argued in other ways.

"The second mistaken idea about the test is that it determines the age of what is written on the paper. It doesn't, at least not to any degree of accuracy. This is because the age of a piece of paper and the age of what is written on it are almost never synonymous. Years can pass between the time a piece of paper was manufactured and when someone actually wrote something on it.

"So it appears that paper-dating tests are more interested in the age of the paper, rather than the age of what is written on it. But to be scrupulously accurate, the test doesn't give the age of the paper, either."

As an example that Forger could grasp at once, Librarian spoke about how Washington, Adams, or Jefferson—whose documents are among the more valuable collectibles—used paper that may have been made years, even decades, before they wrote on it. In theory, some of the paper that these men used could have been manufactured even before they were born, thus giving rise to a paradox in which a tested document predates the birth of the person who wrote on it.

"However," Librarian continued, "since paper tests are insufficiently accurate to isolate the year, the decade, or quarter-century within which the paper was manufactured, such anomalies are unlikely to arise, and if they do, they can be explained away."

Then Librarian went to the heart of what paper tests really did. "The entire process of determining when paper was made is a second cousin to an autopsy, because in the final analysis, what it determines is when death occurred. Literally!

"What is really learned from such tests is the approximate time of death of the vegetable material used to create the paper. So what paper-date tests really give you is the time when the grass, flax, cotton, or other material used to make the rags that made the paper was mowed down.

"Those tests are based on a property of all living and dead matter, called 'radioactive decay.' It is an absolute gold-bond standard for confirming that a document said to be from a certain date really was written on paper made some time around that date, generally within a twenty-five to fifty-year period. That is the best that such tests can accomplish at this juncture of science.

"However," Librarian continued, "it is certainly enough to expose the kind of counterfeits that you make."

"So what is my salvation here?" Forger asked.

"Your salvation lies in the nature and physical consequences of the test on one hand, and in the creation of a document so perfect that the test is deemed to be unnecessary, on the other."

"Let's first examine the main flaw in how you perceive paper dating. The scientific principle underlying radioactive-decay tests is this: anything that lives, including all flora such as the vegetable products used in papermaking, and all fauna such as people and animals, contains an amount of a slightly radioactive variation of the carbon atom, known as carbon-14. The amount of carbon-14 in an object depends mostly on weight, and a human thighbone has more of it than a cotton ball.

"This radioactive material begins the unstoppable process of decay immediately upon death, and in a mathematically very predictable way. Should something that once lived need to have the time of its death determined—for example, a human bone or a piece of paper made from rags, themselves made from a combination of grass, flax, and cotton—a destructive examination of a piece of that thing is used to approximate the time of death."

"What do you mean by destructive?" Forger asked.

"Exactly what it says," responded Librarian. "You have to destroy a part of the document to date it, which is why the test is done far less frequently than one might think. The owners of such things rarely permit it, because after the test, the document's worth has been reduced. But let me continue with that idea in a moment.

"It makes no difference to the test if the time of death refers to when the cotton or flax plant was harvested, or in the case of a person, when he or she died—from whatever cause. The test is interested in only one fact: namely, how many radioactive carbon-14 atoms remain in a sample of the thing whose time of death is under investigation. If the death was long ago, fewer such carbon-14 atoms remain because the substance decays over time. Such an examination would expose any one of your counterfeits very quickly.

"However," continued Librarian as he warmed to the task of bringing Forger's thinking in line with his, "you would have a ton of things working for you. An important one is the fact that radioactive-decay tests cannot be casually performed. They require expensive equipment, often found only at the largest of scientific laboratories. But a far better safety shield is the one I just mentioned—namely, the destruction of a piece of the document. That test requires a number of postage-stamp sized pieces to be cut from the tested document. All of those pieces, taken from an expensive and irreplaceable document, are destroyed!

"A technician weighs and burns them. The ashes are ground up and the remaining quantity of carbon-14 atoms determined. In practice, a Geiger counter tallies the quantity, then the mathematics of exponential decay calculates how much time has elapsed from the moment of harvest of the vegetable material that made the rags that made the paper to this moment. For absolute certainty, the test is often performed at multiple locations so as to confirm the results, with each of those locations requiring pieces of the document."

Then, for emphasis, Librarian told Forger the story of a radioactive decay test done on an item of not only unknown antiquity, but of possible theological value.

"There is a linen shroud said by some to be the winding sheet of Jesus. It rests in the Cathedral of Turin, Italy, and is said to contain a miraculous image of him, following his crucifixion. For years its date of origin was not tested because the technology at that time required a number of handkerchief-sized pieces of cloth be cut from the shroud and then destroyed in the testing. Clearly, that was not something the church authorities would permit.

"Finally, in 1988, the technique improved so much that a smaller pieces of cloth could be used, and approval was finally given for the test. It was done at three different locations: one in America, one in England, and one in Switzerland. So, like the Turin shroud, except in the most extreme cases, no one will ask for destruction of a portion of a manuscript in order to confirm the authenticity of the remaining portion. The act of testing degrades the value of the thing being tested. It just won't be called for unless there is some serious suspicion about its legitimacy.

"This is why the test almost never happens to unusually expensive or rare manuscripts. Instead, if suspicions arise, the buyer backs away from the sale or the seller takes the item off the market, but only very rarely are forgeries identified in this way. Paradoxically, even when such tests conclude that the object is not of the expected age—as was the case with the Shroud of Turin—arguments are offered to cast doubt on the accuracy of the test—as was also the case with the Shroud of Turin."

Forger interrupted to ask, "In the case of a paper document, what kind of arguments could be made to discredit the test?"

"In the case of paper," Librarian responded, "one could argue that after the flax and cotton plants were cut down, some extended period of time took place before cloth was made from them. Then the cloth object—a garment, for example—could have been used and preserved in that state for years, even decades. Finally, when discarded, the garments might be collected and stored with other such fabrics until an economically viable amount was available for paper manufacture, again suggesting the passage of considerable time. Then, after the paper was made, one could argue that it was not sold or written on for some indefinite period of time. It's a subject that a technician could successfully dispute for years. In the case of the Shroud of Turin, arguments were made that plant spores on the garment corrupted the validity of the tests.

"It is almost entirely handwriting, formatting, paper, and ink that confirm the authenticity of documents. In fact, several recently-discovered music manuscripts of great worth were never even considered to have such tests performed on them because the experts examining them knew, by visual examination alone, that their authenticity was certain."

"What kind of music manuscripts were those?" Forger asked.

"Well," responded Librarian, "one of them was a manuscript of a Mozart piano sonata found in a safe in Philadelphia. The first expert who saw it took a three-second look at the first page and offered the absolute assurance that it was in Mozart's hand. And he was right, or must have been, because it was sold to the Central Institute of Mozart Research in Salzburg for a very high price."

Without knowing it, by speaking about music manuscripts of great worth, Librarian was touching on the very issue that he would take up with Forger some years later, following the latter's time in prison.

Then, concluding his remarks about paper testing, Librarian said, "The aura of authenticity of the counterfeits that you create will lie in the fact that all of the things tested solely by visual examination can be simulated. I have every reason to expect that documents produced by you are going to be so absolutely convincing that their authenticity will be accepted immediately by any expert who examines them."

It was because of the confidence Forger had after this explanation that his fears were eliminated and their joint business venture began in earnest.

# 14

# FORGER'S WOULD-BE COLLEAGUES

Other than his remarkable skill at counterfeiting documents, his talent at playing jazz piano, and even at a young age his extraordinary popularity with attractive women, Forger had few personal assets. Furthermore, he had a significant weakness in that he had no sense of politics and was unable—or unwilling—to recognize a dominant power when confronted with it.

Then one year before the government's newly designed $100 bills were placed into circulation, three men, built like cigarette machines, approached Forger. With considerable courtesy, the most articulate of the three invited him to a meeting where their superiors wanted to suggest a mutually profitable opportunity for him. At that meeting it was proposed that funding could be arranged to support an early forgery of the new currency, professional photographs of which were shown to him, though how they were obtained was never explained, nor did he inquire about it.

Being completely out of his depth, but not so much so that he failed to pay attention to the samples, Forger turned them down, and not particularly politely either. Instead, he usurped the idea, decided to make the bills on his own, and in theory at least, keep all the profits for himself.

It was a monumentally bad decision, bordering on the stunningly imbecilic, and Librarian wished that Forger had told him of the overture and his response to it before the fact, and not afterwards, during a visit to Fairton prison.

The men from whom he had gotten the idea for the counterfeiting scheme decided to teach him a small lesson about arrogance. They did not intend to make him disappear, which would have been a very big lesson indeed, but instead advised the Treasury Department of Forger's identity. Apparently they came from a county that had never heard of *omertà*. Besides, Forger's skills were so legendary that those thugs hesitated to dispose of such a potentially valuable resource with such finality.

What they expected was that their action would make him less independent the next time they suggested doing business together. Of course Forger knew enough not to identify anyone. If he had done so, those whom he had deceived, and who had deceived him, might rethink the severity of the lesson they wished to impart.

Would you believe that the authorities initially refused to accept the fact that Forger's bills were counterfeit? In fact, they did not even know that the walls of their new currency structure had been breached. That's how perfect the forgeries were. But his misstep of using only one dozen repeated serial numbers caused them to do an astonished double-take, and before you could say "microprinting," Forger found himself in prison.

On the other hand, considering what might have happened, there was a bright side to the picture. Forger got only an obligatory, no-release-early, four-year sentence at a medium-security federal prison, mostly because he had been caught quickly and was cooperative in describing how he had accomplished the supposedly impossible task.

The Treasury Department, thanks to the help of his erstwhile colleagues, was on top of Forger almost at once. He wisely decided to give up an impressively large cache of still-unpassed currency—none of which was ever kept in any of his safe deposit boxes—and most importantly, the details of his process. Then, as an added gesture of good faith, he met with treasury experts on multiple occasions to suggest a number of things that could avoid this kind of problem in the future.

I think the authorities wanted to hire him as an advisor, but couldn't see their way clear, considering what he had done. It went all the way to the office of the Secretary of the Treasury before the idea was rejected. At a minimum, Librarian thought that Forger should have gotten a consultant's fee, not a four-year sentence. Judging from the way that very poor counterfeits of the new $100 bill were now appearing—with many said to be turned out in the Beka'a Valley by the Hezbollah—they would have made a much more intelligent business, political, and technical decision, had they commuted Forger's four-year prison sentence and hired him.

Of course, the men who turned Forger in assumed that when he got out he'd not refuse them a second time. But their plan backfired, and the longed-for currency-counterfeiting opportunity blew up in their faces. Most of the changes that Forger suggested to the Treasury Department had been quietly implemented and this now made perfect counterfeits even more difficult to produce, so much so that there arose a serious question if it was financially worthwhile to produce a perfect counterfeit at all.

On the surface, that sounds absurd. How can it be financially disadvantageous to counterfeit money? You just keep making more of it to cover your costs, or so you might think. But that's true only if the cost of a technically perfect, counterfeit $100 bill is kept really small, and that was now no longer possible, considering Forger's extraordinarily inventive additions supplemented by the government's already significant impediments. The net result was that to make money—no pun intended—one would have to get one's investment back by counterfeiting so much of the stuff that the authorities would immediately notice a statistically measurable change in the volume of currency in circulation. That's why Forger's erstwhile colleagues went to other sources, many of whom are now producing lots of poor quality counterfeit American $100 bills. In fact, so much of it is being made that merchants in some places have signs that say, "We do not accept US currency notes larger than $20."

# 15

# LIBERTY AT LAST

Librarian made certain that he stayed far away from the prison's administrative entrance while seated in his car awaiting Forger's release, an act that minimized the possibility of his being identified at some later time. Even so, he wore a piece, a fake mustache, a cosmetic mole, and wire-rimmed non-prescription glasses, a pair used only for such occasions.

A forged driver's license in a false name and made by Forger five years earlier had a photo on it showing him wearing all four items. It was used as ID during the four years that Librarian visited Forger in prison, roughly every other month. While the disguise was really created for those few occasions when he would meet with a manuscript dealer to negotiate the sale of one of Forger's products, it came in handy during trips to Fairton, because all visitors were required to show identification. While during the early period of Forger's incarceration Librarian had no plans for projects that might be undertaken at the time of Forger's eventual release, he did not want any officials in the prison system to be able to identify him.

However, in light of what he now had in mind and in the likelihood that his picture would get in the newspapers because of it, the last thing he wanted to happen was to have some Fairton official say, "Isn't that the guy who used to visit...uh...that fancy forger...er...? Damn! I've forgotten his name already."

Shortly before noon, several officials of the prison came and stood by the still-open front door of the administrative area. It was clear that Forger would come out that door, the same one through which Librarian entered whenever he visited the prison. And then, as unimpressive as if it were designed to be mundane, Forger came out of the front door, shook the hands of the several administrative personnel, looked around, saw Librarian now standing by the side of the car, and began to walk towards it.

It wasn't supposed to happen that way. In all the movies Librarian ever saw about men getting out of prison, there were always big gates with a small door set in them. And when it opened, James Cagney—or some poor imitation of him—would step out, and the guard by the door would fling a final insult.

"We'll be seein' ya' back here soon, ya' lousy crook!" he'd say, to which Jimmie, accompanied by a supreme bravado and a depraved sneer, would reply, "You'll neva' get me in dis lousy dump again, ya' stinkin' screw!!" And then he would arrogantly turn his back on the prison officials, step out into the free world, and be greeted lovingly by some beautiful female star in a cloche hat who was standing by a Packard convertible two-seater, with a running board and a rumble seat.

On the other hand, Forger came out carrying his few possessions in a torn paper supermarket bag that was missing a handle. When he got to the car, they greeted each other and shook hands. Forger got into the passenger seat and Librarian got behind the wheel."

"I'm glad to get out of that place!" Forger said. "Thanks for picking me up. I didn't want to take the bus to Trenton and then take another to New York. That's eighty miles out of my way." Then, waving his hand at the prison, he added, "In this place, they say that one of the reasons you get let out of here at noon is because the bus to Trenton is at 1 p.m. and it's a mile to the bus stop, about a thirty-minute walk at middle-aged-man tempo. I wonder if they let out the older prisoners earlier than the younger ones?"

Librarian realized that he had been given misinformation about when prisoners were released. Apparently it was always at noon, since Forger indicated that it was part of inmate scuttlebutt. Then, thinking about what else Forger had just said, he thought, *That's him in normal form. In the space of five sentences he articulated several different and unrelated ideas, speculated negatively on the character of the state's public transportation system, voiced an opinion on the curmudgeonly nature of the Federal Prison's management, spoke of his distaste for long walks, showed his tender views on the problems of the aged, and ruminated on alternatives that must be considered when things don't go right.*

Librarian was very alert as to how Forger's mind wandered in a lot of different directions at once, a manifestation of his natural curiosity and inquisitiveness.

"I thought we might take an agreeable boat ride," Librarian volunteered. "It's your first day out and I want to make it pleasant for you. I've got a lunch for the two of us, we'll have a long time to talk, and maybe you'd like to hear about an opportunity that I've thought about for a while. It can make some serious money for us both."

"Ouch!" Forger replied. "I'm not out of prison five minutes and you want me right back in the saddle? I hope it's not making money again. I think I may have outsmarted myself in that department. Besides, I hear that the new $100 bill has a lot of design competition—most of it junk—and the authorities are collecting both the money and its makers with both hands. Anyway, that's the word inside Fairton. At least my stuff was high class, though I should have used more serial numbers."

"Well, you're right that I'm talking about money," Librarian offered, "but you wouldn't have to make it, at least not literally."

"I'm ready to listen to anything," Forger replied. "It's been four years of doing nothing but reading and playing solitaire. I read every one of the twenty-nine volumes of the *New Grove's Dictionary of Music*—twice! It took me almost half my term to do it. And I even kept my hand in at practicing the piano. They have an old, out-of-tune upright model in the room they use for movies. Also, I can now play forty-five different games of solitaire, some of them requiring two decks of cards, and a couple of them are almost impossible to win. For example, take 'Aces Up.' First you deal four cards face up, and then..."

Forger's voice droned on enthusiastically about the rules of "Aces Up" and a variety of other solitaire games that he was now able to play. Librarian turned on the engine, pointed the nose of the car towards the southernmost point of the New Jersey Cape on nearby Delaware Bay—though fifty-three driving miles away—and put Fairton Federal Prison behind them. Forger, describing the details of "Aces Up," showed his total disinterest in sentimentality by never even looking back.

# BOOK 2:
# THE PLAN

# 16

# DELAWARE FERRY

An hour later, Forger was still babbling on about a variety of subjects for which he had numerous opinions and multiple perspectives when Librarian pulled the car onto the New Jersey-Delaware ferry. After parking, he found a place where they could speak without being overheard for the length of the trip—about an hour and a half—during which time Librarian intended to introduce Forger to a novel idea.

The previous evening, Librarian had picked up some food, presuming that he would eat part of it for lunch if Forger were not released by noon. Knowing his friend's favorites—and wanting to pick events and foods that would get Forger's mind off prison and on to his plan quickly—Librarian bought two smoked turkey sandwiches with hot mustard on Kaiser rolls, some pickles, a giant bag of taco chips, and for each of them a can of Dr. Brown's Cel-Ray Tonic and a Milky Way. If the discussions weren't finished by the time they reached Lewes, Delaware, Librarian would continue the conversation on the trip back to New Jersey.

Even before the ferry departed Cape May, the two had left the car and were occupying deck chairs at the bow end of the ship. Librarian carried a cloth travel bag that he would need during the discussion, situating it at his feet after they were seated. He knew that Forger liked boat rides because his friend often said that one of the most pleasant times he ever had was the ocean voyage to Europe when he first traveled there on the Queen Elizabeth to apprentice the various arts of papermaking.

Consequently, Librarian had an edge, because it involved a boat ride on Forger's first day out of jail, and Librarian was exploiting the atmosphere of both events to make his proposal maximally attractive. Assuming that Forger would not be able to turn down an opportunity of a rainbow with a pot of gold this big at the end of it, the two had an uncertain number of months of hard work ahead of them.

Forger sat in the deck chair and looked out at the bay, really the ocean, but if someone chose to define that vast area of water as something other than the Atlantic, that was OK with him. Finally, a few minutes after the engines were turned on and the ferry left its slip, Librarian took a first bite out of his sandwich and asked Forger if he was ready to discuss a business opportunity.

"How much income potential does it have?" Forger inquired.

"Hard to say, but I think it can bring in at least $20,000,000, and probably more," Librarian replied casually, considering the amount of money involved.

"You've got my attention," was Forger's reaction. "Just what kind of thing do you have in mind?"

Librarian dawdled in his response to create a little drama, taking a second bite of his sandwich to extend the pause even longer. He chewed, swallowed after a time, took a gulp of his Cel-Ray tonic, munched on a taco chip, and then opened the floodgates.

"I had it in mind…that we might produce two valuable music manuscripts."

Forger stopped eating, looked quizzical, and was silent for some time. Then he said, "Exactly what do you mean by a 'music manuscript'? And while you're at it, just what kind of a music manuscript would carry a price tag as big as you suggest?"

Librarian didn't answer the questions at once, instead choosing to lay a little groundwork. "First, I want to tell you that I'm no longer at the Forty-second Street headquarters of the New York Public Library. They felt that I had enough NYPL experience and the necessary background in music history to give me a new job. So they moved me from the facility where the rare manuscripts that have textual and literary content are preserved to the Special Collections of the Music Division in Lincoln Center, where the music manuscript acquisitions are housed.

"You know the complex, of course," he continued. "It's the resident center for the Metropolitan and City Opera companies, the New York Philharmonic, the City Ballet, Lincoln Center Chamber Music Society, the Juilliard School, and a sample of just about everything else related to the performing arts in New York.

"I've been there since right after you went to Fairton, though I can still examine anything in the Forty-second Street facility that we might need. But that business we had working with text forgeries can be made to work with music manuscripts, too. There is also the opportunity for much greater financial potential than with text forgeries, and there is absolutely no competition. It is an arsenal that has never been successfully breached," he concluded with an artistic turn of phrase.

Now that Librarian had Forger's attention with the magic words "financial potential," he continued with some basic detail, being careful not to give him too much at any one time. Forger needed to be teased before his jaws snapped shut on the lure, but once they closed on it, one would have a difficult time getting them open. They stared at the water for a long while, munching their sandwiches, and then Librarian continued with more details of his plan.

# 17

# WHOSE MANUSCRIPTS DID YOU HAVE IN MIND?

"There are music manuscripts in the NYPL that are worth some very serious money," Librarian said. "They're mostly the original scores created by a number of composers. By the way, music manuscripts are also called 'autographs,' and in that sense the term means the whole document, not just someone's signature.

"New York's Pierpont Morgan Library also has a large and valuable music manuscript collection, in some areas even more important than those of the NYPL, and the Library of Congress has the best and most valuable ones in America. But the manuscripts at the New York Public Library are very good, and several are extremely precious. What's more important, they're available to me for examination, should I need to do that. So are others at public and private facilities all over the US.

"For example, if I had to I'd simply ask Rigbie Turner, the Curator of Music Manuscripts at the Pierpont Morgan, if I could examine an item or two. There would almost certainly be no problem because my job requires me to handle the NYPL music manuscripts and Turner knows that. Besides, he is a colleague, and the work we do causes our paths to cross on occasion.

"So I'd call him and say, 'Hi Rigbie. Would it be possible for me to see the manuscript of Mozart's *Haffner* Symphony, please? I need to check some ink colors for an article we're considering about a manuscript that the NYPL owns and it was written around the same time as the *Haffner* Symphony. I prefer to use the original and not the published facsimile of the *Haffner,* because I'm uncertain about the accuracy of the ink colors in the photography.'

'Thirty minutes later I'd be viewing one of the most valuable manuscripts in the world, perhaps even working at old J.P. Morgan's big desk. I mention all this so you are able to place my current position with the NYPL in the context of the plan's details. Now let me get back to your question about value.

'You asked about how the worth of rare and valuable music manuscripts are estimated, so let me get to that now, but I ask you to be aware that some of these things are so precious that no price can be put on them.

"As a starting example," he continued, "I'll mention that just last month there was a sale of a Mozart manuscript at Sotheby's in London. It wasn't even a completed composition—only a draft of one. There was hardly anything to it, just four surfaces of paper with very little written on them. In fact, the fourth surface was blank. The manuscript was really a single sheet of paper about twenty-four inches wide and folded in the middle like a book.

'It sold for $300,000," Librarian said, making sure that the story ended with what was called "the hammer price," not with any of the reasons that justified why someone would pay that kind of money for four surfaces of almost empty paper.

'That must have been a very special case," Forger suggested.

"Not at all," Librarian answered. "Furthermore, that is not an abnormal price. A single page—that's just two surfaces—containing some sketches and handwritten notes for a Beethoven symphony—the sixth, I think—was also sold recently for almost exactly that same price. What made this particular auction especially interesting was that the selling price was twice the presale prediction. It was the first major Beethoven manuscript put up for sale in close to thirty years."

'Whose manuscripts did you have in mind?" Forger asked. "Something of Beethoven's, perhaps?"

'Close, but no cigar," Librarian answered. "I had Mozart in mind, and not a fragment, but a complete and well-known composition. In fact, two of them."

Forger had still not grasped the notion, because he said, "Your idea doesn't sound like a smart one to me. In fact, I don't understand how we could sell a forged Mozart manuscript. Think of the one you just mentioned…that Mozart symphony you said was at the Pierpont Morgan."

'Yes," Librarian agreed. "You are speaking about the manuscript of the *Haffner* symphony. They bought it from the National Orchestral Association in 1979. Quite a while before that, it was the property of the tragic King Ludwig II of Bavaria. What about it?"

Librarian wanted to give Forger all the time he needed to fully probe the idea of manuscript value. It was necessary for him to understand that these things were so rare and so precious that even the history of their ownership was documented, so he deliberately gave his friend a lot of gratuitous information that he really didn't need.

Librarian knew Forger didn't care about who owned that manuscript before the Pierpont Morgan got it, or that an insane king of Bavaria was a previous owner. But the fact that Librarian knew this information, and that it was thought of as historical data worth saving, did strike Forger as significant.

Musing for a while, Forger continued his criticism, slowly at first, but his words gathered speed as the thoughts coalesced. Finally, he presented his full set of objections to the plan.

"Presuming we could get some kind of a copy for me to work from, if I made another copy of the *Haffner* symphony and we sold it to somebody as the original, that would be news that might get in the paper; the Pierpont Morgan would find out about it, and we'd be exposed at once."

"That's right," Librarian responded. "The sale of Mozart manuscripts almost always gets in the paper. Things that rare and which sell for such high prices get a lot of press coverage. Why, Rigbie Turner would be on the phone to the police as soon as he heard about it."

"So if you are not interested in having me make a forged copy of a valuable document, where's the business opportunity?"

Now, despite the fact that Forger appeared puzzled, Librarian had him, though he was still six steps out of kilter. He simply needed to be led where his mind wanted to go.

"My dear friend, what we can't do is copy a manuscript that someone already owns. We have to create a manuscript that nobody owns. What you have not yet grasped, though you will in a minute, is that there are many Mozart manuscripts in libraries and other repositories, and copying any of those would serve no purpose.

"But," he continued, "here is the critical part. There are a number of important Mozart compositions for which no manuscript exists any longer. Either it got destroyed or lost or goodness knows what. It doesn't matter. It's gone.

"Your job would be to create something that has not been seen for several hundred years and which almost certainly no longer exists. My job would be to act as your technical consultant and also to create a scenario that would get people to believe that we had discovered the original."

Librarian really did not mean "we," because when dealing with rare documents, it wasn't good that one of the discoverers be a convicted forger. That kind of nuance would get clarified with time.

# 18

# WHICH MANUSCRIPTS DID YOU HAVE IN MIND?

Forger, continuing to look puzzled, said, "I'm still not sure I understand what you are talking about. How could I possibly compose a piece of music that we'd pass off as something unknown, but written by Mozart? I'm know a good jazz pianist, but what you suggest is way out of my league."

"Nobody is going to compose a work and pass it off as a Mozart original," Librarian responded. "What we are going to do is create two Mozart manuscripts that once had to have existed but almost certainly no longer do. And I have the very two in mind.

"The best part of this whole scheme is that it makes perfect sense for both manuscripts to be discovered at the same time and in the same place. That's the beauty and the simplicity of the plan. I'm hanging my hat on the fact that the history of those two manuscripts would make the whole story stick together and everyone in the know would say, 'Of course. That makes perfect sense.'"

"Which manuscripts did you have in mind?" Forger asked.

Answering Forger's question was something that Librarian had practiced for over a year, and he wanted to give it the right dramatic tone.

"My plan is for us to forge, discover, get authenticated, and then sell the manuscripts of two very famous Mozart compositions, namely the concerto for clarinet, and a quintet he wrote for clarinet and string quartet."

"Why those two?" Forger asked.

"Because when the manuscript of the clarinet concerto disappeared, the other manuscript disappeared with it, presumably under the same circumstances. And if we invent the right story for the clarinet concerto, the other composition gets swept along for free."

"What's the story of their disappearance?" Forger asked.

"Well," Librarian replied, "there isn't a great deal of detail known about the matter, which is a situation that is perfect for us. The more the uncertainty about what happened to those manuscripts, the more we have liberty to create a discovery story. But the basic history is this.

"On commission, Mozart wrote these two pieces about two years apart for a clarinet player he knew, a man named Anton Stadler, a really disreputable character who probably didn't pay for either of the two works.

"Anyway, Stadler supposedly kept the manuscripts of both works in some kind of briefcase, and when he ran short of money—which was apparently very often—he supposedly pawned the briefcase with the two manuscripts still inside, and that was the last anyone ever saw or heard of them. At least that's the best that history can tell us, though I believe that the truth is considerably different. The story has more holes in it than Swiss cheese, though it comes from what is supposed to be an impeccable source, specifically Mozart's widow.

"But what the truth is doesn't really matter," he continued. "That's the story in all the reference books. If those sources suggest that he pawned the case with the autograph scores of these two works inside it, that simplifies the matter for us. We will take advantage of the traditional information by finding an eighteenth-century briefcase—the right kind in terms of age, style, and typical characteristics—that we will claim was pawned in the late eighteenth-century and inside which we found those two manuscripts."

Forger asked, "Where is all this supposed to have happened?"

"No one is really sure," Librarian replied, "but there is a Dutch scholar who printed a technical paper on the subject, and he suggested that the works were pawned in Strasbourg, France. That's where I plan on discovering the manuscripts, though I haven't yet figured out a cover story for doing that.

"Further, when the discovery hits the papers and Strasbourg is mentioned as the place where the manuscripts were found, that Dutchman is going to both applaud and support our discovery, because it confirms his theory and improves his position in the academic community. In effect, he will have no choice but to confirm our discovery, because not to do so places him in the position of contradicting himself."

"Wait a minute! There's a problem here," Forger interrupted. He closed his eyes and paused for a long time to get what appeared to be a complicated idea structured enough to articulate intelligently. Then, after a while, he opened his eyes and said, "If what you say happened, what do we hear at a concert when those pieces are played? How did the music survive if the original manuscripts got lost?"

"Great question, easy answer," Librarian responded.

"A professional copyist made performance parts by hand from each of the original scores before they were lost, maybe even during Mozart's lifetime. At worst, that happened in the late 1790s because the guy for whom Mozart wrote the pieces played them then.

"Those performance parts were used to play the pieces. Then, after the original manuscripts disappeared, those same parts were used to produce the first printed parts right after the turn of the nineteenth-century. In turn, those printed parts got copied again and again up until today.

"You can go into almost any music store and for a modest amount of money, buy a set of those parts—the great-great ten times great-grandchildren of the ones made by that unknown copyist from the original manuscripts that we are going to discover and sell."

Forger interrupted, asking, "Well, if printed parts and scores of the compositions are available, why should the original manuscripts be as valuable as you suggest?"

Librarian had made a list of questions that Forger was likely to ask, and this was not one he had anticipated, assuming that because of the money he had made as a forger, he would know the value of an original. However, his question showed that Forger's appreciation of a collector's thirst for the kinds of products that he produced was primitive. He could create a Lincoln letter of extraordinary pseudo-authenticity, but he never fully appreciated the emotions of people who were so desperate to have such precious things that they would pay a fortune for them.

# 19

# THE VALUE OF AN ORIGINAL

Librarian was astonished at the question of why the originals of music manuscripts might have such value, so he began by answering the question with a question.

"Why are the originals of anything valuable? Why would the manuscript of Hamlet be worth a king's ransom when you can buy a copy of every one of Shakespeare's plays for a few dollars? Your text forgeries have been valuable because every one is perceived as an original. Their worth lies in the fact that people believe that Washington and Lincoln and Jefferson signed them. Owning such things, even looking at them, is a way to touch greatness. On the other hand, their true worth isn't really very much, just pennies for the paper and ink involved.

"Similarly," he continued, "things like the manuscript of a Dickens novel, corrections and all—particularly if it has corrections—a poem by Poe, or a Mozart manuscript are valuable only because they are the originals. True, scholars will want to study these things, but other than that and the emotional content contained in them, they have no worth at all. They are nothing but faded ink on old paper.

"Yet I see scholars come into the NYPL to examine an important manuscript, and when it is brought to their table, they are often overcome with fear and emotion. A few become so frightened that they can't move.

"Once a very important scholar flew in from Germany. It was a woman—I forget her name—and she was big in the business. The explicit purpose of her visit was the examination of a Beethoven letter owned by the NYPL. It was a new acquisition, and based on some watermark issues, a copy would not have been satisfactory for her purpose, which had to do with nailing down the name of Beethoven's so-called 'immortal beloved.'

"Anyway, when the library clerk put the letter on her work table, she fainted dead away. I sat on the floor with that woman's head in my lap, fanning her, giving her sips of water, comforting her. It was more than an hour before she composed herself to the point where she could hold the letter without shaking. That's what these things do to people. And that is why they are enormously valuable."

Forger sat quietly for a while and then said, "But how do you know that a score that I prepared wouldn't be seen by someone who would know immediately that it's not the original?"

"*Are you serious?*" Librarian almost shouted. "Who would know that it's a forgery? The originals haven't been seen in two centuries. If we said that the manuscripts were recently discovered somewhere, and your forgeries were perfect in all technical respects, everyone would assume that they were the originals. No one knows what the originals looked like.

"Your problem would be to forge two manuscripts, using a handwriting and paper type that can fool experts, though it is, of course, a great deal more than just the variables of handwriting and paper type."

"But what would I use as source materials to make the forgery?" Forger asked naively. "What would I copy from?"

"That's the easiest part," Librarian said. "I would go to any music shop, buy a pocket score of each piece for a few dollars, and those would be your basic sources. You would have a nice printed version to work from with all the notes for every one of the instruments, though we would have to use several sources to create our score. The editions are not all identical."

"Why not?" asked Forger.

"Because the original manuscript, which of course should have been used, had already been lost and was not available when the first printed score was made in the earliest years of the nineteenth-century. So printed copies of the score—that's what the conductor uses—had to be constructed in a backwards fashion."

Forger interrupted to ask, "What do you mean by 'backwards'?"

"Instead of the performance parts being extracted from the original manuscript," replied Librarian, "a conductor's score was constructed from the performance parts. But even by that early date the parts were already corrupt, so errors and changes crept in. You can pick up two different printed scores of either of these pieces and find hundreds of differences between them."

"In the notes played?" asked forger.

"Perhaps a few," Librarian responded. "But the main differences lie in dynamics, phrase marks, articulations, and other things that composers mark in their scores and which performers depend on.

"The fact is that there is no authentic source to consult," Librarian continued. "The various editions differ from each other—sometimes in small matters, other times in large ones. The problem is not getting a source, nor is the problem being exposed because somebody else has the original that would show our document to be a counterfeit.

"The problems, and there are many of them, lie elsewhere, and they are not trivial, either. I don't want you to think that this is a walk in the park. Both you and I are going to have to do some very remarkable things to make this plan work."

To Librarian's surprise, because he was not paying attention, at that moment the engines stopped and the ferry glided into the slip at Lewes, Delaware. The two of them hustled back to the car—a trail of dropped taco chips showing their path—drove off the ship when their turn came, turned around on some side street in Lewes, came back to the ferry slip, got on the same ship again, and waited for it to leave for New Jersey.

# 20

# RETURN TRIP

Librarian bought two beers in the ferry snack shop, and the two went back to the bow to continue the private conversation. In point of fact, Librarian didn't have an opportunity to restart the discussion because Forger beat him to it with questions about the financial value of music manuscripts, particularly those in Mozart's hand.

Forger began, "Before we go too far with this, tell me again why you think that a manuscript that could be passed off as the original of Mozart's clarinet concerto would be worth a lot of money. I'm particularly interested in an earlier distinction you made between the value of manuscripts of completed works as contrasted with what you referred to as drafts and sketches. What could one get for a manuscript of a complete Mozart composition?"

"Why is a distinction between a complete work and an incomplete one important to you?" Librarian asked, puzzled.

"It's just a matter of unfamiliar territory," Forger replied. "This idea of a sketch or draft of a music composition doesn't have many parallels with what you and I did in the past.

"I never made and sold a sketch of a Lincoln letter or a draft of a Jefferson document," he continued. "What I created were complete and final manuscripts. It was as if each had a particular purpose and was actually sent somewhere or given to someone. And though every one was a phony, each was a completed phony, and in final form.

"In fact, I don't know if sketches and drafts have a place in the historical manuscript market, or else I'm just showing my ignorance of the marketplace. I can conceive that Lincoln might have made a sketch of the address he gave at the Gettysburg Cemetery or a draft of his second inaugural address, but I've never heard of anything like that coming up for sale. However, that may be because I've always been more attuned to the manufacturing end of our business, leaving the marketing end to you.

"But when it comes to a completed composition," he continued, "that really leaves me baffled. I suspect that most of that uncertainty is due to being unable to find a parallel in the jazz music world with which I'm a lot more familiar.

"As far as I know, there is no such thing as the original manuscript—or whatever it would be called—of for example, *Lullaby of Birdland*. It's just a tune with a harmonic structure. Why would someone find the original manuscript of that to be valuable? There is no original except at the moment when it's being played. And then, it's not the tune that's original but the performance, the imaginative improvisations that are made using the tune as a springboard.

"So any performance of that piece is different from any other, and none have long-term reality beyond the time that they're being played. A performance disappears and has no physical manifestation. I suppose that an argument could be made about a recorded performance being the jazz equivalent of an original manuscript, but there is already a thriving business there. It's called 'The Recording Industry.'

"So that's why I'm having trouble getting my head shaped right concerning your proposal. I just find it hard to believe that music manuscripts—either sketches or complete compositions—have any value. Do you understand what's bothering me? Text originals I can comprehend, but music originals are not so clear."

Librarian, shocked at Forger's naiveté replied, "If you don't think that the manuscript of for example "God Bless America," is valuable, or even something as modest as the original of *Yes! We Have No Bananas*, then your interest in the improvisatory nature of jazz has left you blind to the world of music manuscript collectors. And I'm not even sure that your example of "Lullaby of Birdland" is even true. It's rather that whoever wrote that tune…"

Forger interrupted to say, "It was George Shearing."

"OK, Shearing," Librarian continued and then suddenly made a right-hand turn in his thinking.

"Wait a minute! Shearing is blind," he said, "and that would probably make this example a poor one because I doubt if he wrote anything down in the first place, but if he did, then either he didn't know or couldn't comprehend what the first written sketch of that piece might someday bring on the open market, or else he didn't keep it, or he gave it to someone who might have thought it was unimportant and threw it away. Or else Shearing had an amanuensis copy down what he dictated.

"But whatever the case, you are simply going to have to make a dimensional shift in your understanding of a marketplace that you didn't even know existed. Music manuscripts of all kinds are a big business. No, let me retract and rephrase that.

"Music manuscripts are a small part of a very big business. You are going to have to accept that or we'll never get anywhere in this discussion."

"OK," Forger responded. "I'll accept that premise for the moment, though it may be some time before I'm fully comfortable with it. Now tell me about the market for complete Mozart manuscripts, particularly the ones we are talking about."

# 21

# MANUSCRIPT VALUES

"There are few generalizations here," Librarian began, "because the manuscripts of important, complete compositions come up for sale so rarely, but the musical and historic significance of Mozart's clarinet concerto and quintet are indisputable. As such, there is not the slightest doubt that a sale advertising the autographs of both works will be watched by the entire collector's world. That kind of star appeal will have a critical impact on the sale price.

"The way one evaluates these things is on the basis of the sale of comparable items, and there really hasn't been anything in the last half-century that could be considered equivalent to what I propose we do. There were two sales involving two complete compositions about thirty years ago, with two different houses selling them at unrelated auctions, though Pierpont Morgan purchased both. One was the complete score of Mozart's opera, *The Impresario*, and the other was the *Haffner* symphony that we've spoken about.

"As best as I can estimate, each of the two scores was sold in the mid-seven figures. However, that was thirty years ago and prices have at least quadrupled since then.

"There was another sale of a complete manuscript that took place around 1990," Librarian continued, "but it's not comparable to either of our two pieces. It was a piano sonata found in a safe at the headquarters of the Eastern Theological Seminary in Philadelphia. An accountant, looking for tax records, opened the safe and a manuscript with music on it fell out onto the floor.

"No one at the seminary knew what this unidentified manuscript was, how it had gotten there, how long it had been there, or even—for some time—who the owner was. Eventually, it wound up in a Sotheby's auction catalog and was given a presale estimate of $1,400,000. But the part of this story that is of interest to us is not the price, but the authentication process.

"First there was the matter of figuring out what the seminary had. It took some time before this unknown thing was perceived as an item of possible historical importance with, perhaps, considerable value. Since it was music, they called the University of Pennsylvania who happened, by good fortune, to have a knowledgeable eighteenth-century specialist on its staff. The seminary officials did not ask for a Mozart authority, because they didn't know they needed one.

"On arrival, he took one glance at the first page, instantly recognized what the composition was and concluded that the manuscript was probably the original. Within five minutes he was on the phone to a number of Mozart authorities and sent a FAX of the first page to each.

"The next morning, three of America's best experts on the subject showed up, looking to confirm the authenticity of a manuscript whose location had been unknown since the late eighteen hundreds. Following a brief joint examination, they offered a unanimous opinion about the manuscript's authenticity."

Forger interrupted to ask, "Did the experts know it to be authentic because they had photographs of the original for comparison?"

"No, no. Not at all," Librarian replied. "There were no photographs ever taken of that manuscript. But even without ever having seen it before and in the absence of any previously made photographs, the experts immediately knew it to be a Mozart manuscript by both its handwriting and layout—nothing else.

"In that business, you can make a preliminary judgment about a manuscript's authenticity almost instantaneously; that's how distinctive Mozart's manuscripts are. Of course, for a final judgment a great deal of further examination took place, but I don't think I've heard of a single case in which a later examination overturned the initial judgment of the experts.

"So I can't give a general answer to your question about value," Librarian continued, "though I can give you a rationale for my rough estimate of something like $20,000,000, though it could be higher. I'll give you a breakdown in a moment, because the two manuscripts may have significantly different value.

"As I said earlier, mostly what you see today at the auction houses are fragments—individual sheets, sketches, and incomplete or abandoned compositions. These things sell for hundreds of thousands of dollars.

"Complete compositions are so rare that some very strange things happen when they do come up for sale. For example, some twenty-five years ago a consortium of manuscript dealers got together and bought the autograph of one of Mozart's complete compositions. Then they cut it up and resold it a piece at a time."

"Frankly, I was shocked when I heard about that kind of behavior from professional manuscript dealers. They treated that precious, one-of-a-kind document as if it were Elvis' underwear or the curtain at the old Metropolitan Opera House, which really was cut up into thousands of pieces and sold as souvenirs when the old Met closed.

"But I shouldn't be so critical of those dealers. Even Mozart's son cut up one of his father's drafts for a horn concerto. Then he cut each individual sheet up into quarters, giving the pieces away. That was pretty awful."

"What did the American consortium get for the leaves?" Forger asked, indifferent to the sacrilege of their behavior.

Librarian replied, "Well, the market has improved considerably since then, but at that time a single leaf went for anywhere between $15,000 and $35,000. There were about sixty-five leaves in all, so they got over $1.6 million for the whole manuscript. It took thirteen years to sell all the pieces.

"And I add that it was not a particularly important manuscript. It was not, for example, the original score of Mozart's opera, *The Magic Flute*, which, if it ever came up for sale—and it never will—might go for more than $50,000,000. It was just a simple, delightful orchestral serenade written by the sixteen-year old Mozart. Today, those leaves would bring at least $100,000 each. That's $6,500,000 today for the entire manuscript, and that's minimum.

"I understand that the Japanese got some pieces of that manuscript because there is a big craze for Mozart in Japan, and also because Mozart manuscripts are a great investment."

# 22

# WHY DON'T MANUSCRIPTS BEHAVE LIKE REAL ESTATE?

Forger's next question came out of left field, asking, "If rare music manuscripts are such good investments, why aren't they coming up for sale all the time? Why shouldn't they be like real estate where a single building can be resold five times in as many years, with each new owner giving profit to his predecessor?"

"I've often wondered about that, too," Librarian replied, "but when I started work at the NYPL, I realized that many of the owners of such manuscripts treat them more like holy relics than as blue chips held for profit.

"Most manuscripts eventually wind up being donated or loaned in perpetuity to a carefully-selected repository—like a private or university library—and once there, they almost never get back into the public arena. There are other complications, too.

"For example," Librarian continued, "following the end of a war, people in ravaged areas may have lost their fortunes and find themselves in circumstances where they have to sell their most intimate and beloved treasures. That sometimes includes music manuscripts, and when that happens, volume goes up, prices go down, and libraries have a feeding frenzy.

"In the present climate, the supply of the really great complete manuscripts is drying up because the center of gravity of ownership is shifting to repositories that will never sell them. Ever! And that is why I believe that they don't behave like real estate.

"It's possible, of course, that some day in the future, a variety of bizarre and unpredictable circumstances might arise that would cause the Pierpont Morgan to sell some of its manuscript holdings, but the stone lions in front of the New York Public Library will disintigrate before it does anything like that.

"What all of this explains is why the pricing environment for music manuscripts is becoming more and more overheated as time passes. The market reacts to the fact that there is less and less of that kind of commodity being put up for public sale. Further, the market sees that on the rare occasions when something does come up for sale, it generally winds up in a university, a museum, or a library, and that means it goes out of the open market permanently."

"I must admit," Forger said, "that I had no idea of that kind of market in such stuff."

"Believe it," Librarian said. "When a really good manuscript comes up for sale, Sotheby's or Christie's gets inundated with buyers. And those auction houses work hard to get that kind of business, because the publicity is so good. They will occasionally reduce the seller's commission price just for the privilege of selling such a rarity, and to an auction house, reducing a commission is like selling its children."

"OK, then," Forger said, "now that I have some background in the dynamics of music manuscript values, give me the breakdown on the $20,000,000 that you think possible for the ones we're discussing. Just how did you come up with that figure for the clarinet concerto and the string quartet you mentioned?"

"It's not a string quartet," Librarian corrected. "It's a quintet, a quintet for one clarinet and four string players. The value of the two manuscripts is my best estimate, but this is how I derived it.

"First, I suspect that the concerto is going to be worth more money because of its musical importance, and I am almost certain that the manuscript will be physically bigger than the quintet. The price is not only a function of the manuscript's importance, but is also related to the number of pages.

"So using an estimate of $160,000 per page, with an approximation of seventy-five pages for the entire manuscript, I come up with $12,000,000. And since it is a complete manuscript that has never been seen before, which makes it a rarity, I'm bumping the estimate up to $14,000,000. In my opinion, that is an absolute minimum figure.

"The quintet is a wonderful work, less well-known I think, and will probably be roughly a third the page count of the concerto. So I'm estimating

$4,000,000 to $6,000,000 for it. Consequently, the two items have a possible expectation of something like $20,000,000, though they could and probably will bring even more. You never know."

# 23

# CONSIDER A DIFFERENT APPROACH

"Let me suggest an entirely different approach," Forger offered. "Couldn't we get a really good composer, or even a computer, to secretly create a composition that sounds as if Mozart wrote it? I'd then forge the 'original,' and as an unknown Mozart composition, it might make even more money."

"Forget it!" Librarian said at once. "It would never happen. It's worse than impractical, and it's both foolish and unnecessary. Nobody in the world could create such a work, which in any case would be instantly spotted as a fraud by anyone with half a brain.

"Creating a secretly composed contemporary composition that would be offered as an unknown Mozart work is ridiculous, and that's not an avenue worth a moment of our time. Someone tried that with some Haydn piano sonatas some years ago and it damaged several world-class reputations. It's dangerous, quite impossible, and why am I even discussing this possibility?" Librarian asked, raising his voice angrily. "Besides, why create an inferior composition that would never pass muster and then forge a manuscript of it when we already have two fabulous and authentic compositions at our fingertips that we can use instead?"

Wanting to bring the discussion to an end before the ferry reached New Jersey, Librarian began the conclusion of his pitch to Forger.

"My friend, I need to have a serious understanding from you about your ability to do this thing. I estimate that we are going to have to spend something like $30,000 to $50,000 to finance this project. Neither of us has been putting away that kind of money for the past four years, and I don't think we should make that sort of an investment without some statement from you that this thing can be accomplished.

"You are brilliant beyond imagination when you copy or create text," Librarian continued. "I've been watching you do that since we were both eight years old, but this kind of copying is not the same. You have to be able to copy the peculiarities of the style of a man's music manuscript. There are so very many things on the paper that are not notes, most of which are peculiarities in the way Mozart worked. In effect, there is a lot of his personality in his handwriting and layout, and you have to capture that as well as the notes. It is going to be difficult work with lots of problems that don't have anything to do with normal manuscript handwriting. Do you really think you can do that?"

Forger smiled, sat back, and brazenly said, "I can write or copy anything. Hear me? Anything! Don't think of it as word forgery as contrasted with some other kind of forgery. It's all just geometries of ink on paper, and I can place that ink in any quantity, shape, shading, or style I like. I can make it look like the handwriting of any composer who ever lived, Mozart, Beethoven, or, for that matter, the composer of "God Bless America"—who was Irving Berlin, by the way—and I can learn and add the personal peculiarities of that composer's compositional handwriting, too, once I understand some examples of what it is you are talking about."

Then, with a degree of finality, Forger said, "And I can do that standing on my head! The problems of forgeries rarely lie in penmanship," he continued. "There are far greater problems in the choice of materials that we will use than in any difficulties of the handwriting."

As Librarian stated earlier, Forger had a justifiably proud opinion of his technical expertise. His production of the almost-perfect $100 bill counterfeits in the face of the extraordinary complexities of that task allow an understanding of why in his own, Librarian's, and the government's opinion, he could forge anything.

# 24

# PAGE PERSONALITY

The discussion between the two men was coming to a close, and there was a general, but unstated understanding that Forger intended to try and accomplish the effort, but there was still one final item that needed clarification. Forger brought it up because he considered it the most important aspect that needed to be understood for any counterfeited manuscript.

"You've spoken about the personal peculiarities of each composer's music handwriting," Forger said, "and I want to explore that with you. I think I know exactly what you mean, but I would like to see a couple of examples to make sure that we are singing from the same hymnal."

"If my instincts are right," he continued, "what you really wanted to say was something like 'page personality' or 'manuscript personality.' The things that I think you are talking about are the hidden elements that experts look for and which are found on any kind of manuscript. Those are the things that experts know about from experience and study, but that anyone else would either fail to see or perceive as important, even when looking right at them. That's because they have so little to do with the actual content of the text, or in this case, the music notation that appears on the page.

"None of these hidden elements are really handwriting related, and once I am clear on this matter as it relates to Mozart's hand, I'll spot some that even you have never thought about. So to make sure I have my head shaped right, show me some things that you would consider part of what you call Mozart's 'handwriting personality' but that are not penmanship issues."

With respect to this topic, Librarian recollected one of their earliest collaborations, remembering how Forger had created a Jefferson letter. It was an innocuous item of unimportant content allegedly responding to a question of policy, supposedly asked of Jefferson by an imaginary constituent invented by Forger.

Some basic research on Librarian's part brought forward the fact that in letters at least, Jefferson created the document so that the paper on which the text was written could be folded to become its own envelope. The problem on which Forger had spent the most time was not the content of the letter or even the handwriting of the text, but rather the method of folding and the correct placement of the recipient's address.

For absolute confirmation, Librarian went—under pretext of some NYPL business—to the Jefferson library in Charlottesville, Virginia. There he examined and obtained copies of both sides of a number of original letters, and following that, made a trip to the University of Virginia, the great citadel of learning founded by Jefferson, where there were also a number of his letters. Finally, on the way home, he had also gone to the Library of Congress to examine their Jefferson holdings.

It turned out that Forger's instincts on this matter were spectacular. Jefferson almost always put his addressee information in the very same spot, as if he measured where it was to go with a ruler. And had Forger not sensed and executed the letter that way—after seeing the copies Librarian brought home as well as several facsimiles in a reference volume—the two ran a risk of exposure. That vulnerability would have destroyed the credibility of their letter, even though the handwriting itself was perfect.

Librarian later learned that this was the very thing that a Jefferson specialist would look for. So once Forger was certain where to put the address, he wrote one in Jefferson's hand perfectly in a few seconds, almost without thinking.

That is what he meant by "page personality." It was not content, but geometry, and penmanship was not the critical issue. Forger's great talent lay in the fact that everything he turned out had perfect page personality superimposed on perfect penmanship.

# 25

# FACSIMILES

To help illustrate the issue of music-writing page personality with examples—which he knew Forger would ask for—Librarian had brought published facsimiles of four Mozart manuscripts along with him. Three of them were in the cloth bag at his feet and the fourth was in the back seat of the car.

One facsimile was of Mozart's *Jupiter* symphony, the original being the property of the Berlin State Library. Another was a piano concerto that became very popular when it was used as background music for a Swedish movie named "Elvira Madigan," and the third, a photocopy of the *Haffner* symphony. The originals of these last two reside in the Pierpont Morgan Library.

The fourth facsimile was quite large and would be used to show Forger the manuscript of a really long piece. That particular one was left in the car because it was too big to carry around. Back in Paterson, Librarian had another dozen facsimiles of varying sizes.

Now illustrating his points by using the *Jupiter* symphony and the piano concerto, Librarian opened both to the first manuscript page and said, "Look at the first page of both scores. Here's an example of what you call a 'page personality'—and now that you have used that term, I realize it is a better word description than mine.

"Look at the order of the instruments in the scores," he continued. "It's one that turns out to be anything but haphazard. Generally, Mozart arrayed the instrument names only on the first page of each movement.

"But more important than this fact is that he always put the violins and violas on the upper staves, and below them whatever wind, brass, and percussion instruments he decided to use, all in a specific order. Finally, the bass instruments—cello and contrabass—are written on the bottom.

"If he was writing a concerto, the soloist's placement within this order would be very critical. You can't just put it anywhere."

Pointing to the first page of the piano concerto facsimile, Librarian continued. "See how the solo piano music is situated just above the string bass? This is what he did for every one of his almost thirty piano concertos. Any alleged Mozart piano concerto that had the piano part placed somewhere other than immediately above the bass line would create an alarm bell for any expert called in to authenticate it.

"But we're doing a clarinet concerto, and he would not have put that solo instrument in the same place he seems to have reserved for the piano in his concertos."

Forger interrupted at once, saying, "I'll bet anything the clarinet would go on top, above the string instruments. It's the logical place, and if the piano were written on only one staff instead of two, that's where it would show up. Because the piano's left hand is highly dependent on and related to the bass line, it's much more rational to put it down on the bottom near the bass instruments."

"You are quite correct," Librarian said, "and your suggestion is corroborated in the facsimiles of his violin concertos. I checked them at the NYPL, and the solo part always appears on the top staff, just above the orchestral violins. That was probably true with his flute concertos, too, though I can't check that because the manuscripts of those works are lost, except for one surviving movement. However, for that one case, the flute is on top.

"The point here is that the instruments don't just go anywhere on the page we want to put them. If we did a foolish thing like ignoring this habitual pattern, no matter how good the handwriting was, it would be an unexplainable anomaly, and no expert tolerates anomalies."

Librarian then put the facsimiles of the *Jupiter* symphony and piano concerto back in the cloth bag and brought out the photocopy of the third volume.

"Now take a look at the *Haffner* symphony," Librarian said. "It's different, but not simply because it is not a concerto. Another factor intervened.

"The top line is a flute and the bottom line, below the bass, is a clarinet," he continued. "How do you explain the fact that the rule we just discussed about order of instrumental placement—orchestral violins on top except maybe in a concerto and the bass on the bottom—is violated here?"

"It's obvious," Forger answered, looking completely unsurprised by this abnormality. "Look at the ink of the flute and clarinet music. It's badly faded. And that says that he added those two instruments, using different ink, at a later time. It was cheap, over-diluted, or very old. In adding the additional instruments, he had no other staves on which to place their music, because he had already used up staves two through eleven when he wrote the work in the first place.

"However, look at all the other instruments between the flute on top and the clarinet on bottom—that is, the original instrumentation before he later decided to add flutes and clarinets. They are in the very order you suggested they should be."

"It's exactly as you said," Librarian indicated with a big smile of confidence. "That is very much what happened in the accounts of this composition, and all the history books on this piece confirm the conclusion you made, based solely on ink color.

"Those instruments were added," Librarian continued, "after he finished the piece, probably for later performances. Most likely he changed his mind about the character of sound he wanted and added flutes and clarinets because of that, but there could have been an unknown reason about which we can only speculate."

"What kind of reason?" Forger asked.

"Maybe the orchestra he originally wrote the work for," Librarian answered, "didn't have flutes or clarinets. But when he got around to reusing the piece in another location, those instruments were available to him."

"Very logical," said Forger. And then, smiling at Librarian for having explained this eminently practical reason for such an instrumental change, he said, "Now I know exactly what you were talking about. I'm glad we spoke about it in this kind of detail, first because I now understand it, and second, because it is an eminently solvable problem.

"In fact," he continued, "I already see several other page personality items that I can point out to you. Let me show you just one."

Turning to the second and third pages of the *Jupiter* facsimile, looking at them both with a professional eye and then riffling through another dozen pages, Forger said, "See this big squiggly line on the left-hand side of the page? He appears to have used it like a giant left parenthesis, namely to isolate the staves on which he intended to write. And it appears on every page. Right?"

Knowing exactly what Forger was referring to, Librarian said, "You are right on target. The only thing you missed is the name of that item, and I would be amazed if you had ever heard of it. It's called an 'accolade,' and it serves the exact function you described, namely defining the staves that he intends to use for the instruments."

Forger continued with his observation, saying, "It's nice to know the name of that thing as well as its function, but more important is to understand how Mozart wrote those accolades, because there appears to be a mechanical peculiarity to the way he made them. He began by putting his pen by the lowest staff that would be part of his system of staves. Then, in a single stroke of the pen, he made a **U**-loop and went straight up to the highest staff intended for use. When he got there, he lifted his pen and then made the upper loop, **∩**, as a separate piece.

"So every time you see an accolade, it has to show a break in the upper left-hand corner where the inverted **'U'** connects with the vertical line. It's almost certain that the specialists in Mozart manuscripts would look for that, because he does it on every page. In effect, his making of accolades was an integral part of his page personality.

"Let me point out another and very subtle thing to you," Forger said. Turning to several places in the facsimiles, he put the eraser-end of a pencil by a number of smudges in the manuscript. "Do you see how he smudged ink in these places?"

"Certainly do," replied Librarian.

"Well," continued Forger, "there's a world of information in those smudges. First, he did that deliberately to deface what he had written. Second, he did it almost immediately after he wrote the material, because it suddenly offended him. Remember that a smudging technique works only if the ink is wet. And third, the main reason for the smudge was not to deface."

"Why do you say that?" Librarian asked, surprised.

"Because his real purpose in smudging," responded Forger, "was to correct something, not simply to deface what he had just written. See how every smudge has corrected material right next to the blot, or else on top of it? He was fixing something. Maybe it was an error, or else it was simply an example of him changing his mind immediately on having written something.

"Do you have a really big facsimile at home?" Forger asked, changing the subject. "I mean a large work that would show all or at least most of his page personality issues in one composition?"

# 26

# *THE MAGIC FLUTE* AND A PROBLEM'S DISCOVERY

On receiving the inquiry, Librarian smiled, because he was expecting the question. He suggested that they get back to the car because the ship was about twenty minutes from docking in New Jersey. When they got there and seated themselves, Librarian reached into the back seat and found the large volume. Pulling it into the front seat and handing it to Forger, he said, "Look inside."

Forger opened the manuscript facsimile of the entire opera, *The Magic Flute*, at an arbitrary point. It was three inches thick, and if he wanted something with a lot of pages, he was holding it.

"That should keep you busy for a while," Librarian said. "I deliberately bought that one because it was written at almost exactly the same time as the clarinet concerto. That probably makes it a perfect handwriting model," he pointed out, which was an admission of their commonly held belief that one's handwriting is continuously modified with age.

By that time, Forger's professional eye was looking not at the music or words on any page, but rather at the geometry of the ink as it was dispersed to produce the page.

"I need some more facsimiles, of course," Forger said, "but I can do the handwriting part of this job easily. It's clear to me how Mozart held his quill pen. It was almost certainly a goose feather taken from a bird's left wing."

"What possible difference could the wing make? And how on earth would you know that?" the surprised Librarian asked.

"Well, it's obvious to me that Mozart was right-handed," Forger said, "and right wing quills curve in a direction that makes them very difficult for a right-handed person to use. The feather gets in the way. He needed a left wing quill."

And then, again looking down at the pages of *The Magic Flute* manuscript, he continued. "The noteheads look simple enough, but the stems—particularly for eighth and sixteenth notes—are a little more complex. The beams are easy, and I can see the angle at which he held his pen when he made them. And look at the staccato marks above the notes! There appear to be two kinds: the standard form that looks like a period and then a longer form, almost like a vertical line, but short. Those two different symbols are not an accident. You and I learned only about one symbol for staccato, but Mozart appears to have used two, and for some musical purpose that isn't clear to me. It's something I'm going to have to learn about.

"Those blank pages are interesting," Forger remarked as he came across a few at various points of the facsimile. "They are not an accident, either. He may have sent some completed material off to be copied while he worked on later sections. That would account for them. Paper was too expensive to waste. There's a story to be told for every blank page in this manuscript."

With a face that suddenly turned sour, Forger said, "Unfortunately, now I see a problem. Look at the music staves. There are twelve on every page, and each one has five lines. That's sixty parallel lines per page, in groups of five, and they extend over almost the full width of the page. You've got an inch or so of margin on the left and right, and a little more on the top and bottom.

"How were those staves made?" Forger mused, speaking more to himself than to Librarian. "They are clearly not printed, but drawn. That's a very curious thing. I need a magnifying glass to confirm this, but I'm almost certain that the individual lines were not made one at a time. Each line has a distinctive pen tracing.

"Look at the spacing between each of the staves. It's almost certain that all twelve were created simultaneously. The ends of each staff are ragged, though the raggedness is unique from stave to stave and the pattern is reproduced from page to page," he said as he flipped several pages to prove his point.

"What this means," Forger continued, "is that some sort of mechanical device with twelve pens, or twelve rollers or something was used to create the dozen staves on every page. They were drawn with a kind of device that I cannot even conceive of at this moment.

"We'd have to make such a device or have it made for us. You can't draw sixty lines on each page, one at a time, or even twelve staves, one stave at a time. They'd never be consistent from page to page, or even in good or consistent relationship to each other on every page. The bottom line here is that this is an interesting and perhaps difficult technical problem.

"Except for this," he concluded, "I don't see anything in his handwriting or page personality that I can't get on top of, though I have a lot more to study, of course. But how did those twelve music staves get drawn on a page in the late 1700s? That's not only a key question for us, but a very remarkable technical feat."

The two men waited as the ferry pulled into the slip from which they had left about four hours earlier. The ship's engine died down as all the car engines fired up and got ready to head north.

# BOOK 3:
# FROM THEORY TO PRACTICE

# 27

# HOME AT LAST

It was almost 5 p.m. when Librarian drove the car off the ferry at Cape May and headed north, a trip of 136 parkway miles separating them from their ultimate destination. While that meant less than two hours for the equivalent distance from Winnemucca to Wells on I-80 in Nevada, in New Jersey it took two or three times that long. It would be well after dinnertime when Paterson was reached, and this guaranteed that they would get to Librarian's home after dark. This reduced the likelihood of anyone seeing them arriving together, thus keeping Forger's presence in the house unadvertised.

What with Friday night traffic and an auto accident at the exit for the Atlantic City Expressway, it was 10:20 p.m. when the two pulled off the parkway and stopped at an out-of-the-way restaurant for dinner.

Librarian paid the check, because Forger had only a few dollars on him when he walked out the front door of the prison. His $100 bill fiasco resulted in the government confiscating what it believed were all of his known bank accounts four years earlier. However, that activity missed at least three ten-year, prepaid safe deposit boxes, each in a different name and city. The ones that Librarian knew about were in Stroudsburg, Pennsylvania, Danbury, Connecticut, and Port Jervis, New York.

Though Librarian co-owned all the boxes, he had never visited any of them and had no idea how many there were or how much cash was in them. While it was Forger's intention to visit Stroudsburg in a few days, at that moment he had no money.

An hour and a half later, the two approached Librarian's house on Paterson's Thirty-eighth Street, with Forger hunkered down in the back seat. It was a residence Librarian had bought with the profits from a number of their document-forgery ventures, and to get to it, Librarian deliberately chose to drive through the dark, secluded Eastside Park, a recreation area only one block from his home.

Entering directly into the house through the electronically operated open garage door. Librarian closed the windowless door even before turning off the car's motor. Actually, the minute they turned off the road, no one could look into the car or the garage because high brick walls lined the driveway from house to sidewalk. So, considering the fact that it was late and dark, Forger hidden, the view into the car blocked by high walls, and the probability small that any neighbors were looking out their windows at that time of night, it was almost certain that no one would surmise that Librarian was not alone.

Forger would stay in Librarian's home in a well-appointed, windowless basement room until their work was done. He could have stayed in one of the two second-floor bedrooms, but Librarian did not want to run the risk of anyone seeing light coming from any room but his during the evening. While there were heavy curtains on both bedroom windows, it was foolish to take the gamble.

During the day, Forger would use the entire first floor because each room had heavy, floor-to-ceiling opaque curtains that prevented anyone from seeing in or noticing lighted rooms in a supposedly empty house. A part of the large basement—where there was a sink and laundry equipment—was to be used for making the needed manuscript paper.

For the last year, Librarian had deliberately left all curtains closed at all times in preparation for Forger's arrival. This eliminated sudden changes to the house's appearance occurring at the time of Forger's release from prison. During the day, he would have access to every room of the entire house, but only the first floor and basement after 8 p.m.

He would not be a prisoner, of course, having just been one for four years, so he needed to get out and around. Also, he enjoyed sitting in wooded areas, so nearby Eastside Park was a natural place for him to read and research. However, the matter of his leaving and re-entering the house required some planning on Librarian's part.

Both bushes and a covered archway protected the exit from one of two side doors of the house. It gave access to a path that led to the back yard of a neighbor whose business assignment required him to be in France for at least two years. Some six months earlier, when the neighbor had told Librarian that he was planning to rent his house while living in Paris, Librarian insincerely warned him against it, suggesting that his valuable home might be ill-treated by strangers. Instead, Librarian suggested that he would watch over the property during the neighbor's absence—a position to which he wanted to be maneuvered—and this, of course, gave him full access to his neighbor's house.

Since groundskeepers came every two weeks and Librarian visited it frequently to keep the neighbors alert to his caretaker function, people coming and going from the empty home was not an abnormal situation. In fact, his neighbor's empty house was voted as having the best maintained front lawn and flower garden by the neighborhood association.

When any work was needed, Librarian would contact the vendors, pay them, and then be reimbursed by wire transfer to his bank, following an e-mail to the absent neighbor describing what had been done. All of this effort on Librarian's part was because the lot opposite the neighbor's home was empty. That allowed Forger's comings and goings to occur without observation. When he went out, the plan was for Forger to exit through the side door of the house and a few moments later, to appear like a genie out of a bottle a block away on Thirty-ninth Street, facing an empty lot.

Librarian was certain that a favorite place for Forger to work would be the gazebo that served as Eastside Park's bandstand, a block away. He could carry a folding table and chair on his circuitous route to the park from the house, and it would be there, weather permitting, that he would study and prioritize the things to be done.

On Saturday, the first full day of his complete freedom, Forger suggested that they go equipment shopping. It was the weekend, Librarian was free until Monday, and Forger was anxious to get started. The list of things to be bought focused on the matter of highest priority—namely paper. That meant buying a whole pile of things, some of which by themselves were no more than waste products.

It was critical to the success of their efforts that Forger be able to create the right kind of paper, so he planned to set up a papermaking shop in the basement. The actual making of a sheet of paper was a one-man operation, though in the eighteenth-century, two men worked side-by-side producing the sheets, each of which had one of the two twin watermarks so characteristic of authentic eighteenth-century paper.

Forger intended to work both molds alternatively. However, he had to set up his papermaking equipment first, run some batches of paper, and examine the end product—particularly the color. Then he would modify his ingredients and try again. Only after the testing was completed and the watermark selected would Forger create the paper for the actual forgeries. During that time, Librarian would continue his job at the NYPL, ready to supply Forger with any needed research material.

# 28

# BUYING A GREAT DEAL OF JUNK

The list of purchases began with a wooden tub that had a diameter of fifty inches and a depth of twenty-four. It could be bigger, but not smaller. In this tub, the slurry that eventually becomes transformed into paper would be made.

They would need lots of rags, preferably those with a high linen content. These would be washed a number of times, pounded by hand on a hard surface, cooked in a hot alkali solution, and finally macerated to a pulp in a commercial-sized food processor. Their objective was to get as many white rags as possible, because it was unwise to remove a lot of unwanted cloth colors through heavy bleaching.

A light bleaching to get rid of the darkening that the cooking process brought to the rag fibers would eliminate any residual tints, but excessive bleaching could cause the paper to crumble or break on folding, because it weakened the vegetable fibers. It was also important to avoid producing acid-free paper. This manuscript had to show its maturity, and that included the kind of aging brought about by the normal acidity of eighteenth-century paper.

Librarian called an agency in nearby Clifton and rented a pickup because several of their purchases were going to be too big to get in the trunk of the car. Forger hunkered down in the back seat before they left the garage. In a quiet area of Eastside Park, Librarian stopped to put on his piece, mustache, and wire rim glasses while Forger got into the front seat.

Parking the car several blocks from the truck rental agency, the two walked to it, and using Librarian's forged ID, collected the pickup, leaving a substantial cash deposit in the absence of a credit card.

At a giant hardware store chain they bought a number of large plastic buckets, several pairs of rubber gloves, a rubber mallet, a large-volume medium-mesh plastic colander, and some safety goggles. At a lumber yard they got a heavy piece of hardwood that would stand up to being beaten on as well as squeezed in a wine press. They also bought some boards, half of them precut to three feet and the other half to two feet.

A restaurant-supply store agreed to deliver an enormous stainless steel pot, a gas heater on which it would sit while being powered by two propane bottles—to be refilled when empty—and a professional-size food processor for macerating washed, pounded, and cooked rag pulp. There was a bigger, but lighter weight, and much less expensive pot made of aluminum that they could have bought, but it was useless because the solution that would be made to cook the rags was too caustic for that metal. The owner agreed to hold up the delivery of the items while awaiting their return with the other big purchases, things that they wanted delivered along with the stainless steel pot, and all payments were made in cash. The address given for the delivery was that of the neighbor's empty house on Thirty-ninth Street.

Next they visited a fabric store and bought a two-foot wide bolt of felt 120 feet long. Since the color of the felt was unimportant, they got a savings by buying the bolt in a color that the owner had not previously been able to sell. Eventually, forty pieces would be cut from it, each one thirty inches long. It was on each piece of felt that a single sheet of paper, a little smaller than the size of the felt rectangle, would be created. These open sandwiches of paper on felt would be stacked until the pile was about two feet high.

Finally, from a glass store that repaired screens, they bought several feet of fine mesh window screen and two-dozen panes of clear glass, each two-and-a-half by two feet. The window screen would not be used in the final papermaking process because it was so dissimilar to the sort of screen used in the production of the eighteenth-century paper, though it would have to do at this preliminary stage. Eventually, Forger would weave a screen from wire thread, a job that was difficult, time-consuming, and hard on the hands.

In a swap meet, the two got the wooden tub that would eventually contain the paper slurry. It had been used in the past by several generations of an Italian family who made their own wine, and was discolored from years of use, but that could be bleached out. Next to the tub was the big wine press that had been used with it. They got both at a very good price, and the two muscled them into the pickup.

One final ingredient, namely rags, and they were done. For those, the two went to an older section of Paterson down on River Street, which at one time had a thriving rag and junk store business. Unfortunately, all such places had disappeared more than twenty-five years earlier; so much for the recollections of Librarian's youth. However, one storeowner told them that bundles of linen rags were probably still stored in the old jute mills on Spruce Street.

Both should have thought of that in the first place. That was where the two had done their cockroach stomping as children, and of course such a facility would naturally have rags. The storeowner was right, and they bought 400 pounds of rags there. Amusingly, they were among the most expensive items. For rags!

Finally, they drove back to the restaurant-supply store, unloaded their biggest and heaviest items, got an estimated delivery time of between 4 and 5 p.m., paid the additional delivery fee, then drove to where Librarian's car was parked several blocks away from the truck rental agency. There they unloaded and packed all the things that were not to be delivered by the restaurant-supply store into the car's trunk. The pickup was then returned to the rental agency, the cash deposit refunded, and the two walked back to Librarian's car for the drive home.

Librarian was at the neighbor's house when the restaurant-supply store delivered the materials at 4:30 p.m. The deliverymen had no idea that they were delivering to a house that was not occupied by the party who answered the door.

The driver and his assistant were tipped nicely for putting the wine press and the big stainless steel pot in the back yard, where Forger and Librarian later muscled them into the latter's house. The sight of Librarian going in and out of his neighbor's home would raise no eyebrows in the neighborhood; everyone knew he was the house-watcher for the property.

By suppertime, all the items were unpacked and in place, those destined for immediate use in the basement; the rest were put in the unused side of Librarian's two-car garage. Most of the day's activities would be impossible to trace to him and the rest would be very difficult to track, even if someone were willing to undertake the effort.

# 29

# PREPARING TO MAKE PAPER

On Sunday, Forger and Librarian burned logs in the fireplace all day, not because it was cold, but because the papermaking process needs wood ashes. This was a task that had to be done only when Librarian was home, because smoke coming out the chimney of a supposedly empty house during the work-week would raise suspicions. The ashes, placed in plastic buckets, would be used at a later stage of the process.

In the basement on Monday morning, after Librarian had left for work, Forger began the labor-intensive tasks of preparing and arranging the equipment he would need to make paper. Cutting open several of the purchased rag bundles, he used Librarian's Maytag to wash them a number of times in caustic soap and very hot water. Following each washing, the rags were dried on high heat, and after several such cycles, torn into strips and then cut into smaller pieces with scissors. These were put into the wooden tub he had filled with water by means of a hose attached to the basement sink. In this state, the already decomposing rags were left to soak.

With that task done, Forger began making his first mold. Taking four boards, he formed a three by two foot rectangle from them. In order to make certain that the four corners of the box were perfect right angles before nailing—without which the paper would be geometrically unsuitable—he measured the diagonals of the rectangle. The boards were nailed only when the diagonals were of equal length, an absolute Euclidean guarantee that all four corners were perpendicular.

Then he cut the wire screen bought at the glass store to the size of the frame and attached it, using U-shaped, double-pointed nails. This was the wire-mesh mold in which would be deposited the slurry that would eventually become the individual sheets of manuscript paper.

When the final paper, intended for use in the two manuscripts was made, he might choose to have two molds—one for the watermark, the other for its twin. But at this stage, a single mold would do. Work on watermarks would not begin until after the selection of which were to be used.

For the moment, all Forger wanted to do was to create some oblong paper of the right size, test its folding/breaking characteristics, get the color right, and then later refine the process to get absolutely perfect paper on the runs that really counted.

The next task was to cut roughly twenty pieces from the bolt of felt they had purchased at the fabric store. Every piece was slightly smaller than the mold into which it was intended to fit, and it would be on each of these felt pieces that one sheet of paper—twenty-five by eighteen inches—would be deposited.

Later in the process, every paper sheet produced would be folded in half lengthwise and cut along the fold to make two twenty-five by nine inch half-sheets. Eventually, the pair of half-sheets would be folded in half again, this time widthwise, one half-sheet nesting inside the other, so as to produce an end product with eight distinct writing surfaces.

It was almost always in the form of two nested half-sheets that Mozart bought paper. Depending on what he was composing, he might purchase a dozen such packets to have ninety-six writing surfaces at his disposal. If Mozart needed only four surfaces on which to write something, he would use one of the two half-sheets, and on occasions, he might even cut a half-sheet in two so as to obtain two separate leaves. It all depended on his needs, and he was conservative and prudent in its use because it was expensive.

Having completed the tasks of creating ashes from burning wood in Librarian's fireplace, preparing the rags and leaving them to soak for several days, making one mold, and cutting twenty pieces of felt, each which would fit inside the mold, Forger concluded his first full working day by beginning the creation of the chemical mix essential to papermaking.

Taking several plastic buckets, Forger filled a quarter of each with the fireplace ashes. Then he added tap water, filling the buckets to two inches from the top, a mix that was allowed to stand overnight. While paper can be made with a commercial drain cleaner in place of a blend of ashes and water—because both have the required sodium hydroxide—Forger was uncertain what other chemicals might be in commercial drain cleaners. Using only wood ashes and water reduced the possibility of having a modern chemical present in the paper for investigators to discover.

The next morning, the now-caustic liquid was separated from the ash residue. Putting on rubber gloves and a pair of goggles, he poured the contents of the bucket through a plastic sieve into another bucket, and from there the liquid went into the large stainless steel pot seated on the gas burner.

The sieved ashes went into plastic bags that Librarian would later deposit in various garbage cans and supermarket dumps around the city. This process was repeated for several days until the pot was half full of the corrosive liquid solution.

Finally, the gas burner under the pot was lit, the wet rag pulp taken out of the wooden tub in which it had been sitting for some time—though the water in the tub had been changed every twenty-four hours to avoid the development of a sour odor—and beaten on the pounding board with a rubber hammer. That effort was the hardest physical work of all and Forger kept it up, even though his hands became blistered. It had been some time since he had indulged in this kind of physical labor.

When the liquid in the steel pot was boiling, the partly macerated rag pulp was added, and the heat and caustic solution further broke down the cellulose fibers in the linen. One of the byproducts of this chemical breakdown was sugar, which made the entire basement smell like vanilla syrup.

Finally, again using rubber gloves and goggles, the liquid/rag mixture was taken out of the cooking pot, one bucket at a time, and then poured into a sieve in the basement sink. The brown liquid went down the drain while the rag material, resembling something like oatmeal, was rinsed several times, bagged into pillowcases, run through the Maytag's spin-dry cycle, and allowed to stay wet.

The liquid waste was not dangerous to the sewer system, or at least no more dangerous than typical food wastes from a garbage disposal. It was important that this be the case, because Librarian did not want to have a sewer problem, with the city trying to find out the reason behind it.

The last step needed before paper could be made was the final transformation of the rags into pulp. For that, the commercial food processor was used to cut up what remained of the rags after the pounding and caustic boiling. The food processor could chop only small quantities so this step took some time. The resultant pulp was put back into the wooden tub, which had been cleaned in the interim, and mixed with cold, fresh water. This was now the slurry that would be used to make paper.

# 30

# MAKING PAPER

The manual creation of a piece of mold-made paper takes just a few minutes, though the time to prepare all the needed equipment and ingredients is lengthy. The art of creating material on which something could be written predates recorded history, but not until two millennia ago did there appear the first recorded mention of paper as a writing surface. Made of hemp, mulberry tree bark, silk, and old fishing nets ground up into a mushy mess, its invention is credited to the Chinese.

Thirteen hundred years ago, in a war with China, the Arab nations captured an entire town of paper-makers who were brought back as prisoners and forced to create paper for Arab use. It was on such paper that the secrets of Greek mathematics were preserved while Europe wallowed in the ignorance of the Dark Ages. Not until the Crusades did Western Europe learn the art of papermaking, though it was originally perceived as pagan, since only parchment made from animal skins was considered holy enough to carry sacred text.

Today, mold-made paper is rare to find, though a few facilities specialize in its creation for unique uses. It was this art that Forger had studied for six years. While the caustic solution he created could be neutralized, such alterations to his slurry would not produce the kind of paper he needed. Fortunately, he was not going to continue in the papermaking business long enough to endanger the city of Paterson with a plume of pollution.

Forger picked up his handmade mold, approached the wooden tub that held his caustic slurry, and began the process that would eventually wind up as a Mozart manuscript, worth some unknown number of millions of dollars.

Holding the mold, one gloved hand on each side, Forger dipped it into the slurry. Then, pushing it all the way to the bottom, he turned the mold so that its mesh screen acted as a shovel to scoop up the rag pulp where it was at its thickest. Using a side-to-side motion that diluted the quantity of pulp settling on the mesh screen, he lifted the mold out of the tub. On it lay a thin sheet of paper, though it took several redippings before he was satisfied with the sheet he had just made.

Tilting the mold slightly to let the water drain away, he slowly began to turn it until it was almost vertical, the sheet of paper adhering to the wire screen. One of the pieces of felt that he had cut earlier and that was slightly larger than the paper sheet was slipped inside the mold on top of the paper. The two quickly adhered to each other by capillary action.

Turning the entire tray over allowed the paper sheet to be removed from the mesh screen. If the sheet resisted release, Forger blew on it until it came free. The felt/paper open sandwich was placed on a flat surface and the process was begun again to make the next sheet.

After some time, a two-foot stack of paper-on-felt sandwiches had accumulated, and Forger, after placing a final felt rectangle on top of the last open-faced sandwich, carried the bundle over to the wine press. There he put the heavy board used during the pounding process on top of the bundle and turned the press's screw to squeeze out most of the excess water. When done, the two-foot pile had been reduced to one a few inches thick.

He left the bundle in the wine press overnight, and the next morning slowly peeled off the top layer of felt to reveal the first layer of paper. This, along with the felt on which it was sitting, was separated from the layer below and turned upside down onto a clean sheet of glass. With a putty knife, the felt was slowly lifted off the sheet of paper and a second sheet of glass was placed over the exposed side of the paper. Then the process of paper/felt separation was repeated nine more times, at which point the stack of ten glass-paper sandwiches was carried to a basement oven where it was placed inside the oven to dry. With the heat set at a very low 150 degrees Fahrenheit, the pile was left for twelve hours, and then permitted to cool. As the first ten sheets cooled, he repeated the entire process for the final ten sheets still resting on their damp layer of felt. When they had been placed in the oven for their twelve-hour drying cycle, he examined the now-cool finished product.

In this way, the daily production, restricted by the two twelve-hour drying cycles, was around twenty sheets of paper which, after cutting and folding, produced 160 surfaces of writing material, an excellent production schedule that would eventually provide an ample supply of paper.

# 31

# THE FIRST SIGNIFICANT PROBLEM

After about two weeks into the papermaking cycle, Librarian returned home from work one evening to find Forger sitting at the kitchen table, looking discouraged. "There's a problem with the paper," Forger said, "and we have to talk about it. Do you want to do it now, during dinner, or afterwards?"

Jokingly, Librarian replied, "It looks serious. Let's wait until after supper. That way my digestion will not suffer because I won't know anything about the problem until after we have eaten."

Librarian generally got off work around 6 p.m., took a bus to the Thirty-eighth Street ferry slip and in less than fifteen minutes was in his car in a parking lot on the New Jersey side of the Hudson River. With luck and good traffic, he could be home as early as 7 p.m., but most of the time it took longer, so the two generally sat down for dinner at 8 p.m.

On days when Forger required the car for whatever errands and travel he needed to accomplish, Librarian would leave the house earlier than usual, park the car near the New York bus stop on Thirty-third Street, a few blocks away, and catch the first bus that came along. Later, Forger would do the two-back-yard waltz, walk to the general area where the car had been left, find it, do whatever he had to, return the car somewhere near the original parking place, and walk home. Then Librarian would pick up the car after getting off the bus from New York, all this to make it appear that his commute was unchanged. When that happened, it was a much longer trip involving Manhattan buses or subways and was probably a lot of trouble for nothing. However, the two wanted to be prudent in these matters.

This car-switching system had been used only a few times since Forger's arrival at Librarian's home: once for the drive to Stroudsburg so that Forger could visit his nearest safe deposit box and get some money, and once to the jute mills on the other side of Paterson to buy more rag bundles.

After supper and over coffee, Librarian turned to Forger and said, "All right, now. What's the problem and what can I do about it?"

"It's the paper," Forger said. "I've done everything I can to make it perfect, but one item has proven troublesome and if I don't fix it, it's likely to be fatal."

"That sounds serious," Librarian said sympathetically, trying to keep the discussion from becoming excessively gloomy.

"It's very serious," Forger responded, "and to solve it, you are going to have to find a way for me to see an interior page of an original Mozart manuscript dating from around 1790."

Shaking his head in a "No" movement, Librarian said, "That is very unlikely to happen. It would be almost impossible for me to get you into the NYPL's manuscript collection, and in any case, we don't have anything even near that year. I think our latest Mozart manuscript is from 1780."

"Exactly what is the problem with my seeing an autograph in the NYPL?" Forger asked, ignoring the fact that nothing held in the collection would satisfy the dating needs of his request.

"Because such manuscripts are so valuable," Librarian replied, "several people have to grant permission for anyone to use them, and a valid technical requirement is necessary to obtain that permission. Even scholars who come to the NYPL have to undergo some serious questioning before we let them touch any of the autographs. They have to prove to our satisfaction why a facsimile won't do, and most of them don't win that argument because they can't justify a need to see and handle the original.

"Rare manuscripts are not held for miscellaneous viewing by the general public," Librarian continued. "They are old, fragile, and have great worth, but they are not artwork to be looked at for the pleasure or the emotional excitement of the viewer. One has to have an absolute, gold-bond, technical reason to handle an original—reasons like an examination of the ink colors, pagination issues that deal with how the various sheets of the manuscript are physically arranged, the presence or absence of sewing holes needed in the binding of the sheets, or watermark questions. Those things are not examinable on a facsimile.

"So when a reliable scholar who has impeccable credentials—that are checked very carefully, too—makes that kind of specific request and has that need confirmed, he or she is then permitted to handle the manuscripts. Even that's done under conditions that are almost surgical. They have to wear white cotton gloves, the material is viewed in a special area of the library, the manuscript is placed on a Styrofoam cradle to prevent the spine of the binding from breaking, the lights are special, and the researcher is under constant observation."

Forger sat there, listening, with a hangdog expression on his face. Finally he said, "Then I can't do the job."

Now, for the first time, Librarian was really worried. "Why do you need to see an original?" he asked. "What do you need that you don't have with a facsimile?"

Forger's response was simple, but very telling. "The thing that I'm missing, the thing that I can't fix, has to do with the exact color of the paper that I have to make. While it may have been white in the last decade of the 1700s, what is the color now?

"I can make it anything I want from pale tan to cerulean blue to erotic violet, but I can't solve the problem until I've seen what the real color of a piece of Mozart paper looks like today. That paper was one color in 1790 and it has aged and changed for more than two centuries. I have to make paper today and age it quickly so as to produce that same two-century old patina. To be precise, I have a two-color problem. What do I want the paper to look like when I make it, and what color do I need to create through artificial aging? Those two colors have a relationship to each other that has to be considered at the front end of the papermaking process.

"Don't misunderstand me," he continued. "I can solve the second problem the minute I know where I'm going. That's my difficulty. I don't know where I'm going because I don't know how a piece of Mozart paper looks after two hundred years of sitting around. Using a piece of Jefferson or Washington paper instead, under the assumption that all eighteenth-century paper changes in the same way, is an erroneous premise. It's apples and oranges.

"Furthermore, I need to look at an inside page," he added, "because title pages are generally exposed to the air and the appearance and color changes in unpredictable ways. Making a title page is easy, but an interior page is impossible if you don't know what its color is supposed to look like after two centuries."

"Why can't you use the facsimiles I gave you?" Librarian asked, though he really knew what the answer would be. He was simply asking the same questions of Forger that he would ask of a scholarly patron of the NYPL if that person had requested examination of an original.

Forger's reply was very much on point. "The facsimiles have a range of paper colors that are all over the spectrum and the results produced depend on the particular photographer, the lighting, and even the process of reproduction. Some produce a black and white facsimile using color photography. It's dramatic, but not a satisfactory reproduction for our purposes. I don't know which of the facsimiles that I've looked at give accurate paper color, if any. They are simply not good enough for what we are trying to do, and I have no way to gauge how close any of them are to the real thing.

"I cannot create paper of the right color, because I don't know what the right color is. So if you want this effort to continue, you have to find out what has to be done to get me face-to-face with a real piece of inside paper from around 1790 on which Mozart wrote some music…"

His immediate conclusion of that sentence showed the severity of the problem: "…that is, unless you want to run a risk that I'll be as much as fifteen percent off the correct paper color, in which case the first specialist who examines it will notify the police from Sotheby's conference room!"

From Librarian's point of view, Forger was not being unreasonable. The justifications for his request were such that the NYPL would have accepted them as necessary to see any original in the library, but it was unlikely that they would have valued Forger's desire to create a counterfeit as justification for needing to know about paper color.

Librarian asked Forger to continue work as best as he could while the matter was given some thought. This was not an easy thing that Forger was requesting. The Pierpont Morgan facility, which had manuscripts of the right age, could not be asked to give visiting privileges for Forger, either. They were as difficult on this matter as was the NYPL.

Forger agreed to poke at some other items that needed his attention—for example, the device that would be used to make the twelve music staves on each page—while Librarian tried to figure out a solution to the problem of how to solve Forger's genuinely valid reason to see a real Mozart manuscript of a particular age.

# 32

# GERTRUDE CLARKE WHITTALL, WE SALUTE YOU

Over the next few days, Librarian considered every reasonable approach that occurred to him in which Forger could be put face-to-face with a genuine Mozart manuscript. He called New York's two big auction houses to see if any autographs might be coming up for sale, either in the US or in Europe. At such times, sale items are often put on public, though well-protected "do not touch" display, and Forger might have been able to get near enough for an examination of paper color. He didn't need much time, being as skilled at memorizing precise color shadings as others were at recognizing pitch. One summer vacation he worked in a paint store and produced results by eye that were just as good as color-matching devices.

To a large degree, Librarian was pleased when told that no Mozart manuscripts were part of the next several auctions, because he didn't want Forger to be seen in those places. However, if a sale of a manuscript from the right era were imminent, particularly in Europe, he might have taken the risk. Then he tried Bonhams & Butterfield in San Francisco, but rare manuscripts were not their forte. That was mostly a New York and London specialty. The west coast auction houses dealt more in furniture and *objets d'art*.

Next he considered Chicago's Newberry Library, Princeton, Harvard, Yale, even Stanford out in California, but he couldn't get past what would happen if they inquired about the reasons for the request. Besides, it wasn't he who needed to see the material, but Forger, so they would naturally wonder why Librarian was calling for him. The situation was just too sticky.

There were, of course, the big European centers—Paris, London, Vienna, Salzburg and the kings of them all, Berlin and Kraków, the last holding its manuscript treasures as a legacy of World War II. But if the American libraries were strict about whom they let have access to their manuscripts, the European libraries were psychotic. Also, Forger had no credentials, and even if he forged them, they would be checked by telephone or e-mail long before he got there. So a fake document that announced him as a music professor from Iowa or a musicologist from Michigan wouldn't fool anyone for more than a few hours. In effect, exposure as a fraud was almost certain.

The Library of Congress was an iron fortress. Even on those rare occasions when Librarian went there, they would always suggest the use of a facsimile, relenting only when he gave valid technical reasons for needing to examine the original, plus a ton of documentation to support who he said he was. And they knew him personally, so one can imagine how they behave towards strangers.

Librarian suspected that a 1958 defacing of the manuscript of the Mozart *Requiem*, then on public display at the Belgian World's Fair, was responsible for the permanently heightened caution, though it was difficult to see such things even before that time. The incident resulted in public viewing of manuscripts becoming far more rare, though on the infrequent occasions when communal display was permitted, they were well protected.

Towards the end of that week, during which time Forger gave the impression that he was plugging along on the staff writer mechanism—but which both of them knew wasn't getting anywhere because of his preoccupation with the paper-color problem—Librarian's boss brought up the subject of the NYPL lunchtime public concerts of recorded music.

They used to have them once a week and the auditorium was always full of people on lunch breaks. Librarian really had nothing to do with these concerts, but he enjoyed the fact that they invariably had five times as many people attending them as attended the concerts held at the Library of Congress, though their programs were live and the NYPL programs recorded.

Of course it was a ridiculous comparison in any case, because the NYPL auditorium was five times bigger than LC's hall, so it was natural for NYPL to have more people in attendance. However, they never disclosed that piece of information whenever contrasting attendance records and consequently always appeared to be a giant leap ahead of the LC in audience interest. It was during that casual business conversation with his boss that the solution to Forger's problem of seeing a real Mozart manuscript materialized, though it took a little time to penetrate Librarian's brain.

"With respect to the Library of Congress concerts," his boss said to him, "I hear that their audiences are getting much bigger." Librarian suspected that his boss was afraid of losing his "our audiences versus their audiences" argument.

"Are you aware of the special things they do for their evening concerts," the boss continued, "that might be responsible for their increased attendance?"

"No," Librarian replied, "but I don't believe that their audiences are improving, because their auditorium, though small, is always fully occupied whenever they give a concert. Any rumors that their attendance is improving may be propaganda. They have no place to put more concertgoers. Certainly the LC performs magnificent works live and with great artists, but I don't think that their hall seats more than four hundred. It's the Gertrude Clarke Whittall auditorium we are talking about, aren't we? It's a treasure of a hall, and the fact that it's located right in the LC is particularly fortunate because of the physical beauty of the site. In any case, I am not aware of anything special that they do beyond wonderful concerts. What sort of 'special things' were you talking about?"

"Well," the boss answered, "what they have done in some cases is to tie the works performed to their manuscript collection, many pieces of which were bought with Mrs. Whittall's contributions. I thought you knew that," he said.

Alerted by his boss's reference to what Librarian did and did not know, he said, "Yes, I am aware of the tie-ins between the LC manuscript collection and their public concert series. But it isn't a very regular occurrence, and only happens when they perform a work for which the LC happens to own the autograph. What is it that you have in mind?"

"The reason for my inquiry," his boss continued, "is the hope that we might be able to emulate what they do as part of our noontime concerts of recorded music. Every now and then the LC selects a work to be played on their programs purely on the basis of the fact that it is a composition whose original manuscript is owned by them, and they put that manuscript on public display during the performance. People can see it before and after the concert, though they can't touch it, of course, because it's locked under unbreakable plastic.

"For example, a few weeks ago they did the original chamber-music version of "Appalachian Spring," a work whose manuscript they received from Copland while he was still alive. From what I've heard, the excitement of having the autograph score in the room at the very time that the performance of that work is taking place, coupled with the audience's ability to see it both before and after the concert, adds considerably to the evening's enjoyment and excitement."

At that moment, fireworks started to go off in Librarian's head. His boss's description caused him to realize that it was a direct connection to Forger's need to see a Mozart manuscript.

"If I remember correctly," Librarian said, trying to think and respond to his boss's inquiry at the same time, "the suggestion that manuscripts be displayed at the LC public concerts was one of the conditions that Gertrude Clarke Whittall made when she gave the funds for the purchase of an extraordinarily large collection of manuscripts in the late 1930s. However, that collection is so much more vast than ours that I don't think we could compete in that kind of contest."

"Well, that remains to be seen," the boss said, "and that's the reason for my interest. There is a concert taking place at the LC in about two weeks. I think that it's very clever in concept and will be more so in execution. What I wanted from you are some thoughts about us emulating them."

"What is it that they intend to perform?" Librarian asked.

"Well," his boss responded, "they are going to use those four or five Stradivari that Whittall donated to the LC for a performance of the Mozart C major string quintet. And because they own that manuscript, they intend to display it."

If Librarian's heart was pumping rapidly before, it went into overdrive just then. "That's a great idea," he said, trying to hide his excitement about the manuscript display plans.

Finally his boss added, "And there is a second Mozart work on the same program for which they also own the manuscript. It's a serenade, the one with the strange subtitle of *"Gran Partitta."* The reason I got excited when I heard about it is that this appears to be the first time they've displayed two such important manuscripts during a single concert. And that, plus the use of the Strad collection, is going to make this program a wonderful event."

"Do I understand you to say that two important Mozart manuscripts are going to be publicly displayed at the same time?" Librarian asked, practically holding his breath.

"Am I not speaking English?" the boss said angrily. "That's exactly what I said. The event is being sufficiently well-advertised in and around Washington that I thought we might give some consideration to doing that sort of thing for our concerts. So would you mind looking over what we have in our collection and calling the people who put on the noon record concerts? And if we don't have too much to offer, perhaps we could ask Pierpont Morgan if we could borrow something."

"I certainly will," Librarian replied disingenuously. He was anxious to get away from his boss and think about the consequences of the LC event that was, supposedly, going to take place in two weeks. But with his boss, who had more political sensitivity than technical accuracy, it was wise to check everything.

"I'll get right on it," he added, knowing full well that the NYPL had nothing that could possibly compete with the LC in such a contest, that Pierpont Morgan was not in the business of lending things to the NYPL, and that shortly, his boss would probably forget about the conversation when the press of other duties came his way. Later, and with a very unhappy face, he would tell his boss that it was unwise for the NYPL to try and emulate the efforts of a branch of the Federal government.

Librarian went back to his office and contacted the LC by phone, only to find out that the date of the concert was actually three weeks away. However, the works to be performed, and the fact that they would indeed be publicly displaying two Mozart manuscripts from their collection, was valid information. The string players would consist of the Julliard Quartet plus an extra player from the Julliard faculty, and the *Gran Partitta* would use members from both the Dorian Wind and the New York Wind Quintets, supplemented by members of the National Symphony Orchestra.

Because the LC did this sort of thing frequently, Librarian realized that it was foolish of him not to have thought about it. In fact, the LC representative told him that they had displayed a manuscript of the Mendelssohn string octet—another one of their holdings—at a concert on the previous evening. Asking about tickets, he was told that the performances were open to the public without charge, but it would be wise to get there early, because the seats were invariably gone by 7:15.

Then he checked the dates of composition of the two works to be performed. The wind serenade, which had a contested date of either 1781 or 1784 depending on which authority was consulted, was a little early for their needs, but the string quintet, written in 1787, was close enough to be an acceptable substitute. It would have to do.

So excited was he with the news about the Washington concert that he almost had an automobile accident on the way home that evening. He did not call Forger on the telephone, because his partner was under strict instructions never to answer it. So it was with breathless excitement that Librarian went through the front door and called out, "The manuscript problem is solved. In three weeks, you can see not one, but two Mozart manuscripts, one of which is very near the time you need."

Forger ran up the stairs from the basement, a big grin on his face, and asked for all the details. At the end of the story, Librarian's comment was, "It's a weird turn of fate when the generosity of Gertrude Clarke Whittall, a benefactor of the Library of Congress and widow of a former Massachusetts carpet manufacturer, was going to remove a serious impediment to a peculiar counterfeiting problem."

# 33

# MR. FORGER GOES TO WASHINGTON

During the three weeks preceding his trip to Washington, Forger worked with renewed energy on the staff-liner problem. He was giddy with delight that he would see two real Mozart manuscripts, and when the time came, he rode into New York with Librarian by car and ferry, hunching down in the back seat when the two left Librarian's garage. It was Tuesday morning and the concert was scheduled for that evening. The two parted on the New York side of the ferry, with Forger taking a bus to Penn Station, followed by an express train to America's capitol. Librarian expected him back the next day.

They had arranged that should there be any delay in his return, Forger would use a call signal to let Librarian know that he was on the other end. It worked like this: one ring and a hang up followed by two rings and a hang up. When the phone began to ring a third time, Librarian was to lift the receiver and say, "Yes." Any other response from him and Forger would hang up.

When Librarian arrived home Wednesday evening, he was surprised, but not alarmed, that Forger had not yet returned. At 11 p.m. the phone rang and then stopped. Immediately it rang twice and then stopped. When it began ringing a third time, Librarian answered it with the single word, "Yes," and a voice that did not identify itself said, "Technical problem under control. Return date uncertain." Then the phone was hung up.

Forger finally returned Saturday afternoon, making Librarian jealous by telling him the following story of what turned out to be his excellent Washington adventure.

Arriving in the capital at 2 p.m., he took a taxi to the Library of Congress. He had gotten there so early that the musicians playing the *Gran Partitta* that evening were rehearsing in the auditorium. So he stood outside the door of the Gertrude Clarke Whittall concert hall and fell in love with what he was hearing, even though its sounds were coming through a closed door. After a few minutes and with his typical bravado, he tested the door, found it unlocked, went into the darkened room, and sat down in the last row.

Between the front row and the slightly elevated stage where the musicians were sitting there were two display cases of a non-destructible transparent plastic, both empty and awaiting the arrival of the manuscript treasures that were to be displayed that evening. Each case was mounted on a four-foot high pedestal.

Two hours later, the musicians finished rehearsing and left the auditorium, paying no attention to Forger, though they passed him on their way out. He continued to sit there in the otherwise empty and darkened hall, though he was getting hungry. After he had been sitting alone for an additional hour, five string players came in, passing by him on their way to the performing area. They tuned and began to rehearse that evening's string quintet.

Forger was sure someone would see him, demand identification, and then ask that he leave, which he was prepared to do at once, but that never happened. He just sat there quietly, enthralled by the magnificent harmonies of the music he was hearing, and thinking he really would love to play the cello.

It was sometime around 6:15 p.m. that the string players finished their rehearsal and he was once again left alone in the auditorium. Now he was really hungry, but he had no intentions of leaving. Suddenly, four men entered the hall from the rear. Two were museum guards; a third, dressed in a business suit, had a large package under his arm, and the fourth carried nothing. The last had no identifiable role, though he was the oldest and was therefore probably supervising whatever was to go on. Forger remained seated and watched.

The four went to the front of the auditorium, where the supervisor opened the case on the right. The man in the suit put his package—actually a large cardboard box—on the stage. Opening the box, he selected an item from it. It was an oblong bound document, and he opened it to a page in which there was a large red bookmark, put the item in the open case, removed the bookmark, and then stood back as the case was closed and locked by the supervisor. Both men and the two guards tested the fact that it really was locked. One separated himself from his colleague and took a position, arms folded across the chest, at the back side of the case.

The man in the suit repeated his action by opening a second oblong volume to a marked page and put it in the case on the left. It was then locked, checked, and staffed with the second guard. Both men confirmed the locks one final time and prepared to leave the room. On the way out, the supervisor glanced over to where Forger was sitting and said, "I'm sorry, sir, but we must lock the auditorium now. Only the guards may remain here at this time. You'll have to leave."

Forger smiled and said, "Of course. I understand completely. But may I take a quick look at what it was you put in the cases?"

The two men looked at each other and shrugged, as if to say, "Why not?" Then the supervisor said, "All right, but please do it quickly."

Forger walked swiftly to the front of the auditorium, looked in the case on the right and saw that it was a Mozart manuscript. By the handwriting alone, he knew what it was, probably better than any specialist in the world at this state of his development. There were the broken accolades on the left and right pages, a smudge or two, and two pages of music for string quintet in a neat hand.

In the space of only a few seconds, he had memorized the color of the paper just as one might memorize a word. Then, moving swiftly over to the other case, he saw, by the size of the manuscript, that this was a longer composition, one that called for a bigger performing group. Finally, he left the auditorium, making sure to thank both men for the privilege of seeing the two manuscripts in such a private way.

From a technical point of view, he could have gotten back on the train and come home right then. The color of the 1787 paper was in his head, while at the same time he tucked the unneeded paper color of the other composition in some corner of his brain where he could get at if he needed to.

Instead of leaving the Library of Congress for his return trip, he got on line, which had already begun to form for that evening's concert. At 7:15 the auditorium was opened and he went in, this time walking directly to the right hand case—which contained the string quintet—after putting a newspaper on a seat as identification that it was taken. He stood in front of the manuscript for thirty minutes, just staring. Were he a computer, one could have heard the hard drive clicking away as he recorded data.

Others came by and glanced quickly, often in awe, but Forger was reinforcing things like ink colors, sizes of noteheads, thickness of beams, and positioning of slurs in his head, while simultaneously just admiring the neat organization of the manuscript. Most of what he was now seeing could have been obtained from a facsimile—except for the paper color and the fact that nothing was proportionally altered by the photographic reproduction of many facsimiles. But he was also taking a busman's holiday and rememorizing everything from the two pages at his disposal.

At 7:45, he heard a voice say, "Are you eating that manuscript with your eyes?"

He turned to see an attractive woman peering at him admiringly.

"I'm sorry," he said. "What do you mean?"

"I was behind you on the line and have been watching you staring at that manuscript for thirty minutes. You look as if you are eating it visually."

"Yes," he said, "it is something like that."

Following the first half of the program and during the intermission, Forger went back to the front of the auditorium, and this time he examined the manuscript of the *Gran Partitta* more carefully. The same woman came back and made a few more comments about the intensity of his interest, so he invited her to sit with him for the rest of the performance. He did this by requesting the party in the seat next to him to take the one occupied by the woman, whose name turned out to be Shirley Foster.

Following the excellent performances, Forger was ravenously hungry, so they had something to eat in a restaurant that she chose. She asked if he lived nearby, and Forger replied that he was a tourist.

When she learned that he had not yet checked in at any of the nearby hotels, the matter got more serious, because Washington was not a place in which to presume that hotel rooms were available on a walk-in basis. Because Shirley Foster was attracted to Forger and suspected that he felt the same, she suggested that he spend the night at her place on a couch. So they went there and spent Tuesday night through Saturday morning in bed together.

Well, not all the time, of course, but Forger made a considerable dent into his now more than four-year hiatus from sexual activity. It turned out that Shirley was a programmer and also a very good amateur pianist who attended almost every concert given at the Whittall auditorium. When they were not making love or eating, they played piano four-hand sonatas, often completely naked. Forger was a good sight-reader, as was Shirley, and he got better as their time together passed.

Forty-eight hours after the Library of Congress concert, they went to a jazz club where Forger sat in. She was dazzled with his improvisations on a tune called "Take Five," so named because it was in 5/4 meter, something unusual in the jazz world, at least at the time of the work's composition.

Friday night they went to a concert given by the National Symphony Orchestra and heard a song cycle by Gustav Mahler called "Das Lied von der Erde." It was the first large scale orchestral piece Forger had ever heard live, and the sensuality of the music both overwhelmed him and worked like an aphrodisiac for his last night in bed with the ever-vigorous Shirley. In the morning she made breakfast for him, got what she thought was his telephone number—he never gave her his real name—and he returned to New Jersey via New York City, refreshed, sexually exhausted, and with the exact state of color of the manuscript of the C major string quintet fixed in his memory.

# 34

# GOOSE WING
# QUILL PENS

For anyone who must create text or music manuscripts by hand, a quill pen retains one distinct advantage: the writing end is built like a chisel—wide on one side, narrow the other—so one can draw either thin lines or broad strokes, depending on how the pen is held.

True quill pens, made from real bird's feathers, are available commercially, but their cost is high, the quality of the product uncertain, and the longevity questionable. For those reasons, plus the fact that he did not want to leave a trail of evidence about purchased quill pens, Forger made his own.

With the paper color problem now solved, he began to concentrate on the matter of the pens critical to the project, because they would be used in the writing of the Mozart manuscripts. That meant that he had to buy them from poultry slaughterhouses.

On Washington Street in downtown Paterson, there were several such markets where one could select a live bird, have it slaughtered, gutted, plucked, wrapped, and delivered—head on or off, your choice—in ten minutes. They had everything from rabbits, squirrels, quails, pigeons, partridges, pheasants, and guinea hens to an occasional swan—who eats swan?—but mostly they focused on chickens, ducks, turkeys, and more rarely, geese.

Forger's quill pens were all made from the three or at the most four largest feathers taken from the end of a goose's wing, preferably plucked while the bird was still alive. It is said that Thomas Jefferson kept geese at Monticello for the sole purpose of supplying feathers from which he made his pens.

After Forger removed enough barbs from the bottom of the quill to allow room for the fingers and hand, the partially denuded tube end was allowed to soak in water overnight and then plunged into a tuna fish can full of hot sand. This made the tube less brittle, very flexible, and not likely to split during subsequent cuttings. Because quill pen nibs wear down, the writing point—really the writing chisel—will be re-cut at the most five times, after which the quill's useful life is ended.

The most important phases in the making of the quill pen are cutting the slit and shaping the nib. If the chisel edge of the nib is too wide, it will become dull quickly. If it's too narrow, it flings the ink fed to it from the slit uncontrollably in all directions and wears down rapidly. It is for the completion of these edge-sizing tasks that one must have a tool whose very name hearkens back to the time when everyone made their own writing devices: "the penknife."

Despite the few benefits of using a bird's feather, Forger recognized the numerous disadvantages that caused quill pens to be almost more trouble than they were worth. First, there was a great deal of nib dipping because the pen had no reservoir except the ink adhering to the tip. Second, because of the constant dipping, coupled with the position of the fingers low on the tube, the scribe got ink on his hands and clothes. Third, the curve of the feather had to go around the arm so as not to get in the line of sight. Therefore, unless the scribe was ambidextrous, this resulted in a loss of half a bird's usable feathers; that is to say, for a right handed scribe, the feathers were selected from the left wing of the bird, and vice versa. Add to these disadvantages the necessity to remake the nib periodically and that pressure on the tip occasionally caused breakage and could ruin a page, one can understand Forger's attitude.

However, whatever his feelings, he could not choose to ignore the use of a quill and select a more contemporary writing implement in its place. This was because the differences between something written with a quill pen and something written with a steel-nibbed pen are visible to the naked eye.

For example, on a steel-nibbed pen a blob of metal on the tip of the nib keeps the width of what is being written uniform, no matter at what angle the pen is held. Nor does it show any of the irregularities produced by a quill pen whose stroke is less uniform and whose inability to retain very much ink disallows long unbroken lines.

It was precisely the ability to distinguish between the two types of writing implements that made it obligatory for Forger to use a quill pen in writing his eighteenth-century manuscripts. Steel nibbed pens were not available at this juncture of history and only a specialist in such manuscripts who was asleep at the time of inspection would fail to spot a page written with anything other than a quill pen.

In effect, Forger had no choice in the matter, and though he never really cared for quill pens, he was an expert at making and using them. So, biting the quill-pen bullet—which happened to be on a weekday when Librarian was at work—Forger left the house by the traditional side door method and walked to the bus stop that would take him into downtown Paterson.

Arriving at Washington Street where the live animal markets were located, he selected the largest store and examined the birds there. There were no geese. Going to a second, and then a third market, he found the same situation. The problem was, of course, that geese were reserved for special occasions so it was not surprising that he could find none that day.

A trip back to the first and largest of the three markets, followed by a discussion with the owner, resulted in a business arrangement for twenty-five goose quills at four dollars each, to be delivered over the next four weeks. Most would be taken from living birds, but a few might come from slaughtered animals.

While Forger had the right of rejection of the quills should any be of poor quality, he was not worried that he would be cheated and some substitute supplied in place of the requested goose quills. The items were very identifiable by size, color, and tube dimensions, and any substitutions would be noticeable at once.

A price of four dollars per feather may sound expensive, but that was a great deal cheaper than the finished product bought from stationary stores that maintained calligraphy corners. When the animal-market owner asked why Forger wanted this many quills, he replied that he made a living creating quill-written, elaborate wedding invitations, place cards, and specialized wall hangings.

It isn't easy to get twenty-five goose quills. There are not that many geese slaughtered every day and the number of good pen feathers is limited. Geese are such nasty, aggressive animals that the feathers generally come from slaughtered birds, but in that case they are often bloodied making the quill distasteful to work with. So Forger was prepared to wait the four weeks to get as many as possible from live animals. The owner took a deposit of $50 and asked to be called in one week. Strangely, he got all twenty-five quills in two weeks, which left a lot of birds with aching left wings.

# 35

# THE STAFF LINER—PART 1

Now that paper was no longer a significant issue—the pens never really were—Forger turned his attention to the matter of a device that would be used to draw twelve music staves on each writable surface of the paper simultaneously. Originally he had expressed considerable concern about this device, with the result that Librarian also developed hostility to the problem. Forger's concern began to change when his detailed examination of a variety of facsimiles allowed him to conclude that the staves were all created with metal points. Exactly what those metal points were and how it was done was not clear to him, but that they had to have been metal was, in his view, incontestable.

"Look at those staves," he said to Librarian one night, pointing at four facsimiles each open to an arbitrary page. "Those staves were not made with quill pens, and the fact that none of the twelve are the same as any of the other eleven demonstrates that they weren't printed, either. They were drawn, but not in any way that I'm familiar with. And I'll even take a bigger leap while speculating about them.

"They were not made by pulling or pushing something across the surface of the paper. It was the other way round. The paper was in motion and the device that made the lines was stationary. The pens were held in a fixed vertical position, penpoints down, and the paper pulled underneath them. It's the only way that makes technical sense.

"But," he continued, "what I can't figure out—except for the fact that every one of those sixty lines was the result of ink coming from a metal point that touched paper—are the design characteristics of the thing that made those staves. Look how evenly they are spaced on the page. It's the ends of the staves that are different from staff to staff, with each having its own characteristic raggedness, sometimes even different from one page to the next."

"What is the significance of what you are saying?" Librarian asked.

"Well, if my view that those lines were made with metal points is correct," Forger answered, "then the problem of this staff liner construction goes away. I can use almost anything I want to make the staves, even the ends of paper clips, provided I get them plated with whatever that metal or alloy is, because different materials leave different tracings when drawing lines."

"Suppose," Librarian said, "I do a data base search for articles using the key word 'staff' and its Latin equivalent 'raster,' which is the most common-use term."

"Why Latin?" asked Forger.

"Because the science related to all aspects of the making of music staves is taken from the Latin term for the word 'rake,'" said Librarian.

"You mean there's a science on this subject?" asked Forger, looking astonished.

"Absolutely," replied Librarian, "It's called 'rastrology.'"

The next day, Librarian's search of the appropriate international databases turned up a vast collection of articles in five different languages, with each article containing the key words either in the title or in the body of the text. Choosing those that looked promising, Librarian—who had immediate access to every single one of the technical journals that contained the needed articles—made copies of the most likely ones. He had a big enough pile for a first go round, and if it did not produce a satisfactory result, he'd get a second as soon as it was needed.

When he got home that evening, Forger asked if he had found anything. In response, Librarian opened his briefcase and dumped fifty articles on the table.

"It appears that you've had a very successful day," Forger said. "If I can't find anything in this group, are there more that you can get tomorrow?"

"Well, let's first see if anything useful is here," Librarian replied. "It's easy to find articles on almost any subject. The hard job is to find one that contains what you need."

The two finished supper by 8:45, had fully cleaned up by 9:15, and then jointly began reading the technical papers. By 11 p.m. they had a complete, though as it turned out, not very practical solution to the staff liner problem. It was due to a remarkably detailed article on how a single staff was drawn in the eighteenth-century.

There was no doubt about it. The machines that were used to line paper employed a variety of techniques, but except for some speculation about rollers in place of rasters, what touched the paper was a metal alloy, specifically a brass plate, that was creased, folded like an accordion, and then snipped with shears to achieve a five-pointed surface that looked like this: **VVVVV**. When those points were inked and passed over the surface of a sheet of paper, a single, five-line, four-space music staff was produced.

So what began to coalesce in Forger's mind was how he could create a device with twelve such creased, folded brass plates attached to something he would hold and draw across paper, or vice-versa, to produce his twelve staves. He decided to try to make one staff writer and see how it worked.

Getting a thin brass plate was not a difficult job, though he did have to go to a machine shop to get it scored and bent properly. Snipping the five **V**-points at the place where the ink would run onto the paper required small, but very strong tinsmith shears, for which he had to visit a number of specialty hardware stores.

However, no matter how he held the staff writer to draw it across a sample paper, it didn't work right. The problem was the flow of ink. The five grooves into which he put drops of ink did not tolerate uniform ink flow onto the paper. Some channels fed too much and blotted the paper. Others stopped feeding ink completely. It became impossible to draw a neat staff for more than three or four inches. Making a device to create twelve unbroken parallel staffs simultaneously, each ten inches long, was not going to work if his basic tool was the folded brass plate. It had to be something else. But what?

The next few days involved visiting a number of music stores in the area, and despite his very precise request, he could not get the thing about which he was inquiring. What he wanted was a straight pen nib—actually twelve or more of them—just like the kind that his second grade piano teacher, Miss Spetgang, had given him so he could line his own blank paper and do some music writing exercises. One elderly clerk at a place called "Regent Music" knew about them, but said, "They were a very specialized pen point, and like most straight pen nibs, they haven't been made in twenty years, as far as I know."

# 36

# THE STAFF LINER—PART 2

Forger was not very good at moving on to waiting problems as long as an unsolved one was chewing at his insides. A few days after giving up on the folded brass plate approach, he told Librarian that he needed the car to buy a few more bundles of rags. The fact that about half of the cloth in most of the already bought bundles was not white was causing both too much waste and bleach, as well as reducing the usable quantity of rags. So he intended to buy some more, this time bargaining for as much white cloth as he could get. But the staff liner problem was still in the front of his mind.

It was after completing another purchase at the jute mills on Paterson's west side that he decided to stop at Corrado's fruit market for a few things. Traveling on Main Street in the direction of Corrado's, he passed by PS 3, the school in which both he and Librarian had begun their education. Woolgathering about his first piano lessons with Miss Spetgang at that very school, he was suddenly struck by a thunderbolt of an idea.

He pulled the car to the side of the street, close to the school, parked it and entered through the large doors on the Main Street side. It was 11:30 a.m. and the students were in class. Completely without directions, because he remembered the way well, he went directly to the administrative offices and asked if there was still a teacher named Miss Spetgang at the school.

The secretarial assistant confirmed that Miss Spetgang still taught there, asking what it was this stranger wanted with her. Forger described himself as a former pupil who was just passing by and wanted to speak to her about something that was on his mind.

He was told that the lunch bell would ring shortly and that he could probably meet with her in her classroom during the lunch hour, because she generally ate at her desk. After identifying himself with a counterfeit driver's license—the name on the license was not written down by the secretarial assistant, only examined—Forger was told where Miss Spetgang would be. He was also requested to sit in one of the nearby benches of the administrative area to await the lunch bell, after which he could go to her classroom.

The school was not much different from the time he and Librarian were in attendance there. It still had no cafeteria and the children all went home for lunch, just as he had done. Meanwhile, he structured what it was he wanted from Miss Spetgang.

When the bell sounded and the children flooded the halls, he left the administrative area, found her room, and knocked gently, though he could see her through the pane of glass in the door. She looked up, did not recognize her visitor, of course, and signaled him to come in. She was as thin as he remembered, though her hair was now all salt and pepper.

"I am certain that you do not remember me," Forger began, "but I was a pupil in your class many years ago; in fact, you were my first piano teacher."

A light of recognition came to her face at once. "Of course," she said, "but I have forgotten your name. I do remember you, and I also remember how you tried to change the rhythms of all the tunes I taught to you. You were a devil, though an intelligent student. What is it that you want of me? Is this a social visit?"

Forger replied, "No, not entirely, though it makes me happy to see you well. One of the great gifts that you gave to me, besides your inspiring teaching, was a simple thing, and as hard as I have tried, I can't seem to get another. They aren't made any longer. So I've come by on the outside chance that you might have some more of them, which, I tell you frankly, I am willing to pay a high price to get."

"What on earth was it I gave you that you can't get today?" she asked. "I have no recollection of anything like that."

"Well," Forger said, "it wasn't a big thing, but it was unique. It was a pen nib with five points that you gave me so I could practice music writing. We couldn't afford printed music paper at home, but with that nib I made my own music staff and was able to do the assignments you gave me. Now do you remember?"

Miss Spetgang replied, "I don't remember the specific event you are speaking about, but now I know what it is you are referring to." Getting up from her seat, she went to the closet where she kept what both he and Librarian were convinced was a treasure chest of miraculous boxes. Reaching way in the back, she came up with a box the size of a cigarette pack and brought it back to her desk. Opening it, Forger estimated that it contained more than two hundred penpoints that could be used in a straight pen, many of which were of the five-point variety.

"We don't teach penmanship any longer," she said, "and certainly not with straight pens. There hasn't been a need for these in the last ten years or more. Until you mentioned it, I had completely forgotten about this box of nibs. You are welcome to the whole box if you wish. I have no need for it, and as small as it is, getting rid of it will help relieve my clutter. Here, take it."

Forger thanked her for her generosity, not being sure if she would have given the box of nibs to him had she known what his intentions were for them. He stayed for another ten minutes before excusing himself, saying, "I've taken up enough of your time and you need to eat lunch yourself before the students return. It has been wonderful renewing our acquaintance, and are you sure you will not let me pay you for the nibs?"

Miss Spetgang shooed him out of her office, saying, "I think I paid one penny for each one of those nibs, perhaps two pennies for the more complicated ones such as the five pointers that interest you. And I have no time to figure what is probably a bill of perhaps eighty-seven cents at most. Take them with my thanks, and it was lovely seeing you after so many years. Whatever happened to your friend who sat through your piano lessons with such interest?"

Now Forger had to lie, because he did not intend for her to be aware that the two men still knew each other. "I'm not really sure," he said. "I haven't seen him for years."

"Too bad," she commented. "It's always nice to know what happened to one's students," at which point she stood up, offered Forger her hand, which he took in a friendly shake, and walked with him to the door. He turned as he got to the end of the school corridor and saw her still by the open door. He waved, and she returned the gesture.

On the way back to the house—Miss Spetgang's pen nibs had put buying fruit from Corrado's market out of his head—Forger stopped at a hardware store and bought two-dozen quarter-inch-wide headless screws—flat on one end, pointed on the other—one dozen for immediate use and one dozen extra, a lock wrench for driving the pointed ends into wood, and some epoxy that came in two tubes and which needed to be mixed before use. One end of each of the five-pointed music nibs was a rounded piece of metal that fit nicely over the screws near the flat end. Shortly, it was his intention to glue one nib on that end of each screw.

To begin, he drew a line down the middle of a scrap block of wood about fourteen inches long and one inch wide, marked off one dozen equally-spaced points on that line, and then drilled a pilot hole into each of the twelve marked places, this to ease the imminent insertion of the pointed ends of the headless screws into the wood. Using the lock wrench with dozens of small turns, each screw was then mounted deeply and perpendicularly into the wood block. Finally, the other end of each screw, the flat end, had one of the music nibs glued to it, but not until Forger was certain that the ends of the nibs were all aligned, both vertically and horizontally. It was essential that all twelve touched a flat surface simultaneously. He then put two or three drops of ink into the reservoir on the back side of the nib hanging on the flat end of the screw, and taking a scrap sheet of handmade paper, drew one dozen perfect five-line staves, each one eighteen inches long. The lines were straight because one end of the wooden block was dragged along the surface of a wall that acted as a straightedge.

The next day, Forger borrowed the car and took two-dozen pen nibs to a metal plating house in nearby Clifton. It was a shop that was built to plate large industrial items such as car bumpers or metal pipe. There he requested that his two-dozen pen nibs be plated with the thinnest possible alloy of sixty-nine percent copper, twenty-nine percent zinc, and two percent aluminum, this last metal to prevent corrosion from contact with ink. The owner of the shop looked surprised.

"That's a brass alloy you want, isn't it?" he asked.

"That's right," Forger answered. "Do you see any problem?"

"Not really, just surprised you knew the details that well," the owner replied. "How thin do you want it applied?"

"What's the least you can put on?" Forger asked. "What I want to avoid is to have the plating significantly change the dimensions of the nib's points."

"I can make it micron-level thin," the owner answered, "but it probably won't last more than two months, depending on how frequently you use those nibs. Will that do?"

"Perfectly," replied Forger. "However, there's another issue. Can you protect the nibs from the application of the alloy in certain places?"

"Yes," the proprietor replied. "I paint certain coatings on the metal where you do not want the alloy applied. What is it that you don't want coated?"

"The holes in the nibs," Forger said. "They are an essential design aspect of how the pen nib works, and if you should fill them with metal, it would impede the proper flow of ink."

"I'll paint the edges of the holes with a fine camel's-hair brush," the proprietor said. "That will prevent them from becoming coated. I'll also use the end of a toothpick in the holes so that no alloy fills them through capillary action."

"That sounds fine," Forger said. "Would two weeks be reasonable?"

"More than enough," the owner answered.

Forger went back two weeks later and picked up his plated pen nibs. The total job was $240, or $10 per nib. If he needed more, he still had about another dozen unused nibs at home.

At that point, and for all practical purposes, the staff liner ceased being a technical problem. Librarian, occasionally the worrywart, told Forger that his use of relatively modern pen points might expose the two of them.

"Don't count on it," Forger said. "The tracings made by this staff liner will be able to pass even a microscopic examination, and that's not something that is going to take place when they see the final copy."

# 37

# "I DON'T DO INK!"

"Do you remember the day when I got out of prison and we took the ferry to Delaware and back?" Forger asked one Saturday morning. "You showed me a facsimile of the manuscript of *The Magic Flute*. I've been over that manuscript with a fine-toothed comb a hundred times. Did you ever notice the first dozen pages or so of that facsimile?"

"Not especially," Librarian answered.

"Well, there's a reason why I'm asking this question," Forger continued, "and it has to do with the ink that Mozart used in writing the music for the overture. It was either very poor quality ink or else it was thinned out too much, because most of those pages have faded into complete illegibility. The only things visible on some of those pages are the twelve staves, because the paper was professionally lined with both a different technique and different ink.

"Following the overture, Mozart used a much better quality ink for the rest of the manuscript. What that says to me, though this is unimportant to our work but interesting nevertheless, is that he must have written the overture last, probably after the opera was all done."

"How do you figure that?" Librarian asked.

"Because if it was the first thing he wrote and if he continued using that ink anywhere in the rest of the opera, some other part of the manuscript would also be faded and unreadable. It appears to me that in the body of the opera he used many different inks, all good quality. And his use of these different inks shows how he worked, at least to a careful observer. I can see where he would leave off. He might write a section or two using a particular ink, then he'd go off and do something, and when he got back he'd simply grab the nearest ink-bottle, which probability dictated to be a different mix, and then work on the opera some more.

"Those different ink mixes show his break points in the composition very clearly. It's also quite possible that the colors delineate different days, or even his traveling schedule, which caused him to work on the manuscript in different places where he might have used whatever ink was available locally.

"We work that way today," Forger continued. "You keep a jar full of pencils on your desk, and each time you sit down to do some writing, you grab the nearest one. Well, when Mozart was working on *The Magic Flute*, he did the same thing, except that it was ink and not pencils. In his case, it was even more complicated than that.

"He wrote his manuscripts in layers. One day he might write nothing but a violin and a bass part, using ink from a particular bottle. Then, on another day, he might fill in the wind parts, using a different bottle of ink, and so forth. So the variety of his inks was influenced by how he composed, as well as being influenced by both time and place.

"You can see the differing qualities and tint alterations as you go through the pages. Some writing is dark black. Some has faded to brown, and some, like the overture, for example, has disappeared entirely." Forger concluded by saying, "The reason I'm bringing this up now is because I want to talk about the ink we are going to use."

"Aren't you going to make the ink?" Librarian asked.

"I don't do ink!" Forger responded. "It's an absolute nightmare to make. Do you have any idea what a long, messy, and fundamentally unnecessary job it is to make the right sort of ink? Just for starters, you have to go out and find galls."

"What's a gall?" Librarian asked.

"What kind of library school did you go to?" Forger teased. "A gall is a bulbous growth found on the limb of a tree. The tree creates it as a response to insect attack. Wasps drill into the bark and lay eggs there and the larvae hatch and start to feed on the tree. In doing so, they irritate the tree and that causes the creation of a bulbous growth around the infected area. Of course it encloses the larvae as it grows, too, which is exactly what those smart bugs wanted in the first place.

"Once they are enclosed, the bugs are happy and they continue to feed on the tree. Simultaneously, the gall protects them from being eaten by birds or other insects. When they become fully formed wasps, they chew their way through the gall to get out."

"What on earth do you need galls for?" Librarian asked.

"Because they have tannin in them," Forger said, "and tannin, combined with iron sulfate, makes a liquid that becomes a jet black ink. Unfortunately, just tannin and iron sulfate alone make lousy ink. It doesn't adhere to anything. You have to add a water-soluble material, like gum arabic, to act as a binder. Without it, the ink has no body, won't flow, and doesn't stick to the paper."

Librarian asked, "Isn't there something else you can use besides galls?"

"Of course there is," Forger answered. "You can use pomegranate rinds, horse chestnuts, hemlock, and even pine bark. But galls are the best, particularly galls from oak trees."

Librarian, in admiration, said, "You astound me. How on earth did you find out about this?"

"I'd be a dreadful forger if I did not know a lot about inks!" Forger replied. "To you they are strange and bizarre, but I need them to do the kind of work that I do best, so I had to study them. Further, when I apprenticed in the Netherlands, we had to make our own ink because the master papermaker was a madman. He would scream that you had to know a lot about non-paper things to be good craftsmen, and he said that paper unable to hold ink—that could not be written on—that would decompose in a few years, and was not aesthetically beautiful, was worthless. His favorite expression was, 'If you know nothing about inks, you can't tell if your paper is good.'

"But making ink was the one thing about the paper mill that I hated," he continued. "He'd take everybody in a bus to the middle of nowhere and make us tromp through the woods, looking for trees with chancres on them. We never knew if we were in Germany or the Netherlands. The worst part was when we found a tree with a lot of galls on it and tried to get them off the tree. If there were adult wasps present, they would sting us and we'd come back with lumps on our hands and faces."

"If the problems are that severe," Librarian asked, "how do you propose we get the right kind of ink?"

"We are going to buy it," Forger replied. "It's not terribly expensive and its both easier and less trouble than making it. Buying it is a time saver, too. The best inks come from fermented galls and that process can take two months.

"Because of the fermentation, your place would smell bad for weeks. We'd have ugly, black stains over our hands and clothes, and the neighbors would complain that you were stinking up the entire neighborhood. It might even result in the Health Department calling on you to ask about the odor.

"Look on the web for a site called 'Kremer Pigments,'" Forger continued. "That's not 'K-r-a-m-e-r,' but 'K-r-e-m-e-r.' They're in Germany. I remember visiting their factory in Aichstetten when I was an apprentice in Hechingen, but they have franchises in the U.S. Call their American distributor—I think it's in New York—and ask about black iron gall ink. Make sure that you are inquiring about the product in undiluted form. That's where we mix all the ingredients. We'll probably use two quarts of the stuff, because I have to practice for some time before I can begin on our manuscripts and there is always waste. No, better make that three quarts. I don't want to take the risk of running out."

Librarian, making notes, said, "I'll contact that guy in Los Angeles who used to sell our manuscripts to dealers out there. He can order the ink and pay for it using a California bank check. It would look strange to ask the seller to ship ink to California but then send a New York check."

Out of curiosity, Librarian then asked, "What risks, if any, do we run using purchased iron gall ink?"

"Well," Forger answered, "there is always risk, no matter what you do, but Kremer Pigments is the best. They supposedly use water that is absolutely unpolluted. One of the easiest ways to establish that a document is a forgery is through a mass spectroscopy test on the ink, because it invariably reveals modern chemicals, like chlorinated hydrocarbon pesticides, that contaminate the water used to mix the ink.

"I heard of some men who thought they had gotten around the problem by using natural spring water to make ink, but it turned out that their spring was polluted. Kremer Pigments has a well that is tested every thirty days and the water from it is very pure. Nonetheless, to be 100% safe, we are going to add our own water, only the kinds listed in the US Pharmacopoeia such as sterilized water. I probably won't need more than a quart, but whatever the minimum quantity is, that's what we'll have to buy. There is nothing in such water to indicate a modern chemical contaminant.

"If our manuscripts are perfect," he continued, "no one is going to be interested in the ink or making tests on it. Ink is rarely a problem. In fact, I am going to have to have several adulterations of the ink, because I want it a little faded and brown in some places and dark in others. We'll need several ink adulterations for the clarinet concerto.

"Now don't get too excited about what I'm going to say, but I'll probably have to include some very bad things in the ink: materials like lead, mercury, antimony, and even some human or animal waste, too."

"What?" Librarian exclaimed. "What do you need that stuff for? Why are you buying such pure water only to contaminate it? What would happen if those things were detected?"

"If there were any examination of the ink, I would expect them to be detected," Forger said. "That's why I'm going to contaminate it. The water that was used to make ink in the eighteenth-century wasn't pure. It was swill. The wells were contaminated, people got sick and even died from drinking it, sewers ran into it, and those kinds of contamination have to show up in the ink. What I don't want are modern chemicals that didn't exist in 1790, but the ink cannot be so free of all contamination as to be suspicious in and of itself. It has to have the kinds of pollutants that existed in water of that era.

"If anyone asks you for permission to test the ink," he continued, "let them do it, but resist it at first and then give in graciously. It's no big deal and we're taking steps so they won't come up with anything except normal readings for ink made with the water of the eighteenth-century. In any case, it's unlikely that anyone will want to test the ink if the manuscript, the paper, and the watermarks are good enough. I'll tell you right now that even Mozart would not be likely to produce a more representative autograph than I will when the time comes. Good forgery is ninety percent hard work—most of which is study so you know what to use and what not to use—and ten percent strong light. There is very little inspiration involved. It's mostly mechanical and intellectual."

The next day, Librarian contacted the American representative of Kremer Pigments, called his fence in Los Angeles from a public phone, mailed him a money order for both the ink and his services, and in two weeks had the materials to make a great deal of black iron gall ink. It came in a wooden box on which their California agent had written, "Fragile: Antiques," though probably with his tongue in his cheek.

On the other hand, as Librarian thought about it, the description wasn't entirely a bad fit.

# 38

# WATERMARKS 101

Italian paper makers of the thirteenth century were the first to use watermarks, the purpose of which was to identify and advertise a particular paper manufacturer. Early symbols included a square, a cross, a circle, or other simple geometric figure.

Watermarks were created by sewing wires in the shape of the desired picture onto the mold's screen. The placement of those wires reduced the amount of water that drained through the mesh of the mold. In turn, this lowered the amount of vegetable fibers deposited on that area of the screen, causing an image to be left in the wet paper. A light source placed behind the paper would forever allow the image to be seen, entombed in the fibers of the final product. Until around 1850, this was the only method of watermarking paper.

Forger now came to the matter of which watermarks to use for the paper of both forgeries, and no further manuscript paper would be made until the selections had been completed. It's the kind of problem that sounds, on the surface at least, to be totally unsolveable and there are at least four reasons—none technical, all administrative—that would cause anyone to come to that conclusion.

First, Forger would need facsimiles of all the eventually chosen watermarks, or else photographic reductions of them with, in both cases, the precise percentage of reduction known. That leads to the question of quantity: how many different watermarks did Mozart use in his lifetime? It's potentially off-putting, because it could be a big number, but the reality of the situation is not that bad. He could, and often did use a particular brand of paper for an entire composition, maybe even for several compositions. He would buy some paper, all of one watermark type, and then write one or more compositions, using only that paper. So there are not thousands of different watermarks, only something between 100 and 120, but that's still big enough to worry about.

Second, he needed a list of all of Mozart's compositions, classified by both date of composition and watermark usage. For example, the facsimile of the *Jupiter* symphony that both Librarian and Forger had seen shows a picture of the single watermark found in all the pages of that paper. So if one were to forge a composition written at the same time as the *Jupiter* symphony, it would be logical to create paper with that same watermark. But if one were to forge a composition written ten years earlier, knowing what the watermark was for the paper of the *Jupiter* symphony might not be valuable information.

Third, he would require a concordance of compositions by paper type, stating how many paper types—and which ones—were in every composition. The *Jupiter* symphony has only one paper type, but was this normal practice, or was it common for him to use two or even more paper types in a single composition? Could one find a work written when he was thirty-five containing a paper type that he also used when he was twenty?

Fourth, he had to have some critical measurements of the watermark's components. For example, the three half moons of the *Jupiter* symphony's watermark was a symbol representing a certain manufacturer, maybe even an Italian firm owned by a family named "Luna." The precise size and spacing of those moons was critical. They could not be made any size or placed anywhere on the page, or separated by arbitrary distances.

While Forger had the ability to create paper with any watermark he chose, that skill was not enough. Instead, he had to know which watermarks to use and in what compositional period of his life Mozart used paper containing those particular images.

Once this set of peculiar problems was understood, Forger would begin to turn out the paper for the production of both forged manuscripts. He estimated a manufacturing schedule of twenty sheets, or 160 surfaces of paper a day, though some unknown part of that production would be imperfect and have to be destroyed.

So then, how does this seemingly impossible collection of inquiries get organized, understood, and resolved?

# 39

# WATERMARK GRADUATE SCHOOL

It was because Forger had too many other things on his plate that Librarian had not brought the solution for the watermark puzzle to his attention. Whenever he was asked about the problem, all Librarian would say was, "Don't worry about it. One war at a time." But now that the matter of paper and the staff writer were out of the way, his collection of goose quill pens ready for use, and bottles of undiluted iron gall ink delivered and on the shelf, it was time to come to grips with the choice of the historically correct watermarks for a manuscript, about which no one really knew anything.

"It's time to bite the watermark bullet," Librarian said one evening. "Here's our work for tonight." Saying that, he took two large books from one of the many bookcases in the living room and put them on the table. One volume was in a traditional portrait, or vertical format, but the other was in a landscape or oblong format. Forger had no idea what they contained.

Opening the oblong volume to an arbitrary place, which turned out to be pages 112 and 113, Forger saw a hand-drawn sketch on each of the two exposed pages. Page 112, on the left, showed three half moons, the word **"REAL,"** and the letters **"A"** and **"W,"** all in a stylized text and placed on the page in a seemingly random fashion.

The sketch on facing page 113 was almost, but not quite a mirror image of page 112. The shape and form of the letters were also very similar, though not exactly the same.

Page 112 was described as "*Wasserzeichen* 56: A" and page 113, as "*Wasserzeichen* 56: B."

*Wasserzeichen* is German for "watermark." Each of the two pages also included other things, such as parallel vertical lines extending from top to bottom. The four quadrants of both pages were numerically identified, clockwise on page 112 and counterclockwise on page 113, though this identification was not part of the watermark itself. Its presence simply allowed one to identify placement of the quadrants after folding and cutting the paper to its final size.

Forger stared at the two pages for a while, looked up and said, "Well, those are watermarks. That's certain. The one on the right is the twin. I've seen and even created a great many like them in Germany. There weren't that many papermaking houses in Europe at the end of the eighteenth-century, and I can even identify some specific manufacturers from the watermark. This particular paper," he said, pointing at the two open pages, "came from Northern Italy. But who made the paper is not important. The real question is in what Mozart compositions, if any, this manuscript paper may be found."

After some time and further inspection, Forger added, "These two pages represent the twin pairs of the same watermark. They aren't identical and rarely are, because watermarks are twins, not clones. I recognize those three half moons, too. They were part of the watermark of the *Jupiter* symphony that we spoke about. But this watermark is different. There are things here not found in the watermark of the *Jupiter* symphony paper and vice versa. Do you know anything about the compositions Mozart wrote using paper with this watermark?"

Librarian did not respond to Forger's question verbally. Instead, he reached over and opened the second volume of the pair. This one had few sketches and was mostly text. Riffling through it until he came to a page marked in bold with the words "*Wasserzeichen* 56"—the same words identifying the sketches of the first volume—he put his finger on the text and said, "This is what you want to know.

"The description here," he continued, "lists every Mozart composition using paper of watermark type 56. There are about fifty such compositions, and type 56 is only one of approximately 110 known watermark types that he used during his lifetime.

"Further," he went on, his finger still pointing at the same text, "here is the list of those fifty compositions." Librarian moved his finger down the entries of that list, title by title. Then, turning to another quite arbitrary page in the oblong volume, he displayed the sketch of a completely different watermark, described as "*Wasserzeichen 41*," and asked, "Would you like to see a list of the compositions that use this paper?"

As Librarian looked up for a response, Forger's face showed astonishment. *"What are these volumes?"* he asked excitedly, his eyes wide with wonder.

"I won't keep you on pins and needles any longer," Librarian said. "One volume contains the tracings of every watermark found in every Mozart manuscript, while the other volume classifies his compositions by which watermark he used. Isn't that a pretty good description of what you need?"

"Furthermore," Librarian went on, "that describes only the surface of what's in those books. There is a lot more stuff there. Not only is the location given where the various referenced manuscripts reside, there are also detailed measurements of the size of the objects that make up the watermarks, a list of Mozart's paper makers, and many other things that I haven't gotten into, but I think you need to know them intimately."

"Does it say anything about Mozart using more than one paper type for a single composition?" Forger asked.

"Do you remember that C major string quintet you heard at the Library of Congress?" Librarian asked in response. "Well, according to this book," he continued, flipping through the vertical volume until he found the right page, "that quintet is written on three different paper types—55, 66, and 82. I can even tell you which of the three paper types corresponds to which page of the manuscript."

Forger looked up from the books with eyes as big as saucers. "I absolutely do not believe this! You've made it all up. It's a joke, right? I can't conceive that anyone could have gathered this data. No. That's not strong enough. It would not only be impossible, it would be insane, because there is no financial incentive to have this kind of information.

"If what you say is correct," he continued, looking around at the two volumes still open in front of him, "these constitute a catalog of specific watermarks used in all of Mozart's manuscripts, as well as a concordance of their distribution by composition. I can't believe that you ever found such a thing. I can't believe that anyone would have built such a thing. Have you any idea of the value of these books to our effort? I was going out of my mind trying to figure out how we could learn which watermarks might appear in paper he used around 1791, and this book seems to have solved that problem in the blink of an eye.

"I was almost ready to use the '*Jupiter*' symphony watermark because it was relatively late in his lifetime, and more to the point, the only one whose precise graphic details I had. And then, I would have expected some specialist to say of the completed manuscript, 'Hmmm. These are the wrong watermarks for this period of Mozart's life,' at which point you and I would have had to get on the first plane to Katmandu.

"God bless all the hundreds of people who compiled this data. It must have taken them years to do it. Who are the authors?" he asked.

"Not hundreds," Librarian answered. "Just one—an English scholar named Tyson. Remarkably, he was a physician and psychiatrist, though he spent a great deal of his working life dealing with chronological issues of the music of both Mozart and Beethoven. That was his destiny and all he really wanted to do in life. He traveled great distances to examine every Mozart manuscript in the world on which he could lay his hands. After Mozart himself, he probably handled more paper on which Mozart worked than anyone who ever lived. He went from one library or repository to another, carrying his watermark reader—a light box on which he examined every page of every manuscript—and he created this incredible collection of data. To support himself while doing this, he would occasionally go back to the practice of medicine. Periodically, he lectured on his findings."

"Where does he live?" Forger asked. "This is a guy I'd like to meet."

"You can't. He died recently," Librarian said.

After a few moments, Forger picked up both books, went into the room in which he usually worked during the day, flopped in a big, comfortable armchair, and the two didn't speak for thirteen days. That was because every time Librarian tried to talk to him, Forger raised his hand in a shushing gesture, never taking his eyes off whatever page he was on in the watermark catalog. These were two quiet, but very productive weeks, and later Forger told Librarian that those two books broke the back of whatever significant problems acted as impediments to the forgery of their two manuscripts.

# 40

# RESEARCH FOR FUN, RESEARCH FOR PROFIT

During the time that Forger was completely occupied with the watermark volumes, he would come out of his deep-study mode only to ask Librarian to do a piece of research, some of which was accomplished using the world-wide web. Then he would immediately return to his intense examination of the details of the watermarks found in Mozart's music paper.

Use of the world-wide web was a technique at which Forger felt he was not yet skilled, having been in prison during the formative years of that tool and now too busy to take on anything else. Besides, like most computer illiterate people, he was afraid of automata. Librarian didn't mind doing the work, because it enabled him to keep himself current about Forger's progress. However, Librarian did notice that, from time to time Forger would spend a spare half hour online, and his experience in making inquiries was improving.

Now, having digested a great deal of the watermark information he needed, Forger said that he was almost ready to make the molds for the concerto paper. However, first he wanted to read everything he could about the clarinet concerto to be certain that no major technical considerations had been overlooked. In effect, he wanted to search for two things: first, historical details that might influence the choice of paper type for the job, and second, information about the musical content of the composition that was derived from the nature of the clarinet in Mozart's era.

Considering the fact that Mozart's clarinet concerto was played so often, presumably so well-known, and with the details of the music assumed to be so secure, the two of them expected almost nothing to exist that might influence the manuscript's musical substance. However, as it turned out that was completely incorrect. In fact, it was a scholarly minefield.

Librarian got on the Internet, and using a search engine, began to investigate the matter of music for the clarinet. With a keyword argument of "Mozart clarinet concerto," he had 100 pages of sources in just a few minutes. Of course reading them took a great deal longer.

Many were record reviews of performances of the work and those appeared to be of no special interest. However, that also turned out to be a failure to recognize the significance of certain performance details. There was also a great deal of technical material about the history of that composition and all of those web entries had to be carefully read for content, though much of it turned out to be useless, for their purposes.

However, the good discoveries often led to other areas of study. It was fully three evenings of work before Librarian was able to give Forger a list of the things that appeared to have value for them.

In many of the technical documents, there were references to reports found in scholarly journals. There were even references to entire books that contained what appeared to be interesting and possibly valuable material. While it was clear that many of the cited articles had to be obtained and read, there was one item that appeared to be absolutely indispensable: a book entitled *Mozart—Clarinet Concerto* by an Englishman named Lawson. A blurb from the book's back cover was included, and it appeared to contain some very provocative material:

> "Mozart's clarinet concerto is of supreme importance as his last instrumental work. Yet there are a number of special problems surrounding the piece, since the autograph is lost and the unique instrument for which it was written has not survived. This book traces the origins and development of the clarinet, Mozart's encounter with it, and the composition and subsequent reception of the clarinet concerto."

Now while all of that struck both Librarian and Forger as vitally important, it was one remark in that text that brought both to a complete stop: "…the unique instrument for which it was written has not survived."

Forger focused on that comment as potentially very important. Further, he found it quite peculiar, because he did not understand it at all. What was "unique" about the instrument, and in what way has it "not survived"? Who has not seen a clarinet? And while there have been technical improvements to the instrument over the years, this comment gave him the impression that the author was speaking about something very different than technological advancement. It was an item that had to be explored, understood, and, possibly factored into the manuscript effort.

Later in the day, both men concluded that they could move no further until that book had been read and digested. Forger suggested that it would almost certainly lead to some additional research, saying, "It's beginning to appear to me that not only is there a critical problem in the selection of the paper to be used for the manuscript, but also hidden instrumental questions that I don't yet understand. I've also found a few references in the watermark books for which I'll need to read the original material, too, and several references that you found on the web also need to be obtained."

"That request reminds me," Librarian said. "I meant to ask you about something. You were reading the watermark book, but that's in German. Since when do you read that language?"

"You forget that I apprenticed in European paper-making shops," he responded. "One was in the Netherlands, but in Arnhem, close to the German border, and everyone in that town was either bi- or tri-lingual. But the other shop was in Hechingen, Germany, and hardly anyone spoke anything but German there, though in a dreadful dialect, as bad as any in Bavaria. So I learned the language, of course. I'm not fully fluent, but I can get along."

"Well, if that is the case," Librarian said, "there are several German technical papers mentioned on the web that I think you also need to read. For example, there is one called "Mozart und die Klarinette," printed in Salzburg in 1985. Interested?"

"Sounds like a winner," he responded.

"And there is one in English that appears critical," Librarian continued. "It dates from 1948 and is entitled 'The original text of Mozart's Clarinet Concerto.'"

"That looks like a winner, too," Forger said. "When can you get me some of those things, particularly the clarinet concerto book?" he asked.

"I'll know that in the morning," Librarian answered.

If there was a copy of it in the circulation department of the NYPL, and if it was on the shelves, he would have it by that evening. Then he immediately reversed himself, realizing that it was not at all wise to borrow the book. It would have to be bought in any case, because he did not want there to be any knowledge within the NYPL that the subject held particular interest for him.

Even though library records were not kept about who took out which books, he did not want anyone to know that he had borrowed a book about Mozart's clarinet concerto months before he allegedly discovered the manuscript. What he bought privately could be kept secret by paying cash, but borrowing a book on a particular subject from the library could be seen and remembered, even without formal documentation.

A quick check of the web showed that Cambridge University Press published the concerto book, and unless the edition was a total sellout, he would be able to get a copy at Barnes and Noble during lunch break. Checking on several on-line bookstores, he saw that it was available from a number of them.

As for the technical papers, obtaining those were easy and completely without risk. The NYPL had a magnificent collection of scholarly journals, and all he had to do was to locate the ones containing the papers needed and make photocopies of them.

Forger had one final question, "These two watermark volumes appear to be part of a much larger set of books dealing with Mozart's music. Am I correct in that observation?"

"Yes, you are," Librarian answered. "It's a German edition. We have the complete set of about 120 volumes in the NYPL, and while anyone can come in and use them, they don't circulate, because the volumes are reference material. I had planned to buy the one containing the clarinet concerto when you start making the score. Why do you ask?"

Forger replied, "I don't want to wait that long. Can I get it sooner? And while you are at it, can you also obtain the volume that has the clarinet quintet in it. I don't need it now, but let's get that out of the way. Oh, yes. One more thing," he said, smiling. "I think it is time that I listened to performances of both works, don't you? Could you pick up several different recordings of each?"

"I'll have them tomorrow," Librarian answered.

And so at lunch break on the next day, Librarian went to Barnes and Noble for the concerto book, to Patelson's for the German publisher's scores, and to Tower records for the recordings. In the afternoon he went to the NYPL stacks for the needed technical articles and copied them.

Though they did not yet know it, from the viewpoint of things having to do with the musical content of the concerto and the quintet, their discussion of research material was the most significant contribution to the success of the counterfeit.

# 41

# THE PLANNING PHASE
# COMES TO AN END

Except for bad weather days, Forger had been working in Eastside Park's gazebo since he got out of prison; not all the time, of course, and never on the weekends when there were lots of people in the park. But during the week, if the weather was nice, he was there for six to eight hours a day, returning to the house only for lunch, getting more books and technical reports from the ever-growing pile that Librarian was bringing home every night, or using the necessaries. Then he'd go back to the park, carrying his small, collapsible table on which he would put a pad for making notes—mostly the titles of more papers that he needed to read—some books, and an armload of unread technical reports.

Every now and then some retiree from the area who was taking a walk through the park would see Forger working and come over to say hello. Librarian wasn't happy about that, because he did not want too many people to get to know Forger's face. As far as it was possible to determine, no one knew or suspected that Forger was staying at Librarian's house. On the rare occasions when someone asked him where he lived, he'd wave his hand in some general direction and say that he was renting an apartment "over there." No one asked for more specific details than that.

Librarian, besides supplying Forger with technical documents, had a lot on his mind. What occupied him was that in the not-too-distant future, he was going to open negotiations with Sotheby's and Christie's, and the logistics of those negotiations required careful planning. Particularly important to him was the desire to avoid all personal publicity. Specifically, he did not want to be part of any situation that would wind up with his picture in the paper. And while he intended to take steps to avoid that from happening, he also had to be prepared in the event that there was a slip-up somewhere.

The news media are so alert, so devious, and so utterly ruthless to get their stories—particularly when a great deal of money is involved and the story is both dramatic and heroic—that eventually his identity might get out, no matter what precautions were taken. Somehow, somewhere, and in some unpredictable way, someone might make a mistake, and if that happened, he needed to be so well-prepared that the situation could be dealt with gracefully. But if his name or picture or both did get into the paper, he wanted no one to be able to link him with Forger, who was at that moment sitting in the Eastside Park gazebo talking to an eighty-six year old retired, but still mentally alert gynecologist named Dr. Gold.

Ever since he had begun bringing home all the books and articles Forger requested, Librarian had not been able to get much out of him, and it was getting worse. Forger would read for a day, then Librarian would find a note on the kitchen table the next morning which read, "Copy pages 165–176 of Bärenreiter Mozart volume V/14/4. Enlarge it, please." And the next day, at the music division of NYPL, Librarian would get the needed volume, copy the requested pages, and go back to work.

Or else Forger wrote, "Get Newhill's article in *The Music Review* of 1979, Volume 10, pages 90–122, 'The Contribution of the Mannheim School to Clarinet Literature.'"

This appeared to Librarian to be a stage of work that might take some time, though he was not bothered by it, because it was all grist for the mill, and the work was for the sole purpose of assuring that the forgeries were masked in perfect authority. Forger was making a professional's effort to know everything written about music for the clarinet during this period of music history. So that was why every night Librarian would bring home photocopies of a half dozen articles and a book or two, and Forger would spend all day in the gazebo digesting this material, occasionally interrupted by Dr. Gold telling him about a set of triplets he delivered in 1949, or some gynecological nightmare that he had detected and cured in 1953.

Forger didn't mind the stories. He just smiled and nodded from time to time, giving Dr. Gold the impression that he was listening, while actually reading and making notes. Everyone was happy, including Dr. Gold, who was delighted to find someone to talk to in pleasant surroundings and who appeared to be interested in his repertoire of baby-delivery stories. From all the literature Librarian was bringing home, it was clear that Forger was working hard.

When solid progress was being made in every single area of their joint effort, something else popped up. Librarian's boss asked him to attend an international conference on paper acidity scheduled for Munich in three months. Librarian had known about the conference and expected to be the one asked to attend, so the invitation did not come as a surprise. The timing for the event could not have been better. Within four to six months, Forger would be close to completing the concerto manuscript, maybe even done with it, and following that, he would begin the preparatory work for the quintet autograph. This meant that Librarian had to begin to arrange for the manuscript's discovery story. Since Munich was only four or so hours by train from Strasbourg, he planned to take two weeks of vacation after the Munich conference and lay the cover story for the discovery. He also needed about a month of research in preparation for the Strasbourg visit.

So while Forger spent all day in the gazebo, Librarian would arrive home with armloads of things for him to read, as well as a pile for himself, then the two would work half the night—Forger on manuscript issues, and Librarian on the history of money-lending in eastern France.

Why money-lending? Keep in mind that the stories about the disappearance of the two manuscripts involved them being in a briefcase of some sort that was supposedly pawned in Strasbourg by Mozart's clarinetist, Anton Stadler. Now to whom would Stadler have gone to pawn something? He would have gone to a moneylender, that's who, and that's why.

# 42

# POLITICS AND THE
# WATERMARK CHOICES

"I've chosen the paper types for both manuscripts," Forger said one evening after dinner. "What that means in terms of schedule is that I'm now ready to weave the screen for the mold, create all the paper that we'll need, and then line it. After that, I'll do a lot of handwriting practice using rejected paper, the iron gall ink, and some quill pens. When I get done with all that, I'll create and age both manuscripts. We're talking six months at the most, and probably closer to four. First, however, let me show you the watermark choices and why they were selected."

And flipping open the oblong watermark catalog to the page showing watermark type 82, he said, "This is one of the two concerto papers, and..." flipping back almost thirty pages to watermark type 55, "...this is the other. As for the quintet, I'm going to use only type 55 paper."

Librarian asked, "What is the reasoning behind the choice of those two paper types?"

"A couple of things," Forger responded. "The most important are the watermarks found in another work, one that probably immediately precedes the creation of the clarinet concerto and shares its history to some extent. It's a long story, but I'll give you the short version.

"In almost every research document I've read about the concerto's history, there are references to an earlier concerto that Mozart began, but did not finish. It's an incomplete draft of only twelve pages for an instrument very similar to the clarinet—one called a 'basset horn.' That's a..."

"I know what a basset horn is," Librarian interrupted. "It's like a clarinet, but lower, and the sound character is different. What does this abandoned basset horn concerto have to do with your choice of paper for the clarinet concerto manuscript?"

"Two things," Forger answered. "The paper and the music itself. The fact is that Mozart recycled the melodies of the abandoned composition right into the clarinet concerto. In doing so, he plagiarized himself. But that only shows his good judgment," Forger said smiling.

"Nobody knows why he stopped work on the earlier composition," Forger continued, "but that is not information that concerns us. What does matter is that Mozart took the little bit of music he had written for the basset horn concerto and reused it almost unchanged for the clarinet concerto. So the two works—one abandoned and one complete—may be considered as consecutive, or almost consecutive sister compositions.

"The manuscript of the abandoned concerto has survived and is in a museum in Switzerland. Take a guess as to the paper types it uses," Forger said, smiling. "It is because of the presence of both 82 and 55 in the draft of the basset horn concerto that I plan on using the same paper for the clarinet concerto. Do you see my logic?"

"Of course," answered Librarian, admiringly. "What you are doing is called 'setting up a straw man.' If those two compositions are presumed to be consecutive, then it is almost certain that he had a supply of both paper types as he began the clarinet concerto. And any expert who examines our concerto manuscript should recognize the same two paper types in both works. It makes perfect sense for the two types to show up in consecutive compositions. That's very clever of you. I take back all the negative things I've said about your poor sense of politics."

"Now, as for the quintet paper," Forger said, ignoring the compliment, "I've chosen type 55 because he used a ton of it for other compositions written about the same time as the quintet. For example, half of the opera *Don Giovanni* was written on paper type 55, though that was a year or so earlier. He used that paper, though not exclusively, in composition after composition from 1787 until his death. All of that makes its use for the quintet very logical."

"Are the watermarks on those two types complicated?" Librarian asked.

"Not really. They hardly ever are," Forger replied, turning the watermark volume around so Librarian could see the design. "Three half moons, the word 'REAL,' that sort of thing. But the text is placed differently and the size of the characters are not the same as the *Jupiter* symphony paper where we met it first."

"Does the word 'REAL' have meaning in this context?" Librarian asked.

"It denotes the paper size," Forger answered. "Oh, yes, that reminds me. There is an important tactical issue here. You need to be careful about the extent to which you speak of the watermarks when the authentication process begins. You should not let on that you know about the relationship of the paper types between the clarinet concerto and the abandoned basset horn concerto. This is a fact that we need to let the experts discover. For one thing, if they don't, it's a sign that they don't know anything and that gives us an enormous advantage. But the more important reason for your pretended ignorance is that it is unwise for you to admit you know this information.

"Your role is that of the person who discovered the composition, not someone who contrasted its physical makeup with other Mozart compositions. As a manuscript specialist, you would, of course, be expected to know what the watermarks of your discovery were, but there is no reason that you would have made any connection between the discovered manuscript and the draft of the abandoned basset horn concerto. On the contrary, it could raise suspicions if you demonstrated knowledge of this watermark similarity.

"Once the experts find out that the watermarks of our forgery are the same as the watermarks of the paper used for the abandoned basset horn concerto, it will strengthen their authenticity attitude. It's exactly the kind of news that along with everything else places the seal of absolute authority on our manuscripts. So let the experts discover these things and get the honor. We'll make the money.

"But you haven't heard the most interesting news of all," Forger said. "I've decided that I will incorporate a few of my own improvisations while copying out the music of the clarinet concerto and the quintet. Happily, Mozart will get the credit for my creations."

"You are putting me on," Librarian said.

"Not in the least," he replied. "The most creative part of my work is yet to come. I may even include a chorus or two of 'Lullaby of Birdland,'" he said, smiling.

# 43

# THE PLANNING ENDS WITH
# AN INTERESTING TWIST

"So tell me about this improvising business," Librarian asked Forger the next evening.

"Well," replied Forger, "it's all related to the fact that Stadler, the guy for whom Mozart wrote the clarinet concerto, owned a unique instrument. It was made especially for him and was the only one of its kind. Like many such efforts aimed at advancing the technology of musical instruments, the developments contained in Stadler's new clarinet didn't last beyond his lifetime. In fact, knowledge of the instrument's existence was lost until the middle of the twentieth-century, at which point it miraculously began to make a comeback. That recovery was entirely due to the desire on the part of a few clarinet players to perform Mozart's concerto on an instrument similar to the one for which it had been composed. In order to distinguish Stadler's instrument from a traditional clarinet, it bears a special name: a 'basset clarinet.'

"The difference," Forger continued, "between Stadler's basset clarinet and a traditional one is simple—only a matter of four extra notes at the low end of the instrument. But those four notes will have an enormous impact on our concerto manuscript. It is absolutely certain that, in the concerto, Mozart wrote passages which employ those four low notes, and we have to worry about them."

"I don't understand," said Librarian. "How did those extra notes disappear? Where, how, and when did they get lost?"

"It happened around 1800," Forger answered, "at the time of the concerto's first printed edition. The printing had a built-in marketing and sales problem unless something was done. Specifically, the publication of an edition with the solo part as Mozart wrote it was not likely to be a big seller, because no one besides Stadler had a clarinet that could play it.

"So the publisher hired an editor," Forger continued, "to rewrite the solo part, eliminating all the offending notes that could not be played on a clarinet of traditional compass. The orchestral parts were, of course, not affected and required no tinkering.

"How much of the solo part was rewritten to get rid of those four low notes is unknown. But when the editor got done with his work, the clarinet music was irreversibly corrupted."

"What do you mean by 'irreversibly'?" Librarian asked.

"Think about it for a second," responded Forger. "What the editor did was take the original solo part, modify it in some undocumented way, and leave no record of the changes. Given that state of affairs, you can only know what today's music is, but you know nothing of what it was before being changed. And it gets worse. Because that kind of undocumented tinkering occurred, it can be argued that not one single note for the solo instrument can be guaranteed as being authoritative. How could it be otherwise? The original manuscript is lost. What we have is a version produced from that original by a person paid to change it, and we have no idea what he did.

"However, from a practical point of view, it's not nearly as serious as that, because a lot of the music probably does represent something very close to what Mozart wrote. The main thrust of the changes came from the four extra notes of Stadler's basset clarinet, but there could be other differences too. For example, Mozart may have written one articulation pattern——a slur, for example. Stadler preferred another, writing that in his part, and the editor preferred a third, which is what wound up being in the printed edition."

Librarian interrupted him to say, "But that kind of thing happens all the time, even today. It's called 'editorial authority,' and I can't think of anything that could be better for us than this kind of uncertainty about what Mozart wrote originally. It makes whatever we put in our manuscript more authentic than what is out there. We are, in theory at least, acting as Mozart himself. So what we have to do is some heavy-duty guesswork about what that first editor did and then try to reverse it. In terms of being the guys who will unring the bell, we are in the catbird's seat."

"That's right," Forger said, "but it's a better situation than you might think. We don't have to do all that guesswork to figure out what to put in the concerto with respect to the four low notes. We've got lots of help, because at least four printed editions exist in which scholars have tried to reconstruct exactly that. However, they have no pipeline to the infinite, either. Every one of those efforts may be a good try, but in the final analysis, what's been done represents a guess, presumably an educated guess, but it's a guess nevertheless. Maybe they're right and maybe they're wrong.

"What we must not do," Forger cautioned, "is take what those others have done and simply incorporate it unchanged into our manuscript. That would be a giveaway. Fortunately, the various efforts to recreate the original text of the concerto do not agree. There are technical papers by other experts suggesting that all the published low-note solutions have some flaws."

"So what do you intend to do?" Librarian asked. "Are you going to reject all existing solutions and improvise your own?"

"On the contrary," Forger said. "I'm going to include at least some part of all of them! I'll take some from this and some from that, and do you know what is going to happen? Every one of those editors will be able to say, 'See? I'm right. Mozart did exactly what I said he would have done.' And so will every other person who attempted to solve the problem, because unless their proposals are musically preposterous, which I doubt very much, I'll use their ideas in our manuscript. I'll also make some changes to what they've done and incorporate them. Those are the places where my improvisations will come in to play. Why not? I have good musical instincts. It's not too dissimilar from playing jazz piano, though I presume you know I was teasing when speaking about 'Lullaby of Birdland'!

"What we must not do is use everybody's ideas uncritically. That would generate suspicion. It's important that my readings in some places be different from those of the modern scholars. Then what we'll have is a bunch of excellent scholars and players agreeing that our manuscript has to be absolutely authentic because it concurs, *to some degree*, with what they said it would be, even if only in one or two places. And not one of them will realize that it agrees with them solely because we stole what they wrote and put it in our manuscript."

"Chalk up another political brilliancy in your column," said Librarian. "When do you start?"

"I'm going to take a few days off and go to Stroudsburg to get some more money," Forger answered. "When I get back, I'll begin the real work. At the end of that, we are going to have two manuscripts ready for sale."

# BOOK 4:
# CREATING AND
# DISCOVERING THE
# MANUSCRIPTS

# 44

# THE ARITHMETIC
# OF MUSIC PAPER

Forger was almost ready to begin making the two chosen types of paper. With the required twin forms of each of the two types, the actual need was for four separate manufacturing tasks. One would produce type 82 paper, a second type 82-twin, a third type 55, and the fourth type 55-twin. The reason behind twin representations of the same paper type is not entirely clear. One view is that the creation of two slightly different forms of the same watermark picture was related to quality control.

In actual operation, two men, each having a unique mold and working in a confined area around the dipping tub, improved the efficiency of production. The use of any watermark was restricted to a fixed period of time and careful records were kept to show when any particular image was used. This permitted the manufacturer to know the approximate creation date of any batch of paper at a later time. As part of the quality-control scheme, the two molds used by the two workers were made very similar, but they were not identical.

In the final analysis, the reasons for twin forms of the same paper type are irrelevant. The only important issue was that alternating twin forms were present in Mozart's manuscripts, so their creation became part of Forger's manufacturing process.

The nature of the work facing Forger would now change dramatically as the transition was made from the theoretical to the practical. Of the several labor-intensive tasks that would occupy him over the next few months, the first was the weaving of the wire mesh screen.

Following Forger's release from prison, he had constructed a papermaking facility in the basement and embarked on some testing phases. During those stages he used a commercially available window screen in his mold, the kind used to keep flies out of a house, but that would not do for the final paper. The real production mold required a screen to be woven by hand from wire filament. On its completion, it would be affixed to the wooden mold and the first of four watermark patterns wired into it.

Originally, they planned to make one mold corresponding with every needed watermark image. The advantage of this approach was that the molds remained available in case they misjudged the needed quantity of a particular paper type and required more of it.

However, each mold mandated the weaving of another screen, a task made especially difficult by the need to wear heavy gloves to prevent the weaver's hands from getting cut to ribbons by the wire filament as it was repetitively pulled taut. It also would have greatly increased the overall job time for Forger, because it took several weeks of hard work to weave a single screen.

Instead, Forger decided to weave only one screen, after which he would wire it with the type 82 watermark, and make an ample batch of paper using that mold. Then he would unwire the old watermark and rewire the screen with the twin of type 82.

When they had enough type 82 paper, both original and twin—and they had to be very careful to keep the two papers separate and well-identified because no external markings distinguished them—he would rewire and create a third batch of paper, this with watermark type 55, followed by a fourth and final rewiring of the screen for type 55-twin.

There were three disadvantages of this approach. One was that the multiple wiring and rewiring of four different watermarks on the same screen had to be done without damage to the screen's weave. Second, once a batch of paper was complete and the wires for that watermark removed, it was almost impossible to recreate it—should that become necessary—so as to have a perfect match with its original wiring. Third, it would take an especially watchful scholar to recognize that the screen's weave of four supposedly separate paper types was identical, but if that happened the jig might very well be up! To minimize this admittedly small likelihood of discovery, Forger intended to alter the weave of the screen as much as he could prior to the installation of each new watermark. This would be done with a nail file, inserted to disturb the wire's position in every course of the screen's weave.

Therefore, underestimating the quantity of any paper type would cause the entire project to be significantly slowed down by the recreation of that entire batch. Each of the four batches of paper required a generous quantity to be manufactured, in fact far more than their best estimates had predicted.

How much paper did they need? Theoretically, the whole job for the concerto needed approximately 102 surfaces, the equivalent of a little less than thirteen sheets, each twenty-five by eighteen inches, and producing eight surfaces after cutting and folding. That expectation of a need for thirteen sheets wasn't a guess, but a calculation based on an average of what Mozart wrote on a single typical surface, as testified to by their examination of many facsimiles.

In his orchestral works, he wrote an average of eight measures on each surface of music paper. It all depended on the width of the surface's most note-filled measures. The clarinet concerto would require 810 measures: 359 for the first movement, ninety-eight for the second, and 353 for the third. So at an average of eight measures for each surface, the concerto needed approximately 101 surfaces and a fraction of a 102nd, at least theoretically.

Therefore, it appeared that thirteen sheets would be ample. But since the actual manuscript would consist of alternating sheets of type 82 and type 82-twin, along with some type 55 and its twin, they appeared to need only three sheets of each type, assuming equal distribution of usage. However, in actual practice they would require much more paper than the predicted quantities.

Some sheets would be rejected because of imperfect manufacture, while bad staff lining would spoil others. Blank pages would be deliberately included in the final manuscript because Mozart did that for a variety of reasons, such as the convenience of sending a completed movement—with unused pages at its end—to a copyist as he worked on later movements.

Here and there passages would be deliberately defaced and then rewritten to give the impression that the composer had changed his mind about the musical content of a few measures at that point, something found in many Mozart manuscripts. An entire sheet could be rejected because of a single imperfectly counterfeited measure on one of its eight surfaces. A good deal of music paper was required for handwriting practice, though imperfect sheets might serve some portion of that need. In effect, many reasons made the theoretical calculations insufficiently precise. These things caused Forger to make a great deal more paper than theory predicted. Since he could make only twenty sheets of paper a day, production capacity was on the critical path to the completion of the counterfeits.

They expected to lose half of their manufactured paper. This translated into five days of production for each of the four needed paper types, a schedule that would almost certainly result in far more paper than they could possibly need, but extended the time needed to conclude the job.

One final need dictated their decision to get all the papermaking out of the way in one effort. Once they had sufficient quantities of paper, the cleanup of the mess of papermaking activities would begin. That included disposing of all equipment used for the job because they wanted no potential visitors to find remnants of a papermaking factory in the basement.

For the moment, however, their production schedule placed them in the position of needing more supplies, including both rags and firewood. This shopping trip would not need the rental of a flatbed truck, though they would need one eventually when disposing of the largest items, such as the wine press and cooking pot.

# 45

# THE RHYTHM
# OF MUSIC PAPER

It took Forger almost four weeks to complete his wire screen, attach it to the wooden mold, and weave in the type-82 watermark. The creation of the watermark took ever so long to get right, what with the constant checking of sizes and distances against the sketch in the watermark volume. That the printed sketch was a one-quarter-size reduction of the real watermark made the already-difficult task of maintaining accuracy even more intense. Forger confirmed the measurements of the placement of the three half moons to the paper's edges, to each other, and to the other components of the watermark, with thirty-one distinct distance measurements, each taken multiple times. He was like a carpenter about to use rare woods who followed the admonition, "Measure twice. Cut once."

Next he began to create the rag pulp that would eventually become the paper slurry. There was no slurry left over from the paper-creation experiments of many weeks previous, because unused for a long period of time, slurry develops a sour odor and must be discarded. So that, plus the fact that the color of the experimental paper had to be modified as a result of his Washington visit, required the creation of a new batch of slurry.

The first stage of his work was slowed down because he could only obtain the needed ashes by burning wood during the evenings or on weekends. Even with that impediment, in two weeks he had cooked and pounded and pulverized enough rags to create four clean garbage cans, plus several plastic buckets full of the pulp that would, when mixed with water, become the paper slurry.

To avoid the pulp developing a sour odor, he drained and refreshed it daily with cold water.

Because he was now permanently finished with the creation of rag pulp, he cleaned and scrubbed the large stainless steel pot in which the rags had been cooked. Barring a major miscalculation, he was done with this phase of the work, though for safety he would not immediately get rid of the cooking equipment.

Now, as he created the paper, he moved the rag pulp into the slurry tub by the bucketsful, as required. From that wooden tub of the old winepress, formerly stained a dark purple and from which some local Italian family had extracted rich, homemade, robust, red wines for at least three generations, the paper for two forged Mozart manuscripts was about to be created.

He then began a rhythm of work that lasted approximately twenty days. To begin, he made some sample sheets of paper for the sole purpose of getting the color right. It was still locked in his head like a computer's gray scale. He would make a sheet, examine it, and add a mentally calculated amount of bleach to the slurry. Then he would make another sheet of paper and adjust the slurry again. At one point he must have added too much bleach, because on the next cycle he chose to dilute the mixture with water. After several hours, he had achieved the paper color he wanted. Unfortunately, due to the fact that the colors of the rag pulp added to the slurry were so unpredictable, there was no practical way to fix the proportions of the ingredients. Thus these kinds of empirical adjustments were necessary every time he added rag pulp.

On 6 a.m. of the first day of making real paper, he donned a pair of surgical rubber gloves. He had never done that before, and when Librarian inquired about them he smiled and said, "Remember that my fingerprints are on file with several federal agencies. While I've never heard of an authentication process for valuable manuscripts that included a fingerprint test, you never know. That's why the gloves.

"Your fingerprints," he continued, "are probably on file somewhere too, but that's not a problem, because they would be expected to be on the paper. As for a search for fingerprints remaining from the eighteenth-century, you can forget about that. The volatile oils in fingerprints evanesce over time. Even if Mozart had handled the paper, as would have been the case for a genuine manuscript, his fingerprints would have vanished a century or more ago. But I doubt if anyone will request the test in any case, because it's messy and you could claim that it would hurt the value of the manuscript. That's probably not true, but say it anyway if asked."

On that first day he created twenty sheets of paper—the maximum daily capacity of Librarian's oven—in three hours. After squeezing the water out of the felt-paper-felt sandwiches with the wine press, he made ten glass-paper-glass sandwiches that went into the oven at 11 a.m. for a ten-to-twelve hour baking at 150° F. When those ten sheets came out of the oven, they were cooled and then sprayed with sizing. Next, new sandwiches were made up from the ten remaining sheets still in the wine press. They baked all night and were taken out of the oven around 7 a.m. the next morning. With the night-bake safely in the oven, the day's work was ended.

Over a total of five days, Forger made 100 finished sheets of type 82 paper, though how many sheets might eventually be rejected was not yet known. Once the entire batch of type 82 paper was made, he began, using the time that paper was drying in the oven, to multitask several jobs simultaneously every day. First he would make twenty sheets of watermark type 82-twin, place ten in the oven for drying, and while that was happening, he would go back and make the uncut, unlined sheets of the previous batch of type 82 paper completely functional.

This involved cleaning up the edges and cutting and folding each sheet to produce eight surfaces. When finished, he had 100 sheets, or 800 writing surfaces. On each of these surfaces, he then, using his homemade rig of twelve pen points affixed to headless screws, carefully drew the twelve stave lines. The total production time of those 800, lined surfaces from the original 100 sheets took seventy hours, a job that had to be done three more times before all of the paper was made.

His daily work rhythm was an approximation of the following: he began by making twenty sheets of paper from his slurry, each twenty-five inches wide by eighteen inches high, all of which would go into the wine press and have as much liquid squeezed out of them as possible. Then he removed the glass-paper-glass, night-bake sandwiches that had gone into the oven on the previous evening.

Unmaking those sandwiches by separating the glass from the dry, flat, unlined paper, he sprayed that paper with sizing, a gluey material that filled the pores of the paper. That sizing was another benefit of his years in the Netherlands because it was said to be a "secret mix," invented by the mill's master paper maker. When Librarian asked Forger what the ingredients were, his response was, "You don't want to know."

Following the spray, Forger washed and squeegeed the glass sheets and created ten new sandwiches that would become the day-bake. The sheets for that day-bake—the first half that day's paper manufacture—were taken from the wine press. Once the day-bake was in the oven, he refreshed his slurry, made his color tests, adjusted his mix, and prepared to make another twenty sheets of paper the next morning. It was when he was not doing these papermaking day-bake and night-bake tasks that he folded and cut the completed sheets of the previous paper batch, lining the eight surfaces of each sheet with twelve music staves. Before going to bed, he took the day-bake out of the oven, sprayed sizing on the now dry ten sheets, washed and squeegeed the glass, and created and placed the night-bake in the oven.

Because he was working with the paper types 82 and 82-twin simultaneously, he kept them in separate areas of the basement so as not to mix them up. The only way to distinguish them was by inspection of the watermark. Externally, the two paper types were identical.

When he finished making the 100 sheets of type 82-twin, he rewired the mold and continued in his rhythm of manufacturing the new paper type—which was type 55—while simultaneously folding, cutting, and creating the staves on the pages of the previous batch, the twin of type 82.

Finally, he rewired the mold a fourth and final time, producing the 100 sheets of type 55-twin. Following the folding, cutting, and lining of this final paper type, he had four stacks, one in each corner of the basement.

At last he inspected all 400 sheets—the equivalent of 3200 surfaces of paper—and extracted those that did not satisfy his critical eye. These sheets became practice paper. When finished, he had sixty-three perfect sheets of type 82, seventy-one of type 82-twin, an amazingly high eighty-nine of type 55, and a disappointingly low forty-four of type 55-twin. On the top of his stacks of perfect paper—each sitting on a piece of thick brown wrapping paper so as to avoid direct contact with the floor—was a piece of butcher paper that identified that particular watermark type and gave the count of the sheets in that stack, a tally that would be reduced by a count of one as each sheet was placed into use. Then, to avoid any household dust and dirt from discoloring the paper, he covered each of the four piles with a large white bed sheet. The basement looked as if it were Halloween with four short ghosts standing, one in each corner.

# 46

# HANDWRITING PRACTICE

It was on a Friday evening following dinner that Forger told Librarian of his readiness to begin practicing the penmanship that would be used for the manuscripts.

From Forger's point of view, it was just another handwriting style that he had to master. However, unlike Lincoln, Washington, Jefferson, Poe, and the others whose manuscripts he had duplicated quite perfectly in the past, here there were very few words, just geometries of ink on paper that would reproduce Mozart's music handwriting, including all the peculiarities of personality found in his music manuscripts.

Librarian took a chair opposite Forger as he began to set up his supplies and tools in the dining room because he wanted to observe the process of how Forger went about accomplishing the task of mastering another person's hand. It was a chair that he would occupy for the two days of the weekend, watching everything Forger did, but learning very little about how he did it.

Forger's preliminary work in preparation for the next day's practice session included the creation of scrap music paper from all the rejected sheets. He cut most of these sheets into separate leaves, though he left a few in uncut form for a purpose that was not immediately clear to Librarian. All of this paper was then neatly placed on the dining room table in the largest room of the house—a table on which both manuscripts would eventually be created.

The room had excellent light from the street when the ceiling-to-floor opaque window shades were raised—which was irrelevant at that moment because it was dark outside. However, the room was protected from prying eyes, because the window faced a small garden surrounded by thick hedges more than ten feet tall. There was also a chandelier in the room providing additional light, to which Forger had added three floor lamps from around the house and a table lamp with an intense halogen bulb. He was serious when he told Librarian some time back that good counterfeiting was ten percent strong light.

Forger put several different solutions of iron gall ink, a half-dozen quills from his collection, a penknife, a magnifying glass, a jeweler's loupe, the facsimile of *The Magic Flute*, and a pair of surgical rubber gloves on the table. Librarian asked him why he intended to wear gloves when his fingerprints on those scrap sheets would be of no consequence?

"I'm using gloves during practice," Forger said, "because I'll be wearing them when I'm creating the manuscripts, so I want my hands to become comfortable working in them."

On Saturday morning the actual practicing began and Librarian took his seat of the evening before so as to be directly opposite Forger. Opening *The Magic Flute* facsimile to an arbitrary place, Forger scanned the page, looking for a quarter note that was written on the first line of the staff in treble clef, namely the note 'e.' Finding one, he then copied it, making the vertical line—called the stem—first, and then the note-head connected to it. He did this on the first line of the first staff of the first surface of the first leaf of his practice paper. Then he did it again, and again, and again, about forty more times, until he got to the right end of that first staff.

While it appeared to Librarian that Mozart could have written any one of those quarter notes, that was clearly not Forger's view. He circled four of the notes, looked at each for some time, first with a magnifying glass and then with his loupe, his head only an inch above the surface of the paper. After this he wrote another set of approximately forty quarter notes on the second staff, this time reversing the order of the note's components; that is, the notehead first and then the stem.

Forger then examined every one of those forty notes with his loupe and when he raised his head, his beaming smile told his friend that he thought them to be perfect. Librarian was unable to tell why he was satisfied with the notes, because from his perspective there were many differences between them. The stems on some were longer than on others. The sizes of the noteheads varied, as did the angles at which the two elements of the note connected, with some stems leaning left and others leaning right. Yet apparently it was not uniformity that interested Forger, but some other quality of similarity. And truth to say, to Librarian all the notes looked like Mozart's manuscript, despite the fact that there was only modest affinity between the measurable elements of their handwriting.

Next, Forger did a third staff, placing a vertical line as a measure separator after each four quarter notes. When he finished, there were exactly thirty-two quarter notes presented in eight evenly spaced measures. Then he searched the facsimile again for another example of an '*e*' and copied it perhaps 150 times onto several staves, using a variety of pen strokes.

For one hour Forger wrote nothing but an '*e*' in quarter-note form, using as his model copies of Mozart's quarter-note writing of that same pitch. He would select one note, seemingly arbitrarily, and then would make forty or so copies of it. Once again, those forty notes did not bear many similarities to each other or to the previous ones he had written. He made some close together and some far apart. It appeared to Librarian to have no method, just random selection and writing.

Forger used every available quill, sometimes stopping in the middle of a line to change from one to another, though not because the end had worn down. Apparently he had another reason, one that Librarian could not discern.

He might turn a quill this way and that so the angle of strike on the paper was different than the previous note. Finally, he smudged a series of notes and made a sour face. He then put a Band-Aid on the smudging finger and did it again. He still was not happy and went to the medical cabinet to search for a roll of surgical tape, from which he cut off a piece to cover the Band-Aid, then he wrote another note and smudged it with the same finger. Now he appeared happy.

Librarian had a thousand questions about which he had kept silent, but that business with the Band-Aid and surgical tape broke his resolve. "What did you just do?" he asked Forger.

"The smudge response from the rubber gloves is terrible," Forger replied. "It's not at all the way flesh smudges ink. I put the Band-Aid on to simulate human skin. It was a little better, but not good enough. The surgical tape works fine." At no time during his response had he looked up or even stopped work.

After an hour, with both sides of six leaves full of only the note '*e*' in quarter-note form and apparently satisfied with his ability to write it well enough, Forger then found an '*e-flat*' in *The Magic Flute* manuscript and filled a page, both sides, with copies of it, changing his model every so often by finding another '*e-flat*' in Mozart's handwriting somewhere else. Then he wrote the note *f* for close to thirty minutes, and after that, he chose an *f-sharp,* writing several surfaces of that. He skipped the note *e-sharp* because that was not, apparently, a note Mozart used and he could not find one as a model. Then he went up the scale by making two surfaces of *g,* and kept going upward by half-steps until he reached *f-sharp,* the last note he could write within the confines of the five-line, four-spaced staff.

That exercise took close to four hours. At no time did Forger rush the work or give the appearance of being bored or tired. He worked methodically, tirelessly, critically, and unceasingly, making sour faces at things he did not like, or in his opinion he did not do well. Then he cleaned off his pens, took all the paper on which he had written, put it in a pile of material eventually scheduled to be burned—though he saved it until the manuscripts were completed for what Librarian presumed was a possible later consultation—and took a nap. His concentration during those four hours of work was a sight to see, and based on the number of pages he had created, Librarian estimated that Forger had written close to 40,000 quarter notes.

# 47

# MORE HANDWRITING PRACTICE

Librarian continued to observe Forger's progress after he arose from his nap. Following a light lunch of tea and toast, he began his practice again. This time he made eighth notes, from '*e-flat*' at the bottom of the staff to '*f-sharp*' on its top. Then he wrote several pages of sixteenth notes, an equivalent number of half notes, one page of whole notes, and when Librarian thought him close to being finished, he then filled up eight surfaces with dotted quarter notes followed by pages of dotted eighth and dotted sixteenth notes. His practicing was still restricted to writing individual notes, most with stems, many with flags, but none with beams.

When he appeared to feel that there was nothing left for him to learn about individual notes of almost every rhythmic form written entirely within the five-line, four-spaced staff, he showed Librarian some of his pages. It was the first time all day that he had paid any attention to his friend. Although what he wrote on the pages made no musical sense whatsoever, Librarian was convinced that he could have sold every one of them for at least $50,000 each, so perfect a match was the handwriting to Mozart's own. It was a faultless copy and could have passed for Mozart's manuscript under the most intense scrutiny. Librarian gulped and said nothing as he put the pages in the pile that would eventually be destroyed.

Forger began to copy quarter notes that lay both above and below the staff. He appeared to be having difficulties in writing ledger lines; that is, the lines above and below the staff that must be created by hand so that the noteheads may be written at the correct pitch. Then he stopped writing notes and spent two hours practicing ledger lines, constantly examining models in the facsimile of *The Magic Flute*. Most of his problems appeared to center around the angle at which he was holding his quill, and Librarian believed this to be the case, because Forger was constantly adjusting the angle until it appeared to him that he had it right. Finally, he seemed satisfied with ledger lines and went back to writing a variety of notes above and below the staff.

Now he began to experiment with clefs, some of which he wrote both forward and backwards, as is the case for certain instruments on Mozart's manuscripts. When those apparently gave him no problem, he went on to his next adventure, which turned out to be the writing of conjoined or connected notes. He wrote pages of eighth note pairs joined with a beam, several pages of four sixteenths joined with two beams, and eight thirty-second notes with three. Then he practiced notes of all rhythmic values, in, above, and below the staff: triplets, quintuplets, sextuplets, and septuplets though Mozart rarely used certain of these groupings.

All during this time, much, though not all, of what he copied was based on one or more specific examples in which Mozart did those very things. He was not only practicing invented note combinations, he was copying specific examples, and finally he was writing them in groups that had no precedent in the facsimiles available to him. It was because of this random behavior that Librarian finally saw a small piece of his methodology. Since he had no original score to copy from in the case of the two manuscripts that Librarian was supposed to discover, his skill had to be a great deal more than an ability to copy something that already existed. In fact, it was the exact reverse of that skill. He needed to be able to make a flawless manuscript, not written down as a result of any compositional process but derived from a printed score. Further, by no regularities in its presentation could the end product show that to have been the case.

About midnight, after he had been going for seventeen hours, including the time for his nap and during which time he ate only a very small sandwich in addition to the tea and toast he consumed after his nap, Forger said, "OK. I've got the notes and clefs. Tomorrow I'll work on the rest."

When Librarian came down on Sunday morning, Forger was already practicing at the table. Librarian sat opposite him, nibbling at an orange, and watched what Forger was working on that day.

He began by practicing instrument names, tempo indications, and dynamic markings such as *"pia."* and *"for."* which were Mozart's abbreviations for *"piano,"* meaning soft, and *"forte,"* meaning loud. He created four sheets with nothing but these two abbreviations on them, repeated over and over. Then he worked on a variety of words and abbreviations used by Mozart for the various detailed instructions whose purpose was to be read and interpreted by a manuscript copyist. These included terms such as "colBasso," "colVno 1°," and *"unis"* (meaning "same as the bass," "same as first violin," and "unison"). Then he did an hour of symbols used as rest indications. By lunchtime he seemed to be looking more and writing less. He studied his completed sheets very carefully, then he made a peanut butter sandwich and began to work on what turned out to be his final practice task, namely numbers.

Apparently Mozart's number "4" and "7" caused him to stumble a little, because he did 6 pages of each, both sides, but did fewer pages of all the other integers. When Librarian asked him why numbers were of interest, he was reminded that one of the scores would contain quantities for the instrument names, such as "2 corni in A," meaning "two horns pitched in the key of A."

"But you have no need to be able to write numbers like '6' or '9,'" Librarian said. "So why have you practiced writing all the integers, some of which you don't even have a model for."

"You're right," Forger said, "but I like to be careful. One never knows what might come up."

Forger continued to do further practicing on Monday while Librarian was at work. By the time he got back from New York, around 8 p.m., Forger said, "OK. I've got it now. I can write just as he did in every way. Tomorrow I'll have a special surprise for you when you come home."

On Tuesday evening, the surprise lay on the dining room table. It consisted of two sheets of paper, face down, each being seventeen inches wide by eleven inches high. Forger explained, "I went to a copy center by bus and made photocopies of both the original of a page from *The Magic Flute* facsimile and the same page that I hand-copied today. Each photocopy was made on oversized paper with a five percent enlargement. Our manuscript will not be this big, but copy centers have very discrete paper sizes and that is what happened to be loaded into the machine that I worked on. I made copies because I did not want you to be swayed by the obvious physical differences that would exist if I had shown you the facsimile page in the volume on one hand and a single page made by me on the other." Handing Librarian both pages, Forger said, "Tell me which is the original and which is the copy."

Librarian turned the pages over and stared in both shock and admiration. Each was a one-page excerpt from a scene in *The Magic Flute* in which a character—The Queen of the Night—makes her first entrance. In his opinion, no one in the world would have been able to spot the forgery on the basis of handwriting and layout alone. Using a dilution of the purchased iron gall ink, even the ink shadings of the original were brilliantly mimicked.

But the two pages were not indistinguishable. The layouts of the two were quite different, because Forger had not taken the simple road of just copying the original. Instead, one page—and Librarian could not identify it as Forger's or Mozart's—presented the same music, though it differed in many details of layout and handwriting. For example, the stems of certain notes went up on one copy and down on the other, and their angles were different. One page had a blot at a certain point, while another had smears at three places where notes had been corrected. The widths of the individual measures were not the same, either, though the sum total of the measures on each page fit the same width. The placement of the dynamic markings varied. Even the position of a few words of German text from the Queen's aria was not identical. It was almost as if Mozart had written out the music of that same page twice, at two different times, with some differences in appearance between the two, as would be the case for anyone who wrote something out a second time.

As Forger gathered up the last of his practice sheets, it appeared to Librarian that at least from a handwriting point of view, they were in excellent shape. Watching the intensity of Forger's creativity and work habits for several days was an experience Librarian did not think he would ever be privileged to see again.

# 48

# THE CREATION OF THE MANUSCRIPTS BEGINS

For the moment, everything was proceeding satisfactorily. In six weeks Librarian would leave for his Munich conference on paper acidity. After that, he would take his trip to Strasbourg for the creation of a manuscript-discovery story. But the best news was that Forger had begun making the concerto manuscript.

On a Monday morning, as Librarian was getting ready for work, he found Forger arranging his entire repertoire of tools on the dining room table. Every light in the room was on. Besides his variety of ink bottles, quills, the surgical tape used for smudging, and approximately a dozen facsimiles of Mozart's manuscripts including, of course, *The Magic Flute*, Forger had laid out five different published scores of the clarinet concerto, all opened to the first page, as well as several technical papers. The published scores were all brand new when they were bought but now were dog-eared, marked up, and scruffy.

Something needs to be said about the responsibility that Forger was about to assume. His work was going to result in a great deal more than simply a rediscovery of a previously lost manuscript. Because of the composition's peculiar history, his efforts were going to create the *de facto* absolute authority on the musical content of this glorious composition. Players would no longer be able to say, "We have no idea what Mozart wrote" at this or that spot. Librarian sensed Forger's willingness to accept that heavy responsibility, but he also sympathized with him, because he'd never get any credit for the work.

Forger sat down at the dining room table and said, "You'll have to excuse me because I'm anxious to begin and I have a great deal to do. It will require me to be at this table many hours every day. But because the effort is very intense, I need to rest occasionally.

"I think my early output will be one to two surfaces every day, about sixteen measures of music. That's going to get faster after some experience. At that rate, it will take me anywhere from six to eight weeks to complete the concerto manuscript."

"Are the issues of penmanship the ones that act as the main gating factor in your work?" Librarian asked.

"Absolutely not," Forger said emphatically. "That's the easiest part. The problems derive from having to examine every reading of every measure that I am about to create. Then I'll listen to several recordings of the work at that point in the music. Only then will I actually write the music in Mozart's hand. And I may do some practice sketches first. The phrasings have to be chosen, many lines of music must be written, and every now and then I'll have to show a change of mind in Mozart's intent. That will involve crossing out what I just wrote and writing it differently. Those are the things that are the gating factors. If we were sure about what he wrote by virtue of having an authoritative score to copy from, I'd be done in two weeks.

"Now, no more questions, please! It's time for me to get to work."

And with that, Forger put on his rubber gloves, went to the basement and took one sheet off the top of the pile of type 82 paper, reduced the quantity remaining by one on the count sheet lying on top of that stack, came back upstairs, placed the sheet on the table, sat down, and began to create the manuscript. The first thing he wrote on the page was at the center of the first staff and on top of it. It was the single word, "Concerto."

Despite his admonitions about interrupting him, Librarian did it anyway, asking, "Are you going to give the manuscript a date?"

"Absolutely not!" Forger said. "Anything that can lead to a possible paradox has to be avoided. I just don't know enough about what Mozart did in 1791 to choose a date for this composition. But in the specialist's world, there are probably a dozen people who know what he did every day of that year. And they can find something wrong with almost any date I choose arbitrarily. They'll say, 'He could not possibly have written this concerto then,' and we're in trouble right out of the gate."

Librarian realized that he was right, of course, and decided to leave him to his work. Forger went back to the manuscript's first page, which had only the word "Concerto" written above the center of the first staff, and following a properly written accolade, he began to label the next ten staves with the names of the instruments in the orchestration. Beginning with the second staff, he wrote "Clarinetto in A" at the very left, and then continued with "Violini," covering two staves, "Viole," covering one, "2 Flauti," and "2 Fagotti," each pair of instruments requiring two staves with the instrument names written between the two, "2 Corni in A," the horn pair written economically on a single staff—the tenth one—with two G clefs, as was his custom when a pair of instruments shared the same staff, and finally, on the eleventh staff of the manuscript, "Bassi." The twelfth staff would remain unused. Forger did not write a tempo indication above the second staff where it would normally go.

The handwriting, as least as much as he wrote down, was a perfect counterfeit of Mozart's; to Librarian's eyes it was an absolute miracle. Though it was undoubtedly annoying to him when Librarian ignored his admonition and interrupted him, he decided to risk his anger one final time and ask him why he did not specify a tempo indication.

His not entirely pleasant response was, "There have to be some areas of this manuscript where I do not supply neat solutions. The lack of a tempo indication is a good place to do just that, particularly in light of the fact that two centuries of tradition exist about how fast this piece is supposed to go, at least for this movement. I'll probably be explicit for the second movement, but for the last, 'Rondo' will have to suffice. *Now be quiet, please,* or else I am going to include an electric guitar as part of the instrumentation and that will do the authentication process little good."

Months had passed since Forger and Librarian had discussed this very moment, and finally they had reached it. The work had begun.

# BOOK 5:
# THE COVER STORY

—

# 49

# DEVELOPING A COVER STORY

While Forger was producing both manuscripts, Librarian occupied himself with the creation of a fiction that would explain their discovery. The ability to do that successfully would be almost as critical to the accomplishment of their effort as Forger's skill was in the creation of the counterfeit autographs that could pass the scrutiny of authentication.

On one hand, Librarian's task was made simple because the documentation about the manuscript's loss was so scant, being only a few remarks in one letter written by Mozart's widow nine years after her husband died. In it, she made reference to the disappearance of clarinetist Stadler's briefcase, and after that the not unreasonable, but far from established conclusion that the briefcase contained the manuscripts of both the clarinet concerto and the quintet.

The sequence of events in her narration about what she was told is not a smooth one. First she stated that the briefcase was stolen in Germany. Then the widow Mozart went on to add how she was also informed by unnamed others that Stadler pawned the briefcase for a specific amount. The reasons behind the case's disappearance notwithstanding, she did allude to a number of things that might have been in it, though there is certainly no explicit identification of either the clarinet concerto or the quintet. Her brief commentary concludes with the suggestion that Stadler also left one or more musical instruments in the case.

This kind of uncertainty and lack of precision was perfect for Librarian's situation. Since there was no way to know what really happened to the manuscripts, he was at liberty to bend the story to his needs.

On the other hand, the absence of reliable information did not allow Librarian to have free reign in the invention of any kind of a tale. His cover story needed some rational essence that had two critical components. First, it had to contain something that would make at least one contemporary scholar jump on the bandwagon and say "Hooray!" That was something Librarian thought he had by centering his discovery plan in Strasbourg, where a Dutch scholar had, in 1991, published a strong technical paper on Stadler's visit there. Second, it had to have corroborative pieces of evidence supplied by several absolutely innocent and completely trustworthy people who would agree on the roles that they had played when Librarian supposedly discovered the manuscripts.

He began with the only piece of information about the disappearance of the manuscripts that had general acceptance in the scholarly community. Conventional wisdom—a fancy name for a conclusion arising from the absence of any hard factual information—was based entirely on Mozart's widow's story of the stolen or pawned briefcase. Because any story surrounding a stolen object would be far more difficult to construct than one about a pawned item, Librarian dismissed the first assertion and focused his energy on the pawning scenario.

Even that story made Librarian choke with disbelief because it was ridiculous as transmitted, and it failed to pass tests of reason from almost every direction. That Stadler might have the two manuscripts in the case—manuscripts of significant compositions that he personally had commissioned but probably didn't pay for—and then have that fact slip his mind during the pawning of the briefcase beggars the imagination. That his memory loss would even extend to his clarinets being in the case is too bizarre to be considered even a distant possibility.

If he pawned that case, it seems much more likely that he pawned it knowing that it contained valuables. And that leads to a more likely possibility, one that is quite unexplored in the extensive literature on the subject. Stadler could have pawned the briefcase not for the pittance of its worth, but *because* its contents had become valuable.

By 1800, Mozart's reputation was such that his manuscripts were worth some real money. In that context, the pawning became rational, but since such a scenario worked against Librarian's scheme, he abandoned it. His cover story worked only if Stadler was thought of as a simpleton, one who would pawn a briefcase without thinking about what was inside it. Therefore, a pawning story based on Stadler's simple-mindedness became the vehicle of choice.

Now came the next step. If Stadler pawned something, with whom might he have pawned it? No, the word "might" is not strong enough. That rhetorical question needed a stainless steel center.

With whom *must* he have pawned it?

What kinds of money lending organizations were in place in Strasbourg in the late eighteenth-century? This was a subject to which Librarian had devoted considerable research and study. If money-lending organizations existed, he had to find them, identify some people who were involved in the business, and use them—or rather their descendants—to establish a direct connection to Stadler. That was not going to be an easy task.

Out of these slowly coalescing ideas arose one strong fact about the past. According to his research about the lending of money in eastern France at that juncture of history, there was no difference between pawn brokering and money lending. It was one business. As such, if *ca.* 1800 Stadler pawned something in Strasbourg, he would have gone to the Jews of that city. That is where all money-lending activity took place, either on the basis of a promissory note for people of known substance, or else a collateral loan based on the value of a thing to be offered, such as a briefcase. Depending on its condition, size, and quality, he might get something for it.

But why Jews?

At that time, the lending of money was a trade almost exclusively managed by Jews, not by choice, but by virtue of church and state policy that forbad Christians from lending money at interest, a policy derived from biblical references critical of the act. There were also pre-Christian objections to the lending of money, and since they were consistent with and supportive of church policy, it influenced church thinking.

Aristotle had taken the position that money was a dead substance, one that could not be used to create wealth. In effect, the use of money—unlike land and labor—was not perceived as a moral way to make money. Worse, to the medieval mind it was an act perceived as having incestuous characteristics. Therefore, lending money at interest was thought of as an unnatural act.

In the face of these attitudes, coupled with the fact that until the revolution Jews could not own property, farm, belong to trade guilds, or do almost anything to make a living except be animal traders or deal in animal hides, the Jews gravitated to the only business permitted them in a land in which they had neither citizenship nor rights. This disenfranchised people lent what little money they had at high rates of interest as their only way to survive.

It was because of the research Librarian had done while Forger was studying scholarly papers on early clarinet music that he was able to have this understanding about the dynamics of money lending in eastern France in the eighteenth century. Armed only with this knowledge, he left his house on a Saturday afternoon in an airport limousine to take the Lufthansa Newark-to-Munich flight where the paper-acidity conference he was directed to attend by his NYPL management was to take place.

# 50

# TO MUNICH AND STRASBOURG

Newark airport was a madhouse, and though Librarian arrived at the terminal fully three hours before the flight, he almost didn't make it, so long were the check-in lines!

The flight was very normal for Lufthansa—an on-time departure followed by indigestible food covered with a gravy of uncertain provenance. Arriving at the Munich airport on Sunday morning, he took the U-Bahn to a stop near his hotel—a Holiday Inn of all places—where breakfast was still being served. He ate some slices of magnificent black bread with butter and sharp cheese, and following that took a walk. After several hours he went to sleep and stayed that way, on and off, until Monday morning.

While the paper-acidity conference was interesting, useful, and valuable, it was technical information for which he felt he would have little use in the foreseeable future if his forged manuscript scheme worked out. The conference ended Thursday evening with a banquet, and early Friday morning he took the train to Strasbourg, arriving at noon, where he caught a taxi to his hotel, the Sofitel, just a few blocks from the Cathedral. With two weeks of vacation in front of him, he parked his bags in his room and asked the *concierge* where there was a pawnshop. That raised some eyebrows.

There were three pawnshops in the city; two within walking distance of the hotel, and one near the *Place d'Etoile*—a tram ride of perhaps fifteen minutes from the city center. The first two pawnshops proved to be of no value. Non-

Jews who were newcomers to the pawn business owned both shops, and neither had purchased the proprietorship from anyone.

A Christian merchant also owned the third shop, but his father had bought
the business in 1938 from a Jewish former owner named Hemmerdinger. As
far as the current owner knew, at the time of the sale in 1938 the Hemmerdingers—father, grandfather, and great-grandfather—had been proprietors of
that pawnshop for at least a century. In fact, it was the longevity of that family
in the pawnbroker business, as well as their reputation for fair and honest
dealings, that convinced the current owner's father that it was an advantageous
investment. Unfortunately, being too young at the time, he had no idea if the
former proprietor had any children or even siblings in 1938.

Librarian went back to the hotel and found seven entries in the Strasbourg
phone directory for that unusual name, and one of them, a certain Benjamin
Hemmerdinger, was proprietor of a leather-goods shop near his hotel. Going
there, he asked, in his moderate French, if he could speak to the proprietor.

"I am so sorry," said the clerk in good but accented English, "but M. Hemmerdinger is not in for the moment. However, he will return at 17 hours to
close the shop shortly after that time," he said, using the twenty-four hour
European clock time as a point of reference.

"Will he be in tomorrow?" Librarian asked.

"Regrettably, no. M. Hemmerdinger keeps his shop closed on Saturday
and city law requires that it be closed on Sunday. However, I would hope that
he could give you a few minutes before closing this evening."

Librarian promised to return at 17 hours and left, spending the rest of the
day walking around the great Cathedral of Strasbourg to observe the external
statuary, looking at the remarkable astronomical clock in the interior of the
sanctuary, and staring at the appetizing food displays in the windows of several
*charcuteries*. On his return to the Hemmerdinger leather-goods shop at 16:55,
the clerk whom he had met earlier introduced him to the owner.

"What is it that I can do for you?" Hemmerdinger said in perfect and unac-
cented British English. "I must apologize, but I have very little time because in
a few minutes I will close the shop and go home to prepare for the Sabbath.
Unfortunately, I will not be back here until Monday morning, but if it is
something that we can discuss quickly, I shall be delighted to help you."

"Thank you for your courtesy," Librarian said. "I ask this. By any chance,
are you related to a man named Hemmerdinger who owned a pawnshop out
near the *Place d'Etoile* as late as 1938?"

A surprised look came over Hemmerdinger's face. "Indeed I am related," he said. "You are speaking of my late father, of blessed memory, Aron Hemmerdinger. How do you know of him?"

Librarian replied, "I am afraid I know nothing at all of him, but I am on a quest searching for something. Since I was informed that your father's family were pawnbrokers and moneylenders for some time, may I presume that he was not the original owner?"

"Oh, my," the leather-goods merchant said. "This is going to take some time, which I do not have, unfortunately. Briefly let me state that my family has been in the money-lending business in and around Strasbourg for almost three centuries. The store you visited dates from about 1850, but the Hemmerdingers have been lending money and dealing in animal skins for a long time," he said, spreading his arms to show the merchandise of his leather-goods business and its relationship to the trade in animal skins. "I'll be happy to tell you the story, but we simply do not have time. Please, let me give you my card. It has my home address on it and I invite you to lunch there tomorrow. Please do come. It is just a short distance from here, an apartment near the *Place de l'Ancien Synagogue*. It will be very informal. Will one o'clock be satisfactory? Good. I shall see you then and tell you the whole story. Now, you must forgive me, for if I do not hurry I will violate the Sabbath."

"That is something I do not wish to be responsible for," Librarian said, "so I will see you tomorrow at one o'clock."

He left the shop and went back to his hotel. After a pleasant dinner at the Maison Kammerzell, he went to bed early, sensing that tomorrow would be an important day.

# 51

# LUNCH CHEZ MONSIEUR HEMMERDINGER

At almost 1 p.m. the next day, Librarian knocked on the door of the Hemmerdinger apartment. The leather goods owner opened it, greeted him with a handshake, and said, "Thank you so much for coming, and I do ask you to forgive me for delaying my response to your interesting question about my father. I simply had no choice in the matter."

"It is I who am grateful for your help," Librarian replied, "and I promise not to take up too much of your time with my silly questions. But before we begin on the matter of the pawning business, can you tell me the circumstances that permit you to speak English so perfectly? You have no accent at all, and your grammar is without flaw."

"Thank you. That is very kind of you," Hemmerdinger replied. "My English dates from the years I spent in Manchester from 1936 until 1948. I was there, along with my father's younger sister Ella. He chose to send both of us to live there with a cousin in England when he realized how badly things were progressing in Germany. In fact, after he sent us away he took steps to sell his business, but you already know about that from your discussion with the current proprietor of what used to be his shop."

"Is your father still alive?" Librarian asked.

"Oh! Unfortunately, no," he replied, "and he would probably not be alive in any case, because he would be more than 100 years old today, but his death was under unpleasant circumstances in the center of France. Almost the entire Jewish community of the city of Strasbourg—in fact, all of Alsace—evacuated itself and resettled in various locations in the center of France following the German invasion. Many elderly people, including my father, had to do hard manual labor. Had it not been for the unselfish kindness of many of the Christian citizens of the area, he would have died much sooner. Eventually he did die, and I think it was partly from sadness.

"My father was a decorated officer in the German army during the First World War, but that did little to protect him. However, let us not dwell on these unpleasant subjects. You are my guest and I have invited you here to have some lunch. As we eat, I'll try and clarify the nature of my father's business to you."

Taking the part of a gracious host, he placed a platter of cold cuts on the table, some sliced bread, mustard, and a bottle of white wine—a local Gewürztraminer. Librarian inquired if Mme. Hemmerdinger was to join them and was told that, sadly, she had passed away a year earlier.

"Now," Hemmerdinger said, taking the conversation away from chitchat, "tell me why you want to know about my father's business?"

"It may sound preposterous," Librarian began, "but I am searching for an object that was used as collateral for a loan made in Strasbourg many years ago. My research tells me that at the time that the object was pawned, only Jews were in the business of money lending in this area of France, perhaps all areas of France, but I have not investigated that. Therefore, it seemed to me that the best thing to do was to inquire of someone from the Jewish community who might have knowledge of the business of accepting items for pawn at that earlier time. That is why I began my search by going to every pawnshop in Strasbourg. The first two owners told me that they had not bought their business from someone else; they simply rented quarters and began to make collateral loans. Therefore, since they are the first in their line to be in that business, as well as not having purchased the business of a predecessor, they would have no knowledge of what took place before their involvement.

"The third pawnbroker told me that he had bought his shop from your father, whom he also described as a Jewish merchant in the very business that I was investigating. That is why I approached you. I recognize, of course, that your father could not have been involved in the transaction that interests me, but perhaps some ancestor of his was. So the first thing I need to know is how far back your family was involved in money lending and pawn brokering."

"Fascinating!" Hemmerdinger said. "You are trying to trace the location of an object...what is the object by the way?"

"A briefcase," Librarian replied, "and the time period is around 1800, though I have less knowledge than the precision of that date might suggest."

"A briefcase. How interesting," Hemmerdinger said. "If I understand you correctly, you are trying to trace the location of an object that perhaps someone used as collateral with one of my ancestors in a loan that took place at the very beginning of the nineteenth-century."

"Exactly that," said Librarian.

"Well, I can tell you that it certainly could have been one of my ancestors," Hemmerdinger said. "My family—and I speak here only of my direct paternal line—has been living in this area since perhaps 1650. I cannot be sure of the exact date, but we have documents and letters going back at least that far, though my paternal line might have been here even earlier. We lived in the village of Scherwiller, a small town that is some fifty kilometers south of where we are, directly opposite the city of Sélestat. My family was not permitted to reside in Sélestat, but they could live outside the city and travel into it when necessary.

"The earliest ancestor of whom I have information was an animal merchant. He bought and sold animals, mostly horses and cattle, to the military and also dealt in animal skins. In addition, he lent money at interest, because that was one of the few trades permitted to him at that time.

"For those activities he would travel into Sélestat a few days each week, make his loans, and then take his collateral back to Scherwiller with him. His sons did the same, and that is the way it has been now for almost three centuries. My father was the last in that business, though the fact that I own a leather goods shop does show some continuity to the days when my family dealt in animal sales, including skins.

"Sometime around 1760, my many times ancestor Aron Hemmerdinger—there are many with the name 'Aron,' so don't get confused should you hear it in several different generations—bought a small house in Fegersheim. It was little more than a shack, just south of here, and he began to travel to Strasbourg several days a week for the purpose of continuing the family collateral loan business. He would take items for pawn in Strasbourg and also make known what items he had available for sale from his supply in Fegersheim. Then, if interest was shown, he would bring an object or two into Strasbourg on his next visit, and perhaps a sale would be made. If not, he returned the items to his supply in Fegersheim to await a possible future sale."

"Why did he not live in Strasbourg?" Librarian asked.

"As it was in Sélestat, he was not permitted to live in Strasbourg," was the reply, and judging from the brevity of his answer, Librarian chose not to pursue the issue for further details. "However," M. Hemmerdinger continued, "he traveled into the city a few days each week, plied his trade in a miserable little back room somewhere, and carried that day's pawned goods back to Fegersheim.

"After the revolution, he was given French citizenship and eventually permitted to live in Strasbourg. He found a small apartment of some sort and ran his business from there, and that is how the family eventually came to this city, where we have lived continuously as moneylenders, pawnbrokers, and merchants of animal skins for the last two hundred years.

"My father took over the store from his father in 1918, right after the war. He also took French citizenship at that same time. It was a strange moment in Alsatian history. One day he was a German citizen, and because Alsace had been ceded back to France in 1918, he opted for French citizenship. His father—that is, my grandfather—had assumed the role of head of the business in 1870, just around the time of the Dreyfus affair, of which I presume you know. Captain Dreyfus' grandfather was a butcher and also in the business of money lending, but in the village of Rixheim, a different area of Alsace. Our families were on friendly terms. In any case, it was during the era of my grandfather that the store was moved to the *Place d'Etoile* in Strasbourg, sometime before I was born, perhaps 1910. I'm not really certain."

"Can you tell me how your father's business was operated?" Librarian asked. "In what way did transactions take place?"

"Probably the same as they do today, both here and in the United States, I suspect," he responded. "A person needs money. He takes an object of some value to a pawnbroker, who appraises it as low as possible and offers a pittance for the item. Both men know that the lender is not likely to come back and retrieve it, but they play their *petite comédie* very nicely. The lender leaves with some money and is generally never seen again. He or she has only a brief time to retrieve the pawned object—perhaps ninety days—after which it will be made available to the general public at the highest possible price, often very much overpriced. This allows for bargaining. But the bargaining battle is unfair, because the person who made the loan knows very well what he gave for the object. On the other hand, if before the elapsed time the original owner should return to reclaim it, he must pay back the initial amount lent to him plus some very high interest. In theory, the lender can even do this as long as the object has not been sold, but it almost never happens."

"Did your family ever accept things in pawn that could not be sold?" Librarian inquired.

"Oh, yes," Hemmerdinger said. "My great-great grandfather, also named Aron by the way, was a notorious—what do you call it?—a man with a generous nature…"

"A 'softie'?" Librarian suggested.

"Exactly!" said Hemmerdinger, smiling. "The British also use the same term. Yes, he was a softie. He often took in objects that were worthless and could not be later sold at any price, but he did so out of pity. We had many such objects for years and years. I suspect that at the time of my father's sale of the business in 1938, there were things that had been in the dead pawn for 100 years, probably more."

Librarian caught his breath when M. Hemmerdinger said that, because these were issues likely to arise after the forged Mozart manuscripts were made public. The press might ask, "Is it true that the briefcase in which the manuscripts were found remained in the possession of the original money-lender for two centuries?" And from M. Hemmerdinger's statement, the answer would be, "Absolutely," which the Strasbourg leather-goods merchant would confirm to be the case if asked.

"When your father sold his store, what happened to the merchandise that was in it?" Librarian inquired.

"Well, I was not here at the time, and suppose that the buyer got most of the stock. I was with my aunt in England, but my father did write to say that he carted a truckload of unsellable items down to his sister's empty house in Scherwiller. My father, in writing to his sister in Manchester, was simply stating that he stored a lot of things in her cellar. As far as I know, they are still there. I would have to ask my aunt, of course."

"That would be most kind of you," Librarian said. "I should appreciate looking over that material if you and she would not mind. Perhaps the item I seek might be there. Would it disturb your aunt if I were to do that?"

"I doubt it very much," Hemmerdinger said. "She is now ninety-two and loves company. It will be an adventure for her. Would you believe that the woman still rides her bicycle to the baker on the *Rue de la Mairie* every morning? I promise to call her this evening and tell her you are coming for a visit. She enjoys using her English. In fact, both before and after the war she taught English and German in Sélestat. You will find her a charming woman. At first, when I went to England in 1936 I objected to my aunt because she was, in effect, a baby-sitter. But she was such a loving woman and a comfort to me when I was away from my parents that we have remained close all of our lives. I hope to have her with me for many more years, but I'm being realistic and have fairly much decided that when she goes, I will retire from my leather-goods business, give it to my children to run if they wish, and move to Scherwiller into the family house. But I am wandering. Tell me, what day would you like to see her?"

"Would tomorrow be satisfactory?" Librarian asked.

"Why don't I call you tonight at your hotel? Which one is it?" Hemmerdinger inquired.

"The Sofitel," he replied.

"Nice hotel. Quiet. Good location. I shall call my aunt and let you know if she can see you tomorrow, or when it might be convenient. Whenever that is, there is a train from the central station in Strasbourg to Scherwiller. I'll give you both her address and the train schedule after I speak to her. From the Scherwiller train station it is only a ten-minute walk to her house. In the meanwhile, let us finish our lunch and then you can tell me what about this briefcase is so interesting to you, that is if it is not violating some sort of secret, of course."

It was almost 3 p.m. when Librarian left the apartment of the exquisitely courteous and helpful M. Hemmerdinger, whose excellent memory enabled him to invent a path connecting Stadler's supposed briefcase with today's Strasbourg. In just a few days—two or three at the most—he had to find a briefcase that would serve his purposes and if that was at the home of Ella Hemmerdinger in Scherwiller, that was fine. If not, he might be in some trouble.

# 52

# SCHERWILLER AND MLLE. HEMMERDINGER

On Tuesday morning, Librarian took the train to Scherwiller from Strasbourg's main station at 9 o'clock, arriving at his destination fifty-nine minutes later. He had spent Sunday and Monday in anticipation of this trip, following a call from M. Hemmerdinger on Saturday evening to say that as much as his aunt was looking forward to meeting with him, she preferred that they meet Tuesday morning. The reasons for the delay were not explained to him.

While waiting for his Tuesday appointment, he spent the free days looking around Strasbourg, taking a bus tour of the area—which included a stop at one of the few underground bunkers that was part of the militarily ineffective 1914 Maginot Line. He also took the time to learn how to use the city's strikingly modern tram system and did most of his touring on it.

On arriving in Scherwiller exactly on time, he inquired about the location of the Rue Giessen, the street on which Mlle. Hemmerdinger lived. It was barely 100 yards from the train station and he arrived at her home at 10:30.

All one can say about Ella Hemmerdinger is that even at the age of ninety-two, she was an energetic, absolutely charming, and warmly courteous woman. Yes, her nephew had called her and explained the circumstances. Yes, she was aware of what Librarian was seeking. And yes, she would try to help as much as she could, though there really wasn't much she could do. The reason for that was because almost every single item that her brother had deposited at the house before the war was gone, and recently, too. There had not been very much in the first place, and finally, the previous year, she had decided to donate it all to the local Emmaüs thrift shop.

"What is the Emmaüs thrift shop?" Librarian asked her.

"It is a private, charitable, faith-based organization that accepts donations of many things," she said, "then they sell them at various locations throughout France and use the profits for good works. We have such a facility here in Scherwiller, which is really the reason why I suggested that this visit be on Tuesday. That is one of the two days of the week that the Scherwiller Emmaüs is open to the buying public, and I felt sure that you would want to visit the facility to see if you can find what you are looking for."

"Do you know the origin of the name, 'Emmaüs'?" Librarian asked. "It is not familiar to me. Is it an acronym?"

"No," she replied. "It's a place name, I believe, though why that name is used by the charitable organization is not known to me."

"Is it likely that any donation you made to them would be sold at the Scherwiller store?" Librarian asked.

"That is the most likely place where it would be sold," she said, "or I would not have had you make the trip here. The Emmaüs organization generally moves goods from one facility to another, but only when there is no longer any room at the location nearest to the point of donation, which is not true here in Scherwiller. There is still a great deal of room, and I suspect that most of what I donated is still there."

"That's good," Librarian said. "Even though you have told me something about the name 'Emmaüs,' I am still not very clear about what that is or what it does, and I wonder if you might explain that to me."

"You have several such organizations in America," she replied. "If I remember correctly from my readings, there are both Salvation Army and Goodwill Industry Thrift Shops that accept donations and make goods available at various outlets. Am I not right? Well, Emmaüs is the same thing here in France."

"Ah, now I understand," Librarian said. "You are quite right, and if Emmaüs is the same kind of facility as are the Salvation Army and Goodwill shops, I will be quite familiar with how things work here. As a child, my parents purchased a good deal of our household furniture from just such a place. Can you tell me where the shop is and what time of the day it is open?"

"You probably did not realize it," she said, "but when you arrived in Scherwiller by train, you passed their store coming here. The main facility is right next to the train station. I can point it out to you when we go for lunch."

"I did not know that we were to go to lunch, but that sounds like a wonderful idea. Is there a restaurant nearby?" he asked.

"You ask that question in France?" she said. "Tell me, can you ride a bicycle?"

"Well, it has been many years," he replied, "but at one time I could."

"Good," she said. "I always keep two bicycles in the event that I get a visitor who comes here without one. But to answer your question, there are one or two restaurants in the center of Scherwiller—*A la Couronne* and the *Weinstub a l'Ortenburg*. However, there is a much better one called the *Auberge Ramstein* at the edge of town, but it is too far to walk. That is why I asked if you could ride a bicycle. We will go there for lunch, and on the way I will point out where the Emmaüs is. They don't open until two o'clock in the afternoon in any case, so we will have ample time to ride through the village to the Auberge Ramstein, which has an excellent kitchen. But for the moment, you must tell me about yourself. I notice that you speak like a New Yorker, what with that peculiar accent."

And she then launched into an imitation of the, to a Frenchman, hilarious New York speech patterns. Librarian spoke to her of growing up in New Jersey, of his current position at the NYPL, and of his interest in the items held in her brother's store at the time of his sale of the business in 1938, though he went into no greater detail with her than he did with her nephew. Around noon she told him that it was time to go and they left, she on her bicycle and he on his. It took only half a block for him to get back into the spirit of bicycle riding and he followed her down the Rue Giessen to the main street leading both into the center of the village, and in the other direction to the main north-south highway. When they came to the intersection of *Rue Giessen* and *Rue de la Gare*, she stopped, pointed, and said, "You came from that direction when you left the train station. Do you remember? Well, if you go back to the railroad tracks and turn right, you will find the Emmaüs shop perhaps fifty meters on your right, and the train station just a little further. The Emmaüs has a big sign; you cannot miss it."

At that point she turned left towards the center of the village and he followed her to the Auberge Ramstein, where they had an excellent lunch of *choucroute*. The meal consisted of an enormous amount of spiced and braised sauerkraut, served with a number of different kinds of sausages, plus mustard, potatoes, bread, and cold Alsatian beer. It was a magnificent and filling meal.

Mlle. Hemmerdinger spoke of her love for Alsatian food, saying that when she and her nephew were in England during the war, it was one of the things she missed most. "Unfortunately, my nephew's dietary restrictions do not tolerate his eating this kind of thing. His father was always more observant than I. Still, he is a wonderful nephew to me, and I love him dearly."

Then, realizing that it was getting late and that Emmaüs would be open shortly, she suggested they leave, knowing that he needed a lot of time to hunt through their inventory. She also made it clear that the only remaining train from Scherwiller to Strasbourg that day would leave the village's station at 18:22.

Librarian paid for their meal and followed her back to her home to drop off the bicycle. There he thanked her for her help and also for telling him what happened to the remnants of her brother's Strasbourg pawnshop. He promised, following her request to that effect, to send her some postcards from America. She said that she loved to get mail and at her age, she was not getting as much as she used to or would like. "Perhaps a picture postcard of Niagara Falls or the Empire State Building might be nice," she said.

# 53

# THE EMMAÜS BRIEFCASE

After leaving Ella Hemmerdinger, Librarian walked to the Emmaüs thrift shop. A crowd of some two-dozen people were milling around the door, awaiting the beginning of the Tuesday sales. There would be no further sales until the following Saturday. By the time Librarian joined the waiting group, the doors were open and everyone began to go inside in a search of bargains.

Librarian wandered through the furniture section, dishware and glassware, linens, pots and pans, books and recordings, and household appliances, coming finally to a walled-off area that had a variety of travel containers. There was no order to how the many things were stacked. Large, bulky cases sat on little ones; backpacks were lumped together with cardboard suitcases. It was a large mess. To find something, one had to be prepared to attack the enormous pile, relocating everything to get a view of what was in the back.

After an hour of moving things around, getting closer and closer to the back wall, as well as dirtier, Librarian suddenly saw what he had come so far to find. It was not a briefcase in the sense of the flat kind in use today. Instead, it was like a doctor's bag, wide on the bottom and rectangular until it got within six inches of the top. Then it slanted in and closed by means of two leather straps. It was genuinely a case in which a legal brief could be kept, which was exactly how the name "briefcase" originated. It was also a case in which an inch or two of music manuscript could lie flat on the bottom of the case without having to be folded. However, it was questionable that it could hold the pair or triplet of clarinets required of a working professional, if indeed Stadler had used his case in such a fashion. That part of the history would simply go by the wayside.

Librarian opened the case, looked inside, and saw nothing but dust. The bottom of the case was kept in shape by a scuffed-up rectangular piece of wood, cracked, but not split down the middle. He lifted it carefully, saw nothing but the leather on the bottom of the bag underneath, and pushed the wooden panel back into place.

The outer surface of the bag was constructed from heavy, rigid leather—like saddle leather—but it was scratched, torn, and scarred. There were no metal pieces anywhere in or on the bag except for the old-fashioned buckles that were used to close the two straps. Librarian didn't know how old this briefcase really was, but that it could be two hundred or more years old was very evident. What he had found would pass for Stadler's briefcase nicely.

Librarian spent some time making the room neat again after his rearrangement of its contents. Then he took the briefcase to the cashier's desk to pay for it. Instead of taking his money, he was sent back to a clerk in a blue smock who sat at a very official looking table near the luggage room and to whom he should have gone originally with his planned purchase. Apparently, the way things worked was to get the item priced by the blue-smocked clerk and then to present oneself, the item, and the bill at the front desk for payment. Showing the bag to the clerk, it was returned to him with a slip that read "3€," the equivalent of $3.88 at that moment. He paid for it, asked for a receipt so as to sustain his planned story about the location where he bought the item as well as the price paid, walked to the train station and waited for the 18:22 to Strasbourg. By the rarity of the trains that stopped there, Scherwiller was clearly not a frequently-used station.

When he got back to his hotel, the local Lufthansa office was closed, so he was unable to schedule a return flight to New York. The briefcase—should he now call it Stadler's briefcase?—was sitting on his bed, and he was ready to return home with his trip having been completed successfully. His cover story was locked in solidly by virtue of his conversations with Benjamin Hemmerdinger and his aunt Ella, and he had a perfectly suitable briefcase with dated proof of purchase. There was no need for him to remain in Europe.

The next day, Wednesday, the Strasbourg offices of Lufthansa Airlines advised him that the Thursday flights to New York and Newark out of both Munich and Frankfurt were completely booked, but that he could go via Düsseldorf at 10:30 a.m., though at a slight increase in ticket price. He then checked the train schedule, confirmed that he could leave Strasbourg at 1:25 p.m., change trains in Offenburg, and arrive in Düsseldorf at 7:27 p.m.

He booked the flight, had a hotel room reserved for him near Düsseldorf airport by Lufthansa, went back to the Sofitel, packed his bags, paid his bill, had a light lunch, and left Strasbourg with Stadler's briefcase tied neatly onto his suitcase with a bungee cord that he bought from a street vendor at the plaza outside of Strasbourg's train station.

After the pleasant train trip, a quiet night at a small, soundproofed hotel near Düsseldorf airport, and a good breakfast, he left for New York on time. Eight hours later, when he should have been passing through customs in JFK, he was circling over Westchester County, due to an unexpected series of rain-squalls over New York City. The flight was finally rerouted to Boston for more fuel, and by the time he landed at JFK, it was 5:30 p.m. The customs agents thoroughly examined Stadler's briefcase—probably because it looked bizarre—but were satisfied that it was nothing other than what he told them: namely an antique. One bus, one subway trip, and a second bus later brought him to Paterson at 8:50 p.m., where—except for Stadler's briefcase which he would not let out of his sight—he left his luggage at a drug store by the bus stop. The proprietor of the drugstore knew him and permitted him to leave his luggage there until he got home, with intent to return by car the next morning. He probably could have muscled all his luggage up the hill to the house, but he was too tired to do so.

When he came through the front door, Forger was asleep in a living room chair, the TV showing a World Wrestling Federation championship match, and the worktable in the dining room, which should have been covered with papers and books, was completely empty. It was then that he got worried. Had something gone wrong?

"*Hey!*" Librarian shouted. "Is there a problem? What's wrong?"

Forger woke with a start, rubbing his eyes, and stretched. "Stop yelling. Nothing's wrong. The work is all done. Both manuscripts are finished. I've just been sleeping a lot because I was working twenty-hour days to get done with the job. Everything is fine."

"Is that the bag?" Forger asked, pointing at the briefcase.

Smiling now, Librarian said, "It sure is. I left everything else at the drug store, but it's closed now, so I'll pick it all up tomorrow morning. However, I'm hungry. Want to go out, have some dinner, and celebrate? Then I'd like to see the manuscripts. Is that OK?"

Forger said, "How about a pizza?"

# 54

# THE FINISHED
# MANUSCRIPTS

Lying down on the floor in the back of Librarian's car for one of the last times that he would have to undergo the indignity, Forger prepared to be chauffeured to nearby Patsy's Restaurant for pizza, and more importantly, a draft birch beer, a refreshing soft drink that Librarian and Forger learned to love as children when they were given glasses of it in Dugan's bar on Grand Street and told that it was real beer.

Librarian was unable to contain his impatience, so as soon as they were seated in a booth with their order placed, he spoke first, saying quietly, "Please tell me what happened." He had to keep his voice down because the restaurant was crowded.

Forger poured the birch beer from a pitcher into both glasses as soon as it arrived and told Librarian how he had been getting far ahead of his schedule even before Librarian had left for Germany. The original prediction of two surfaces or sixteen measures of concerto manuscript a day turned out to be far too conservative, and even checking the various editions for significant differences between them didn't slow him down. This was because the editions were similar in all the important aspects. When there was a difference, he selected the least invasive presentation of the music.

After a while, Forger was doing from four to as many as six surfaces of manuscript every day, averaging around five surfaces a day, which cut his production time to about twenty days. When Librarian asked why he wasn't told of this important development, Forger said it was because Librarian had enough on his mind. The surprise ending to this part of the story was that Forger was effectively finished with the concerto manuscript even before Librarian had left for Germany.

The day after he had left for Munich, Forger indicated that he began his preparation for the clarinet quintet manuscript. However, that work was a great deal easier to do. There were fewer instruments and the layout on the page literally doubled the number of measures he could produce on a single surface.

"I should have realized that when I saw the string quintet manuscript in Washington," Forger said, describing how the organization of the clarinet quintet autograph simplified the task.

"It needed only one staff for each of the five players. And the way Mozart wrote music for any group that size was to have a blank staff on the top of the page, five staves for the music, another blank staff, and finally, another five staves for the music, an organization that's perfect for twelve-stave paper. That changed the average number of measures on a surface from eight—for the concerto—to sixteen for the quintet. Even though the clarinet quintet has more movements than the concerto, it has only 547 measures, and the whole work fit on thirty-five surfaces.

"On the other hand," he continued, "each of the five players had a lot to play. The piece was not really a solo work as much as a composition for five equal participants. The concerto was not that kind of a democracy, and as such, the instrumental accompaniment for the concerto was much simpler. The only significant problem I faced with the quintet was where to put in the infamous low notes, and that's because there is no published edition that suggests a solution to that problem, though there were some technical papers that addressed the subject. I used them, but the fact is that there has not been as much done to reinvent the low notes in the clarinet quintet as has been the case for the concerto, even though both works were written for Stadler's basset clarinet. Fortunately, the recordings you got for me included two quintet performances with invented solutions to the low-note problem, so I stole from those.

"Anyway, I finished the whole piece in nine days," he continued. "And since you were gone and I had nothing else to do, I loafed a lot and planned my schedule for the next couple of months. During the time that you will be dealing with the announcement and sale of the manuscripts, I don't think I should be here. You might get a visitor and then my presence would have to be explained. We don't need that kind of a problem."

Their pizza arrived and both wolfed it down, Librarian burning the roof of his mouth, which always happened when he ate pizza too quickly. Fortunately, the cold birch beer acted as a temporary palliative.

For the trip back, Forger hunkered down in the back seat as they neared the house and drove into the garage, closing the door electronically as fast as its mechanical components would permit. Inside, Forger turned on all the lights in the dining room, reached into a drawer in the buffet where Librarian kept several generations of dishes, and pulled out a large manila envelope.

"I need to tell you about the several assumptions I made concerning the environmental factors that would have influenced the present physical condition of the manuscripts. Perhaps the most important was that both documents would, theoretically, have lain undisturbed inside a briefcase for two centuries without a light source shining on them. That means that the ink would not have faded significantly between then and now. However, the bottom page, being in contact with leather for two centuries, would have become stained a dark brown. This would not have happened to the top page, because it would have been in contact with the briefcase's wooden panel. In order to avoid any curiosity about the condition of the outer pages being so good, you must say that the manuscripts were wrapped in a linen garment when you found them. Don't even try to identify what the garment was. And say that after two centuries of contact with the leather, it had become so fragile that it crumbled when you unwrapped it. We would not want to try and emulate a two-century old piece of linen. Because of this wrapped environment, the manuscripts would not have become terribly dirty, even on the first and last pages. Also, the paper's edges would not be likely to have received the normal dings of documents that pass from hand to hand. All of this is by way of saying that both manuscripts would be expected to be in very good physical condition, with the ink and paper a little faded over time, but nothing else. That's why the copies are so pristine."

And with that, Forger put on a pair of rubber gloves, reached into the manila envelope and took out two oversized plastic envelopes. Both were opaque, so Librarian could see nothing. Forger opened the first and took out the concerto manuscript. Then he did the same for the other plastic envelope, which held the quintet autograph.

Though Librarian was leaning against the table as Forger exposed the pair of manuscripts, his legs suddenly became so weak that he was forced to sit down or he would have fallen down. Even seated, his legs were trembling and he was not immediately able to catch his breath. This was because—except for the fact that he knew them to be forgeries—the table held two magnificent, almost pristine but forged Mozart manuscripts on whose authenticity he would have gambled a great deal of money. And he made that judgment even though he could see only the first page of each document. His heart was thumping and it became difficult to draw a full breath.

Until he had calmed himself, something that took close to thirty minutes, he did nothing but simply sit and stare. Finally, with shaking hands, he drew the two manuscripts close, afraid to touch them, but unable not to, and began to turn the pages. They appeared to him to be perfect presentations of the music of the two compositions. At the end of the first movement of the concerto, Forger had used a half-sheet, because the final music of that movement required only two surfaces. The third and fourth surfaces of that half-sheet were left blank. Further, the half sheet was type-55 twin paper, though Librarian could not know this. Forger later told him that the inclusion of this paper type with its half-empty contents was done deliberately so as to stir the academic pot, so to speak. The combination of the two blank pages, plus the half-sheet of type-55 twin paper, would cause some scholarly debate for the next century about how much time had elapsed between the composition of the first and second movements of the concerto. To the average person, blank pages are uninteresting, but to the research scholar they hold hostage the details of a historical puzzle. The choice of paper type would also give rise to discussions designed to explain why Mozart would suddenly revert to that type of paper at this juncture of the composition.

Towards the end of the final movement, the handwriting became somewhat more rushed and sloppy. When Librarian looked up, Forger anticipated his question and said, "A number of the facsimiles show his handwriting deteriorating as he got towards the end of a composition. Perhaps he was in a rush; perhaps he became tired. It doesn't matter what the reasons were. For confirmation, just look at the facsimiles yourself. That's why I emulated the condition."

The quintet manuscript was equally beautiful, and Librarian stared in wonder and admiration at the familiar opening string music, whose first four notes exactly duplicate the melody of the old chestnut, "The Sidewalks of New York" *(East Side, West Side)*.

"These manuscripts are exquisite," Librarian finally whispered.

"What are you whispering for?" Forger said.

"I don't know," Librarian answered, smiling. "Don't bug me. I'm excited. If I didn't know what these things were, I'd swear that they were the originals." And then, pointing at some defaced measures, he commented, "I see that you crossed out six measures in the middle of the first movement of the quintet and then reworked them."

"Indeed I did," Forger replied. "It was extremely hard work figuring out what to write down so as to reject it in favor of what Mozart really wrote, and it was also necessary to make the crossed-out version slightly inferior and a little awkward so as to justify its rejection. That's not easy to do. Actually, I should say that it's very easy to do, because if you change a single note of what that man wrote, it diminishes the composition. It turns out that the most difficult thing in the entire manuscript was to modify the music in preparation for rejecting it, but not produce something completely ridiculous. I finally worked out a way to do that by starting with Mozart's passage as it would ultimately appear and alter it—here in the harmony, there in the melody—until I had it just a little bit awkward. Any more than that and it would have been obvious that Mozart didn't write it, no matter how good my copy of his handwriting was."

The two spent almost three hours going over a number of details in both manuscripts so Librarian would not be surprised when specialists noted this point or that in their examination. Of course it was not for him to defend these peculiar matters. In theory, he wasn't even supposed to know about them at this level of detail. But Forger wanted him aware that he had considered every possible objection to them by finding a precedent for every instance in another Mozart manuscript. For example, at the end of the slow movement of the concerto Forger had inserted an unusually large melodic leap downward, using an interval that looked most peculiar. Forger pointed out an identical passage in Mozart's opera, *The Marriage of Figaro*, and once precedence was established, it was a closed issue. In effect, one could not say, "Mozart never did that," if an example of him doing that very thing could be demonstrated.

Carefully, and with gloves still on, Forger put the manuscripts back into their separate plastic envelopes, then inside the manila folder, being exquisitely cautious not to bend or fold any of the paper. Finally, he put the package back into the buffet's drawer. By that time Librarian was exhausted, what with the flight and the excitement of the evening. Before closing out the day, he identified the most immediate action that needed to take place.

"Tomorrow," he said, "I'll find a facility to get the manuscripts photographed. After that I'll put them in a safe deposit box in New York. That is when the authentication process will start."

The most perilous phase of the work was about to begin.

# BOOK 6:
# AUTHENTICATION

# 55

# PHOTOGRAPHY—PART 1

The fun part was over, and it is accurate to say that to no small degree, the making of the two manuscripts really had been dizzyingly exciting. The task had required both men to show enormous skill, bravado, intuition, an ability to accomplish highly-specialized research, intimate knowledge of a broad collection of particulars from a host of unrelated disciplines, and some unfettered and imaginative vision about making money illegally. Now, however, the ominous work was about to begin. Though it may have appeared more menacing, the two men were already neck-deep in legal hot water.

In theory, at least until that moment nothing Librarian and Forger had done in the preparation of the two manuscripts appeared to be criminal. One could take the view that it is not illegal simply to create something whose purpose is to deceive, and it would appear that one has to try and sell the false thing before fraud places its foot on the drama's stage. But that bit of shoddy self-justification would never fly. Their conspiracy to commit an illegal act began the day Forger got out of prison, and it was the conversation that took place during the boat ride on Delaware Bay that was the first overt act taken in furtherance of their conspiracy. So the step that Librarian was about to take was not one whit more perilous than what the two had done over the previous few months. It just seemed more threatening.

That step would occur following the storage in a safe-deposit vault of the manuscripts, along with photographic and microfilm copies of each. It was the logical place where Librarian would have safeguarded the material were it real, and also where the auction house representatives would expect to go for any preliminary technical examinations.

Since Librarian still had one week of vacation left before returning to work, he chose the photography job as the first critical task. During his time at the Forty-second Street headquarters of the NYPL—and before his transfer to duties at Lincoln Center's music manuscript collection—Librarian had observed a particular self-employed professional who specialized in facsimile photography. The man was invariably used by the NYPL during the preparation of all facsimiles. One of the reasons Librarian decided to solicit that same individual's help now was because the photographer ran a one-man shop. That meant Librarian would not have to be concerned about some unknown number of additional people being made aware of the existence of his manuscripts.

Interestingly, all his previous business arrangements with this professional involved a need for discretion. This was because the documents they dealt with were rare and valuable, the main reason why facsimile editions of them were being made in the first place. It was a security problem when anyone knew about the movements and locations of valuable things that temporarily had left the premises and protection of the NYPL. Librarian was impressed with how this particular photographer handled such confidences and how expertly he did his work. The technical results were outstanding, though not inexpensive. He was reliable in meeting schedules, and he never discussed what he was doing nor for whom he was doing it.

On calling the photographer's business number, Librarian was connected to an answering service and told that the office had not yet opened for the day. He left a message, stating that he wanted to consult with the proprietor about some needed photographic work, and that he would arrive at the shop in less than two hours. Then he drove to the New York ferry with a large backpack on the passenger seat near his right hand. It contained both manuscripts. All car doors were locked, all windows closed.

Not only was the backpack big enough to avoid crushing any part of its contents, the manila envelope containing both manuscripts was sandwiched between fitted slabs of wood designed to prevent accidental bending.

The moment he got out of his car in the parking lot on the New Jersey side of the ferry, Librarian slipped his arms into the pack, snapping its waistbands in place for further security. While he had no negative experience in this matter, the last thing he needed at this juncture was to be mugged for his backpack. Arriving on the New York side of the Hudson River, he took a taxi to the Greenwich Village shop of the photographer, finding him there and in possession of the telephoned message.

Librarian introduced himself—reminding the owner of their earlier work together—and showed his NYPL employee ID. However, he made it clear that he was there on personal, not library business and would pay for all services himself. Then he described the work he wanted done.

"I have some music manuscripts that I need professionally photographed," he said, "and that will involve me getting three things. First, I want a set of highest quality contact negatives for use in preparing a facsimile edition of the original. I'm not really certain if I will do that, but it's the kind of end product that you should keep in mind as you consider your work options. Second, I'll also need a set of photographic positives made from the contact negatives. Third and last, I want a microfilm copy of the manuscripts. That last item can be done in black and white, but the contact negatives must be done in color."

The owner shrugged, suggesting that all of Librarian's needs were business-as-usual requests. The photography was the simplest and fastest task, though preparing for it took time. Each shot would take at the most only a few minutes once everything was ready. However, his statement that the remaining tasks would involve the use of subcontractors caused Librarian to react.

"I'm afraid that I need you to handle every task personally," he said. "You see, I'm trying my best to keep the nature of what I have confidential. The more people who are involved with access of any kind to the material, the greater the exposure that word of these manuscripts will be made public. So how can we arrange it so that no one but you is to have a hand in the production of any stage of the total task? That request is not dissimilar to those I asked of you in the past when the NYPL required absolute confidentiality, and is the main reason why I am here now."

"Ah, I see," the photographer said. "Well, that complicates the task, makes it considerably more expensive for you, because it occupies me in ways that eliminate my availability to other customers. But if you are prepared to meet the price, I'll do it any way you wish. It really depends on the value to you of the costs arising from confidentiality considerations, though there is a schedule advantage if I work that way. The whole job will be done more quickly because I don't have to farm things out and get in a queue at the subcontractors. That always takes the longest time. Could you leave your manuscripts with me overnight?"

"No," Librarian said. "I can't do that, though you should not interpret my reluctance as a slight against your excellent reputation. Until that photography is done and these manuscripts are placed in a safe deposit box, I won't let them

out of my sight. This means that I need to be present even during the photography. However, my presence is not necessary for any of the work that follows
the photography. I'm confident that I can count on your discretion, and that
no one but you will see, or for that matter even get near the negatives, positives, or microfilm. But the manuscripts themselves must be under my personal supervision at all times."

The photographer shrugged and then, to establish the price for librarian,
inquired about the number of surfaces. That was the gating factor for both the
job's time and cost.

"There are exactly 140 surfaces," Librarian answered. "The material con-
sists of one manuscript of ninety-eight surfaces plus two blank pages, and a
second of thirty-five surfaces plus one blank surface and one blank page. The
photography must include all blank surfaces. I brought the original material
with me in the unlikely event you were free to do the photography today."

The proprietor stated his inability to do that because of previous commit-
ments for both that day as well as Saturday. However he would be able to start
early on Sunday morning and barring any complications, could finish all the
photography in an estimated ten hours. When Librarian indicated his agreement with that schedule, the photographer asked to see the manuscripts.

Before going to the nonpublic area of the shop for the inspection, the photographer told Librarian that there were no confidential documents being
worked on at that moment, so there would be no restrictions against Librarian
entering the nonpublic area. Then the two went into the large, well-equipped
back room, where the manuscripts were taken out of the backpack. The photographer had no music training whatsoever and Librarian was grateful for
that, since he could have no idea of the identity of the music that he was being
asked to photograph.

After examining all the pages, the photographer concluded that there did
not appear to be any significant technical problems. After setup, he estimated
that no more than three minutes would be necessary for each surface to be
photographed. The microfilming would take an estimated hour and a half. He
felt that the total job would run close to his earlier-estimated ten hours,
including setup. Then Librarian could take the original material and leave.
Development of the plates and microfilm, and the printing of the positives
would take several days and would be done only in the evening when the shop
was locked and no one could enter it.

Librarian carefully repacked the manuscripts and the two left the back
room for the storefront where the owner made his cost estimate of the work.

"My time for the Sunday shoot is $500 an hour, assuming no more than my estimated ten hours," he said. "After that, the costs for my time will be $300 per hour, or any part of one, until the photography is done. The negatives will run $50 each—you pay only for the good ones—the positives $25 each—same story—and the microfilm $300 for the entire shoot. Because I have to handle the whole job myself, there will be a twenty-five percent supplement. That comes to...er..."

He was working his calculator very quickly and Librarian intended to check the accuracy of his figures when he got home.

"...er, that comes to $19,375. Let's round it up to $19,500 and I will throw in a second copy of the microfilm. You really need an extra one for safety so it can be stored in a separate location. If the job takes less than ten hours, I'll adjust the price downward on the final bill, and I will require a deposit of twenty-five percent at this time, please."

Librarian was shocked by the price, but had no good alternative. He wrote a check for $4,875 and thought about reminding the photographer again about the importance of confidentiality. Then he decided against it and signed the check.

The fact that such a large amount of money was paid out of his personal bank account and could be traced was unimportant now, because it was not a security breach. The work had entered into another stage, one where the details of *his* involvement did not have to be concealed. On the contrary, they needed to be documented so that any suspicious searcher could stumble upon them. For example, as the discoverer of a valuable manuscript, Librarian would have been expected to order and pay for a complete set of photographic prints.

Librarian was now ready to leave the photographer's shop, but he asked what time he should be there on Sunday. The owner suggested 7 a.m. and Librarian agreed. Slipping his arms through his backpack straps, he left the shop, flagged a taxi, and went to an already selected bank on Park Avenue near Fifty-fifth Street to complete all the paperwork for the rental of an oversized safe deposit box. He even examined the box in a small private room to confirm that the material fit satisfactorily. Then he left the bank and went back to Paterson via the Thirty-eighth Street ferry, where his car was waiting on the New Jersey side. The manuscripts were, of course, still in his backpack by his side, because he needed them for the Sunday morning photo shoot.

# 56

# PHOTOGRAPHY—PART 2

Sunday morning, a few minutes before 7 o'clock, Librarian arrived at the front door of the photographer's shop. The street was empty and the door locked, but following his knock, the proprietor appeared from the back room where he was completing his preparations for the shoot. Only after recognizing his client did the photographer unlock the door and let Librarian in. Then he relocked it and lowered a shade over the door's glass panels. The two went into the back room where Librarian emptied his backpack, placing the manuscripts on the photographer's worktable.

An inquiry by the photographer about who might have written the manuscripts—made in a casual way, more as small talk than with genuine interest—was parried by Librarian. Disingenuously, he replied with the names of two minor composers from the middle of the nineteenth-century and added that the matter wasn't clear. He was still working on the author's identity.

The photographer, who really wasn't listening in any case, stated that he was ready to begin as soon as the matter of surface identification was decided on. Did Librarian want each page to have an identifying manuscript and surface number? These would appear only on the photographs. The manuscripts would not, of course, be altered in any way.

Librarian knew about that kind of identification, had decided on what it should be, agreed to its inclusion, and described several alternative identification schemes, any of which would be acceptable. The photographer chose the one with the fewest letters, since each surface required the creation of a unique identification template.

He then placed the concerto manuscript on a worktable directly under-neath a large camera, set on tracks that allowed it to be omnidirectionally moveable. Taking a metal template, he selected the needed identification text from a box full of alphabetized black letters and numbers, inserting them into the template and placing it on the lower right hand corner of the manuscript's first surface. The template's contents read, "M1–1r" in forty-eight point Times New Roman type font. The "M1" defined the manuscript number while the "1r" stood for the first "recto" surface, the traditional name used to describe the odd-numbered surface of any sheet of a manuscript.

The photographer took some measurements with a light meter at several places on the manuscript and made a few adjustments to nearby lamps and the position of the camera. Then he took a single, contact-plate photograph—the negative almost as large as the surface it was expected to copy—and disap-peared into a darkroom to develop his shot. When he reappeared, he made changes in the camera's position and orientation, moved one light source a few inches forward, took a second photo of the same surface, and returned to his dark room.

He came back with a developed contact print, showed it to Librarian, and stated that it was now perfect. Librarian, on seeing what might someday be a facsimile of both manuscripts, was pleased to have chosen a color photo of a black and white surface. In his view, it was always the most dramatic way to show autograph pages. The total elapsed setup time was forty-five minutes.

Librarian took the first of the two preliminary negatives and both sample positives when the photographer suggested that he, as owner of the manu-scripts, handle the destruction of all material that would not be part of the fin-ished packet. Since the second photograph had already been accepted as a satisfactory negative of the manuscript's first surface, the photographer would continue his work with the second shot.

Librarian seated himself on a stool located opposite the worktable to avoid getting in the way. The photographer turned the page, installed a new, unex-posed contact negative, ignored the second surface, modified the number in his template to "M1–3r" and photographed the third surface. Not knowing the mechanics involved because he had never been present during the actual shooting of a facsimile, Librarian asked, "Haven't you forgotten the second surface?"

"No," the photographer responded, without stopping work. "We do all the recto surfaces at one time, and then the verso surfaces next," making reference to the traditional term for an obverse or even-numbered surface of a page. He explained that the sequence he followed required only the page to be turned following each shot. By not moving either the sensitive camera or the manuscript until all recto photographs had been made, he eliminated the possibility of ruining one or more shots. Since ruined photos would not be detected until after the positives were made a day or more later, it would require the customer to return with the manuscripts for reshooting. By taking the shots out of sequence, the photographer moved the camera only once during the entire session.

When he finished all the recto surfaces of the concerto, he readied himself to continue with the photography of the recto surfaces of the quintet manuscript. Only when that was completed would he return to do all the verso surfaces of both manuscripts. Librarian was informed that there was no need to worry, because everything would be interleaved properly at the end of the job and nothing would get lost or be left out.

Then he initialized the template to "M2–1r," took a test photo since the second manuscript had been freshly placed in its position, developed that shot, concluded that it was satisfactory, and quickly completed all the recto surfaces of the quintet. For the first and only time in the shoot, he moved the camera on its tracking mechanism so it would be above the verso surfaces of the manuscripts. Going back to the concerto, he turned it to the first verso surface, set the template to read "M1–2v," and took a trial photograph. "Couldn't be better," he said after developing it, and then completed the entire set of even-numbered surfaces of both manuscripts, taking his last test case on the first verso surface of the quintet autograph.

Librarian noted that the photography of both manuscripts had taken an average of three minutes per surface, a time that included changing the template's identification information. The two had been working uninterruptedly for seven hours, almost eight including setup. They would continue, without interruption, for the two additional hours needed to end the entire job.

The photographer then took both manuscripts over to another worktable that had a different kind of camera above it and began photographing for the microfilm copies. These pages were shot in the natural order, because each photograph copied two surfaces—a left and a right—simultaneously, so the second microfilm shot showed "2v" on the left and "3r" on the right in a single photograph. When all pages had been filmed, the owner handed the manuscripts to Librarian and asked how he wanted to receive the completed work, which he estimated would be ready no later than Thursday noon. The total elapsed time was ten hours and seven minutes. The photographer forgave the seven minutes and said that the charge would be for only ten hours.

Librarian requested that, when finished, all material be sent via messenger to his New Jersey home and asked if the photographer would mind being called on Tuesday to confirm that the schedule was unchanged. In addition, he asked that all materials slated for destruction be wrapped separately and identified as such.

Then he wrote a check for another twenty-five percent of the work, confirming that the remaining balance would be given to the messenger on delivery. In the event of a delay in the completion of the job, he suggested that they negotiate a new delivery time and possibly a new delivery location in that eventuality. Then he thanked the owner for his quick service and left his shop at 5:25 p.m.

As the photographer was closing the door, he said, "Come again. No job is too small, you know."

Librarian smiled at him and said, "At those prices, I'm not surprised."

# 57

# HOUSE CLEANING AND FORGER'S DEPARTURE

On Monday, following the photography session and in the final week of Librarian's vacation, he went back into New York with the manuscripts again housed in his backpack. With luck, New Jersey would never see them again. Taking a taxi to his Park Avenue bank, he put both manuscripts in his safe deposit box—the one he had rented on the previous Friday. Its rectangular dimensions were large enough to contain the manuscripts and its vertical dimension high enough to hold the negatives, positives, and one reel of microfilm when he got them. The large manila envelope that previously held both manuscripts, as well as the two wooden panels that prevented his backpack from folding over, were no longer needed, and except for the backpack that went home with him, all were tossed into a New York City waste-disposal can.

For the identification required to obtain his safe deposit box, Librarian used completely accurate information, including his correct name, home, and business addresses, as well as phone numbers. There was no reason for any disguise at this juncture. Besides, it's hard to maintain a masquerade. One has to do too much lying, and after a while you trip yourself up.

His second wife had done that. She had an affair with an ophthalmologist and within ten minutes of his first inquiry about where she might have been that afternoon, he knew everything but her lover's underwear size. She kept falling over her facts, contradicting what she had said earlier, and creating scenarios that failed all tests of reason. Within three weeks after he confronted her confused and incomprehensible story, she ran off with her lover, and following the divorce, the last he heard was that she was living alone in a mobile home in the desert outside of Kingman, Arizona. That kind of tripping over one's narrative was not going to happen to him, even though he still had plenty of lies left to tell before the story was over.

Librarian returned to Paterson before noon, and with Forger's help began the housecleaning process that would eliminate all traces of their work. The cooking equipment, wine press, unused bottles of propane gas, and everything else that could not be burned or dumped in various locations around the city, were stacked in the unused side of the garage waiting for Sunday, when all would be transported by rented pickup truck to a local flea market, where he intended to sell everything. If that failed, it would be given away. He would have preferred simply to dump everything, but how and where does one dispose of a giant stainless steel pot? A joke that came to mind in any effort to dispose of the heavy, bulky wine press in an inconspicuous location was that of the miscreant stealing an elephant. When confronted by a policeman, he said, "What elephant, officer?"

On Tuesday, Librarian called the photographer and was told that everything was on schedule and the material would be brought to him via special messenger around 1 p.m. on Thursday. He was to have two checks ready, one for the unpaid balance for the photographic work and one for the two messenger services. He wrote down the amounts and told the photographer that he was looking forward to seeing the complete package, also thanking him for his rapid work and for having the kind of reputation that relieved his anxiety about confidential matters.

On Wednesday he called his NYPL office and confirmed that he would be back at work the following Monday. Then Forger and he completed every last detail of the cleanup and took all the miscellaneous debris to a number of dumps in and around Paterson, making sure that no one location got too much of their stuff. All unused paper had been burned, the ashes were bagged and dumped at a variety of other locations, and the fireplace was thoroughly vacuumed.

By Thursday morning the house was spotless, and except for the large items in the garage, was empty of all materials associated with the development of the forgeries. Even the unused iron gall ink had been dumped into the Passaic River in Fair Lawn, the next town. That river separates the two towns, and on driving over a bridge leading to Fair Lawn, Librarian parked by the side of the road, walked to the water's edge and poured the ink into the river.

The local environmental officials would have skinned him alive had they seen his action. However, as a child, he remembered seeing the river bright red and occasionally bright yellow from dyes casually dumped by Paterson's cloth mills, so he figured that some bottles of ink made from all-natural products would not create much contamination. The labels on the inkbottles were removed and destroyed, and the bottles put in a supermarket dumpster.

By mid-afternoon Thursday, the materials, perfectly prepared, arrived from the photographer. The positives, with border, were fourteen by eleven inches and as clear as only good photography can be. If this was an example of what the color transparencies were capable of producing, any facsimile derived from them was going to be dramatic. He paid the messenger, took one of the two microfilm reels from the package, and put it in the buffet drawer where the manuscripts had been stored. A package of scrap work from the photographer was set aside for shredding and disposal. The rest of the delivery went into his backpack. On Friday he took everything into New York and placed it all in his safe-deposit box, stopping first at a local Kinko's to make a color reproduction of the first page of the photographs of both the concerto and the quintet. These were destined for use in his initial contact with both Sotheby's and Christie's.

He thought carefully about what things should go where in the safe-deposit box, figuring that the pressure of both the transparencies and positives lying on top of the manuscripts might cause some ink transfer from one page to another. Consequently, the manuscripts were put in last, on top of everything else, except for the second reel of microfilm, which was quite light in any case. The other reel was to remain in the Paterson house for extra protection.

Finally, early Sunday morning, he rented the pickup truck, drove back to his house and backed it up to the garage door where the loading of it would be out of sight. With Forger's help, he muscled everything into the truck, covered and tied it down with a large tarp, and drove alone to the site of the flea market out near Morristown. Within an hour he had sold all of the items because he practically gave them away just to get rid of everything. He played the role of the simple country boy in pricing things, and when someone offered him a fee lower than the requested amount, he pretended to be awed by their bargaining acumen. For example, the stainless steel pot in which Forger had cooked rags, cost a fortune when they bought it at a restaurant supply house. He sold it for $25, with the buyer assuming that it was hot merchandise. Driving the empty pickup back to the rental agency, he paid his bill in cash and drove home in his own car, which he had parked a half-mile away from the truck rental agency.

Except for the fact that Forger was still in the house, the efforts needed to start what would, it was hoped, end in a sale of the manuscripts were ready to begin. This, sadly, included Forger's departure. He had packed all of his belongings and planned to leave that afternoon. This time he had a suitcase and was spared the indignity of leaving with all of his possessions in torn paper bags, as had been the case when he left Fairton Federal prison.

Forger had no precise plan for where he would be during the weeks that Librarian was be presenting the manuscripts to the two largest auction houses, but they arranged to keep in contact in the following way, should the need arise. If Librarian wanted to speak to Forger, he would place an advertisement, to run for three consecutive weekdays in the "In Memoriam" section of the obituaries found in the national edition of the New York *Times*. The ad would say, "I miss speaking to the expert." In almost any large city in which Forger found himself over the next few weeks, he would be able to buy the New York *Times*, and when he saw that notice he was to call Librarian's NYPL office from a public phone, identifying himself as "the expert." Forger was also told to have at least $20 in quarters for every pay phone call, this to avoid being cut off in mid-conversation.

If Librarian answered the phone, he would give Forger a ten-digit number that was an arithmetically altered version of the real telephone number of a nearby public phone in Manhattan. The altered number was constructed by subtracting each digit of the real phone number from nine. Forger would repeat the number and then hang up after Librarian's confirmation. Then he would reconstruct the original digits of the phone number by reversing the process and subtracting each digit of the coded number from nine, allow Librarian about fifteen minutes to get to that particular public phone, and then he'd call the number.

If the line was busy or no one answered, he'd try again every fifteen minutes until he got Librarian. Eventually, the two would speak to each other, using two public phones, and Librarian could communicate what was necessary, since it would have been he who asked to be called in the first place.

On the other hand, should Forger need to speak to Librarian, he was simply to call his New York office, tell him that it was the "expert" calling, and leave a ten-digit number, which included the area code—altered using the same nines-complement method—of a public phone where he could be reached. Librarian would then unscramble the number, go to any convenient public phone, call back, and they would do their business. Neither of them believed that very much contact would be necessary. If Forger were to see something in the newspapers about the sale, he could understand what was happening from that publicity. When everything worked out well and the sale was completed—the two did not consider any other alternative—the plan was for the two of them to meet and take off for Switzerland, where Librarian kept a bank account. There Forger would open his own account, using half the money they got from the sale, minus taxes and commission of course. Then they would simply become permanently unavailable. It was Librarian's intention to sell the Paterson house through an agent who would deduct his commission and deposit the balance in his local bank. When an electronic query showed that the deposit had been accomplished, Librarian would transfer the balance to his Swiss account. By that time he would have quit his job, notified the neighbor living in France that he could no longer handle the care of his home, and turned that task over to the same real estate agent who was responsible for the sale of his own house. The owner in Paris and the agent would be put together through electronic mail. God bless technology. Unfortunately Librarian and Forger had badly misjudged the need for better communications.

That afternoon, the two drove to Port Jervis, New York, where Forger intended to stay the night at a local motel, empty a safe-deposit box that he kept in that town, buy a car, drive to Danbury, Connecticut, where he would consider emptying out a second safe-deposit box, and then travel by car throughout America. Forger loved driving the Interstate highway systems—his favorite being I-80, which runs from New York City to San Francisco—but even more than that, he adored the old US routes, telling Librarian once that he would prefer to be a long-distance truck driver than almost anything else. That, however, was not his destiny.

In the next few days, after he had his car and enough money for some unknown number of weeks that he would be on the road, he intended to drive across America by a specific backcountry route about which he had been dreaming for years. When he got to California, he would wander up to Sacramento and then head home, slowly traveling east on US 50, a road that begins in that city and ends up on the waters of the Atlantic at Ocean City, Maryland. That was probably four to six weeks' worth of casual travel, and by that time Librarian would have some good information about the sale of the manuscripts.

The trip to Port Jervis took them up New Jersey route 23, passing by High Point Park, the highest elevation in the state. While the last months had been tiresome, it was an adventure that neither of them would ever forget and Librarian was sorry that Forger was leaving. They had been friends their entire lives and Forger had just finished a miraculous piece of work that was now Librarian's responsibility to bring to a $20,000,000 end.

There was a Comfort Inn in Port Jervis and Librarian did not leave until Forger was registered. He supposed that Forger could have stayed around Paterson, gotten an apartment, and kept in close touch, but it was too dangerous. Neither of them felt that his presence as a known forger and convicted felon was good for the sale of the manuscripts. Despite the fact that there was no public knowledge of any contact between the two of them in years, there was no need to take that risk. The two shook hands, Librarian asked if Forger had enough money on him, to which he smiled cryptically and said, "I think that with my safe-deposit boxes, I've got a lot more than you."

"I remind you," Forger continued, "that you are listed as a co-owner of all of my safe-deposit boxes. You know about three. There's this one," meaning Port Jervis, "but I'm emptying it tomorrow, the one in Stroudsburg, and the one in Danbury. But there are some others, too. There's a list of them in the Stroudsburg box."

Librarian responded, "I kind of figured that, but I have no idea which banks are involved and I don't have any keys."

"That's why I chose small towns," Forger said. "If you ever need to go to any of the boxes, there are only a few banks in each of those cities. You can visit them all in half an hour. Then show your ID, state that you lost the key, pay the fee needed to get a locksmith to open the box, and you can clean it out. Most of them still have about five years to run."

"That's all well and good," Librarian replied. "But I have no need to get to any of them, so they are going to sit there."

The final remark Librarian made to Forger before leaving was, "On your trip, will you send some picture postcards to Ella Hemmerdinger in Scherwiller? She told me that she enjoys getting mail and explicitly asked for some cards. I haven't sent any, so you can do it for me. Keep your eyes open for some pretty postcards and send them to her at 7 Rue Giessen. Will you do that, please? It will make an old lady who was very helpful to me quite happy."

Just to keep in practice, Forger wrote her name in a small notebook in the handwriting of Abraham Lincoln, and said, "Sure. I'll send her a card every now and then."

Librarian got back in his car, waved to Forger, and drove home to an empty, lonely house. "All right," he said to himself, "now let's get busy and sell this stuff!"

# 58

# AUCTION HOUSES, FIRST CONTACT

On the following Monday morning, Librarian returned to work at the NYPL and began his duties with a one-hour briefing to his management about the Munich seminar. Most of the time was spent reviewing the various techniques—some proposed, some in use, some tried and rejected—to save the many books and documents that were literally being eaten by the acid in their own paper. Since the NYPL was already in the forefront of book preservation technology, much of what he had heard in Munich was not new, and some of it had even been developed either at the NYPL or the Library of Congress. The NYPL had been employing almost every successful technique for book preservation for some time. Still, Librarian did not want his boss to think that the trip wasn't a wise use of scarce resources, so he spoke glowingly about a far-out and new approach then under test in several European archives. Further, he volunteered to give a presentation on the subject, the method, and the European experience with it for the entire department at Lincoln Center and separately, the personnel of the Rare Books and Manuscripts Division over on Forty-second Street.

Librarian then brought up the, to him, key item for this discussion. He told his supervisor that he had made a significant personal discovery of some music manuscripts while on vacation in France. The boss seemed delighted that Librarian had appeared to take a busman's holiday.

"What did you find?" he asked, followed by two other questions in quick succession. "Do you think it has some importance? What are you going to do with it?"

"It's not one thing, it's two, though I'm not really sure if the manuscripts have any value," he said dishonestly. "I plan on taking them to both Sotheby's and Christie's and see what they say."

"But why?" his boss said, surprised at Librarian's modest response. "I would expect you to know what you've found. I'm no manuscript expert, of course. That's not my specialization, but you have experience in that arena."

Librarian realized that, considering his level of expertise, he had to be more careful when he played the fool, so he changed direction in mid-air, saying that he thought he knew what he had, but he wanted to keep the information under his hat until he got an independent confirmation. Then he apologized for being secretive, but said that he preferred to say nothing about the matter until the details were certain. He also added that he was mentioning the matter now in case his boss got a call from any of the big auction houses asking if any NYPL manuscripts had suddenly gone missing.

The boss giggled at the peculiar twist of the story—though he made a mental note to confirm, without Librarian's involvement, that the inventory of NYPL music manuscripts was unchanged—saying that the matter was none of his business, in any case. He was curious to know what Librarian had found and would value being told that information whenever Librarian that the need to maintain confidentiality was over.

With that, the conversation ended and Librarian went back to work in his office. He knew that when the auction houses understood that he worked in the Rare Books and Manuscripts Division at Lincoln Center's Music Library, while at the same time, was offering manuscripts for sale that he had allegedly found, they would want to confirm that he was who he said he was. There had been some recent and unfortunate cases of scholars who had stolen property from a research library and then tried to sell it on the open market. The auction house would also want to make certain that he was not someone who walked off with a valuable piece of NYPL property.

Back in his office, he cleaned out three weeks worth of backed-up mail and phone calls. It was close to 2 p.m. before he was ready to call Sotheby's and Christie's. He had chosen those two firms as his auction houses of choice because both had excellent technical reputations. People sink fortunes into buying things after the auction-house experts have assessed and confirmed their authenticity, so they had to be careful in their evaluations.

He had no idea of when, if ever, they had claimed authority for something that turned out to be counterfeit. An auction house could not continue to remain in business very long if they made that kind of mistake more than once. It was that quality of their reputation that Librarian was counting on. They did, however, have policies about the extent of their responsibilities, should an object that they originally stated as authentic later be determined to have been a counterfeit. In sum and substance, anyone dealing with either house was dealing with one of the most thorough and technically responsible auction houses in the world. They were not alone, of course. There were other such facilities. But in New York, they shared the ruling of the roost, and each had considerable experience in selling rare music manuscripts.

With the realization that no matter how inept he was in personally selling something through Sotheby's and Christie's—he had only bought things through them in the past—their interest in supplying good customer service would enable him to get through the process successfully. From the buyer's side, it was anyone's guess as to which of the two houses was superior, so professional were they both.

It was very unlikely that either house employed on a full time basis an expert who would examine and be fully capable of authenticating Librarian's manuscripts. No auction house could afford to keep that many highly specialized authorities on its payroll. The normal procedure would be for him to make an initial inquiry, go see their first line of defense, show some impressive evidence of a valuable item, and then wait while they selected a person with world-class expertise in that very thing.

He flipped a coin, and on the basis of that alone decided to call Christie's first. Their web site invited interested individuals who had something to sell to get a free estimate of the object, either by making an appointment or filling out an Auction Estimate Questionnaire and submitting it with a photograph of the item. Since he had no intentions of doing that, he called instead.

Dialing the number at their Twenty Rockefeller Plaza, New York location, he told the answering party that he wanted to make an appointment to have some rare manuscripts examined for possible future auction sale and was immediately transferred to the Books and Manuscripts department. A cheery-voiced woman answered on the second ring.

Librarian identified himself, and to avoid being forestalled as a casual caller who had an item of uncertain identity, unknown provenance, and limited value, he gave a brief survey of his job with the NYPL, stressing his not-inconsiderable experience in dealing with rare manuscripts. Only after he had given the clear impression that he was a man who knew the manuscript business intimately did he state that he had two possibly important music manuscripts that he was interested in placing at auction. He added that he would not describe them in any detail over the phone, but was prepared to come into Christie's with photocopies of the first page of each of the two manuscripts. If the party examining them thought it worthwhile to pursue the matter, a further appointment could take place at his bank, where the originals were kept in a safe-deposit box.

"Well, that certainly is interesting," Christie's cheery-voiced representative said, somewhat disingenuously, and then went directly into stonewalling mode, "but we would *much* prefer if you sent a fax of those two pages rather than taking the trouble to come down here. We can certainly examine the facsimiles and get back to you. Does that sound reasonable?"

"Unfortunately, no," Librarian replied. "I am of the opinion that the manuscripts are the originals of two extremely important and very well-known compositions whose autographs have not been seen in two centuries. Consequently, I don't want to have copies of anything sent anywhere until after some preliminary evaluation. If they are obviously false or nineteenth-century copies, I don't want there to be the slightest chance that any material that I sent to you by fax could be seen by anyone."

The Christie's representative became very defensive, stating that they, too, were concerned about the confidentiality of both their clientele and anything they got, including faxes, so he need not worry that some inadvertent action might allow the material to be seen by anyone other than authorized employees of Christie's.

"I am supremely confident in Christie's integrity in handling this sort of thing," Librarian said, "but because my call is personal and not professional, I could be embarrassed if my management ever heard that I confused an original manuscript with a nineteenth-century copy. I am prepared to consider Christie's as a possible agent for the sale only if I can begin our dialogue by bringing my photocopies over personally. If they are of no value, I'll take them away and no one will be the wiser for it. Can we do that?"

Librarian had made it very clear that his heels were dug in and he was not going to budge one millimeter on this matter.

The Christie's representative got the message and reluctantly agreed, saying that she understood the situation completely now, though she really did not. It was her job to prevent the wasting of time of the firm's experts, so he did not expect any different reaction than the one he got. However, if he came on too strong, she could get hard nosed, so he had to be careful. The comment about "Christie's as a possible agent for the sale" was about as tough as he would get at this stage.

What happened next was very much expected by Librarian. The Christie's representative asked if in his work for the NYPL he had occasion to deal with rare manuscripts. What she was getting at, very delicately, was the possibility that perhaps the subject manuscripts really were not his, but were lifted from the NYPL collection.

"I do indeed," he replied. "It would not be possible to work in the Rare Books and Manuscripts Division specializing in the music manuscripts held at Lincoln Center's Music Library and not be constantly handing rare and valuable items."

"Ah, I see," she said. Librarian suspected from the change of character in her voice, that she was now paying very careful attention. "Let me set up an appointment with one of our music manuscript experts. That would be Mr. Carter. He is currently out of town and will not be back until Wednesday of this week. Would 2 p.m. the day after tomorrow be convenient for you?"

Librarian agreed to both the date and time.

"And I must also tell you," cheery voice said, "that Mr. Carter's expertise may not be in the era associated with your manuscripts. In that case, there may be a need for another examination with an expert who has a more specialized knowledge of the epoch or composer. May I inquire what period you believe your manuscripts to be from?"

"If I am correct in my assessment of these manuscripts," Librarian replied, "one of them is unquestionably from 1791 and the other from 1789."

There was a silence from the other end. When she spoke again, it was with a much greater seriousness of purpose. Here she was speaking to one of the NYPL's experts in rare manuscripts, telling her that he believed himself to have two valuable autographs from a particularly propitious and collectible epoch.

"Do you think," she said, "that you might have a manuscript of Joseph Haydn, early Beethoven, or even Mozart, perhaps? Or might it be a minor composer of the period, perhaps a lesser-known individual such as Fiala or Dittersdorf?"

"I'd really rather not speculate on that," Librarian said while silently admiring her knowledge of the era's minor composers. "Should Mr. Carter express interest in the material, I will tell him, under a confidentiality agreement, of course, where I obtained them and what, in my opinion, I think they might be."

"I understand," she said, though now he sensed evidence of greater interest in her voice. She was professional enough not to be overwhelmed with what she heard, because he really had told her nothing of substance, but 1789 and 1791 were important dates in music of that period since Mozart was still alive, Haydn was busily composing for Esterhazy, and Beethoven was a young man. The woman was definitely making connections. Librarian smiled at her acumen.

"You did say earlier," she inquired, "that these manuscripts were your own property. Did I understand you correctly on that matter?"

"You did indeed," Librarian said. "This transaction has nothing to do with the NYPL. I was recently in Europe, during which time and while on vacation I came across and purchased these manuscripts. I have discussed the matter with my employer, and Mr. Carter will be welcome to confirm this with him after he has seen the materials, should he wish to do so."

"All right, then," she said. "Let me confirm that you have an appointment with Mr. Carter at 2 p.m. at our offices at Twenty Rockefeller Plaza on Wednesday, the day after tomorrow. If there is a problem with that date, please call us. May I have your phone number in case Mr. Carter's return is delayed for some reason?"

He gave her both his NYPL and home numbers, as well as his e-mail address, thanked her for her generous help, and that was the end of the first contact. He wouldn't buy any champagne yet, but it was certainly a move in the right direction.

The next morning he got on line to Sotheby's web site. There he had a similar, in fact almost identical conversation with an employee who responded to pushing the computer screen's "Instant Help" button. He was unable to tell if it was a man or a woman responding to him, because gender is unidentifiable in on-line conversations, but it was a fast and efficient way for the firm to deal with potential customers. Unfortunately, in the absence of tones of voice, he could not read vocal cues and had to be especially careful not to come on too strong. That's not easy. When speaking, tone character conveys feelings, but in writing, care must be taken not to offend. Written requests can appear aggressive, though they can sound different when the same words are spoken.

Whoever the party was, he or she appeared to be curious about his NYPL connection and confirmed that what he had for sale was his personal property and not that of the NYPL. The party also requested faxes of the material, and again Librarian politely declined, saying that he would prefer to bring in a suitable copy personally. After a little more hassle about that issue, his appointment was finally set for Friday morning at ten o'clock, at which time he was to be seen by a Mr. Jonathan Kincaid of their Music Manuscript Division.

Things were definitely moving forward.

# 59

# CHRISTIE'S

The next day, following his appointment-setting calls to the two New York auction houses, Librarian received a call from the intuitive Ms. Cheery Voice of Christie's at 4:30 in the afternoon.

"I'm sorry to call you at such a late time," she said, knowing full well that things had a tendency to pile at the end of the day, "but I wonder if you might be free to come in to see Mr. Carter a little earlier than your currently scheduled appointment tomorrow? I just spoke to him, and he seemed intrigued by the nature of your request. Would an appointment at 8 a.m. be possible?"

Librarian's opinion of the request was such that if she said Carter was intrigued, he was probably on fire. "That time will be fine," he said, trying to sound casual, though his heart was thumping. He perceived that Carter sensed something important, but he had no idea how important it was going to be.

To make absolutely certain that he would be there on time, Librarian left his house at 6 a.m. on Wednesday morning. The big traffic problem in his getting to New York was always the Palisades Park cutoff near the New Jersey side of the George Washington Bridge. From that point, it was only twenty minutes to the ferry terminal, ten minutes to park his car, ten minutes for the Hudson crossing, and another fifteen for the bus ride uptown. He got to Christie's at 7:45 a.m. and presented himself to a guard at the receptionist's desk, giving his name, showing some identification, and waiting while the guard called Carter. Librarian suspected that their regular reception personnel came on duty at 9 a.m. He was directed to the elevator by the guard and told which floor to punch. As Librarian got off, he found a smiling, middle-aged man waiting to greet him.

"Hi there," he said. "I'm Frank Carter of Christie's staff. Thank you so much for changing your schedule around at the last moment. I appreciate the accommodation. My afternoon schedule is all jammed up, but I am most anxious to see what it is you have. How about some coffee?" he offered as the two walked towards what Librarian thought was his office, but which was, in fact, a conference room that Carter had reserved for their meeting.

"I prefer tea if I may, please," Librarian replied as Carter led him into a moderate-sized room containing a magnificent mahogany table capable of seating twelve comfortably. It was centered under some very strong lights. On one corner of the table there were croissants, bagels, and Danish pastries. On the adjacent corner, there were two thermos jugs, one holding hot water with a small Meissen dish of tea bags next to it, the other holding coffee. There was also some fresh fruit placed very engagingly in an exquisite silver bowl. The coffee and teacups were china, not Styrofoam, and the silverware—not plastic swizzle sticks—was sterling in a late nineteenth-century pattern, not a copy. Napkins were linen. Sugar bowl and creamer were in a matching sterling pair, polished to a fare-thee-well. They certainly knew how to do things elegantly at Christie's. Carter took coffee, Librarian took Earl Grey tea, each selected a pastry, and both sat down at the other end of the table.

"Why don't we get right down to business, if you do not mind?" Carter said. "I am told that you found some manuscripts in Europe that you believe are from the late eighteenth-century. Is that correct?"

Librarian confirmed Carter's information with a nod of his head and the simplest of responses, saying, "Yes, that's correct."

"Do you own these manuscripts or are you acting for another person?" Carter asked.

Once again, Librarian confirmed that the materials were entirely his property, though he did not have them with him at that moment, saying, "They're in a safe-deposit box nearby. I am prepared to take you to them whenever you wish, should your initial reaction to the copies I made of the first page of each manuscript be favorable."

Librarian went on to say that it would not have been wise to transport the manuscripts with him that morning because, if they really were valuable, that would involve some risk.

"I understand completely," Carter replied. "I was told that you would not bring the originals this morning and presumed that I can see them later if the occasion warrants."

*Nicely put,* Librarian thought to himself. *This man is a very careful person. I'll bet he wears both suspenders and a belt.*

"I confirmed with my bank that they have several moderate-sized conference rooms," Librarian said, continuing their dialogue, "though they need to be reserved in advance but…" looking around at the intense lights in the room where they were seated, he added, "I doubt if the lighting will be as good as this."

Carter smiled, but said nothing.

With that, Librarian reached down to where he had placed his briefcase, put it on the tabletop, took out a manila folder containing the reproductions of the manuscripts' pages that he had made a few days earlier, and said, "Here are copies of the first page of each of the two manuscripts." He then handed Carter the closed folder.

Carter opened the folder, separated the two pages placing them face up on the table so that one was by his left hand and the other by his right. It was at that moment that he looked at them carefully for the first time. Librarian heard a deep intake of breath and Carter flushed bright red. He didn't say a word, nor did his expression change. He just sat there and looked at both pages in absolute silence, his face the color of a bowl of borscht. The man certainly had restraint, but he could not control his blood pressure. Considering the shade of his face at that moment, his systolic must have shot up to 220. Whatever was going on in Carter's head, he could have been looking at a banana for all the emotion visible on the mask of his face. His eyes darted from the left to the right. After a few minutes, he reached into his left-hand jacket pocket, took out a handsome magnifying glass, and began to look at various portions of the two pages through it. It was close to twenty minutes before he said a single word. Librarian drank his tea, refilled the cup with hot water using the same tea bag, chose and ate a chocolate croissant, thought about taking a banana but didn't, and waited silently. Strangely enough, he had ceased to be nervous.

Finally, Carter spoke. "I cannot," he began slowly, "say anything definitive until I examine the original manuscripts. Nor, I sadly admit, is this music in my area of expertise, though I recognized both compositions at once. Mostly my qualifications are in Italian operatic manuscripts of the mid-to-late nineteenth-century—Verdi mostly—and this is clearly not from that epoch. As a consequence of that I am going to have to call on the services of one of the world's leading scholars of music from this period as well as an expert on the composer of this music. His name is Dr. Alfred Elias, and he is a professor of musicology at Princeton. I think he will want to see these as soon as he can, and after that there may be further examinations by other experts who also specialize in this period."

*He certainly is being careful in his use of words,* Librarian thought, as Carter tiptoed through a minefield of studiously selected adjectives, avoiding any that might have made comments about his mental state. In effect, his words revealed nothing to suggest what he did or did not know.

"Further, please excuse me, because I know you are anxious about this matter," he continued, "but I don't even want to speculate on whose hand this music might be written in. That this page," he said pointing to the left, "is music from Mozart's clarinet concerto, and that page," he said, pointing to his right, "is music from his clarinet quintet is very clear to me. But that is because the works are favorites of mine. However, I am not prepared to venture an opinion about whose hand wrote this music down because I am not qualified to do so. I will set up the appointment with Professor Elias as quickly as I can. But may I please have your permission, under the strictest of confidence of course, to send these two pages to him by special messenger in Princeton, presuming he is there today?"

Librarian responded, "I appreciate your unwillingness to speculate about the person who may have written these pages. I think I know who it is, and I suspect that you have an inkling of that, too. I am also grateful that you are going to solicit the help of an expert in getting that important question resolved. But until we have a firm idea of what it is we have here, I am opposed to allowing anyone to see this material outside of my presence. This is no reflection on you, on the integrity of Christie's, or that of Professor Elias, but the only way I can be 100% certain that someone will not make a copy of this and allow some newspaper to have an exclusive, is by refusing all requests for examination of this material out of my sight. If it turns out to be in the handwriting of some unknown person, then as a possible copy of the original it probably will have little value, but that remains to be seen. Or if some unknown person wrote this down before the first printed edition of around 1800, it might have some residual value as a historical document. So until we know what we have here, I just don't want anyone to see this material without me in attendance. I hope I have not offended you by my attitude. Indeed, I would be devastated if you were to take my comments personally."

Then Librarian put a more specific restriction on the matter, requesting that Carter not identify which Mozart compositions were involved to anyone, including Elias. In that way, the opportunity for rumors to begin was minimized or eliminated.

Carter looked at Librarian and said, "I'm disappointed, of course, but I understand. It's clear to me that you have done some serious research on this matter, as demonstrated by your reference to the time of the first printed edition. And you are not an amateur, judging from the fact that you are employed in the Rare Books and Manuscripts Division of the NYPL. If I were the owner of that manuscript, I would probably insist on the same course of action. I agree that it might be better if I simply told Professor Elias that we had manuscripts in an unknown hand of what might be early copies of some of Mozart's music, without being specific as to the compositions or the scribe. That way he cannot anticipate what he is to see. I will not even give him the benefit of my ideas on the matter, but I doubt that he would ask in any case, because he knows that I am not an expert in this area. However, I would like him—and myself too, of course—to see the complete manuscripts and not these copies," he said, holding up the pages Librarian had brought. "That will probably take either one minute or else several hours. Would an examination of that length be convenient for you during the workweek? Would you be able to get the time off from work for the examination?"

"There is no problem with that," Librarian said, adding that only the workweek was possible for the examination in any case, since the bank was not open on the weekends. He also stated that he had informed his manager about unidentified manuscripts that he intended to sell, so his boss was aware of what he was doing, though he had no knowledge of what the pieces were or their possible value. Then, Librarian concluded with a very disingenuous statement.

"To be accurate, I don't know their value either, so to avoid being disappointed, I have presumed them to be copies of no particular worth or importance."

"Good idea," Carter replied. "As for seeing them on the weekend, we could transport the material to the safe here at Christie's for that purpose and then return everything to your safe-deposit box afterwards. Do you think that might be possible?"

"Let's cross that bridge when we come to it," Librarian answered. "After you have spoken to Professor Elias we'll know if that is necessary."

"Excellent suggestion," Carter said. "I apologize in advance for being indiscreet, but may I ask if you have consulted with any other auction houses?"

"Not as yet," Librarian replied, "though I do have an appointment for a first meeting with Sotheby's on Friday morning. At the current preliminary stage of negotiations, I see no reason why I should not interview several reputable auction houses in order for me to obtain the best possible leverage for my manuscripts should they turn out to be genuine. Do you see it differently?"

"Not at all," Carter replied. "In fact, I was going to suggest that you do just that to place yourself in as advantageous a position as possible. I only hope that when you are ready to make a final selection about which house you might want to represent you, assuming that what you have is both authentic and valuable, you will think pleasantly of this, your first visit. If what you have is important, Christie's will very much want to represent you."

Carter continued with the suggestion that he would hold off the many other questions he had until he was able to reach Elias, but he was curious to know how and where Librarian had found the manuscripts, asking if it would violate some confidence were he to discuss it.

Librarian indicated that he was able to discuss the matter, but only to the extent of where they were when he found them and how they probably got there. He admitted that there was a great deal of history prior to his obtaining the manuscripts and about which he had no personal knowledge.

He then described the scenario that he had established with his visits to Benjamin Hemmerdinger of Strasbourg and his aunt Ella Hemmerdinger of Scherwiller. Beginning with the discovery of the manuscripts in an old brief-case, he spoke of where he found it, the circumstances of the discovery in the secondhand thrift shop in Scherwiller, why he was searching there in the first place, and the assistance that was given to him by the Hemmerdingers—both nephew and aunt. He made sure to mention the fact that Benjamin Hemmerdinger was a direct descendant of a Strasbourg money lender with whom he believed the briefcase was originally pawned in the early part of the nine-teenth-century, the manuscripts still inside it. He spiced the story with a hypothesis that the borrower—almost certainly Stadler—never returned to reclaim the pawned satchel. Then, he opined, the money lender was unable to sell it, the shop moved over the intervening years, and the satchel simply went from one location to the other, though under the same family management.

He concluded his story—parts of it very true and confirmable, much of it entirely invented—by going over the events since 1938, when a descendant of the original money lender sold the pawnshop business. The satchel, still unpurchased at that time, was one of several items not included in the sale of the business, probably because the new owner considered them unsellable.

Certainly, by 1938, the shop's former owners were alleged to have been unable to sell the briefcase in the approximately 138 years since they had supposedly acquired it.

"The son of the owner who sold the shop in 1938," he said, bringing his telling of the story to Carter right up to the minute, "still lives in Strasbourg, and it was through him that I was able to trace the briefcase further. I'm not surprised that no one bought it. It's really a very old and quite dreadful satchel. The price I paid for it at the thrift shop attests to its lack of worth. I have it in my home in New Jersey. Would you like for me to bring it to the meeting with Professor Elias?"

"You can if you wish," Carter replied, "but this first meeting will deal almost exclusively with the examination of the manuscripts. While the item is an important part of the provenance, let's first see if there is any provenance worth knowing about. If Elias doesn't see the briefcase on this trip, he will absolutely want to see it if the manuscripts are of interest."

Carter seemed ready to conclude the meeting, and Librarian sensed that it would be best for him to initiate that. It was time to get going.

"I really must not keep you any longer," Librarian said. "Both of us have some work to do."

Carter replied, "Indeed. I certainly do. And the first thing on my agenda will be to contact Professor Elias, make an appointment, and then confirm it with you. Let me see," he said looking down at a folder that he had been carrying with him. "I have both your business and home numbers, so that's fine. Here are the photocopies of the music, copies that I reluctantly part with, and I hope to be able to do business with you."

"You have been more than helpful," Librarian said, "and I am very pleased by your conservative approach to this matter, and anxious to see you again."

With that, Librarian left at 8:55 a.m. and went to work.

The next morning, Thursday, Carter called his office and said that Professor Elias was free the next day, asking if a meeting at 9 a.m. would do.

Librarian, knowing of his Friday meeting with Sotheby's said that the time was too close to his ten a.m. appointment that same morning, and asked for one in the early afternoon instead.

"Let's do it at 2 p.m. then," Carter suggested, adding a request that Librarian reserve a conference room at the bank and confirming the address and location where they would meet. Finally, he suggested that if their meeting lasted well into the afternoon—a tacit admission that Carter thought the manuscripts to be genuine because if Elias thought them to be phonies, they would be done at 2:02—that the three of them have dinner together.

"I'd like that very much," Librarian replied, confirming all the requested information. "I'll get back to you if there is any problem with the conference room. If not, I'll see you in the lobby of the bank as close to 2 p.m. as you can get there."

After hanging up the phone, Librarian knew right then that Carter's suggestion for a morning meeting the next day was to try and get Sotheby's out of the loop. Good thinking on his part, but it was not going to work. And if he was trying to ace out Sotheby's, then he knew what it was Librarian had, except that Librarian knew a great deal more than he did.

He called the bank and reserved a conference room for 2 p.m. the next day, making certain that they were aware of his intentions to use it until five that afternoon. At 4:30 p.m. he received a call from Sotheby's, reminding him of his meeting with Kincaid the next day. He wondered if that was a standard business practice. He wondered about that very much.

# 60

# SOTHEBY'S

Librarian didn't expect his visit to Sotheby's to be significantly different from the one he had with Christie's, but it turned out to be revelatory, and he was the recipient of some first-class tactical, strategic, and political advice. It reinforced his realization that whatever his extensive previous auction experiences as a seller of Forger's early manuscript counterfeits, as well as his consultant's role for auction purchases made by the NYPL, he had a lot to learn when dealing in the rarefied atmosphere of items worth many millions of dollars.

Kincaid was waiting for him at the reception desk when Librarian arrived a few minutes before 9 a.m. On giving his name to the receptionist, Kincaid stepped forward and identified himself.

"Welcome to Sotheby's," he said in a friendly way while shaking hands. "I'm Jonathan Kincaid. Call me Jon. Shall we go to my office and chat?" His genuinely friendly manner, as well as being thoughtful enough to be at the front desk awaiting Librarian's arrival, allowed Librarian to sense that the two would get along well.

On arriving at Kincaid's office, the discussion was a parallel of the one he'd had with Carter at Christie's. However, it very quickly went off on an unexpected tangent dealing with the protocol of the big-time music manuscript-selling business. What he had done in the past with Forger's earlier efforts was small potatoes, at least when contrasted with the thin strata in which he now found himself. The most that any of Forger's pieces had ever gotten was $250,000 for a Louis XVI letter. But once the price got as high as he believed the Mozart manuscripts would bring, it appeared that the whole process metamorphosed itself into something resembling a political phenomenon with international ramifications and considerable ego management.

Kincaid's examination of the manuscripts was professional, but perfunctory. Librarian produced his photocopies. Kincaid looked at them with a loupe, which he apparently preferred to Carter's magnifying glass, pursed his lips, and then said, "Very interesting, indeed." And that was that. No big hoo-ha, no jumping up and down with excitement, no kissing his fingertips and looking heavenward. Instead he took the time to bring Librarian into the world of the dynamics of major-league music manuscript sales.

"Let me tell you immediately," he said, "that I think you have two very important manuscripts, though I do have to see the originals, of course. But I specialize in the late Romantic literature—Brahms, Mahler, that sort of thing—and no one will care what I say about these," he said, pointing at the photocopy pages. "I'm going to presume that Carter is calling in that young genius, Alfred Elias, from Princeton, and if he's doing that, then he's impressed, too. But let me tell you some of the political dynamics involved.

"Elias' approval is necessary, but by no means sufficient, though his rejection of the authenticity of your two documents would ruin you. His technical reputation is very strong, but no single person's assertions about your manuscripts will suffice, particularly the declaration of an American, and Elias knows that. Following his examination, assuming he generates a high-confidence level about authenticity, he will then recommend a second meeting with two or more of the really big guns.

"I'm going to suggest that we skip all the intermediate steps and go directly to two of the bigger guns in the business. If they like what you have, you're home free and an auction can begin immediately after that. If they don't like what you have, then we would not be interested in pursuing this any further, no matter what Elias says."

Librarian asked who the bigger guns in the business were.

Kincaid responded, "One is an important official in the hierarchy of the Salzburg *Mozarteum*. He lives there, of course, and has an international reputation that is impeccable. The other is head of manuscripts for the Berlin *Staatsbibliothek*, and while he is not as prestigious in the world of Mozart scholarship as the Salzburg official, the Berlin facility has an enormous collection of Mozart manuscripts. In fact, it was the largest in the world until the events of World War II dispersed the collection, though they did get some of it back, and what they didn't get back is in Poland.

"And these," he said, pointing to Librarian's copies of the manuscript pages, "will have to be passed on by them in any case. It would be political suicide not to do so."

Librarian asked, "Why is that the case?"

"First, because one of the two represents Salzburg," Kincaid said, "and that is the center of gravity in the Mozart universe. The reasons are complex. After all, Mozart didn't live in Salzburg very long and his most mature work was done elsewhere. It's safe to say that he never liked the city, and apparently during his lifetime, the city didn't much like him. However, today a big piece of the city's economy is based on the fact that he was born there. So even though a great deal of the world's expertise is elsewhere, Salzburg still remains the galactic center for Mozart research, and you can't do much in that world without being in Salzburg's good graces.

"Their approval of a manuscript discovery alleged to be by Mozart is sufficiently authoritative for any auction house in the world to accept it as a guarantee of authenticity. If they say it's good, it stops all arguments. Furthermore, if we were to ignore them and attempt authentication entirely with people outside of Salzburg, that would create a political problem for you that we don't need and you couldn't surmount or survive.

"Second, the Berlin State Library is, after Salzburg, an important place for Mozart manuscript expertise, but it is infinitely more than that. It has enormous political clout in Germany, and therefore in the scholarly world. At one time, it may have been the wealthiest facility of its kind on the planet. For example, the archeologist Schliemann took the antiquities he found at the site of the city of Troy and deposited them in Berlin. The Russians have them now, but Berlin will get that stuff back some day. The aura of greatness still hangs over that facility, and we need them to be in bed with us.

"Having both Salzburg and Berlin making kissy-kissy noises about your manuscripts will probably improve the auction price by twenty percent, at least. So if both of those men like your manuscripts, you will have the entire scholarly world supporting the authenticity of your discovery. And don't kid yourself. While the idea of scholarship may be a synonym for ivory tower uselessness in some corners of America, in Germany and Austria it draws money from stones.

"Fundamentally, these guys and their institutions are the best, and they know it. But equally important is that they've learned not to trust anyone else's opinion because they've been burned in the past. A few years ago, somebody found a manuscript and the first words out of his mouth, and to the newspapers too, was 'Genuine Mozart!' It happens all the time. There is no value in discovering a work by an unknown klutz. Finding the originals of the great masters makes reputations, even if unknown klutzes really did compose them. You have no idea how much rubbish is out there under Mozart's name that is completely inauthentic. For example, that claim of 'Genuine Mozart!' that was leaked to the press turned out to be a manuscript copy of a bad edition, composed by a hack in 1813. And the biggest mistake that guy made was not getting Salzburg's or Berlin's *imprimatur*—which he would not have gotten in any case—before he opened his mouth.

"The Salzburg and Berlin *Mafiosi*—and to a great extent, the Austrian National Library, too—see themselves as guardians of Mozart's name. They take that job very seriously, and they do it very well. On several occasions they saved us from making public fools of ourselves, not that I'm saying anything negative about your manuscripts for one second.

"And most importantly, when the European press gets word of these manuscripts, the first calls they will make will be to Salzburg and Berlin. And the last thing you need is for those experts to be placed in the embarrassing position of saying, 'We know nothing about this, we have not been consulted, and we have nothing to say.' That would place you and your manuscripts in a very disadvantageous position. Furthermore, it would serve you no purpose to solicit their opinions following that embarrassment. You'd be a dollar short and a day late."

"I didn't know that the politics were so cutthroat," Librarian ventured.

"At the level of the really big money and the most significant discoveries, you better believe it," Kincaid said, "and we are going to have to work within the confines of that political situation or come out losers. Besides, if you have rubbish—and I don't think you do—then I am motivated to find out about it early. It will save me money, time, and effort. So I'm just doing my job, which in the final analysis is for Sotheby's benefit and yours. That way, everybody wins. Any other course of action is perilous and should be avoided.

"So what happens next?" Librarian asked.

"I have a very good contact in Salzburg," he said. "As soon as I see the originals of both manuscripts, I'll call her. She's an American woman from Texas, by the way, and she knows her business. Unless she's off examining something or on vacation, she should be there. With the right words from her, I can probably get those two experts I spoke of on a plane within twenty-four hours, barring war and the simultaneous discovery of Mozart's unknown gravesite. Sotheby's will pay the bill, of course. It's all part of the authentication process.

If nothing works out, some money has been spent, but not much. If things go well, we'll get our money back in commissions, plus some sensational publicity. Now, when can I see the originals? Would this afternoon be OK?" he asked.

Librarian liked Kincaid's take-no-prisoners attitude, but that afternoon wouldn't do. He advised Kincaid about the meeting with Carter and Elias at the bank at 2 p.m., looked at his watch and said, "But it is only 9:45. Why don't we go to the bank right now? We'll be back in an hour or so."

Kincaid ruminated for a few seconds, looked at his watch, consulted his Palm Pilot, called his secretary to cancel some appointments, and said, "OK. Let's go."

Librarian suggested that he call and confirm the availability of a conference room, but Kincaid said he didn't need one. His view was that he could tell what he needed to know, even if he saw the manuscripts in a phone booth. Besides, he reminded Librarian that banks have booths for people who need to examine the contents of their boxes and don't mind standing up, saying, "In a pinch that will have to do."

Twenty minutes later, the two were at Librarian's bank. Luckily, a conference room happened to be free, and with an attendant, Librarian went through the pseudo-mystical and quasi-religious safe-deposit box unlocking ceremony. Then, walking next to the rolling cart on which his box was being transported by a uniformed guard, Librarian went to the conference room. Kincaid, not permitted into the area where the safe deposit boxes were kept, was waiting there for him.

The guard left the box on the rolling cart and then went out of the room, closing the door behind him. Librarian opened the lid, took out the reel of microfilm, the two manuscripts, each in its own opaque plastic envelope, and placed them on the table.

Kincaid took the two manuscripts, opened the thicker one, which was the concerto, put on a pair of white cotton gloves, extracted the manuscript, turned to a surface here and a surface there, closed it up and put it back in its folder. Then he examined the other manuscript, essentially the same way, and put it back in its folder. He was so used to handling treasures that seeing another—or what one thinks is another—is not a scary experience.

"What else is in the box?" he asked.

Librarian took out the contact prints and negatives, and then tilted the box to show that its interior was now empty. Kincaid shook his head in confirmation and turned his attention back to the manuscripts.

"OK," he said, "I've got my work cut out for me. Let's get this material back into protected storage."

Librarian repacked everything, including the copies of the first page of each manuscript that he had taken with him for that morning's meeting with Kincaid, pushed the cart to the door, and signaled the guard. He and Librarian then went through the cabalistic ritual of the unfathomable safe-deposit box locking procedure and went to lunch, Kincaid's treat. At 1:45 Librarian left Kincaid, who got into a taxi to go back to his office. "Expect a call from me this weekend," he said, and the driver took off.

Librarian turned around and walked back to the bank. It was time for his appointment with Carter and Elias.

# 61

# AH, PROFESSOR ELIAS,
# I PRESUME

On entering his bank for the second time that day, Librarian saw Christie's Frank Carter in the lobby, chatting with the anvil salesman from *The Music Man*. The central character of that successful musical is a con man—a band-instrument salesman named Harold Hill. There were legitimate salesmen in the musical, too, and one of them sold anvils. His equipment, kept in a single giant suitcase that its owner carried in one hand, presumably included a full-sized sample of his product, so whenever he put the suitcase down, it went "SMASH!" This seeming irrelevancy is mentioned here because the man chatting with Frank Carter in the bank's lobby was a *doppelgänger* of that anvil salesman. He had the biggest suitcase Librarian had ever seen. Furthermore, he appeared to be very insecure about it, because every fifteen seconds he reached down to verify that it was still where he confirmed it to have been fifteen seconds earlier. He was built like a young Arnold Schwarzenegger. In the brief walk Librarian took between the front door and where the two of them were standing, the anvil salesman confirmed twice more that the monstrous case was still in its place and had not been spirited away.

"Ah," said Carter when he looked up and saw Librarian approaching, "good to see you, and on time, too. Let me introduce you to Professor Alfred Elias of Princeton, one of the world's leading Mozart authorities."

Elias, in the midst of verifying the presence of his case yet another time, drew his hand back from the handle and extended it to Librarian. "Nice to meet you," he said without either vocal inflection or even the tiniest hint of a smile. Librarian sensed that this was a man who had little time, comfort, or patience with social amenities. If he could get by the anvil salesman, he might make it to the end of the race.

"Likewise," Librarian said, with a big smile, and the battle lines were drawn. Librarian didn't know where Elias' attitude came from, but it was like an aura about his person. Perhaps Carter, in stating to Elias that the man they were to meet possibly had two important Mozart manuscripts, coupled with the fact that Librarian was not in Elias' data base of people important to the Mozart world, may have set him off on the wrong foot. This was a man to be handled with caution.

"Shall we get right to business?" Librarian asked, and the three of them went downstairs to the safe-deposit area that he had visited with Sotheby's Jonathan Kincaid only a few hours earlier. First Librarian confirmed his reservation of the largest of the several conference rooms, and then went to it with both men, assuming that Elias would want to put down his suitcase. After that, Librarian intended to do the formalities and fetch the safe-deposit box. When he began to leave the conference room, Elias said rather gruffly, "If you don't mind, I'd like to accompany you."

"If the bank doesn't object, then I certainly will not," Librarian said, wondering why Elias would want to follow him into the bank vault. When the two got to the security desk and Librarian identified himself as the bank's client, the guard said to Elias, "Sorry, sir, but vault entry is restricted to those whose names appear on the box renter's contract."

Elias looked unhappy, but positioned himself by the two-foot thick steel-door entrance to the vault where Librarian and the guard would—because the vault was L-shaped—be out of sight for a brief period. Librarian could not figure out what Elias was thinking. Perhaps he perceived a plot in which Librarian could be transported instantaneously to a secret location, return at once with some stolen manuscripts in his possession, and then calmly walk out of the vault to present the treasures as his own.

The guard and Librarian entered the vault, did the two-key unlocking together, and came out with the box on the rolling cart. It took no more that two minutes. As it was being pushed out of the safe for the second time that day, Elias followed them, seemingly satisfied that no trickery was going on. It was clear that he was a suspicious and a careful man. Librarian thought that he would hate to try to bribe him.

With the three men in the conference room—the door having been closed by the guard on his way out—Librarian opened the lid of the box, slid the reel of microfilm out of the way and took out the two plastic envelopes, saying, "The first one is the larger of the two. Is there anything you would like to know about this matter before I show you the manuscripts?"

Elias said that if necessary, he would ask questions after he examined the material. The tone of his voice was as if to say, "Your story is of no interest to me unless what you have is something important, which I doubt in any case, without even having seen it." It was clear to Librarian that Elias had no idea what he was about to see. Librarian had asked Carter not to identify what the manuscripts were, and that should have been the state of Elias' mind at that moment. His attitude might have been derived from the fact that he was being presented with a potentially important piece of Mozart knowledge that was totally outside of his database, and he was uncomfortable being put in that position.

Elias then opened his suitcase—in which Librarian really did not expect to see an anvil—and took out a variety of things, including an impressively sized, portable watermark reader. It was identical to a thirty-five millimeter slide-viewing table and consisted of a large, flat, glass plate, behind which was a light source. A page of manuscript would be placed on the glass and the light beneath that page would illuminate the watermark in the paper. Elias plugged the reader into an extra-long extension cord, also carried in his case, looked around the room for a wall plug, found one, and completed the connection. Additionally, from the case he extracted cotton gloves, a loupe, two magnifying glasses, a dozen thick books—a pair of which Librarian recognized at once as the two-volume catalog of Mozart's watermarks—and a number of bottles, which looked suspiciously like chemicals to Librarian.

"Professor Elias," Librarian said with a smile that got nowhere near his eyes, "do those bottles contain liquid chemicals?"

"Yes," he replied. "They do. I was only laying them out on the table in case the occasion necessitated it."

"I understand completely," Librarian said unctuously, with the teeth-only smile pasted on his face conveying the idea that he actually understood nothing of the sort, "but until you decide to use them, would you mind keeping them off the table on which the manuscripts are located. I just want to avoid any accidents."

"Sure," Elias replied somewhat unhappily, and he put the chemicals off to a side table. When everything was unpacked, he put on the pair of cotton gloves, reached over, extracted the manuscript of the concerto from its folder, and placed it face up in front of himself.

*Well*, Librarian thought, *it's show time!*

Elias looked at the first page intensely for a full five minutes, his head held at a peculiar angle. It was as if he had seen the Medusa and been turned to stone, so unmoving was he. His hands were on the table with the fingers of the left overlapping those of his right, the thumbs hanging over the edge. Librarian didn't think anyone could remain so motionless for that amount of time. Although it was impossible, of course, he even appeared not to blink his eyes during the entire interval. Somewhere around the fifth minute of his emulation of a marble statue, he said two words, perhaps not even aware that he spoke in such an unacademic fashion.

What he said was, "Holy shit!"

And then, as if those words were a light switch that turned the world back on, he came to life—not even realizing what he had just said—reached over, and flipped the switch on his watermark reader. A light went on inside the box, and handling the manuscript like a holy object, Elias picked up its first sheet, carefully separated it into its two half sheets, and placed the outer one, unfolded, on the watermark reader.

"Oh, my," he mumbled, "It's 82," and it was now Librarian's turn to be impressed. Elias apparently had the shapes and content of more than 100 watermark classifications—actually more than 200 if you count twins—memorized and, at a moment's glance had instantly recognized the one Forger had chosen for much of the paper of the concerto manuscript. Reaching over, he picked out the watermark catalog from his collection of volumes and turned to the page showing the details of watermark type 82. Measuring the three half moons, the distance between them, and the distance from the left-hand moon's outer semicircle to the right-hand moon's inner semicircle on both the manuscript page and the image of it in the manuscript catalog—proportionally adjusting for the difference in size between the printed catalog and its watermark reality—he got a perfect match. That was due to Forger's careful measuring of thirty-one critical points at the time he wired the watermark into his hand-woven mesh. *Forger's genius has always been in his careful management of details*, Librarian thought to himself.

Elias then reassembled the manuscript sheet from its two half-sheet components, put it back on the pile, turned off his watermark reader, and slowly started to go through the entire manuscript, one careful half sheet at a time. Other than the unacademic expletive and his reference to the paper type, he had said nothing thus far. As he examined the manuscript, he made a number of notes in pencil on a small pad—pens are never used near an important holograph—and after almost forty-five minutes, completed his visual examination of all the surfaces of the manuscript.

Then he turned his watermark light box back on and, one at a time, catalogued the watermarks of every half-sheet in the manuscript, making notes about which watermark appeared on each sequential half-sheet. He got a surprised expression on his face when he came to the final half sheet of the concerto's first movement, saying, "Wow! That's the 55 twin."

When everything was reassembled, he carefully placed the concerto manuscript on the left side of the table and turned his attention to the plastic folder containing the clarinet quintet, though before he opened it he excused himself and went to the facilities. So did Carter, who had not said a single word during the now one-hour-and-fifteen-minute long still-unfinished examination. Librarian stayed by the manuscripts. Frankly, he considered the fact that Elias was willing to leave him alone in the room with the autographs as a positive sign. He apparently no longer thought that Librarian would instantaneously teleport himself to a secret location, returning with more treasures.

On their return, Librarian could tell by Carter's sour expression that Elias had said nothing to him, which meant that the only thing Carter heard during the time they were together was the sound of Elias urinating. Clearly, Elias was not a man who revealed information until he was ready to do so. Back in his seat, his cotton gloves replaced on his hands—Librarian presumed that he had taken them off before relieving himself—Elias opened the second plastic envelope.

Once again, he came out with an expletive, this one an even greater display of astonishment. He said, "Oh my God!" his hand rising to the middle of his chest. Librarian again doubted that he was aware of what he had said.

With equal intensity and for some forty-five minutes, Elias examined the quintet autograph, checking watermarks and making more notes on his pad. Then he placed the quintet manuscript near that of the already examined clarinet concerto, turned his light box switch to the off position, and sat back, putting his fingertips over his closed eyelids. It was almost 4 p.m. They had one more hour before the bank closed.

Elias appeared to be done and for the first time since he began his examination, he looked directly at both Carter and Librarian. Obviously very much emotionally moved, he said, with wonderment in his voice, "I never thought that in my lifetime I would ever take part in an event such as this." Then, to Librarian, he addressed the following in a tone so affected that it was almost out of control: "You have what is perhaps the most important Mozart discovery in two centuries. I have to check a number of points, particularly the quadrant watermarks found on each half-sheet, to confirm that the jigsaw puzzle fits. But with that and a few other small caveats that I want to confirm at the Princeton University library, and in the unlikely event that there is something here that I have missed—which I doubt very much—there is not the slightest doubt that these manuscripts are absolutely authentic. I consider myself fortunate, indeed honored, to have been given the opportunity to be the first to examine them. But having said this," he continued, "There is a caveat involved. You should not be prepared to accept my examination alone as establishing the authority of this material.

"A find so enormously important as this has to be confirmed by several experts. If we were talking about something less important than the rediscovery of two complete, major manuscripts that have not been seen for two centuries, I would recommend several other scholars to whom you might wish to show these treasures for confirmation of my opinion. But not these manuscripts. For the powerhouse that you have on this table, I think you have to get Salzburg involved. I can make that happen, of course, but first you need to think about the implications of all of this," he said as he turned his palms upward and spread his arms out to cover the scope of the manuscripts lying on the table. "I believe there is a great deal of money involved here, though I am not yet prepared to estimate the value of these treasures. That will take considerably more research. The fact is that there is no precedent for this event, and I have almost no way to judge the worth of these two miracles."

When he finished his monologue, no one said anything for some time. At first, Librarian wanted to get the discussion off the emotional roller coaster by allowing Elias to speak about the factors that convinced him of the manuscript's authenticity, but he decided that it was best to wait until after Elias had calmed down. That could be done during the dinner that the three would shortly be having together.

Finally, Elias said almost pleadingly, "Judging from the microfilm reel you took out of the safe-deposit box earlier, can I assume that you have had these manuscripts photographed?"

When Librarian confirmed that to be the case, he continued, saying, "Would it be possible for me to have a copy of these manuscripts so that I may do some further analysis? And from a personal point of view, I'd love to continue studying them. Further, I'd like to prepare a paper on them for inclusion in the next issue of the *Mozart-Jahrbuch*," making reference to the annual publication of the world's most prestigious technical papers on Mozart and sponsored by the Salzburg Mozarteum.

"Unfortunately," Librarian said with the perfect out, "I have not yet entered into a contractual relationship with Christie's, or anyone else for that matter. And until I do, I prefer that no one have access to this material outside of my presence. Should I enter into such an agreement with Christie's, I would have no objections if they allow you to see the material, presumably at their site, and I certainly would not object to your preparation of a technical paper on the subject. However, I would insist that no chemical tests be employed, no cuttings or scrapings taken. That sort of thing."

Librarian was being very insincere. He said nothing about his real intentions to allow no one to see any of the manuscripts alone until they were sold, but at this time, there was no need to bring that possible irritant to the surface.

"Of course I would make no tests!" Elias said, almost in panic. "I only use those chemicals when the material may possibly be counterfeit, and only then to confirm a point or two such as the presence in the ink of chemicals that did not exist at the time Mozart was alive. I would no more think of doing any physical tests on these manuscripts than I would take an unauthorized scraping from The Sistine Chapel. But I would be most grateful for the opportunity to study them further, should you decide to complete an agreement with an auction house."

Since the time was now close to 5 p.m., the bank would be closing soon. The group had been there just short of three hours. Carter suggested that they all have a drink and then supper, during which time they could talk further about what might happen next. With that agreed to, Librarian repacked the safe-deposit box, Elias his anvil case, the guard was summoned, the box taken to the vault, and they left the bank.

Carter indicated that he had made a reservation at a restaurant called "Atlas" on Central Park South for 5:30 p.m., and they managed to get a taxi with a trunk large enough to hold Elias' suitcase. In Manhattan at that hour of the evening, getting a taxi with a trunk that big was no easy task.

# 62

# DINNER AT ATLAS

The attractive attendant at the Atlas Restaurant took one look at Elias' suitcase, and immediately opened both halves of the cloakroom's Dutch door to allow him to carry his case inside and place it in the corner with a CRASH! After being escorted to and seated at their table, Carter spoke quietly to the *Maitre d'* and a bottle of *Dom Perignon*, 1975, miraculously appeared, along with three delicate, tall champagne glasses.

Because it was early, the beautifully appointed restaurant was not yet crowded, and that—plus a corner table—allowed them privacy. Carter appeared to be extremely satisfied with the results of the examination and offered a quiet toast to honor Elias' authentication of the manuscripts. Librarian felt no guilt about participating in the act of honoring the confirmation of fraudulent documents. Instead, he took the pragmatist's point of view: business is business.

"Let me say," Carter began quietly so no one could overhear his words, "how thrilled and excited I am with the results of Professor Elias' examination." And then, turning directly to face Librarian, he continued, saying, "I earnestly hope that you will choose Christie's as your agent for the sale of your fabulous manuscripts and that we will be able to bring this matter to a profitable conclusion for you.

"From the moment I laid eyes on copies of the two pages you brought to my office," he continued, "my heart leapt with pleasure at what I then believed—and now know—to be one of the most important discoveries of known works in manuscript form ever accomplished. Personally, I consider it nothing less than miraculous. The only way you could have excited Christie's more is if you had discovered a lost Vermeer."

The three clinked their glasses, drank their *Dom Perignon*, and Librarian saluted Professor Elias for the excellence of his knowledge and his remarkable skills.

Elias responded in such an appreciative way as to embarrass Librarian with his gratitude, saying, "In years to come, when people ask me what in my lifetime was my most memorable moment, I will say without an instant of hesitation, 'The day that I first saw and confirmed the authenticity of the manuscripts of these two compositions.'"

Those words caused Librarian to realize how he had misjudged Elias because of the initial appraisal of his aggressive attitude. He was really a shy person whose only goal in life was to protect the authority of the man whose music he most admired in the world. It was amazing to Librarian how Elias' initial posture of caution, and even mistrust, had been completely neutralized following his examination of the manuscripts. He was now smiling, happy, and glad to be part of what was, to him, one of the high points of his life—just as he had said. It was one of life's high points for Librarian, too, though for different reasons.

"Now I would like to know, Professor Elias," Librarian asked, "what was it that you saw in the manuscripts that allowed you to conclude that they were genuine? While I have a little experience in doing that sort of thing," he said, minimizing his real skills and puffing up Elias' ego as if he were a pillow being fluffed, "I'm light years behind you in terms of real skill and knowledge."

Librarian asked that question for two reasons. First he wanted Carter to hear what Elias had to say on the matter, though Librarian was sure that Elias would put a great deal of this in his formal written report to Christie's. Such a report was not only needed for the obvious end of asserting legitimacy, it was also required for insurance purposes. And second, as a small conceit, Librarian wanted to see how many of the things that Forger put into the manuscript to create a patina of authenticity had directly influenced Elias. Librarian's compliment to him at the end of his question was only partly to plump his ego. The man's expertise deserved the praise, though it was paradoxical to assert expertise about someone who had authenticated a fraudulent document.

Elias responded, ignoring the tribute and about which he was plainly embarrassed, "The immediate thing, of course, was the penmanship of the manuscript. That is to say, the handwriting is unmistakably Mozart's. But although I have never seen it happen, I am of the opinion that forging his hand is not out of the question, so it wasn't the most important thing that led to my conclusion. Let me say that in reverse. If the handwriting were clearly not Mozart's, I would have dismissed the manuscript at once, but that it was his did not, by itself, cause me to accept the documents as genuine."

He took another drink of his champagne, the wine steward appeared as if from nowhere to refill the glasses, disappeared at once, and Elias continued. "If I were to rank the several key elements of the manuscripts, I would first and foremost point out the variety of special things that invariably appear in all of Mozart's mature autographs, and even in many early ones. In fact, when these things don't appear, that is *prima facie* evidence to allow a conclusion that Mozart was not involved with those documents.

"Let me give you a famous example," he continued. "When Mozart died, with his final composition, music for a *Requiem* mass, still unfinished, his widow selected Franz Süssmayr to complete the work, perhaps because his handwriting was similar to Mozart's. In fact, it is difficult to distinguish the penmanship of the two men. But very few of the special things that should appear on almost every page of a genuine Mozart manuscript are present on the pages with which Süssmayr was involved.

"In your case, every one of the non-penmanship things that need to be in a Mozart manuscript of this era were there, including the critical ones such as the way accolades were drawn, the order of the orchestral instruments, and even a few random sums and other mathematical calculations—totally unrelated to the music, by the way—that appear on a few of the pages. It's not terribly important in terms of its content, but Mozart sometimes used his music paper to do calculations, often for an unknown purpose, and he seems to have done a few of those in these manuscripts, not that it is possible to figure out why he was adding a column of figures or doing a multiplication, and occasionally even a long division."

"Excuse me, please," Librarian said, interrupting Elias with intent to draw him into a web from which he would not be able to extricate himself. "What is so special about Mozart's accolades that identify them as having come from his hand?"

Elias fell into the trap with his answer, something whose details Librarian wanted Carter to hear. He said, "I am sure you are aware that the accolades appearing on the left hand side of every page are used to define and frame the staves on which he intended to write his music. Unused staves, usually the highest and lowest, did not get included in the accolade's range. It is not so much that the accolades were present that impressed me, though it is important that they be there, but that every one of them was drawn in a way that is very uniquely Mozartean."

Then Elias took a scrap of paper from his pocket and showed how Mozart drew his accolades, making it in two pieces so a natural break was created in the upper left-hand corner, one that unambiguously demonstrated where Mozart lifted his pen. In Librarian's case, he had not known about this hand-writing peculiarity until Forger, with his laser beam of an eye, had pointed out that phenomenon to him on their Delaware Bay boat ride many months earlier.

"Please continue," Librarian said, wanting Elias to give more details for Carter's benefit. He wasn't sure, but those details might impact Carter's view of the manuscript's value. This, in turn, might raise the pre-auction estimate, should it be Christie's whom he selected as his agent of sale.

"And then, there were the watermarks, of course," Elias said wistfully. "What absolutely sealed the matter for me, even had I not been convinced earlier, was the fact that the paper of your manuscript contains the same watermarks that Mozart used for the draft of an earlier, but incomplete concerto for basset horn. He never finished that piece, though the few pages he wrote have survived."

Librarian was tempted to say, "Exactly twenty-four surfaces, buster!" to show off a little, but he wisely kept his mouth shut.

"However," Elias continued, "he remembered that earlier music and decided to reuse it for the clarinet concerto. Apparently, when he was writing that earlier work, he had a lot of paper with those watermarks around. The fact that the clarinet concerto manuscript uses the same paper is very telling."

At that moment the waiter appeared to take the food order; both Elias and Librarian chose fish, Carter chose a buffalo steak, no one wanted any appetizers, the wine steward made a suggestion or two, and they were left alone again.

"I could go on for an hour about all the many details that were so convincing that I could come to no conclusion other than the one I reached," Elias said. "Even the rastrology of the staff lines are the same as other paper he used for composing at around this same time. And the tracings made show that they were drawn with a brass writing instrument."

*Oh, if only Forger were present to hear this*, Librarian thought. Every single item that Elias mentioned had been foreseen by Forger, and several of them were deliberately put in the manuscripts for exactly the purpose of being found, and thus reinforce its authority.

"That's really very thorough," Librarian said to Elias. "And in light of your analysis, I'd like to make a practical and perhaps financially worthwhile suggestion to Mr. Carter on the matter of what we might do next, but I'm hesitant, for fear that my proposal might be perceived as unethical." Then, waiting for a moment, Librarian said, "Oh well, I'll mention it anyway. If I'm out of line, say so, and I'll withdraw my suggestion.

"It has to do with a conversation I had with Mr. Kincaid of Sotheby's just this morning. He also indicated that the best course of action would be to solicit the help of several European authorities, one in Salzburg and another in Berlin. Of course this was entirely dependent on Professor Elias' analysis being encouraging."

Actually, Kincaid had made his proposal independent of anything Elias might say, but Librarian felt that giving him the pat on the back wouldn't hurt. He continued, saying, "So my suggestion is that since Professor Elias is also of the opinion that other authorities see the material—isn't that correct, Professor?"—at which point Elias shook his head in agreement, "then perhaps it would be valuable if both Mr. Carter and Mr. Kincaid jointly invite additional specialists to view the manuscripts. After all, there is no need for them to write two distinct reports. There is the added advantage of the two auction houses sharing the transportation costs and other expenses. Would that be introducing some sort of conflict of interest?" Librarian asked.

Carter responded, "I'm not sure, but I don't think so. As long as it is understood that we are simply trying to have the same authorities view the identical material with a single written report generated for both parties whose sole interaction would be the sharing of the transportation costs and the *honoraria* equally, I think that my management might be in agreement. I can't speak for Mr. Kincaid, of course, but I will broach the subject with him.

"If management and the attorneys agree," he continued, "then we can contact these additional experts together. I'll have to hurry to speak to Mr. Kincaid, because you met with him this morning and he is not a man who drags his feet. I'll call him at his home right now and see what he has to say about the idea," at which point he excused himself from the table and stepped outside to use his cell phone. It wasn't any electronic interference that caused him to go outside as much as it was his wish to have a private conversation.

Elias and Librarian chatted about a number of things during Carter's absence, and the conversation began to verge towards the story of how the material was discovered when Carter returned.

"Kincaid thinks it's a good idea," Carter said. "He will notify his management by phone tonight. I will do the same with mine. Both of us will get opinions from our respective legal departments, and if the attorneys are in agreement, then both he and I will approach a mutually-agreed-to Salzburg colleague on a three-way conference call."

Then, looking at Librarian, he said, "We have also agreed that you should not continue any formal discussions with either of us until after the conclusion of the examination that we are trying to set up. So any substantive conversations that either he or I would normally have with you at this point are to be put aside until the visitors have finished their work.

"I felt it necessary," Carter continued, "to tell Kincaid that at this moment we were having dinner together here at Atlas. Instead of demanding that we stop at once, he said that it was his proposal that we all have the unique coconut cake for dessert, followed by an after-dinner glass of the house's Alsatian *grappa*.

"Should we agree to combine forces for the technical examination," he continued, "we will both contact you with a conference call to arrange the date and time. Until that happens and following this dinner, during which time I told Kincaid we would no longer discuss the manuscripts, neither one of us will contact you privately. Mr. Kincaid is a most correct and responsible man, and I accept his assertions to this effect completely."

With that, the meal arrived and they had it with a spectacular South African dry white wine. All three remarked on the sensational coconut cake Kincaid had suggested for dessert, and the *grappa* afterwards was thought of as an amazing thing for Alsace to produce. What went through Librarian's mind was that if he had known about the *grappa* when he was in Strasbourg, he would have bought a bottle to bring home.

Elias asked if he could drop by Librarian's house to see the briefcase in which the manuscripts were found, and Librarian said, "If it is all right with you—and under the presumption that you will be there—let me bring it to our next meeting. I realize that you are anxious to see it, but I feel that at the moment you are Christie's representative and showing something to you privately might be misinterpreted by Mr. Kincaid."

"Valid point," said Carter, and the meeting was concluded. Librarian took a taxi, first asking to be taken to the Thirty eighth Street ferry station, and then, changing his mind, requested that he be dropped at the business offices of the New York *Times*. On arriving, he went to their still-open commercial advertising section. There he left an advertisement to appear in the "In Memoriam" section of their national edition as soon as they could get it in, and was told that it would appear on Monday. He paid cash and asked that the ad read, "I miss speaking to the expert."

# 63

# SALZBURG & BERLIN IN THE GAME; FORGER'S MISTAKE

On Saturday evening, just as Librarian finished his dinner and was cleaning up the kitchen, the phone rang. It was Sotheby's Jon Kincaid who said, "Hold on while I click Frank Carter into this three-way conversation."

After a moment, Librarian heard Kincaid's voice say, "Frank, can you hear me?" to which Carter responded with a cheery, "Good evening! I'm here."

Librarian greeted the men and was informed by Kincaid that the attorneys of both firms were in agreement on the matter of making a common invitation to the Salzburg and Berlin authorities, though there were a few provisos. Both houses would share expenses for travel, hotel, per diem costs, and honoraria equally, and a single formal report would be provided to both Carter and Kincaid simultaneously. At that time, either house would be free to reenter negotiations for the sale of the manuscripts or else to terminate them, if it so chose.

Carter then continued, speaking about what had happened thus far and what was to take place next, saying, "Both Frank and I contacted Salzburg this morning on a three-way call and spoke to the party who has the clout to pull this sort of thing together. It is the American woman that Frank told me he mentioned to you, the one from Texas.

"At first her reaction was that the duties and schedules of the men we wanted might result in a wait of several weeks or even longer before they were available. We told her that there were two complete manuscripts involved, though we were not at liberty to identify them, and that they were probably the most important lost Mozart items ever rediscovered. At that point, she asked us to call back in two hours. When we did, she had both men on line with her and they grilled us with a lot of questions. For example, they pressured us about the identity of the compositions, but we stated that the owner had insisted on confidentiality. So they backed off to their next position, which was to ask for faxed copies of a page or two from each of the manuscripts, and we told them that the owner was not willing to do that, either. With responses like that, they turned us down flat, saying that they required a much greater level of comfort or they might run the risk of wasting their time. But when we told them about Professor Elias' activities and his absolute authentication of the material, they seemed to arrive at that level of comfort very quickly, particularly when we summarized the details supporting his opinion without describing what the specific compositions were that he had seen.

"So imposing were Elias' opinions and so strong is his reputation that following our recitation of his comments, they said that they would fly here on Wednesday, evaluate the material on Thursday, prepare a report on Friday, and return to Europe on Saturday. They also made sure we knew that they had to do a great deal of schedule reshuffling to make this happen, and if the manuscripts were not really worthy of that kind of personal and professional discomfort, they would become very unhappy with us, indeed.

"That was not a message lost on either Jon Kincaid or me. It was tantamount to saying, 'If these manuscripts turn out to be worthless or unimportant, don't bother calling on us at any time in the future.'

"Anyway," Carter continued, "that's the way it looks now, so we ask that you free up Thursday and we'll try for something like a 9 a.m. meeting at your bank. Can you please request a conference room there, and it needs to be large enough to hold six people. I'll contact Professor Elias and remind him to bring his watermark reader again. Oh yes," he said, "please don't forget to bring the briefcase in which you found the documents."

"I won't," Librarian replied, and with that the conversation was over.

Going to work on Monday morning, Librarian stopped at three different pay phones near Lincoln Center looking for one that would provide the best privacy when Forger called him as a result of the ad in the obituary section of the National Edition of the New York *Times*. An outside public phone would be a poor choice because the din of the traffic might require him to speak too loudly. Finally, choosing one of the three as better suited than the others, he began coding the telephone number in his head as he walked towards Lincoln

Center. Subtracting each digit of the telephone number 841-2612 from nine, it became transformed to 158-7387. All Forger had to do to reverse the process was to subtract each digit of the number given him from nine and except for the area code, which Forger knew to be 212, he'd have the proper number to call.

Arriving at work at 8:45, Librarian recalculated the number for verification, wrote it down on a "Post-It" for handy reference, and turned his attention to NYPL business. By noon, no call had come through, so he rang a sandwich shop and had lunch delivered to avoid being away from his desk at the time Forger might try to reach him. He also made certain that any business calls were kept brief, and thus, in the absence of call-waiting capability, kept his line as free as possible. At 2:30 in the afternoon the phone rang. Answering it quickly, he heard a voice say, "This is the expert."

Librarian reached for the "Post-it" with the phone number and said, without preliminary remarks, "158-7387."

Forger said, "158-7387," and hung up as soon as Librarian confirmed that number by saying, "Correct."

Leaving his office, Librarian walked three blocks to the location he had selected, went into the building housing the pay phone, and blocked anyone else who tried to use it, saying, "Sorry, but I'm expecting a very important long distance call. Should be here in a minute. Would you mind using a phone over there, please?" which was accompanied by pointing to a bank of phones on the opposite wall, down about twenty-five yards. Within five minutes of arriving, the phone rang and he picked up the receiver at once.

"Yes?" Librarian asked.

"It's me," Forger replied

"Where are you?"

"In Davenport, Iowa. I slept late, ate breakfast around 10:30, and then bought the *Times*. That's why I'm calling so late. Is everything OK?"

"Everything is great here. It couldn't be better," Librarian said, and then gave him a fifteen-minute rundown on what had happened with the various meetings. He concluded with, "This Thursday, two experts are coming in from Europe and then, presuming no difficulties, I should be able to start—and maybe even complete—the negotiations with one of the auction houses next week. When that gets done, I will know when and where the next auction might be. I think both auction houses will want to have the sale in London, not in New York, because the big buyers favor London. It still has an aura of gracious splendor. New York is too frantic for the tastes of some collectors."

"Sounds good," Forger said. "I didn't expect any problems, and it is clear that you are on top of the situation. Myself, I'm having a wonderful time driving across the US on back roads. The only problem with the trip is that I lose track of what day it is and where I was yesterday. How long have I been on the road?"

Doing a quick calculation, Librarian replied, "Today's the ninth day. Just one week ago yesterday I sold the big things including the wine press at the flea market on Sunday morning and drove you to Port Jervis in the late afternoon. Then I started calling the auction houses on Monday and we had our last meeting on Friday, which is when the specialist from Princeton came to look at the manuscripts. The next day I got a call saying that the Europeans would be here this week, and today is Monday. So yesterday was the start of your second week. Tell me what you did after I dropped you off?"

"Well, after you left Port Jervis," Forger answered, "I emptied out my safe-deposit box on Monday morning, bought a used car and drove straight to Boston to catch the ferry to the tip of Cape Cod. I spent the night at a bed-and-breakfast in Provincetown, Massachusetts. That's from where I sent my first postcard."

"Postcard?" Librarian asked, "To whom?"

"To Ella Hemmerdinger in Scherwiller, of course," he replied. "Didn't you ask me to do that? I wrote a nice message of greetings in very good French."

"Of course!" Librarian said. "I just forgot. She'll appreciate any cards you send, and I thank you for doing that. Now tell me about your trip so far."

"On Tuesday morning," he said, "I picked up the beginning of US route 6 and haven't left it since. I also found a hitchhiker to keep me company. It's nice to have someone to talk to on long trips, and even to drive when I want to look at the scenery. Anyway, route 6 goes right through Danbury, where I intended to empty another safe-deposit box in the afternoon and spend the night. But I decided that I had ample money, so I took nothing from that box. On Wednesday morning I took all the cash I had on me from Port Jervis, which was considerable, and at several different banks, bought a lot of traveler's checks. After that I think I spent the night in a place called 'Cory' in north-central Pennsylvania, and yesterday—what day is today? Oh yes, it's Monday—I crossed the Mississippi from Illinois into Iowa and spent the evening luxuriating in the sybaritic excesses of Davenport. Today I'll head out for Omaha and I hope I can find a hitchhiker to drive, because I want to see some scenery instead of just driving through it. My map shows that when I get to Bishop, California, which looks like the end of US 6, I can drive to Las Vegas on some very isolated back roads. Maybe I'll spend a week or so there before I wend my way home via US 50. In the meanwhile, if something interesting happens, put another ad in the *Times*. And I'll contact you by our agreed-to method if anything arises at my end."

After that and a reminder that Forger continue to send postcards to Ella Hemmerdinger, the men broke the connection. Their call took about twenty minutes, after which Librarian went back to work in the NYPL. It was only that evening when he remembered Forger's throwaway line about his intent to detour to Las Vegas. Something about his doing that was bothering Librarian, but because he had lots of things on his mind, he didn't focus on it. Now, because his three-day advertisement had two more days to run in the *Times*, there was no practical way to get back to Forger to discuss the ramifications of that detour. In effect, Forger would not know that Librarian wanted to speak to him again until after the current ad ran its course. And because Librarian was tied up on Thursday with the European experts, another three-weekday run of the ad was not possible before the following Monday. The fact that Librarian could not communicate with Forger at once was a flaw in their plan, a bad mistake that he realized too late to fix.

The next day, Tuesday, Librarian went back to the New York *Times* and reinstated the ad for the following week. As it turned out, his intuition was right and Forger's decision to visit Las Vegas proved to be a grievous mistake.

# 64

# THE BERLIN AND SALZBURG
# TEAM ARRIVES

Wednesday afternoon, when Librarian told his boss that he would take another personal day off without pay on Thursday, the reaction was anything but supportive. "I've been meaning to talk to you," his boss said, "about the number of times that you have been absent since returning from your Munich trip. It's damaging the smooth running of our department."

"Well," Librarian responded, "you will remember my mentioning that I planned to sell some manuscripts I discovered while on vacation and I'm in the middle of those negotiations now. Besides, all the time off I have taken has been coded as unpaid on my timecard."

"True," his boss replied, "and I am grateful to you for having been scrupulous in keeping your time-off accounting correctly managed, but it wasn't the money to which I was referring. You are an important person in the running of this piece of one of America's greatest libraries and your taking this amount of time off, as legitimate as it may be to your personal affairs, is creating a problem with our staffing needs."

Somewhat surprised by the concern expressed, Librarian decided to take a soft approach, and said, "You have raised a reasonable issue and it is one to which I offer the following suggestion. Hopefully by the end of next week I will have an understanding of the value of my manuscripts. If those documents are what I think they are, their authentication will allow me to sell them at an unusually high price, and with the income of that sale, live quite comfortably for the rest of my life without any need to work. In that case, if you wish I'll resign immediately, or at the latest, after the sale, which I estimate to be in about two months. If the documents are not authenticated, then my need for further time off will cease at once and this problem will be resolved by default."

"I'm astonished by your offer to resign!" his boss said. "That's not what I want or need. You are a valuable member of this department, perhaps its most knowledgeable employee, particularly for eighteenth and nineteenth-century manuscripts, and the purpose of my earlier comment was not designed to elicit an offer of resignation from you. Frankly, I don't know what I would do without you. My intention was to bring up a small point, and suddenly I find myself in the middle of what is to me, personally, and the library, professionally, a major problem.

"As for the offer on your part of a resignation, if it is really related to the sale of some valuable manuscripts from which you will profit handsomely, then of course there is nothing I can do about that. From my selfish point of view, I can only hope that your material is not terribly valuable. That way, your need for further time off will cease at once and the problem of which I spoke will become moot. But such a wish on my part is heartless of me, because I genuinely hope you have found something important. In any case, why don't we wait for a week and see what your understanding is of the value of your manuscripts. Then we can take it from there.

"While this is a personal and not a professional request," he continued, "I'd love to know what it is that you think you have found. Would it place you in a difficult position to tell me?"

"I'm really torn," Librarian responded, "because you have been a good friend, as well as a decent and thoughtful supervisor, but I am very hesitant about saying anything until the experts involved tell me if what I have is real or otherwise. Please excuse me for being so close to the vest, but I'd look like a fool if I told you something that I later had to retract."

"I understand," the boss said. "Let's go back to my original suggestion that we wait a week and see what you know then."

"That's unusually generous of you," Librarian said, "and I do promise you that when I know something for certain about the manuscripts, you will be the first to know. If I'm right, you are going to be astonished. And I've already said more than I should have, so let me get back to my desk and my work. I also state that all of the time that I am taking is critical to the authentication process and I would not be requesting it if it were not so important."

"OK," the boss replied, "and good luck, or I should say, though again self-ishly, 'Bad luck.'"

The next morning, Librarian took the Emmaüs briefcase out of the closet where it had lain since he had returned from France, placed it in the back of his car and left for New York, arriving at his bank shortly before 9 a.m. Carter, Kincaid, Elias, and two other men, both European judging from their shoes, eyeglasses, and haircuts, all arrived together at 9:15.

Carter said, "I am so very sorry that we are late, but we needed two taxis, what with Professor Elias' suitcase as well as some additional material brought by our guests from Europe, and it is the middle of morning rush hour, so getting two taxis was not easy." Then, turning to his guests, he said, "Permit me to introduce our visitors to you. May I present Professor Doctor Paul von Waldersee of the Salzburg *Mozarteum* and Professor Doctor Walter Heidenreich of the Berlin *Staatsbibliothek.*"

The two men looked grim, to the point of appearing furious. Librarian's assumption was that the overseas travel, followed by a morning meeting, was certain to reduce any technical specialist's expertise by twenty percent. They shook hands all around and he made a special effort to greet Elias, wondering if he had briefed the two guests. Then he had his question answered immediately with a remark from Elias.

"I have deliberately chosen," he offered, "to say nothing specific about my examination of the manuscripts. Messrs. Carter and Kincaid indicated that they briefly reviewed my findings with Doctors Heidenreich and von Waldersee on the phone last Saturday, but I suggested that until I complete my formal report, I didn't want to make any corroborative statements."

Now it became clear to Librarian. The two Salzburg officials were not so much tired as they were disappointed and possibly angry. Probably Carter and Kincaid had spoken very positively about Elias' conclusions, and here was Elias, refusing to confirm them. Heidenreich and von Waldersee were beginning to think that they had made some difficult changes to their crowded schedules, and a tiring trip to New York on top of that, for possibly no valid purpose. They weren't tired. They were furious.

This was a situation that was absolutely perfect for Librarian. These men were irate as a result of which they had become skeptical, and he was going to ride in on a white horse and make their day, their week, their year, and maybe their lifetimes! It could not have been better for him and the manuscripts. He was aided by the fact that their technical judgments would in no way be impacted by their anger.

"Gentlemen," Librarian said sweetly and with a warm, ingratiating smile, "shall we look at the material?" and off they went to the conference room. Once they were seated, Librarian, as owner of the safe-deposit box, went with the guard, extracted the case from the vault, had it wheeled to the conference room, and thanked the guard as he left, closing the door behind him. He opened his box, took out the two plastic envelopes, put them on the table and said, "Whenever you wish, gentlemen."

Three hours later, as they left the bank for a lunch arranged for by Sotheby's Kincaid, the attitude of the Salzburg visitors had changed from one of anger to one of being flabbergasted and in a state of openmouthed astonishment. They had been that way almost from the beginning of their examination. Librarian thought von Waldersee was going to have a stroke, so thrown was he on his beam's end when he saw the first page of the clarinet concerto.

These were two very professional men, used to being in complete control of a situation, but within ten minutes both had lost their composure. Heidenreich had tears in his eyes and von Waldersee was lost in wonder, saying over and over "*unglaublich, unglaublich!*"

Elias then took out his notebook and reviewed the watermarks, which all three randomly verified, using his watermark reader, and this caused more weeping from Heidenreich, with von Waldersee joining in rhythmic canon, saying "*erstaunlich, wunderbar, verblüffend, außerordentlich!*" the meaning of which was obvious in context, even to a non-German speaker like Librarian.

But it was not until Elias reached over and took out the manuscript of the clarinet quintet that the room went totally insane, with Heidenreich almost going mad with amazement. "*Do you mean to say that you found both lost manuscripts?*" he shouted, and then apologized, saying, "Forgive me speaking so loudly. I am quite overcome." I thought that Kincaid and Carter were going to burst with pleasure, and von Waldersee was now beet red.

Librarian answered Heidenreich's still outstanding question about finding both manuscripts with the statement, "Indeed I did find them both, sir, and my amazement at doing so was no less emotional than yours."

All in all, both very happy European guests spent the next three hours with Elias, going over every squiggle in the manuscript.

It was approximately 12:30 p.m. when Carter asked Librarian to review the circumstances of how and where he found the manuscripts. He would have done so, except that Kincaid suggested that the story be told over lunch, so everything was packed up and replaced in the bank's vault and the six went to a French restaurant nearby, with Librarian carrying the Emmaüs briefcase. Kincaid had selected the restaurant at which a small private room had been reserved.

This time Kincaid sprang for the champagne, a magnum of *Tattinger* 1971 *brut extra*. They toasted each other giddily, and Librarian told his story, passing the $3.88 briefcase around the table, with Elias paying particularly close attention to the wooden panel in the bottom, under which Librarian said he discovered the manuscripts. But it was von Waldersee who asked him why he had concentrated on Strasbourg as the likely place to look. When Librarian spoke of the technical paper given by the Dutch Mozart specialist, von Waldersee slapped his leg and said, "Of course! I remember him delivering that paper in Salzburg in 1991. I was there! At the time I found it difficult to believe that Stadler would have pawned his briefcase in Strasbourg, but it seems that he was 100% right. I must call and congratulate him when I get back to Salzburg."

"Could I ask you," Kincaid interrupted, "not to communicate any of this information until the matter of an auction has been concluded? At that point we will notify the press of the manuscripts and you will be then, of course, at liberty to discuss this with whomever you wish."

"Certainly," Heidenreich said. "I understand, and will, of course, comply."

Following lunch, Carter asked if there was any technical purpose served by returning to the bank, to which von Waldersee said, "There is no technical purpose, but I must see them again," and turning to Librarian, he said, "Would you mind very much?"

It appeared to Librarian that the authentication process was now over. As such, there really was no need to acquiesce to such a request. But not to do so might irritate someone. Besides, he saw no harm in giving von Waldersee a little more of the obvious pleasure he had shown earlier.

Despite his euphoria at this moment, Librarian was thinking about how much he wanted Forger not to make his planned detour to Las Vegas and how impotent he was in communicating that message to him before the following Monday, at the earliest.

# BOOK 7:
# TRIUMPH, TRAGEDY, AND RESURRECTION

# 65

# CONDITIONS OF SALE

At 9 a.m. on the Sunday following the examination by the European specialists, Librarian received a call from Jon Kincaid of Sotheby's. He got to the
point at once, saying, "You are aware that the agreement between Sotheby's
and Christie's that forbade individual communication with you on the matter
of the sale of your manuscripts became inoperative on submission of the technical report by our guests from Europe. My copy of that report—highly positive, I should add—was delivered about fifteen minutes ago. Frank Carter
probably got his at the same time. Both Heidenreich and von Waldersee are
now in a taxi on their way to JFK for the Lufthansa flight to Frankfurt, where
they'll connect to flights that will take them to their respective cities. Therefore, my call to you on the matter of that sale is perfectly legitimate and my
thought was that we might get together today. I know that it's Sunday, but we
should talk anyway. How do you feel about that?"

"I admire your aggressive style," Librarian replied. "How does 11 a.m. at
your office sound?"

"See you then," he agreed. "I'll get some sandwiches. Any favorites?"

"Stay away from anything that looks like liverwurst. Are a shirt and tie
obligatory?" Librarian asked.

"No, it's Sunday," Kincaid said, "and no one's here, but if your clothing is
very strange, you may have difficulty getting by the guard. Of course he'll call
me, in any case. See you later." Then he hung up.

Librarian left his house at 9:45 a.m., and Sunday traffic being light, he was
in front of Sotheby's an hour later. His shorts and sneakers resulted in the

guard giving him a difficult time, but he relented when Kincaid came to the front desk to rescue him.

In his office, Kincaid gave Librarian a copy of both the joint report and Elias' statement, and then he sat back while Librarian read them. The bottom line was that all three men authenticated both manuscripts without reservation, and von Waldersee further stated that as soon as the public announcement was made, the Mozarteum intended to seek financial assistance to be able to bid on the manuscripts even before the auction. They did not estimate a possible selling price, since that was not their job.

Now there was no doubt about it. The manuscripts had metamorphosed themselves into incontrovertibly genuine Mozart autographs, this despite the fact that Librarian saw them being created on his dining room table only a few weeks earlier.

Before the heavy formal discussions began, Kincaid took a small box wrapped with gift paper out of his desk drawer. "Here is a small present for you. However, be aware that the cost of this gift could not, in any way, be considered big enough to constitute a bribe. I'm giving this to you because you did a great thing for the world when you found those manuscripts. Professor von Waldersee said that he would be happy to review anything for us in the future, solely because of the pleasure he had in seeing your manuscripts. He also said that he never thought that he would ever see such a thing in his lifetime. So Sotheby's owes you for getting him so firmly on our side for the future."

Librarian opened the box and found a pair of white cotton examination gloves inside, remembering that when he inspected the manuscripts, he had rarely worn any and Kincaid reacted to that carelessness on his part, in a thoughtful way. With Librarian's spoken appreciation to him for his kindness, the negotiations began.

"Are there any special conditions on which you would insist in any agreement that you might make with Sotheby's?" Kincaid asked.

"Yes, there are," Librarian responded, taking out and preparing to give him a copy of the conditions. He also intended to leave a copy with Carter during his meeting with him, whenever that was.

"The most important personal condition for me," Librarian began, "is that, when this discovery is announced to the press, my anonymity is still to be protected. So please, no personal publicity.

"Second, if Sotheby's is chosen to be the auction house for the sale, it's presumed that the manuscripts would be moved from my bank to your vault, at which point they cease to be under my control and direct supervision. However, without my express knowledge and written consent, there are to be no further tests on those manuscripts, particularly those of a physical nature such as radiological or chemical. What scares me is that someone with very good intentions might think that he or she is authorized to scrape ink from the pages of the manuscripts, or else cut some pieces off for a radioactive decay test, or goodness knows what. To stop any accidents from occurring, I want it made clear that the process of authentication is now over, and were you in control of the manuscripts, Sotheby's would be held responsible for consequential damages should this provision be violated.

"Third, while generally the seller's commission fee is fifteen percent, it is not my intention to pay more than seven percent, unless a buyer offers to pay the seller's commission as a levered advantage. In that case, it doesn't matter to me what the commission is.

"Fourth, if the auction price for the clarinet concerto is less than $15,000,000, there is to be no sale and the manuscript will be returned to me without penalty of any kind. In the case of the clarinet quintet, that sale price must not be less than $10,000,000, otherwise the same conditions apply.

"Fifth, it is my understanding that an insurance policy that safeguards the material as it awaits sale is arranged for by the auction house, though it is paid for by me. If this is correct, then the policy should be one of "all risks," and its value must be for an amount equal to the sum of my minimum acceptable bids, as described in the fourth condition: that's $25,000,000.

"Sixth, the purchasers must sign an agreement to retain the manuscript as it now exists. What has to be avoided is a situation that actually happened some time ago in which a Mozart manuscript was bought by a consortium of manuscript dealers, cut up, and then sold piece by piece. Now this is going to be a challenge for your legal department, because the laws of ownership might be so dominant as to prevent the exercise of control after the sale. But I want the matter explored, not only between myself and the buyer, but for that person's insistence on the same conditions, should he or she ever sell the manuscripts to a third party. And those conditions are to go on in perpetuity.

"Seventh, and last, the manuscripts' negatives and positives, as well as my microfilm, are my property and will be retained by me. They are not part of the sale. The buyer may, if he or she wishes, restrict reproduction of the manuscripts in all forms, for a time to be negotiated and with a maximum not to exceed five years. After that time, whoever holds these photographic reproductions has a right to use that material in any way, including the preparation of facsimile or performance editions based on the manuscripts."

Kincaid sat there during the litany of requirements and didn't blink an eye. "I see two issues," he finally said. "Let's talk about them. Your proposed commission of seven percent is considerably lower than that which we are accustomed to getting from the seller. The buyer's commission is, of course, a nonnegotiable fifteen percent. I'll bring the matter up to the management of the house and see what they say. However, they will probably reject it. Make it ten percent instead, and I think Sotheby's will accept that because the sale will be such a publicized event, and good for our business.

"The second issue," he continued, "is the value of the manuscripts. I think that they are worth what you propose, and further, it's very likely that the hammer price will be higher. But it is good business to give a far more conservative minimum opening bid and then let the dynamics of the auction take over. With that in mind, let me offer a compromise. Let's adjust the presale estimate to $20,000,000. We can have the insurance value set at anything you like, because insurance is cheap. Besides, you want to insure them for what both of us think they are worth, not the minimum expectation. However, getting customers to a sale is one part art, two parts science, and a sprinkling of P.T. Barnum. A $20,000,000 presale estimate for the autographs will entice people without scaring them. Once the auction begins, the dynamics of the sale will take over and the buyers will be swept along with the energy flow."

Librarian replied, "However you wish to set the presale estimate is up to you, but I want the insurance to cover what I think is the value of the manuscripts. If you are suggesting that we could insure them for $25,000,000, or any other value we choose, while simultaneously giving a presale estimate of only $20,000,000, then I'm satisfied."

"Absolutely," Kincaid replied. "Insurance is as cheap as borscht. We can insure them for whatever we wish, but the fact is that one never really knows what they will go for. Items have come to us that should have gone for $50,000,000 and we could not get a bid above $10,000,000. And the reverse is true, too. My opinion is that your manuscripts will go for something around $30,000,000, but even with that view, we should still give a pre-auction estimate of no more than $20,000,000 for both."

"In that case," Librarian said, "let's adjust the two prices so they add up to $20,000,000 for the announcement estimates. However, at a sale price of say $30,000,000, your commission at seven percent for the seller and fifteen percent for the buyer nets you $6.6 million, less expenses. A ten percent seller and fifteen percent buyer commission nets you $7.5 million. I'm not prepared to give you that extra $900,000. Further, the same proposal will be given to

Frank Carter. If Christie's agrees but Sotheby's does not, Christie's will get my business and the almost $1,000,000 difference will go in my pocket."

To which Kincaid said, "Let's not argue about that until the need arises. Since we have no other obstacles, we are in good shape. I'll discuss this with my colleagues by phone later today and call you tomorrow with our answer and our offer. If you accept, we'll need to sign a contract, and following that, transport the manuscripts from your bank to our vault. Because we are thinking in terms of a sale in London, they would be moved to that location at a later time, but that's our responsibility. Incidentally, should the sale be in London, your transportation and expenses to that sale are borne by us, though the insurance fees are borne by you, no matter where the sale takes place, and those fees will be deducted from the selling price."

Librarian said, "Please understand that I would not be in a position to approve or disapprove your offer without speaking to Frank Carter at Christie's. After I see him, my decision will be based on which deal is best for me."

"Of course," Kincaid replied. "It is to be expected that you will have this kind of a discussion with him. Nonetheless, you have made your conditions to me very clear, you have heard my suggestions, and Sotheby's will work very hard to make sure that your manuscripts get the best and most dramatic publicity possible. After you receive our offer, why don't you give me a call if you need anything else, or when you've made up your mind? If you have any items that need further clarification, I'll handle that, too.

"And now, let's have our sandwiches. While we are eating," he said, taking out the sandwiches and several bottles of Evian water, "let me give you my opinion of your sixth condition, the one having to do with your desire to prevent someone from buying one or more of the manuscripts and then cutting them up into pieces. Not being a lawyer, my opinion here may be all wet, but it seems to me that once someone buys something, that person can do with it whatever he or she wishes, and that could include cutting it up, putting tobacco in the pieces of paper, and smoking them. My view is that you will not be able to exercise control over the treatment of the manuscripts once you are no longer the owner. But you have an interesting point, and my attorneys will examine it. Just don't expect such a condition to be really enforceable."

By the time Librarian got home, around 2 p.m., there was a call on his answering machine from Frank Carter. He returned his call, made an appointment with him for first thing Monday. Actually, he was motivated to see him as early as possible so he could get back to his phone at the NYPL. If Forger was in or near Las Vegas, he was two hours behind New York time. Maybe Librarian could conclude the meeting with Carter and get back to his office even before Forger got up in the morning.

# 66

# AN OMINOUS CONVERSATION WITH FORGER

With one significant exception, Librarian's Monday meeting with Frank Carter was a carbon copy of the one he had with Kincaid on the previous day. The difference was that Carter had the authority to agree or reject his seven percent commission limitation on the spot, and did not give a lame excuse such as "the matter is out of my hands," or "I'll have to consult with my management." In fact, after listening to Librarian's arguments, Carter agreed with the limitation almost immediately. Librarian suspected that Kincaid had the same authority, but was a different sort of a haggler. Well, no crime in that.

Carter also voiced identical concerns about the sixth condition—the one designed to prevent the manuscript from being chopped up and sold as pieces in the future—saying that his attorneys would examine it, of course, but he did not believe that any such post-sale control could be placed against a future owner, at least not in an enforceable way. He also gave the same recommendation about the presale estimated price being a compromise of marketing savvy on one hand and something that Christie's felt was realistic and achievable on the other. Comparables, which is the auction house term to describe the recent sale price of items of similar character, had nothing to do with setting the presale estimates for these Mozart manuscripts, because there had not been anything comparable to them for so many years. Carter also agreed that the insurance could be for whatever figure Librarian chose and would pay for.

Librarian liked Frank Carter. He was a decent man, sharp, and very much old school. He never came on strongly and was both conservative and polite. The problem that he had with Carter was that he was not a hustler. He was as intelligent and certainly as ethical as Kincaid, but the latter would drive an armored personnel carrier through whatever was creating a difficult situation for Sotheby's. And if he would work that hard for Sotheby's, then Librarian felt that he would work that hard for him. In effect, with Kincaid, Librarian felt that he had a steamroller for support. It wasn't that Carter was shy, only not as aggressive as Librarian would have liked. His feelings, therefore, were that all things being equal, he was going to go with Sotheby's, though he revealed nothing about that. Who knows what might change his mind prior to the signing of the contract?

The two concluded their meeting, with Carter agreeing to document all conditions in a contract and then notify Librarian when it was ready. By that time, Librarian would probably also have Kincaid's contract, and then it would be decision time. That was likely to happen no later than the end of the next business day, Tuesday, though Librarian intended to insist on twenty-four to forty-eight hours to finalize a decision.

What was really on Librarian's mind at that juncture was not the contract, but Forger and his stated intention to visit Las Vegas. He wanted to speak with him before the auction-house decision was made, a conversation that he presumed would have to take place prior to the end of the business day on Wednesday, because his ad in the New York *Times* ended on that day. Librarian's intention was to get Forger out of Las Vegas before he was seen by anyone who might present a problem for the two of them.

Forger's face and reputation were known by enough men who visited Las Vegas that word could get back to his "friends" from the forged $100 bill days. These were the men Librarian called "the cigarette machines," because Forger's description of them caused Librarian to think they were built like that.

Not only did he not want Forger to run into any of those thugs accidentally, he also did not want him to be any place where he might meet some friends or colleagues of those same men. It was highly probable that those who betrayed Forger into his four-year jail term at Fairton Prison began looking for him shortly after his release.

The Treasury Department was busily making propaganda about how counterfeiters of the $100 bill were being imprisoned by the handfuls. But if those thugs who tried to commission work from Forger more than four years earlier believed the Treasury Department's statements, they would be looking for Forger at that moment. Their reasoning was that if others were losing their hold on the counterfeit-currency market, they were ready to establish their ascendancy in it. They saw Forger as the key to getting them where they wanted to go, thus his going to Las Vegas was a very dangerous thing for him personally, and possibly even for the success of the efforts to sell the counterfeit manuscripts.

By the end of the business day on Monday, Forger had not called. Librarian checked that day's New York *Times* twice to confirm that the ad was present and its wording correct. Jon Kincaid, on the other hand, did call, confirming all the details of Sotheby's position, including their agreement with a seven percent seller's commission. On Tuesday, Librarian received two separate contracts, one each from Christie's and Sotheby's. Both contained typewritten notes advising him that the sixth condition—the one designed to prevent future destruction of the manuscripts—was, according to their attorneys, almost certainly not enforceable, though they included the clause anyway. Librarian called both men separately and told them that he would commit to signing with one or the other no later than the end of the business day on Thursday, stating that he needed a little more time to think about the matter. That was not true, of course. He had already decided on Sotheby's.

There was no call from Forger on either Tuesday or Wednesday, which made Librarian frantic. On Thursday, around noon, just as he was getting ready to deal with the contract matter, the phone rang. A voice said, in a peculiar, almost-frightened way, "This is the expert."

Librarian looked around for the "Post-It" he had prepared under the assumption that Forger would call Monday, Tuesday, or Wednesday. When that didn't happen, he had foolishly thrown it out on arriving at work on Thursday. Fortunately, he was able to retrieve it from his wastebasket and he gave the coded information to Forger as soon as he found it.

After Forger confirmed the number, Librarian hung up and took off for the public phone. When he got there ten minutes later, it was, mercifully, not in use. After a few minutes of standing in front of the phone so as to prevent anyone else from using it, the phone rang and he grabbed the receiver off the hook so fast that it slipped out of his hand.

"Where are you?" he said frantically, not even asking who was calling. "Where have you been? Why didn't you call earlier?"

"I'm in a gas station on US 93 in Ash Springs, Nevada," Forger replied in a timid, almost-frightened voice. "I bought yesterday's and today's New York

*Times* before leaving Las Vegas this morning, but waited until there was 100 miles between me and that town before calling you. It's a good thing that yesterday's edition was still on sale, because the notice is not in today's paper." He paused a moment, as if gathering strength to tell Librarian some unpleasant news, and then said, "Going to Las Vegas was a bad mistake."

Librarian's heart sank. Did the worst happen, or had he just lost a lot of money gambling instead? "What do you mean?" he asked.

"I met some old friends there, and they kept me in my room for three days trying to convince me to do some work for them. You know the parties who are being spoken about, don't you? We had some business together almost five years ago. There is no need to be any more specific than that over the phone. Conversations can be picked out of the air and analyzed entirely by the use and patterns of certain key words, so for this chat, we must avoid all such words."

"It is clear to me who you must have met there," Librarian said. Forger had run into the thugs who tried to involve him in the currency-counterfeiting scheme of more than four years ago.

"I got to Las Vegas last Saturday and stayed at the MGM Grand," Forger continued. "On Sunday night at dinner with a lovely working girl at the hotel's buffet, two of those guys sat down at our table and growled at the pro. She recognized them at once, got the message, and left. It isn't clear how they spotted me, or even if it was they who did the spotting. What they wanted was a talk, and for three days that's what we did in my room. They wouldn't even let the maid in to clean up. Food was sent in. There was nothing physical going on, they just wouldn't let me out, insisting that I make myself available to them for a job.

"They said that they had been looking for me for some time," he explained. 'These guys were not the same personnel as my last involvement with that bunch, but they represent the same corporate organization, if you get my drift. They knew me, though it isn't clear how. And it doesn't matter. What they were looking for was for me to do the same thing they asked me about the last time.

"For three days I detailed how the manufacture of perfect merchandise was no longer financially practical, but these were neither businessmen nor technicians, just muscle trying to convince me of something without hurting me. My descriptions of the technical issues, the costs needed to overcome them, and the vast resources that would be needed to produce perfect goods—now that the product had been improved—went right over their heads. However, I made no comments about the fact that those improvements were because of my suggestions to the Treasury Department. For a full eight hours they got the smallest details of why this was the case, and do you know how those morons responded?"

"No. What did they say?" Librarian replied.

"What those idiots said," he answered, "was 'OK, if it is not financially profitable to make the 100 unit, then make the fifty unit.' That's how dumb these guys are. They even asked about merchandise in a 500-unit denomination, not knowing that no such unit has been around for years. Then I offered two constructive suggestions so they would not think that it was simply a case of trying to avoid doing any kind of a job for them. First I proposed doing European goods, saying that they'd have my best professional opinion about what could be done with that kind of merchandise, but they refused to even consider that option. Those dumb bastards don't recognize European merchandise as a commodity that has value.

"And second, as a fall back position, I told them that goods that weren't perfect could be done, though there was a higher detection rate. But they said that their management insisted that my product had to be as good as the one for which the four-year vacation was my reward."

"Well, how did this thing with them end?" Librarian asked, breathlessly.

"They let me go this morning because the hotel security came to the door and refused to accept their 'come back later' routine. Instead, security insisted on being allowed in, threatening to break down the door if needed. Apparently the maid had told the hotel management about not being permitted to clean up the room for three days. Anyway, rather than make any further fuss, those guys let me take off, but they are not done with me.

"Because of my not making a formal complaint of being held against my will, there was no crime committed, so they had to let those guys go. When they left the grounds of the MGM Grand, the hotel security guards had no further authority either. So my 'companions' just took off. In thirty minutes my packed bags were in the car, my bill was paid, and I was on US 93 heading north out of Las Vegas. Not until I got to Ash Springs—it's in the middle of nowhere—was my comfort level good enough to make this call to you. When we get done, I'll head towards Ely and pick up US 50. Then it's east from Ely in a straight run across America.

"Now you need to know one more thing," he continued, "and it involves you. They asked what had happened to me since my release from Fairton, and I told them about your place. They might contact you to confirm this personally, so be aware that they know who you are, though they know nothing about our manuscript partnership, past or present. Dragging you into this was not a good thing, but it doesn't pay to deceive these guys. If they had asked the right questions, they would have gotten the whole story because they *know* when you are lying or deceiving them or otherwise not giving them the straight skinny, and that's when they get suspicious, unpleasant, and physical.

"Fortunately, they didn't ask what was going on at your place. Instead, I volunteered that we were both Paterson kids simply renewing an old acquaintance from the days of our earliest school years. They seemed to be satisfied when they heard about your profession. I think they hold librarians in contempt, and that's good for us. They're not likely to think we had a business going in which they might be interested."

As Forger gave this critical information to Librarian, the latter knew at once that there was now no choice but to keep his name out of the newspapers. Here he was ready to sign with Sotheby's, and the manuscript story would hit the newspapers very shortly thereafter. If somehow he was identified with that announcement, those thugs—or more likely their bosses—were going to put two and two together. They might be dumb, but the fact that Forger was at Librarian's place for some months and suddenly Librarian becomes identified as the discoverer of two valuable manuscripts was a story that they would see through in a heartbeat.

Forger interrupted Librarian's thoughts to say, "Judging from your silence, is it correct to say that we're close to going public with the manuscripts?"

"Absolutely," Librarian answered. "I'll call both Christie's and Sotheby's in about two hours, cut off negotiations with one, sign with the other, and then this will go public, maybe as early as next week."

"That's wonderful," Forger said. "Just keep your head should friends of those guys visit you. Play the dopey librarian and academician. I'll keep a low profile on the drive east, and maybe we'll get through this thing. Which auction house will you choose?"

"Probably Sotheby's," Librarian said. "And we *are* going to get through this thing, but your greatest flaw is showing in this casual attitude about the dangers involved. You don't have a sense of politics and you refuse to recognize the power of a dominant force. That is what those thugs represent. From this day on, call me every day just to let me know what, if anything, you see on this trip. Look for cars that might be following you. And please, stop picking up hitchhikers. That's another danger to you.

"There will be no further ads in the paper," Librarian continued. "Just call. Every day except weekends, unless there is a real emergency. I'll have another couple of pay phones lined up. Either say 'the expert is calling,' in which case you'll get a phone number scrambled in the usual way, or if no one answers, hang up. I might not be at my desk every time you call, particularly in light of the fact that whatever auction house is selected is going to go public soon. Just keep calling until you get me. Once a day. Do you understand all that?"

"Sure," he said. "But being out of Las Vegas and on the road gives me a real sense of security."

"Those men have long arms," Librarian retorted. "Have you inspected your car for bugs?"

"Oh, come on!" Forger replied. "Those guys are too dumb for anything like that."

"Stop being so damn arrogant!" Librarian almost shouted. "Think 'dominant power' whenever you are awake. Then examine the car and call me tomorrow."

"OK," Forger said. "I'll keep in touch." With that he hung up and Librarian was left with a sick feeling in the pit of his stomach.

# 67

# A CONTRACT IS SIGNED

It was 1 p.m. by the time Librarian finished his telephone conversation with Forger and learned what had happened in Las Vegas. Notwithstanding the fact that Mexican jumping beans were doing a cha-cha in his stomach, he had duties to perform, work to do, and obligations that had to be carried out.

First, he called Jon Kincaid at Sotheby's and asked for an appointment at 2:30 that afternoon. Then he called Frank Carter and requested one at 4 p.m. In neither case did he make a statement about his ultimate intentions for the meeting.

Second, he stuck his head in his boss's office and asked for fifteen minutes of his time. It turned out to be more than an hour, which almost made him late for the appointment at Sotheby's. What the two of them discussed were the details of the manuscripts, and when Librarian told his boss the details of the autographs that were involved, his manager turned ashen.

"You mean to say that…" and then he repeated back to Librarian the very story that had been told to him a moment earlier.

"That's right," Librarian agreed, "and I'm on my way right now to sign a contract with Sotheby's."

"That's some story!" his boss said. "It has to be the most important manuscript rediscovery of Mozart's music ever accomplished, and you have chosen a great auction house to be your representative for the sale. I am so very envious of you for the remarkable thing you have done. Please, tell me everything about it."

And nothing would do but that Librarian give him the details involved, which he did because his boss was a kind and generous man, allowing liberties with schedules, and being so supportive when Librarian had made his earlier offer of resignation to avoid further difficulties for his management. After finishing his story, Librarian requested that the matter continue to be kept in confidence. While his boss agreed to do so, he did ask permission to arrange for a little departmental celebration following the press announcement.

"That is one of the many things that you must *not* do," Librarian said, thinking of the problems of how to continue to maintain his anonymity. He clarified his earlier request for confidentiality by making it much more specific. "I want you to keep the matter in confidence permanently, discussing it with no one under any circumstances. I am insisting on such an agreement with Sotheby's, so I'm counting on you to keep the matter to yourself."

"You mean to say that you aren't going to bask in the publicity and honor of your find?" the boss asked.

"That's exactly what I mean," Librarian said gently. "You see, if there is publicity, a lot of people will be on my neck trying to borrow money, which is what always happens to me whenever I've come in to some. And here there is a lot of money involved. It's a case of my wanting to take the money and run," and looking at his watch, he continued, "which is exactly what I have to do now or my contract signing appointment at Sotheby's will be delayed."

Slipping his copy of the contract into his jacket pocket, Librarian caught a taxi to Sotheby's, got there at 2:25, and went directly to Kincaid's office.

Looking up when he knocked at his open door, Kincaid waved him in, saying, "Nice to see you." Coming right to the point, which was the main reason Librarian liked him, he said, "I do hope that you have some good news for me."

"Indeed I do," Librarian replied. "Sotheby's is the one who will be given the responsibility for the sale of my manuscripts. Here's my copy of the contract, and if you'll give me a pen, we'll be done with the formalities in a moment. My only request at this instant is that you take no action for the rest of the day, because I'm going to see Frank Carter, and I want to tell him of this decision personally. It is important to me that no one has told him of my intentions before I do. Carter has been more than decent, and it would be disrespectful if he were treated like an unwanted cat. Agreed?"

"OK," Kincaid said. "There will be nothing said about it until the end of the day. My management is anxious to hear what has happened as a result of this visit, but they'll be put off until 6 o'clock this afternoon. Is that satisfactory?"

"That will work," Librarian replied.

Kincaid opened his desk, took out a folder with Sotheby's copy of the contract, and after checking it to confirm the inclusion of all conditions, he signed it, as well as Librarian's copy. Librarian did the same and the deed was done. The two shook hands and Librarian told Kincaid how proud he was to be represented by such a distinguished organization.

"We have a little more signing to do," he said, "but that won't happen until the manuscripts are moved from your bank to our vaults. Can we do that on Monday? I need to know, because we use an armored vehicle for transfers of anything worth more than $1,000,000, and that requires some logistics and advance contact."

"Certainly," Librarian replied. "Monday will be fine. Shall we say 10 a.m. to give the morning rush hour a chance to dissipate?"

"You don't think that the New York traffic ever dissipates, do you?" Kincaid asked, smiling. "But suppose you meet me here at 9 a.m., we'll sign the insurance papers, the management will have a chance to meet you, and then we can go to your bank." Except for the meeting with Sotheby's management, Librarian agreed to the plan.

"I'm sure your management handles even more confidential things than my neurotic wish to remain unknown in this matter," Librarian said, "but I'd prefer it if we keep the number of Sotheby's people who know me to you alone."

"As you wish," Kincaid said, "though they will be disappointed, because they were looking forward to meeting you. As for a public announcement," he continued, "I'm going to generate a press release and I'd appreciate it if you would look it over. Will faxing it to your home so you can look at the details overnight be OK? The press conference will be at noon in our auction area, which is not being used on Monday, and I plan to have the manuscripts on display, though in locked cases, of course. Finally, can we also get your photographic originals of the first pages of both manuscripts so that I can have copies made for the media and also for use with the press release that will go worldwide?"

Librarian responded to Kincaid's fax request first, saying, "The FAX is not a good idea. If too much communication is going on between us, that lessens the likelihood of retaining confidentiality. With respect to a FAX, I understand the need for speed, but I prefer to come by personally after my talk with Carter and look over the suggested text. The problem with faxes is that they transmit my telephone number, too, and that's an unneeded exposure. As for Monday, once I place the manuscripts in your hands for transfer to your vault, I want to stay far away from all the activity. I don't want to be seen or have anyone ask, 'Who is that man?' And should you have to call me or vice versa, please do not use a cell phone. Their conversations can be taken out of the air like that," he said, snapping his fingers.

"In the several days following the press release, please don't call me at all, because that is when the *paparazzi* will be trying hardest to find out the name of the anonymous owner of the manuscripts, so my anonymity is best protected by no communication whatsoever. Oh yes, one more favor."

Reaching into his pocket, Librarian brought out a sheet of paper with two telephone numbers typed on it, saying, "Immediately prior to the press release, can you have your Paris office contact Benjamin Hemmerdinger in Strasbourg and his aunt Ella Hemmerdinger in Scherwiller—here are their telephone numbers—and request that they not use my name in any public statements about their role in the affair. I'll contact them after the auction in order to express my appreciation in a more tangible way, namely with a gift, but they are not to know of that at this time."

Kincaid could not know it, of course, but Librarian's main concern was to have his personal relationship to the manuscripts remain absolutely unknown to the thugs trying to get in touch with Forger. Earlier in the process, he was prepared to live with a slip of the tongue and have his identity as the anonymous discoverer be made known. But now, that was no longer an option. Forger's troubles in Las Vegas had precluded that.

"Let me tell you," Kincaid said, "that in this business we know very well how to keep material confidential. In the time that I have been here, I've never seen or heard of an event that was supposed to be kept private going public, either accidentally or even maliciously. So be confident that your name is not going to be released from this place."

"Fine," Librarian replied. "Now unless we have something else, I've got to go and see Frank Carter." The two shook hands again and Librarian was out the door.

Over the next hour he met with Carter at Christie's, told him of the decision to use Sotheby's as his agent of sale, and explained his rationale. Carter could not have been more understanding and he made a great deal out of the fact that Librarian had come to tell him of the decision personally, saying that it was rare to see such courtesy extended.

Strange that Librarian felt no compunction about selling a fraudulent set of manuscripts, but was heartbroken about having to disappoint Carter. Leaving his office, Librarian went back to Sotheby's, reviewed the text of the proposed press release and agreed to it outright. Then he and Kincaid had supper together and Librarian went home, still feeling guilty about Carter and Christie's.

# 68

# TEARS IN ELY, A PRESS RELEASE IN NEW YORK

On Monday morning at 9 a.m., Librarian returned to Jon Kincaid's office, this time signing the insurance papers that placed on the back of Lloyd's of London's the responsibility for a debt of $25,000,000 in the event of loss of the manuscripts due to almost any cause. Perhaps a very unusual condition might be excluded, but he doubted it, though personal experience with automobile insurance companies always caused him to conclude that if there were any way they could get out of paying, the insurance company would find it. Sotheby's arranged for the details of the policy, but its cost would be deducted from the payment due Librarian after the sale. Following that, which took only ten minutes, he was scheduled to shake a lot of hands of the upper management at Sotheby's. However, he asked Kincaid to get him out of that because the fewer people who knew him by sight, the better.

Kincaid assured Librarian of the fact that the management was aware of his wish for anonymity, but also added that these people were used to dealing in extremely confidential matters. Even so, Librarian stated his unwillingness to expand the number of people who could recognize him, ducked out of the meeting, and then took a taxi along with Kincaid to his bank. Because Sotheby's intended to place Stadler's briefcase in their vault along with the manuscripts, Librarian had brought it along with him.

A Brinks armored truck was parked in front of the bank, waiting for them to arrive. Kincaid approached one uniformed guard standing, arms akimbo, outside the truck. He verified the guard's ID, identified himself in a formal way, and then, on signal from the exterior guard, a second Brinks employee dispatched himself through the truck's back door, closing it behind him.

"Big deal," Librarian thought. "There isn't anything valuable in the truck now, so why all the fancy security whoop-dee-doo?" He wanted to see how they behaved once they had the manuscripts in hand.

Librarian was surprised to see Elias and a total stranger join both him and Kincaid. Elias introduced the man as the representative of Lloyd's of London, and who was there to confirm that what was being turned over to Sotheby's were, in fact, the manuscripts that Elias had authenticated.

The six went to the safe-deposit box area, with one guard deliberately separating himself from the group and walking about ten feet behind them. Librarian retrieved his box from the vault, had it wheeled to a conference room, extracted the two plastic envelopes, put them on the work table, rummaged through the photographic positives extracting the first page of each of the two manuscripts, closed the box, and accompanied its return to the vault. He would get the positives back in a few days and replace them in his box.

Meanwhile, Elias—with white gloves on—confirmed each authenticated manuscript as being entirely there, repacked them in the plastic envelopes, and handed them to one of the two guards, who put them inside a very large zippered cloth bag. Then the men went back out to the street. The guard at the rear of the group of six had his pistol unholstered and carried muzzle-end towards the ground, arm fully extended. Then a third guard, in the interior of the vehicle, opened the rear door from the inside and the first guard—the one holding the zippered bag—got in. The door was then closed from the outside by the guard with the pistol, and he, in turn, was let into the vehicle's cab by a fourth man, the driver. With the case buttoned up in the Brink's truck like a Chinese puzzle box, they left for Sotheby's, while Kincaid and Librarian took a taxi, getting to the auction house a few minutes before the truck arrived. The passenger in the truck's cab—the man with the pistol—got out first, walked around to the rear of the vehicle and signaled. The door was unlocked from the inside and both men who had occupied the rear during the brief ride emerged, one holding the zippered bag, the other now also holding an unholstered pistol. All three guards went into Sotheby's, along with Librarian and Kincaid, took the elevator to the floor where the vault was located, and had the contents of the plastic envelopes examined a second time by Elias and the Lloyd's representative. And that, thought Librarian, was probably the last he would see of the manuscripts until the London auction.

Since his involvement was effectively complete, he went back to the NYPL and to work, first stopping to get the number of today's telephone when Forger called. It was 11:25 a.m. when he arrived at his office; the message light on his phone was dark.

At noon, Forger called saying, "This is the expert." Librarian gave him the number of the day, he repeated it, and Librarian took off. The phone was ringing as he approached, and several people looked as if they were about to answer it. A ringing public phone in New York City is a very peculiar thing. The citizens don't know what to do, so they look around to see if anyone else knows what to do. Failing that, they walk away, just in case whoever is calling wants to borrow money from them.

Librarian answered and said, "Yes."

"It's me," Forger said.

"Where are you?" Librarian asked.

"Ely, Nevada," Forger responded.

"Are you serious?" Librarian said. "When we spoke last, which was Thursday, I got the impression that you were only a few hours from Ely, and here it is four days later and you finally got there?"

"No," Forger replied. "I got here Thursday afternoon planning, only to spend the night, but an amazing thing happened, and you'll be astonished when I tell you of it."

"What happened?" Librarian asked, suddenly frightened. "Is it the guys from Las Vegas again? Did they follow you?"

"No," Forger replied, "but I did run into someone here. It's someone from my childhood in Paterson. When I got into town, I decided to stay over, so I looked for a nice motel and found one on US 50 named *La Mireille*" across the street from the Copper Queen Casino."

"Wasn't 'Mireille' your mother's name?" Librarian asked.

"Yes," Forger replied. "And the amazing thing is that it turns out the motel was named after her."

"*What?*" Librarian reacted with a jolt. "How did you conclude that?"

"Do you remember Mr. Lammie from Paterson who taught me to play the piano? Well, he lives here, owns the motel, and named it after my mother. He has been here, first as a motel clerk and general handyman, then as a part owner of the place, and finally full proprietor when the previous owner died and left the motel to him. This was the town he came to right after my mother turned down his proposal of marriage."

"Did he recognize you?" Librarian asked.

"No. He did not," Forger said. "It was I who recognized him, and when I saw his name tag, that confirmed my suspicion. It was an absolutely unbeliev-able situation. My first comment to him was, 'Hello, Mr. Lammie. Do you remember me? You taught me how to play the piano in Paterson.'

"He looked at me for a few seconds and then became very pale. I got him seated in a chair, because it appeared that he was ready to faint. When he regained control of himself, he asked me a thousand questions, most of them about my mother, and when I told him that she passed away a few years ago and is buried next to my father in Clifton, he got all misty eyed. That was more than thirty years ago, and as far as I could tell, he's still in love with her.

"After he learned about mom's death, his legs got all trembly. Nothing would do but that I stay at *La Mireille* as his guest, and being with him almost constantly has been my duty and my pleasure for four days. He knows that I'm leaving shortly after this call, so he is very upset right now. My saying goodbye to him is not going to be easy. He's not well, and it's almost certain that he doesn't have long to live. It's terminal cancer. He told me that, but it was not in any sense of being morbid. He thought it would be helpful for me to know that. Last night we went to his apartment in the motel—he has lived in that room for the thirty or so years he's been in Ely, though he did expand it when title passed to him about ten years ago—and he had me play the piano for him. It's a small upright with dampers on all the strings so as not to bother his guests. I played some jazz, and later he played the Beethoven *Hammerklavier* sonata. For a man his age and physical condition, he plays well. When he got done playing, he was crying, and he told me all about my mother and him, and how miserable his life had been without her. He even converted to Catholi-cism in the hopes that some day he might see her again and she would not reject his plea because of religious differences. I think he forgot the many rea-sons she gave him for not marrying him, of which religion was only one.

"Finally," Forger concluded, "he told me that if I could see my way to stay-ing in Ely, he would give me the motel, lock, stock, and barrel. He sees my mother's face in mine and it broke my heart to say that it was impossible because of important business and other obligations back east. Then tears came to his eyes again. As you can see, it has been a remarkable four days here."

Librarian reacted to Forger's story sympathetically, though he never knew Mr. Lammie personally. After giving him some responsive words to what was an amazing coincidence, Librarian still was vitally concerned about his safety, so he brought the subject back to earth with the question, "Did you search your car for a bug?"

"No, and I'm not going to either," Forger said.

"Why not?" Librarian asked.

"First, because it's dumb, and second because I wouldn't know what a bug looked like if I saw one. I think you've been watching too many spy movies. If those men did not want me to leave Las Vegas, I'd be buried out in the desert right now.

"Look," he continued, "stop raining on my parade. I've just had a magic thing happen to me in a very small and isolated town in a sparsely settled state, and I don't want to deal with a discussion of those Las Vegas guys. What I want to do is thank Mr. Lammie for his many kindnesses to me when I was a kid, and for enriching my life by teaching me how to play the piano. If he had not done that, you recognize that I never would have been able to complete our most recent effort. I know what my mother had to do to get lessons for me, and while Mr. Lammie may have begun teaching me with that motivation, it changed to one of sympathy, understanding, and help. He loved her and I think he loved me, too. He was like a father to me and has been here close to half his life because of his run-in with my mother and me many years ago. So I want to devote my final hours here with him, and not having an argument about electronic devices.

"By the way," Forger continued, "he asked for my address and I gave him yours. He may want to write a letter speaking of things that are still too hard for him to say. So with something as poignant as the one that happened to me when I arrived in this town, do you think I was going to worry about looking for a bug in my car?"

"Suit yourself," Librarian said, giving in to the fact that further pursuit of the subject was useless. Then he added, "That's really wonderful that you saw your old piano teacher in such an out-of-the-way place. And the coincidence of that is remarkable. If you had not chosen to drive across America on US 50, that twist of fate would never have taken place. It was a remarkable and memorable event for you.

"But let me get off this emotional roller coaster and keep you current about what is happening here. The manuscripts are in the vault at Sotheby's and the news conference is today. In fact, it's happening as we speak. I am staying clear of Sotheby's for the next few weeks. When they get ready to send the manuscripts to London I may get involved, but only if I have to. Take a look in the New York *Times* tomorrow and you should see the whole story break there."

Forger responded, "I'm heading out of here right after this call and my goodbye to Mr. Lammie. I'll probably have to get off US 50 and drive to Provo, Utah to get a copy of the New York *Times,* and depending on what time it is when I get there, decide if I should stay the night. Expect my call tomorrow in any case and we can talk some more. Is around noon your time for my next call OK?"

"Yes. That's fine," Librarian said. "Keep your eyes open and please don't pick up any hitchhikers."

"Of course," he replied disingenuously, and hung up.

Apparently the press conference went off without any problems. Librarian did not call Kincaid to ask how it went, but waited until late Monday night when the early Tuesday edition of the New York *Times* hit the streets. There were no places in Paterson where Librarian could get it, so that was when he visited an all-night newspaper stand in Ridgewood and got his copy around midnight.

# 69

# TRAGEDY

Over the two weeks following the press announcement, life got back to some degree of normality for Librarian. He didn't miss a day at the NYPL, although his manager did speak to him privately in a congratulatory fashion on several occasions as the media hype about the manuscripts continued and was expanded on in print, TV, and radio. Out in the open, of course, his boss treated the publicity as little more than news that was important for people who, like the NYPL staff, were manuscript freaks. The department was buzzing with excitement, what with patrons asking a ton of questions about the NYPL's knowledge of the event. The staff—Librarian included—simply advised all inquirers that the NYPL knew nothing more about the details of the event than what was printed in the news media.

There was a particularly fascinating article by New York *Times* music critic Anthony Tommasini in which he spoke of the large number of Mozart manuscripts thought to be in the United States, though in the hands of unknown private collectors who would not acknowledge ownership of the treasures. Recognizing their fear of theft, Tommasini, in his well-written article, spoke of the loss to both scholarship and music history because the location of so many of these long-missing manuscripts was not known to scholars. In fact, some were not even thought to exist any longer.

Within two days of his article, the owners of three complete manuscripts and one sketch whose locations had remained unknown for years publicly acknowledged their status, and one of the manuscripts—the sketch—was donated to Harvard, with a generous tax benefit obtained by the donor.

Forger called Librarian every day, and both of them were at the point of concluding that they had been overexcited about the thugs who had effectively imprisoned Forger in his Las Vegas hotel room. As for the matter of the manuscripts, Forger never once said, "I told you so" when a very detailed technical piece dealing with Mozart's handwriting peculiarities as identified in the manuscripts was commented on accurately and extensively in the Los Angeles *Times*, with the observation made by Dr. Isabelle Emerson, a Mozart expert and Chairperson of the Music Department at the University of Nevada, Las Vegas. Forger, of course, could not help but enjoy the effect that his work had brought about, but his pride was not accompanied by arrogance.

His US 50 trip had taken him onto I-70 because the two roads were coincident for so much of Utah, but he got off the interstate from time to time in order to be able to wander the back roads. There was still a little more than a month before the auction, and Forger did not plan to get back to Paterson until after it had taken place. By that time, Librarian would be back from London, and the plan was for the two men to fly to Switzerland, take a train to Basle where Librarian's Swiss account was located, and then transfer half the money into an account that Forger would set up for himself.

After Forger crossed into Colorado, he continued to stay on US 50, because in that state it was very much a backcountry road. He spent three days in Pueblo, and then later told Librarian that he might like to buy a house there, but when asked questions about Mr. Lammie, Forger choked up and changed the subject. Librarian did not remember him ever being so moved. In Kansas, US 50 became an interstate near Emporia and he spent a few days in Kansas City because the bar-b-que was supposed to be the best in Missouri, though the residents insisted that it was the best in the world.

Librarian's last call from Forger was two days before the manuscripts were to be sent to London. At that time, Forger said he was a little west of St. Louis and would work his way east from there, continuing on US 50 across the bottom of Illinois. Librarian asked him to call the next day, but presumed that Forger had forgotten when no call came through.

Librarian had his meeting to review the Munich paper acidity conference the following day and wasn't at his phone. Since there were no messages, he presumed that Forger hadn't called for a second day in a row. That was peculiar.

Towards the end of that day, Librarian called Jon Kincaid and confirmed that the manuscripts had been picked up for shipment to London, asking him, "How do you send them, by courier with a briefcase handcuffed to his wrist?"

"Not quite," Kincaid replied. "We use FedEx. It's a great deal less expensive than having to rent handcuffs, and we can tell where the package is practically by the minute. Never lost a thing with them," he concluded. They spoke some more, with Kincaid telling Librarian that the expectations for the sale were now up to $40,000,000.

"How do you know that?" Librarian asked.

"First, because we've received a private bid for $35,000,000 from Vienna's Austrian National Library," he replied. "And second, we have an open bid from an anonymous party in Texas, who must have taken the Governor's advice. His agent says that he will pay $5,000,000 more than any bid we now have in hand. If his bid is good, that's $40,000,000. Do you want to sell it at that price? His offer will be withdrawn on the day the sale begins in London."

"No," Librarian said. "I wouldn't miss this auction for anything. There is a question I want to ask, but it's so silly that I'm embarrassed. I'll ask you now, but if you make fun of me I'll take my business to Bonhams & Butterfield in San Francisco," he said jokingly.

"What's the question?" Kincaid asked.

"After the sale, how long does it take before I collect my money, less the seven percent commission and insurance costs, of course?"

"That's not a silly question at all," Kincaid said. "We wait until the buyer's instrument has cleared the bank and are in possession of his money. Then he can claim his purchase, though that has nothing to do with when you get your money. Generally, within twenty-four to forty-eight hours after his check clears you get paid—if it's a check, of course; for amounts this high it's more likely to be an interbank electronic transfer, so that means we can deposit it directly into any bank you wish and in any currency you wish. Do you want to meet the buyer?"

"No," Librarian replied. "Do buyers sometimes ask to remain anonymous?"

"Frequently," he answered, "and for prices this high they are more often than not absent from the auction. Instead they have an agent who acts for them and works within preset limits that the buyer will not exceed."

"Do they know about my conditions related to the sale?" Librarian asked.

"Absolutely," Kincaid replied. "In fact, they are not only told what those conditions are, but the buyer has to sign a statement saying that he read, understands, and will comply with them. If he doesn't, as I have told you on several occasions, there isn't much we can do about it."

"Well," Librarian concluded, "I am going home. Will you call me tomorrow confirming that the package has been delivered safely?"

"Of course," Kincaid replied.

And with that, Librarian was off to the Thirty-eighth Street ferry and home. He showered, went out for a light dinner, and was home, in bed and asleep, by 10:30 p.m.

At 3:30 a.m. his phone rang. That is never a good time to get a call. The phone may have rung several times because he had been sound asleep. Grabbing at the receiver, he mumbled, "Mmfh! Yeah?"

It was Jon Kincaid of Sotheby's. "The news is disturbing and there's been some trouble," he said. "The FedEx flight carrying the manuscripts has disappeared from the flight tracking system. We don't know where it is or what's happened to it."

Librarian sat straight up in bed and asked, "Where was the flight when it disappeared?"

"Somewhere near the eastern coast of Greenland," was the reply, "and it isn't clear if it was over land or ocean."

"Do you think it crashed?" Librarian asked, in shock.

"I don't know," Kincaid replied. "Sotheby's tracks all precious materials from vault to vault and the party responsible for worldwide movement of all valuables called me only five minutes ago to report what I just told you. He waited until he could get through to FedEx for confirmation before calling me, so this whole thing could have happened anywhere from thirty to sixty minutes ago. There are no further details than these."

"How many people were on that flight?" Librarian asked.

"FedEx overseas flights usually have a crew of three, depending on the size of the craft and the length of the flight," he answered. "There are also some FedEx employees on board from time to time. It's not clear if there were any for this flight."

"Well, I'm up now," Librarian said, "and it is not likely that I'll be going back to sleep. Can you keep me informed?"

"Of course," he said. "I'll call you in half an hour in any case. You are not likely to hear much on the news, because as a rule, reporting of air disasters occurs only when there are a great many passengers involved, but you might. The flight left from Memphis, Tennessee and was to go nonstop to London, with a scheduled London arrival time of 7:30 a.m. It could also be any of a number of non-serious problems including transponder failure, so we should not assume the worst."

"OK," Librarian said, assuming that since Kincaid had called, it probably was with an assumption of the worst situation possible. "I'll wait for your call."

He dressed quickly and went down to the kitchen to make some coffee. Except for the tragedy of the loss of life, he realized selfishly that the worst-case scenario had no effect on him. The insurance would pay the contracted amount, or he presumed so.

Turning on the television, he searched for a news channel, coming up with the FOX news network. After twenty minutes, there was nothing reported about the FedEx plane. Then his phone rang and he answered it at once.

It was Kincaid. "The news is the worst possible," he said. "FedEx reports that the craft has gone down either in the ocean or else in an inaccessible place thirty to fifty miles west of Greenland's eastern coast. It simply disappeared from the radar screen. They have to wait until daylight to do any serious searching, but they're not hopeful. What I am about to say is not going to be much consolation to you, but the Lloyd's of London representative said that following an investigation of the craft's fate, you should receive the full insurance payment of $25,000,000, less the cost of the coverage. Also, though you may not have noticed it, your contract with Sotheby's has a provision that we have never before had occasion to invoke. It forgives any commission from you under these circumstances. So except for insurance costs, the entire amount will come to you unencumbered."

Librarian replied, "It's very kind of you to tell me this. I'm going to lie down now because I don't feel well. Unless there is some information of a remarkable nature, please don't call me back. We'll speak by phone later in the week."

"Sure," Kincaid said. "I understand completely. What I'll do…"

"Wait, wait!" Librarian said, interrupting him. "There's something coming on the TV right now."

The FOX announcer began speaking about a plane crash. Behind her was a map of Greenland with a large Maltese cross marking an ambiguous spot that could have been land or ocean by the Eastern coast. "This just in from FedEx," the announcer said. "A London-bound FedEx plane carrying a crew of three has crashed near the coast of Greenland. On board were various FedEx shipments from Memphis to Europe, among which were several recently rediscovered and valuable manuscripts scheduled for auction by Sotheby's of London. The manuscripts, which were the handwritten materials for original compositions by the Austrian composer Mozart, had a presale estimate of $20,000,000. There is no information about survivors or if any portion of the cargo has been recovered. We'll have more on this shortly, but now a word from…"

Librarian stopped listening to the rest and reported all this to Kincaid, who thanked him and said that he would call back only if what he learned was important enough to do so.

With the exception of the tragic deaths of the crew, from Librarian's narrow perspective he had not been hurt at all. The insurance payment, in fact more than he originally anticipated, was going to be made to him. And because the primary evidence was destroyed, there was now no way that the forgery could ever be discovered.

He remained by the TV for several hours, but no new developments were reported, only a rehash of the earliest communication. By 7:30 a.m. he was dressed and decided to go to work. It would not be a good idea if he failed to show up. The coincidence of the destruction of the manuscripts, coupled with his absence from the job that day, might raise some eyebrows. Of course he also needed to be at his desk when Forger called. He would have to call today. This was going to be big news with headlines like "VALUABLE MANU-SCRIPTS LOST FOR 200 YEARS DESTROYED IN AIR CRASH."

When Librarian got to his office, his boss asked to speak to him and the two chatted for a few minutes. The supervisor was extraordinarily sympathetic and asked why he had come to work, considering the circumstances. Librarian told him that he wanted to take his mind off the problem. He also told his manager that the destruction of the manuscripts would not change the necessity of preserving confidentiality of the subject, because according to the Sotheby's representative, Librarian would receive the full insurance settlement.

Forger did not call that day. Where was he? Why wasn't he calling? Newspapers all across America had headlines about the loss of the manuscripts that were even larger and more dramatic than those used when the documents were announced as having been found. It was impossible for Forger not to know about the matter. The news was on all the major cross-country radio news stations. Yet he did not call.

Something else had gone very wrong.

# 70

# MURDER IN ILLINOIS

After three additional days of getting no call from Forger, Librarian was forced to take some action. The situation could not continue.

He reviewed what he knew. When Forger had last called, five days earlier, he said that he was a little west of St. Louis and Librarian presumed that he would stay on US 50 heading east, since it was his intention to go all the way across America on that single, back-country route. He asked the reference librarian just down the hall from his office if she had a Rand McNally road atlas, which she did, and he looked through it.

It showed that after East St. Louis, there were only three Illinois cities of any significant size on US 50 west of Vincennes, Indiana, and he decided to focus on just that geography as his first step in finding out where Forger might be. The towns were—going from west to east—Salem, Flora, and Olney. Librarian could, of course, call the Illinois State Police and ask about auto accidents on US 50. However, the problem with that was it gave them an opportunity, should something bad have happened, to ask him who he was and why was he calling about the matter.

Instead, he went on the internet and did a search for newspapers in Illinois, finding out that Flora and Olney both had daily newspapers, while Salem did not, or at least not one that could be seen on line. The one in Flora was *The Clay County Advocate-Press* while Olney's was *The Daily Mail*. Both could be viewed on line.

The local section of *The Clay County Advocate-Press* had no information about automobile accidents for five consecutive days, beginning with the date of his last call from Forger, but *The Daily Mail* of Olney was a different story.

There, under local news, one day after Forger must have passed through St. Louis heading east, he found the following headline: "Murdered man found in auto on US 50." The few sentences that followed stated only that a body of an unnamed man was found by the Illinois State police behind the steering wheel of an automobile with New York State licence plates. He had apparently been shot twice in the head at close range. The undamaged car was parked by the side of the road near Clairmont, Illinois, a much smaller town just a few miles east of Olney and only thirty miles west of the Indiana border. The murdered man had no identification and the police were investigating.

The next three day's issues of Olney's paper—all of which were still on line—said nothing further on the matter. Librarian decided that he had to call the offices of *The Daily Mail* to see about whom it was they were writing.

The newspaper's telephone operator transferred Librarian to the editorial desk where a man answered, saying, "*Daily Mail* editorial desk. What can I do for you?"

Librarian responded with, "Good morning. I saw a piece in the on line version of your paper of three days ago that dealt with a man found shot to death on US 50."

"Yeah, I remember it," the voice responded. "What about it?"

"I searched the on line version of the next three days and could find nothing further on the subject. Now it so happens that my uncle was traveling across the US and we haven't heard from him in more than a week. We're getting nervous about the matter, so we're checking on newspaper stories about unidentified people being found."

"What makes you think that this man might be your uncle?" the editor said.

"Well, he told us that he wanted to see some family in St. Louis and then visit a cemetery in Vincennes, Indiana, and the most logical way to get from St. Louis to Vincennes is on US 50. It's a straight route across the bottom of Illinois and appears to be the best route to take. Anyway, your newspaper had the only lead for us to follow. Can you tell me if you have anything further on that story?"

"The guy I assigned it to is in and I'm going to transfer you," the editor said. "Just ask him what he knows. He'll be responsive. Hold on. I'm transferring you."

In a few seconds, a phone rang in Librarian's ear and a voice said, "Larsen here."

"Mr. Larsen," Librarian said, "I was just speaking to your editorial desk about a story that appeared three days ago. It dealt with a man found shot to death in his car on US 50. Your editor said that he had assigned the story to you, and if I wanted anything further, I should ask you."

"Yes," he replied. "I'm the one who did the original piece on that murdered guy. It was just one paragraph, because we had nothing else at the time, and since then I've had nothing further from the Illinois State police. Why is this person of interest to you?" he asked.

Librarian gave him the story about the lost uncle and how worried the family was. As the editorial desk said, Larsen was a helpful person.

"You think this might be your missing uncle?" he asked sympathetically. "Well, hold on for a few minutes. I'll call my contact in the Illinois State police and ask where they are in their investigation. On second thought, this call could take half an hour and I don't want you paying for wait time. Call me back in forty-five minutes, will you?"

Librarian agreed and hung up. When he called back, the answering party put him on hold briefly. The she came back in a minute and said, "Mr. Larsen told me that he is almost done with his call to the state police. Hold on please."

When Larsen came on, he said, "Sorry to have taken so long on that, but I have the complete story so maybe it was worth your time. First, the license plates of the car in which the murdered man was found were traced to a purchase made only a few weeks ago in Port Jervis, New York."

Librarian's heart sank.

"It was paid for in cash by a man named 'James Harold,' who used a forged driver's license as ID, according to a communication from the New York State Police who answered the Illinois police's inquiry, so they don't know the identity of the murdered man. When they examined the car, they found six electronic devices in it. Can you imagine that? Somebody was tracking the location of the car very carefully. As to the matter of the murdered man's fingerprints, the Illinois State police are still awaiting a response from the FBI on the matter, but that might take two weeks. Is it possible that this man was your uncle?" Larsen asked.

It was not easy for Librarian to talk, but he managed with, "No, it's not likely. Our uncle never was in New York State and wouldn't have bought a car there in the last few weeks. We're from Ohio."

"Well," Larsen said, "then it's good news for you, because this man couldn't be your uncle."

"You're right," Librarian said. He was effusive in his thanks for the help, and got off the phone.

It had to be Forger. What on earth could have happened? The six electronic bugs must tell the story. Librarian suspected that those thugs in Las Vegas were either going to get what they wanted from him or kill him. When the MGM hotel security forced the issue, they had to let him go. However, they must have had his car bugged while he was packing to leave Las Vegas, figuring that they would get him in their own sweet time and in their own sweet way, particularly when he was far away from Las Vegas and no one would make the connection between him and the MGM security incident.

But why Illinois? Why did they wait so long? The logical conclusion was that they used a hired hit man, or more likely a pair of men from Chicago or St. Louis, so they just kept a tail on him as he traveled across America, like the fly to the spider. Then when he got near St. Louis, they alerted their hit man or men who tailed him east on US 50 and took care of the matter when the occasion arose.

As Librarian's scenario unrolled, he realized that there was an anomaly here. The news report said nothing about a car accident. The vehicle was not smashed up. It was parked by the side of the road near Clairmont and the newspaper account explicitly said that the car was undamaged, so the shots could not have been fired as he rode along.

Did Forger pull over to take a nap and then was jumped? Did one of the men get into the car with him when he stopped for food or gas in Olney, perhaps, and then force him to pull over near Clairmont? Librarian couldn't figure that out. How would these men have recognized Forger? They would not have known him. Recognition must have been by the car alone. They undoubtedly had the license plate number, and they certainly had use of the six electronic bugs. Whatever it was, they had done their work with deadly force and Librarian had lost his friend and colleague.

# 71

# RETURN TO STRASBOURG

Two months after the double disaster of Forger's death and the loss of the manuscripts, Librarian's life had been radically changed, both from within and without. He resigned his position at the NYPL and sold the Paterson house, taking six weeks to close that chapter of his life. No trace of the FedEx plane was found, nor did any announcements allow one to conclude whether it fell into the ocean east of Greenland or on the snow and ice at its eastern edge.

Then there was the issue of Forger's safe-deposit boxes of which Librarian was a co-owner, though he had not been to a single one of them and had no idea other than the most general about what they contained. He considered visiting and emptying them out, but ultimately decided not to. After all, he had more than enough money and it would have made him feel like a grave robber to visit and empty the boxes in Danbury and Stroudsburg. The one in Port Jervis had been closed. Forger had told him that at the time he got the money for his trip and bought a used car. But ever since Librarian's bank in Basle notified him that Lloyd's of London made a very large deposit to his account, he really had no motivation to do anything about Forger's various safe-deposit boxes. In the future, should he decide differently, he'd visit the one in Stroudsburg first. There, as Forger had also told him, he would find a list of all the cities in which he had cash stored in such boxes. The only other one Librarian knew about was in Danbury.

It turned out that not visiting the one in Danbury was a serious mistake. Librarian would have learned something very important.

As for his own safe-deposit box in New York——the one with the photographic copies of the now lost manuscripts—his original thought was to donate everything to a suitable library. It would be a considerable tax write-off because those photographs and negatives had become enormously valuable after the manuscripts were destroyed. But he decided to leave things alone until he got some perspective on the situation. Perhaps, after the passage of some time, he might decide to do something with those things.

So instead of closing out the rental, he did the exact opposite by calling the bank, obtaining the fee for a prepaid period of ten years, and then sending a check to them. After that, the box and its contents were put out of mind. As for the two photo positives Librarian had taken out of the box so that Sotheby's could use them for the press kit, Kincaid had returned them to Librarian within a few days of the plane crash and Librarian had put them back into the strong box.

Flying to Zurich, Librarian rented a car from Hertz and spent several days relaxing, eating well, seeing the countryside, and slowly making his way west to Basle. There, he visited his bank and requested two cashier's checks, each in the amount of 100,000€, crossed the border into France and continued on his way north towards Strasbourg.

Visiting the shop of M. Hemmerdinger immediately after arrival, he was made to feel very welcome. Because the leather-goods owner was busy with customers, the two could not talk, so Librarian suggested that they go out for dinner, and this time, he would be Librarian's guest. M. Hemmerdinger agreed, providing that he could choose the restaurant. In the meanwhile, Librarian registered at the Sofitel, unpacked, sent some clothes out for cleaning, and took a walk around the city. By 7 p.m. he was back at the leather goods shop and they walked to a restaurant that served kosher food, thus enabling M. Hemmerdinger to observe his dietary restrictions.

After the two were seated, M. Hemmerdinger said, "You must permit me to extend my congratulations to you on the discovery you made in Scherwiller, though I am, of course, saddened beyond measure by the loss that you suffered subsequently. The finding of those manuscripts was the most talked about item in the press for days, and even I was interviewed because of the public references to my aunt and me having been of help to you. Frankly, I thought I did very little and said so when asked. I did not, of course, mention you by name, because I had been asked not to do so by a representative of Sotheby's. And then there was the tragic conclusion of the entire story when the plane, on which your great discoveries were being transported to London, crashed near Greenland. That was so very terrible, both for you, personally, and for the music world. The news stories of the loss were reported in the *Dernières Nouv-*

*elles d'Alsace* even more extensively than those of their discovery. It was a terrible tragedy, made even more awful because those treasures had lain undiscovered for two centuries, and then, so soon after rediscovery, were lost again.

"Incidentally," he continued, "I had a moment after you left the shop earlier today to call and speak to my Aunt Ella. She invites you to visit with her again, perhaps even for another *choucroute*. She also wants to thank you for the many postcards she got from your friend who was touring the US and sent to her from so many interesting places. He even sent one of a motel in Nevada that was named after his French mother. What a charming man, and such excellent French for an American."

"Actually," Librarian said, "I am here to do much more than simply fulfill my social obligations to both you and your aunt. Had it not been for your family's history, coupled with your personal recollections, to say nothing of the help of your aunt, I would never have been successful in my search. Of course it is tragic that the manuscripts were lost, but I did have photographic copies made of the material and have been considering donating them to a worthy institution, perhaps even the University of Strasbourg. But that is a decision I will not make for some time. As for myself, I was richly rewarded for the discovery, even if only by insurance.

"I felt that you and your aunt should share in my good fortune," Librarian said, as he reached into his pocket and came out with an envelope that had M. Hemmerdinger's name typed on it. "And so, I make this gift of appreciation to you."

Hemmerdinger took the check out of the envelope and held it in his hands, looking at it for a moment and finally saying, "I am so very grateful to you for this most generous gift. Would you object if I shared this good fortune with my children? It will not only help them personally, but will enable an even greater bond to be formed between them and their Hemmerdinger ancestors. My son intends to take over my business when I retire, and that will certainly help maintain the continuity."

"How could I possibly object to you sharing this gift with your children?" Librarian said. "That money is yours to do with as you wish. For your information, I have an identical amount that I intend to present to your aunt, but please don't tell her. That way I will have the pleasure of surprising her."

"She is going to be quite astonished," he said. "And I can assure you that very little in this world is capable of doing that to my aunt. Should the two of you go out to dinner, I do ask that you try and create a situation in which she will not ride her bicycle. She is almost 93 now and I am terribly afraid that she will fall and break something. But I am being rude. Here you are making this generous gift to both my aunt and me, and, instead of being appreciative I'm asking you to stop her from riding a bicycle," and both laughed a great deal at that.

# 72

# SCHERWILLER REDUX, AN
# IMPOSSIBLE POSTCARD

The next morning, Librarian called Ella Hemmerdinger and made arrangements for dinner for that evening. She seemed happy to hear that he would be able to visit with her, inquiring if he wanted her to select the restaurant. Librarian thanked her but said that he would do that, and further, he had a rented car and intended to drive to Scherwiller. In this way they would not be restricted as to where they might go.

Librarian asked for a recommendation from the hotel's *concierge,* and when he said that he would be meeting his guest in Scherwiller, the *concierge* immediately suggested a restaurant by the name of *Auberge de l'Il* in the nearby town of Illhaeusern. "It is one of the greats of the restaurant world, a real experience, though expensive as are all such remarkable places," the *concierge* said, and called at once for a reservation. He was extremely fortunate to find a table free, because in such places the wait can be months. However, they had had a last-minute cancellation and Librarian benefited from it. The *concierge* also supplied him with directions, saying, "From Scherwiller, take the *autoroute* south to the town of Illhaeusern. You won't be on the *autoroute* very long, perhaps 20 kilometers. Once you leave the highway, you enter the village. Just follow the road to the center of town and you cannot miss it. The restaurant will be on your right, perhaps two kilometers from the *autoroute* and well lit up."

He left Strasbourg at 5 p.m., following the street signs that would take him to the A35 north-south superhighway. Exiting the quiet expressway at the city of Sélestat, he found signs that took him to Scherwiller, and the moment he entered the city he recognized exactly where he was. Going straight to Ella Hemmerdinger's home on 7 Rue Giessen, he arrived at 6:15.

"How nice to see you," she said on answering the door. "It has been a long time, and one in which your good fortune at Emmaüs allowed you to make a wonderful discovery. I am so sorry that fate snatched it from you at the last moment. This was a great tragedy for both you and the world."

Librarian replied, "I must tell you that I am really here for a purpose other than simply to thank you for your help. I have a small gift for you. Over dinner will be a nice time for me to give it to you, don't you think?"

"Of course," she said. "Over dinner is a wonderful place to make a gift. I do hope that it's blue. I just love blue. Just a moment while I get my things and we can leave. Where are we going?"

When Librarian told her that it was the *Auberge de l'Il,* she was impressed. "You know," she said, "it is said to be the best restaurant in all France, which if true, means it is the best in the world. I hope that they have not slipped," she said wistfully.

"I'm looking forward to it," Librarian said, and the two got back on the highway, heading south. Thirty minutes later they were at the restaurant and greeted by one of the two owner-brothers. After being seated at the elegantly set and beautifully decorated table, they were offered a small plate of exquisite pre-dinner snacks.

"What would you like to drink?" Librarian asked.

"Champagne," she answered. "It's for special occasions."

It was almost two hours later that they finished their meal and he gave her his gift. There was no need to apologize for the color, because the Swiss bank check was on blue-tinted paper. As her nephew suggested, there was genuine astonishment on her face. "How magnificent of you!" she said. "I thought that you had gotten a handkerchief for me, or something like that. But this amount of money is extraordinarily generous of you," at which point she rose out of her chair, kissed him on both cheeks and sat down, with tears in her eyes. Then she said, "I'm quite breathless, but I still must show you the postcards sent to me by your friend who writes such beautiful French."

Librarian was a little taken aback and then remembered how Forger told him that at Librarian's request, he was sending postcards to Ella Hemmerdinger as he traveled across America. She reached into her handbag and took out at least two-dozen cards. As she put each one in front of Librarian, she remarked on the beauty of the pictures. The order closely followed Forger's trip. First there was a postcard showing the very tip of Cape Cod, then one from Danbury with a picture of a hat and the announcement that it was a souvenir of "The Hat City," and, following those, Mlle. Hemmerdinger was given a tour all the way to California, one card at a time, with one usually sent every few days. Then there was a card from Las Vegas showing a scantily dressed showgirl, next, a picture of the motel *La Mireille* on US 50 in Ely, Nevada. Librarian found that particularly touching. The next-to-the-last card she showed him was of the "Gateway Arch" from St. Louis. As she handed it to Librarian, he saw that she still had one card left in her hands.

"Your friend told me how you asked him to send cards to me," she said, "and I very much value the pictures of his trip across America. What a beautiful land. He has such a quaint and old fashioned handwriting."

"Yes," Librarian responded, seeing that Forger had used his Abraham Lincoln penmanship, though she would not know that, of course. "His handwriting was very..." as he searched for the right word, "...uh...adaptable," Librarian finally said.

And it was then that Ella Hemmerdinger, very quietly, dropped the anvil salesman's case on Librarian's head.

She said, "Of course your friend must be in Europe now, because I got his latest card postmarked from Germany just a week ago. However, he sent it to you, not to me. I presume he thought you might visit me and that is why he sent it to you at my address."

As she extended the last card, picture side towards him, Librarian said, "There must be some mistake. My friend was killed in an automobile accident." There was no need to tell her when this happened, or that he was murdered, or any other specifics about it. "Perhaps you received a card from someone else and simply presumed that it was from him."

"That is terrible information about your friend," she said, clearly shocked by the news of Forger's death. "I am so sorry to hear it. But this card is not addressed to me. It's for you. Look at the address information."

Librarian took the card from her outstretched hand. There was a picture of a highway that turned out to be a portion of the German Autobahn near Stuttgart. Turning it over, he saw that she was correct. It was addressed to him, in care of Ella Hemmerdinger at 7 Rue Giessen, Scherwiller. There was no message. Other than the address information, the postmark, and a pre-printed remark about the Autobahn, the card was blank.

"But what makes you think that this is from my dead friend?" Librarian asked.

"Because of the handwriting," she said. "It is the same old-fashioned and quaint handwriting as all the others."

Librarian looked again, and saw that she was correct. The address was Forger's Abraham Lincoln hand. The card was dated only eight days ago and the postmark read Hechingen, Germany.

Ella Hemmerdinger looked at him and said, "Why, you're as white as a ghost! Is there something wrong?"

"It's nothing. Perhaps something I ate," he said with a forced half-smile.

"Be careful," she said seriously. "In this restaurant, they take any statements about problems arising from eating something most seriously."

And as gently and politely as Librarian could, he told her that he was feeling tired, particularly after his long car voyage of the day before, and suggested that he take her back to Scherwiller. The two left the restaurant and he had her home in thirty minutes.

"Let me thank you again for this very generous gift," she said. "I hope that the postcard I gave you did not upset you too much. I'm so sorry to have heard about your friend, but I think I know what must have happened. He probably sent the card to you a week ago, and then, after traveling back to America, became involved in that automobile accident you spoke of. It was that shock that must have upset you."

She did not realize the dynamics of what had happened. Librarian simply told her that Forger had died in an auto accident, without stating when or where that happened. Therefore, she thought that the sequence of events was final postcard first, and death second, when in fact it was the completely absurd other way round. It was death first—or certainly what he thought to have been death first—and postcard second.

The circumstances of this postcard were quite impossible.

"You are so kind," Librarian said, anxious now to get away and think about the matter. "I think you are right. Yes, it was the shock of seeing my friend's postcard that upset me, but I am fine now and I very much thank you for showing me this card. I do not know what I would have done had I not seen it."

Librarian walked her to her door, promised that he would call again soon, got back in the car, and headed north towards Strasbourg, thinking as he drove about what might possibly explain the situation. Suddenly, the name of the town of Hechingen came back to him. That was the city where Forger had apprenticed at a German papermaking mill immediately following his first apprenticeship in The Netherlands. It was there that he had learned German!

That's where he had to be now, though how he got there and who that dead person was in Illinois was a complete and unfathomable mystery to Librarian.

He arrived back at the hotel at 11:30 p.m., asked for an early wake-up call and a map with directions to Hechingen, laid out what he would need for the next day, packed his clothes, and went to bed. But his mind was in such a dazzled state that it took a long while to fall asleep.

The next morning, he left the hotel at 5:15 a.m. and was on the German autobahn heading towards Karlsruhe by 5:45, arriving at Hechingen at 10 a.m. with only a short pause for breakfast at one of the autobahn's rest stops. Hechingen was a small town, and he was going to have some difficulty making himself understood. Finally, he saw a moderate-sized hotel, went inside, and spoke to the *concierge*. Any *concierge* in any hotel in Europe is going to be at least trilingual, and that included English.

Spotting the *concierge*'s desk, he approached it and said, "Excuse me. Is there a paper-making factory here in Hechingen?"

"I'm sorry. What kind of a factory?" the *concierge* answered in perfect English.

"It is not so much a factory," Librarian replied, "as a shop that manufactures handmade paper—antique paper similar to that of the eighteenth-century. The facility trains people to make paper the old-fashioned way. I had an American friend who was an apprentice at such a shop here in Hechingen a number of years ago."

"Oh, yes," the *concierge* said. "I know the facility. It's the only one of its kind in Germany, and once you described it, I realized what you meant. It is quite well known, though I never thought of it as a factory. It's very close to where we are now, perhaps ten minutes by car," he said, writing the directions down.

On arriving at a large, gray-painted, unmarked building with the address given him by the *concierge*, he went inside. There, at a large vat, throwing handfuls of rags into a tub of boiling liquid was Forger. He looked up, saw Librarian, got a big smile on his face and said, "Well, you certainly took your time about it!"

# FINALE: DA CAPO SENZA REPLICHE

Following happy hugging and hand shaking, it took some time before Forger could break free of his papermaking duties, because he was doing work on which a number of young apprentices depended. But that he was alive was quite enough for the moment.

"Be patient. I'll be with you as quickly as possible," Forger said. "Besides, you should have been here a month ago," which Librarian interpreted as an extremely cryptic remark. How was he supposed to be there a month ago when Forger sent his coded postcard to Ella Hemmerdinger only one week earlier?

An hour later, the two were seated at an outdoor café and beer hall, drinking coffee. Forger opened the conversation by wryly stating the obvious, saying, "I presume you want to know what happened."

"That's the understatement of the year," Librarian replied. "You have no idea what I did to get information about what supposedly happened to you eight weeks ago."

Then Librarian told him the story about the telephone calls to the Olney *Daily Mail* and his conversations with the reporter. He also realized, as he was telling the story, that the most significant error he made was in not calling back a week or two later. Had he done so, he might have learned that the fingerprint examination requested by the Illinois State Police did not identify Forger as the deceased. Had he called back, the reporter would have immediately become suspicious, keeping in mind that the inquiries made of him earlier were about a so-called lost uncle of the caller. So there really was no cover story that Librarian could have used, had he called back to find out the identity of the murdered man in the car.

Forger listened intently to the information about his own supposed death and said, "Well, the first thing you should know is that you were right about hitchhikers. Do you remember telling me several times not to pick up anyone? Unfortunately, the last one I picked up was just outside of East St. Louis, and it led to exactly the kind of problem about which you were concerned.

"As it turned out, however, that man saved my life but lost his own in doing so. He was hitchhiking, holding a big, handwritten sign that said, 'East On US 50.' Hitchhikers who advertise where they are going generally make good risks and pleasant companions, but this man was an exception.

"We were going through Salem, Illinois, the first town of any size after East St. Louis, and my gas tank was down to a quarter full, so the first gas station that showed itself got my business, probably because a pit stop was called for, too. A sign on the pump said, 'Pay before fueling,' and I was going inside to put down some cash. Suddenly my hitchhiker moved into the driver's seat, turned on the engine—because of my stupidity in leaving the keys in the ignition—and took off.

"While the car-jacking was seen by me," he continued, "the owner of the gas station was not paying any attention. This caused me to go straight to the men's room instead of the cashier's desk."

"Why did you do that?" Librarian asked.

"Because me yelling 'Help! That man is stealing my car!' would have resulted in the owner calling the police. You know my feelings about never dealing with police. Keep in mind that I'm a convicted felon, so no matter what the reason, my position is invariably one of no police involvement. Besides, it was a used car that cost only $800, and after driving across the US, it needed a lot of work. It wasn't my intention to keep that car after getting back to Paterson anyway."

"So what did you do?" Librarian asked.

"After ten minutes of calming down in the men's room I came out, bought a cup of coffee and a donut, took them outside, sat on a bench, and tried to figure out what was the best course of action. From a practical point of view, all that was lost was my car, a bit of luggage, and some dirty underwear. My travelers checks were in a money belt around my waist, all my cash was in my wallet, and it seemed to be best to say nothing.

"After about thirty minutes, I went back into the gas station office and asked if there was a used car lot in town. The owner rubbed his hands together like Uriah Heep and told me that he had a few good cars for sale himself, and that he might be willing to let me have one for a good price. Perhaps he viewed my recent purchase of coffee and a donut as showing my worthiness to get a discount on a used car. So only an hour after that hitchhiker stole the car I got in Port Jervis, my trip east on US 50 was being continued in a second one. For the car's paperwork, I used the same phony ID as for the car bought in Port Jervis. It was paid for with traveler's checks.

"After passing through a town called Olney—that must be the town with the newspaper you called—there were troubles on the road ahead. A little to the east of town, the traffic came to a dead stop with flashing lights, state police cars, and an ambulance by the side of the road. You can pretty much figure out what was there."

"It was your stolen car with a body inside it, right?" Librarian said.

"Correct," Forger replied, "and that scared the wits out of me. At first I thought it might have been a car crash or some other kind of accident, but there was no damage to the car's body. It was simply parked on the shoulder of the road."

"Did you investigate when you saw your stolen car?" Librarian asked.

"Yes," Forger replied. "I passed the parked car when the State Police let the traffic through. A lot of cars stopped further down the road beyond the accident and a number of people got out to see what had happened. It was easy to attach myself to the larger group, so I did, though there was a lot of discomfort for me because of the police at the scene. However, I had to find out what happened.

"In the driver's seat of the old car was my hitchhiker. The top of his head was blown off, though how it happened was anything but clear. Perhaps it took more than one man to bring it off. Certainly he was not shot from outside the car. The glass from the driver-side window was all over the road. If he had been shot from the outside, there would have been almost no glass on the road, because most of it would have wound up in his lap.

"And then it became clear to me what must have happened," Forger continued. "Whoever shot the hitchhiker must have thought that it was me. Then I saw one of the cops shine a flashlight into the interior of the left rear-tire well, reaching in to pull out what looked like an electronic device the size of a quarter. That's when the pieces fell together, and it's the second thing for which you are owed an apology."

"You told me to examine my car for electronic devices and I ignored you. What must have happened was that two men got the hitchhiker to stop his car, using some pretense. The Las Vegas crew, or more likely their bosses, probably hired them out of St. Louis as soon as my cross-country route was understood. That would have been easy to do, considering the bug in the car."

Librarian interrupted to say, "You should know that the information given to me was that there were six bugs in the car."

"Wow!" said Forger, bug-eyed in amazement. "No wonder they were able to follow me so well. When they concluded that my route was going through St. Louis, they must have called some local talent, who then followed the car electronically until it got into the eastern end of rural Illinois. Perhaps they deliberately touched his bumper with theirs and hailed him down, as if to apologize for the error. Then, when he stopped, one man forced his way into the car with him, they drove ahead to the final location outside of Olney, made him stop, and shot him twice. These men didn't know who was in the car. They were tracking it electronically, not visually, and they mistakenly shot a man they thought was me.

"Going back to my new car, I got out of there as fast as possible. From that point until reaching Danbury, Connecticut, eighteen hours later, my only stops were for gas, food, toilets, and once to get some sleep in a rest stop by the Newburgh/Beacon bridge near Poughkeepsie, New York. Arriving in Danbury, I put the car in the Holiday Inn's indoor parking garage, walked to my bank, emptied the cash out of it, took two different passports that were made by me six years ago, bought travelers checks in one of those names, left a detailed letter for you in the box, and then took a Greyhound bus to Boston, via Hartford. Boston was much preferred, because it would have been suicidal to go anywhere near New York. From there I flew to Frankfurt, took the train to Hechingen, and have been here ever since, waiting for you. Didn't you find my letter in the Danbury safe-deposit box?"

"The idea of visiting that box never occurred to me," Librarian answered. "Sure, you told me about the shared ownership, but I had no need for the money. My first hint that you were still alive came when Ella Hemmerdinger showed me your postcard."

"That is what I figured must have happened," Forger said. "The safe-deposit note had the address of the paper-making shop, and when I didn't hear from you, that's when the postcard was sent to the Hemmerdinger woman. You had to show up there eventually to give her the cash gift about which you told me. If my postcard had a Hechingen postmark, I knew you would put two and two together. The fact that the card was addressed in Lincoln's hand was just a little extra to convince you that I wrote it.

"Anyway," he continued, "after getting here, I wanted to do something productive and not just sit around waiting for you to give me my half of the insurance money. So they gave me this job at the paper shop, though there is no pay involved, just room and board. It helps pass the time. And speaking of papermaking, that reminds me about the loss of our manuscripts. When I read about it in the newspapers, it really hurt, but the article also indicated that insurance would be paid. How much insurance did you have?"

"It was $25,000,000," Librarian said, "though no taxes have yet been paid. Also there is the matter of the insurance costs and the 200,000€ given as gifts to the Hemmerdingers. The rest is still sitting in my bank in Basle."

"Weren't there any commission costs?" Forger asked.

"No," Librarian replied. "There was a contract provision that forgave the commission in the event of loss or destruction of the manuscripts. The loss of our manuscripts was the first occasion for which that provision was ever invoked."

"That's fantastic," Forger said. "You deserve congratulations for your handling of the administrative and financial end of the job! Here in Hechingen, there are still some people who remembered me, but all they had available for me to do was work the slurry bucket. It didn't matter to me. What counted was the fact that this place is very much out of the way and no one is going to look for or find me here. If those Las Vegas thugs ever figure out that it was not me they murdered, they might try it again.

"So what this all says," he concluded, "is that I'm in Europe to stay for a while. And now that you're here, I'd like to open my own Swiss account."

"We can do that tomorrow if you wish," Librarian offered, "though we will have to go to Basle for that. What did you have in mind to do after you get your money?"

"Is there any reason," Forger replied, "why we can't do a little manuscript business here in Europe just to keep our hand in the game? The food is good here, the living is easy, and paper can be made anywhere. We still have the people in Los Angeles, San Francisco, Chicago, and elsewhere who helped us sell our pieces in the past. They can continue to do that for us in the future. Prices for rare articles are going up every day. We don't need the money, but we can have an impact on history. I'm anxious to do several preliminary sketches of Lincoln's letter to the woman who lost her five sons in the Civil War. It was learning about Mozart's sketches and drafts that awakened me to the possibility of preliminary sketches of famous letters. It's an untapped market."

"It would be harder," Librarian said, "to do work like that without my having the same kind of access to libraries that we had when the NYPL opened all doors for me."

"We'll manage somehow," Forger replied.

"But maybe there's another option for us," Librarian suggested, an idea popping almost fully formed into his head.

"What's that?" Forger asked.

"Before leaving Paterson," Librarian answered, "I called the public relations officer at FedEx headquarters in Memphis and got some details about the crash."

"What were you told?" Forger inquired.

"It seems that the plane with our manuscripts did not crash into the ocean," Librarian replied. "It crashed on land, about eleven miles west of the eastern coast of Greenland. The place where the wreckage lies is said to be inaccessible. But I am not sure that a statement about the inaccessibility of Greenland's geography from someone living in Memphis, Tennessee can be accepted at face value. To them, two inches of snow shuts down the state for a week. Even if we were able to get to the wreckage in some way, there is no assurance that anything survived the crash, and within a few years it will all be buried under a great deal of snow. However, there might be another way to get our manuscripts back."

"What way is that?" Forger asked.

"We could do them all over again!" Librarian replied.

"There's no advantage to that," Forger said. "You'd have to pay back the insurance money."

"Almost certainly, yes," Librarian responded, "but the circumstances surrounding the value of those manuscripts have changed dramatically, and their worth is now considerably more than the presale estimate of a few months ago. At that time, I supposedly rediscovered them in France. But then, they were lost again, and in the most dramatic fashion possible. Before my rediscovery of those manuscripts, maybe a hundred people—scholars and historians—knew anything about them and their strange history. Now the whole world knows what happened to the manuscripts of Mozart's clarinet concerto and clarinet quintet. We got some heavy-duty press on that rediscovery. If they were to be re-rediscovered, their worth would almost certainly be much higher, particularly because of the dramatic loss after the terrible plane crash in which three men died so tragically.

"So if you made another set of manuscripts, and I created a believable story about how an expedition to Greenland found and miraculously saved them—please don't ask me for details now, I haven't had time to figure anything out—they could be sold for as high as $60,000,000. We had a bid for $40,000,000 before both the auction and the crash, and I was an idiot not to increase the insurance value of the manuscripts. Who knows what we might have gotten, had the auction been held?

"As for the insurance company, were we to remake the manuscripts and then announce that we had located them in Greenland, we would have to pay $25 million back to them, less insurance costs. But if we can sell the lost-in-the-crash-found-again manuscripts for $60,000,000, that would be the financial deal of the century. We'd give back $25 million to the insurance company and then get it all back again as part of the sales price. And I'll bet that we could hold off the debt to the insurers until we sold the manuscripts. We'd need some legal help, of course, but I'll bet that Sotheby's would be on our side in order to get the opportunity to sell those manuscripts at a new auction. Have you any idea of the publicity that such a situation would place us in?"

It was then that Forger asked a key question. "What did you do with those photographic positives of the original manuscripts that you had made?"

"They're in my safe-deposit box in New York, waiting for you to copy them, of course," Librarian answered, an ear-to-ear grin spread all over his face.

# ACKNOWLEDGEMENTS

I am especially grateful to two Mozart specialists who, at my request, read and commented on an early version of this book, both paying particular attention to technical issues. To refer to Professor Robert D. Levin of Harvard University and Dr. Faye Ferguson of the Neue-Mozart Ausgabe in Salzburg as "two Mozart specialists" is a serious understatement. The two are, in fact, among the world's most knowledgeable living Mozart experts. Between them, they have probably examined the details of as many Mozart manuscripts as any other living authority. I borrowed on our long-standing friendships to have them independently review and comment on the accuracy of my various remarks about eighteenth-century paper, watermarks, inks, goose-quill pens, and staff lining, to say nothing of the details of Mozart's music handwriting and manuscript organizational peculiarities.

Professor Levin, one of the world's most brilliant, dynamic, and inventive Mozart pianists, spent weeks reading and commenting on the manuscript while touring the world as part of his extensive concert career. Levin sent emails from distant locations—Australia one day, Germany the next—in which he told me the many things that he believed would improve the flow of the tale, identifying the offending text in an attention-getting but unnerving bold red color.

Dr. Faye Ferguson, who is the Salzburg-resident, cello-playing Texan who had a minor role in the events of the story, has a Mozart manuscript authority rivaled by few living people. Her knowledge of these matters is encyclopedic, and in her reading of my book, she was magnificent in isolating specific technical problems in short, pithy statements that went directly to the heart of the matter, all done while traveling in Africa.

Whatever technical insight and accuracy this book has is due, in no small measure, to their contributions. Whatever might be discovered in the future as being technically soft (and it is earnestly hoped that there will be no such discoveries) is, as my beloved mother Rose Sandow Leeson enjoyed, reminding me on multiple occasions prior to her death, entirely my fault.

Los Altos, California
May 23, 2004
Email: dnleeson@sbcglobal.net

# About the Author

Daniel Leeson is a 30-year veteran of the IBM corporation, a professional performing musician for much of his life, one of the editors of the *Neue Mozart Ausgabe's* 120 volumes of Mozart's music, and, following retirement from his business career, a teacher of college-level mathematics. An officer of the Mozart Society of America, he is also an award-winning writer of nonfiction, the author of more than 100 technical articles, the co-author or co-editor of four books, and a published fiction writer.

0-595-31676-X